THE GRELL MYSTERY

'THE DETECTIVE STORY CLUB is a clearing house for the best detective and mystery stories chosen for you by a select committee of experts. Only the most ingenious crime stories will be published under the THE DETECTIVE STORY CLUB imprint. A special distinguishing stamp appears on the wrapper and title page of every THE DETECTIVE STORY CLUB book—the Man with the Gun. Always look for the Man with the Gun when buying a Crime book.'

Wm. Collins Sons & Co. Ltd., 1929

Now the Man with the Gun is back in this series of COLLINS CRIME CLUB reprints, and with him the chance to experience the classic books that influenced the Golden Age of crime fiction.

THE
DETECTIVE STORY
CLUB

LIST OF TITLES

THE PERFECT CRIME • ISRAEL ZANGWILL

CALLED BACK • HUGH CONWAY

THE MAYFAIR MYSTERY • FRANK RICHARDSON

THE MYSTERY OF THE SKELETON KEY • BERNARD CAPES

FURTHER TITLES IN PREPARATION

THE GRELL MYSTERY

A STORY OF CRIME BY
FRANK FROËST
Ex-Chief Inspector of Scotland Yard

WITH AN INTRODUCTION BY
TONY MEDAWAR

COLLINS
CRIME
CLUB

COLLINS CRIME CLUB

An imprint of HarperCollins*Publishers*
1 London Bridge Street
London SE1 9GF
www.harpercollins.co.uk

This edition 2015

1

First published in Great Britain 1913
Published by The Detective Story Club Ltd
for Wm Collins Sons & Co. Ltd 1929

Introduction © Tony Medawar 2015

A catalogue record for this book is
available from the British Library

ISBN 978-0-00-813717-5

Printed and bound in Great Britain by
Clays Ltd, St Ives plc

INTRODUCTION

FIRST published a hundred years ago, *The Grell Mystery* is best regarded as an early example of what has become known as the police procedural. However, it is also one of the earliest instances of a novel written by an individual who has already attained fame, in this case Frank Froëst, a former Superintendent at Scotland Yard and once the most famous policeman in the world.

Frank Castle Froëst was born in the West of England around 1858. He joined the Metropolitan Police in 1879 and was promoted to detective two years later. In 1903, Froëst attained the rank of Chief Inspector and in 1906 he was appointed Superintendent of the Yard's premier division, the Criminal Investigation Department. According to contemporary newspaper reports, 'Frankie' Froëst was a genial, kindly-faced man, broad-shouldered and thick-set with twinkling blue eyes, a short greyish moustache and a misleading air of innocence. There are also numerous references to Froëst's extraordinary strength and, in particular, his ability to bend coins and to tear a pack of playing cards in two.

There are therefore some similarities between Froëst and Heldon Foyle, the detective who resolves *The Grell Mystery*, and if its central puzzle has little in common with any of the crimes that Froëst himself investigated, the detective's experiences and knowledge of what happened at a real crime scene give the novel a more realistic feel than many of its contemporaries. Heldon Foyle also works closely with the newspapers, something that Froëst was renowned for, but it is hard to believe that the real detective ever used disguise as Foyle does in *The Grell Mystery*. The book has a strong sense of place and the locations and minor characters are vividly realised.

Froëst achieved international renown in 1894 with the arrest of Jabez Balfour. In 1869, Balfour, a Liberal Party politician and one time Member of Parliament for Tamworth, founded the Liberator Permanent Benefit and Investment Society. The society grew to become one of Britain's largest but its success was built on false accounting and, inevitably, it collapsed, owing millions and leaving thousands of small investors defrauded and penniless. Balfour promptly fled to South America with his wife and sister-in-law, and he must have believed himself far beyond the reach of the Metropolitan Police. But he had reckoned without Frank Froëst. Tasked by the Assistant Commissioner at Scotland Yard with bringing the financier to justice, the detective travelled to Argentina where, after a year of battling officialdom, he tracked down his man. However, the business of returning Balfour to England was far from straightforward. Working with a British diplomat, Froëst chartered a train and, narrowly evading arrest for murder en route when a local sheriff's officer was killed trying to board the moving train, the two men reached the coast with their prisoner. Froëst chartered passage for Britain and as soon as the ship reached international waters he arrested Balfour who was later sentenced to fourteen years. The arrest was Froëst's first major success and in the course of his long career there would be many, many others, including the resolution of the Liverpool Bank Fraud and the arrest of Dr Hawley Crippen after he too had fled from justice.

When Frank Froëst retired in September 1912 after over 30 years' service, he was by general acclaim 'the best known of all the detectives in the world'. His fame was even such that the speech marking his retirement was given by King George V, who a few months earlier had awarded the detective the King's Police Medal, an honour then given rarely to officers of Froëst's rank.

On his retirement, Frank Froëst and his wife Sarah moved to Axbridge in Somerset, where he became a justice of the peace. Working with the journalist George Dilnot, he wrote *The Grell Mystery* and in return he helped Dilnot with his history of the Metropolitan Police, *The Story of Scotland Yard* (1915). The newspaperman and the former policeman got on well together and co-authored two further works of fiction: *The Crime Club* (1915), an entertaining collection of short stories; and *The Rogues' Syndicate* (1916). A silent film was made of each of the two novels by the Vitagraph Company of America and released in 1917 with *The Rogues' Syndicate* re-titled as *The Maelstrom*. Both films starred Earle Williams, an American actor, who played Heldon Foyle in the film of *The Grell Mystery*.

After his wife died in 1916, Frank Froëst lost his appetite for writing about crime. He moved into politics instead and was elected to Somerset County Council on which he served for some years before a second retirement after the onset of blindness. He died in 1930 in a convalescent home at Weston-super-Mare. Froëst's passing was marked around the world with one obituary describing him as 'one of the most brilliant, courageous and resourceful men who ever graduated through Scotland Yard'.

TONY MEDAWAR
February 2015

CHAPTER I

OUTSIDE the St Jermyn's Club the rain pelted pitilessly upon deserted pavements. Mr Robert Grell leaned his arms on the table and stared steadily out through the steaming window-panes for a second. His shoulders lifted in a shrug that was almost a shiver.

'It's a deuce of a night,' he exclaimed with conviction.

There was a faint trace of accent in his voice—an almost imperceptible drawl, such as might remain in the speech of an American who had travelled widely and rubbed shoulders with all sorts and conditions of men.

His companion lifted his eyebrows whimsically and nipped the end from a cigar.

'It is,' he agreed. 'But the way you put it is more like plain Bob Grell of the old days than the polished Mr Robert Grell, social idol, millionaire and diplomat, and winner of the greatest matrimonial prize in London.'

Grell tugged at his drooping iron-grey moustache. 'That's all right,' he said. 'This is not a meeting of the Royal Society. Here, in my own club, I claim the right of every free-born citizen to condemn the weather—or anything else—in any language I choose. Great Scott, Fairfield! You don't expect me to wear my mantle all the time. I should explode if I didn't have a safety valve.'

Sir Ralph Fairfield nodded. He understood. For years the two had been close friends, and in certain phases of temperament they were much alike. Both had tasted deeply of the sweets and hardships of life. Both had known the fierce wander-lust that drives men into strange places to suffer hunger, thirst, hardship and death itself for the sheer love of the game, and both had achieved something more than

1

national fame. Fairfield as a fertile writer on ethnography and travel; and Grell equally as a daring explorer, and as a man who had made his mark in the politics and finance of the United States. More than once he had been employed on delicate diplomatic missions for his Government, and always he had succeeded. Great things were within his reach when he had suddenly announced his intention of giving up business, politics and travel to settle in England and lead the life of a gentleman of leisure. He had bought a thousand acres in Sussex, and rented a town house in Grosvenor Gardens.

Then he had met Lady Eileen Meredith, daughter of the Duke of Burghley. Like others, he had fallen a victim to her grey eyes. The piquant beauty, the supple grace, the intangible charm of the girl had aroused his desire. A man who always achieved his ends, he set himself to woo and win her with fierce impetuosity. He had won. Now he was spending his last night of bachelordom at his club.

A man of about forty-five, he carried himself well and the evening dress he wore showed his upright muscular figure to advantage. Every movement he made had a swift grace that reminded one irresistibly of a tiger, with its suggestion of reserve force. His close-cropped hair and a drooping moustache were prematurely grey. He had a trick of looking at one through half-closed eyelids that gave the totally erroneous impression that he was half asleep. The face was square, the chin dogged, the lips, half-hidden by the moustache, thin and tightly pressed together. He was the type of man who emerges victor in any contest, whether of wits or muscle. Plain and direct when it suited his purpose; subtle master of intrigue when subtlety was needed.

A nervous gust of wind flung the rain fiercely against the window. Sir Ralph Fairfield uncrossed his knees with care for the scrupulous crease in his trousers.

'You're a great man, Bob,' he said slowly. 'You take it quite as a matter of course that you should win the prettiest girl in the three kingdoms.' His voice became meditative. 'I wonder how married life will suit you. You know, you're not altogether the type of a man one associates with the domestic hearthstone.'

Their eyes met. The twinkle of humour which was in the baronet's did not reflect itself in the other's. Grell, too, was wondering whether he was fitted for domestic life. He had a taste for introspection, and was speculating how far the joyous girl who had confided her heart to his keeping would fit in with the scheme of things. He roused himself with an effort and glanced at his watch. It was half-past nine.

'You make a mistake, Fairfield,' he laughed. 'Eileen and I fit each other, and you'll see we'll settle down all right. Care to see the present I'm giving her tomorrow? It's to be a little surprise. Look here!'

He inserted a hand in his breast pocket and produced a flat case of blue Morocco leather. He touched a spring: 'There!'

Soft, shimmering white against the sombre velvet lining reposed a string of pearls which even the untrained eye of Fairfield knew must be of enormous value. Each gem was perfect in its soft purity, and they had been matched with scrupulous care. Grell picked it up and dangled it on his forefinger, so that the crimson glow of the shaded electric lights was reflected in the smooth surface of the jewels.

'Pretty toy, isn't it?' he commented. 'I gave Streeters *carte blanche* to do the best they could.'

He dropped the necklace carelessly back in its case, snapped the catch, and placed it in his pocket. Fairfield's jerk of the head was significant.

'And you are fool enough to carry the thing around loose in your pocket. Good heavens, man! Do you know that there are people who would not stick at murder to get a thing like that?'

The other laughed easily. 'Don't you worry, Fairfield. You're the only person I've shown it to, and I'm not afraid you'll sandbag me.' He changed the subject abruptly. 'By the way, I've got an engagement I want to keep. Do you mind answering the telephone if I'm rung up by anyone? Say I'm here, but I'm frightfully busy clearing up some business matters, will you?'

The baronet frowned half in perplexity, half in protest. 'Why—forgive me, Bob—why not say that you are gone out to keep an appointment?'

Grell was plainly a little embarrassed, but he strove to disguise the fact. 'Oh, it's only a fancy of mine,' he retorted lightly. 'I shan't be gone long. You'll do it, won't you?'

'Of course,' agreed Sir Ralph, still frowning.

'That's all right, then. Thanks. I'll be back in half an hour.'

He strode away with an abrupt nod. Shortly afterwards Fairfield heard a taxicab scurry away down the sodden street. He leaned back in his chair and puffed a cloud of smoke towards the ceiling. There was a dim uneasiness in his mind, though he could have given no reason for it. He picked up an evening paper and threw it aside. Then he strolled up into the card-room and tried to interest himself in watching a game of bridge. But the play only bored him. Time hung heavily on his hands. A servant spoke to him. Instantly he rose and made his way to the telephone. A call had been made for Grell.

'Hello! Is that you, dear? This is Eileen speaking. . . . I can't hear. What do you say?'

It was the clear, musical voice of the girl Robert Grell was to marry. Fairfield wondered if his friend had expected this.

'This is not Mr Grell,' he said. 'This is Fairfield—Sir Ralph Fairfield—speaking.'

'Oh!' He could detect the disappointment in her voice. 'Is he there? I am Lady Eileen Meredith.'

Fairfield mentally cursed the false position in which he found himself. He was usually a ready-witted man, but now he found himself stammering almost incoherently.

'Yes—no—yes. He is here, Lady Eileen, but he has a guest whom it is impossible for him to leave. It's a matter of settling up an important diplomatic question, I believe. Can I give him any message?'

'No, thank you, Sir Ralph.' The voice had become cold and dignified. He could picture her chagrin, and again anathematised Grell in his thoughts. 'Has he been there long? When do you think he will be free?'

'I can't say, I'm sure. He met me here for dinner at seven and has been here since.'

He hung up the receiver viciously. He had not expected to have to lie to Grell's *fiancée* when he had promised not to disclose his friend's absence from the club. It was too bad of Grell. His eye met the clock, and with a start he realised that it was a few minutes to eleven o'clock. Grell had been gone an hour and a half.

'Queer chap,' he murmured to himself, as he lit a fresh cigar and selected a comfortable chair in the deserted smoking-room. 'He's certainly in love with her all right, but it's strange that he should have used me to put her off tonight like that. Wonder what it means.'

Two hours later a wild-eyed, breathless servant, bareheaded in the pouring rain, was stammering incoherently to a police-constable in Grosvenor Gardens that Mr Robert Grell had been found murdered in his study.

CHAPTER II

THE shattering ring of the telephone awoke Heldon Foyle with a start. There was only one place from which he was likely to be rung up at one o'clock in the morning, and he was reaching for his clothes with one hand even while he answered.

'That you, sir?'... The voice at the other end was tremulous and excited. 'This is the Yard speaking—Flack. Mr Grell, the American explorer, has been killed—murdered ... yes ... at his house in Grosvenor Gardens. The butler found him....'

When a man has passed thirty years in the service of the Criminal Investigation Department at New Scotland Yard his nerves are pretty well shock-proof. Few emergencies can shake him—not even the murder of so distinguished a man as Robert Grell. Heldon Foyle gave a momentary gasp, and then wasted no further time in astonishment. There were certain obvious things to be done at once. For, up to a point, the science of detection is merely a matter of routine. He flung back his orders curtly and concisely.

'Right. I'm coming straight down. I suppose the local division inspector is on it. Send for Chief Inspector Green and Inspector Waverley, and let the finger-print people know. I shall want one of their best men. Let one of our photographers go to the house and wait for me. Send a messenger to Professor Harding, and telephone to the assistant commissioner. Tell any of the people who are at the house not to touch anything and to detain everyone there. And Flack—Flack. Not a word to the newspaper men. We don't want any leakage yet.'

He hung up the receiver and began to dress hurriedly, but methodically. He was a methodical man. Resolutely he put from his mind all thoughts of the murder. No good would come of spinning theories until he had all the available facts.

For ten years Heldon Foyle had been the actual executive chief of the Criminal Investigation Department. He rarely wore a dressing-gown and never played the violin. But he had a fine taste in cigars, and was as well-dressed a man as might be found between Temple Bar and Hyde Park Corner. He did not wear policemen's boots, nor, for the matter of that, would he have allowed any of the six hundred odd men who were under his control to wear them. He would have passed without remark in a crowd of West-end clubmen. It is an aim of the good detective to fit his surroundings, whether they be in Kensington or the Whitechapel Road. A suggestion of immense strength was in his broad shoulders and deep chest. His square, strong face and heavy jaw was redeemed from sternness by a twinkle of humour in the eyes. That same sense of humour had often saved him from making mistakes, although it is not a popular attribute of story-book detectives. His carefully kept brown moustache was daintily upturned at the ends. There was grim tenacity written all over the man, but none but his intimates knew how it was wedded to pliant resource and fertile invention.

Down a quiet street a motor-car throbbed its way and stopped before the door of his quiet suburban home. It had been sent from Scotland Yard.

'Don't worry about speed limits,' he said quietly as he stepped in. 'Refer anyone to me who tries to stop you. Get to Grosvenor Gardens as quickly as you can.'

The driver touched his hat, and the car leapt forward with a jerk. A man with tenderer nerves than Foyle would have found it a startling journey. They swept round corners almost on two wheels, skidded on the greasy roads, and once narrowly escaped running down one of London's outcasts who was shuffling across the road with the painful shamble that seems to be the hallmark of beggars and tramps. Few, save policemen on night duty, were about to mark their wild career.

As they drew up before the pillared portico of the great house in Grosvenor Gardens a couple of policemen moved out of the shadow of the railing and saluted.

Foyle nodded and walked up the steps. The door had flown open before he touched the bell, and a lanky man with slightly bent shoulders was outlined in the radiant glow of the electric light. It was Bolt, the divisional detective inspector, a quiet, grave man who, save on exceptional occasions, was with his staff responsible for the investigation of all crime in his district.

'You're the first to come, sir,' he said in a quiet, melancholy tone. 'It's a terrible job, this.'

He spoke professionally. Living as they do in an atmosphere of crime, always among major and minor tragedies, C.I.D.

men—official detectives prefer the term—are forced to view their work objectively, like doctors and journalists. All murders are terrible—as murders. A detective cannot allow his sympathies or sensibility to pain or grief to hamper him in his work. In Bolt's sense the case was terrible because it was difficult to investigate; because, unless the perpetrators were discovered and arrested, discredit would be brought upon the service and glaring contents-bills declare the inefficiency of the department to the world. The C.I.D. is very jealous of its reputation.

'Yes,' agreed Foyle. 'Where is the butler? He found the body, I'm told. Fetch him into some room where I can talk to him.'

The butler, a middle-aged man, nervous, white-faced and half-distracted, was brought into a little sitting-room. His eyes moved restlessly to and from the detective: his fingers were twitching uneasily.

Foyle shot one swift appraising glance at him. Then he nodded to a chair.

'Sit down, my man,' he said, and his voice was silky and smooth. 'Get him a drink, Bolt. He'll feel better after that. Now, what's your name?—Wills?—Pull yourself together. There's nothing to be alarmed about. Just take your own time and tell us all about it.'

There was no hint of officialdom in his manner. It was the sympathetic attitude of one friend towards another. Wills gulped down a strong mixture of brandy and soda which Bolt held out to him, and a tinge of colour returned to his pale cheeks.

'It was awful, sir—awful,' he said shakily. 'Mr Grell came in shortly before ten, and left word that if a lady came to see him she was to be brought straight into his study. She drove up in a motor-car a few minutes afterwards and went up to him.'

'What was her name? What was she like?' interrupted Bolt. Foyle held up his hand warningly to his subordinate.

Wills quivered all over, and words forsook him for a moment. Then he went on—

'I—I don't know. Ivan, Mr Grell's valet, let her in. I saw her pass through the hall. She was tall and slim, but she wore a heavy veil, so I didn't see her face. I don't know when she left, but I went up to the study at one o'clock to ask if anything was needed before I went to bed. I could get no answer, although I knocked loudly two or three times; so I opened the door. My God! I—'

He flung his hands over his eyes and collapsed in an infantile paroxysm of tears.

Foyle rose and touched him gently on the shoulder. 'Yes, then?'

'The room was only dimly lit, sir, and I could see that he was lying on the couch, rather awkwardly, his face turned from me. I thought he might have dozed off, and I went into the room and touched him on the shoulder. My hand came away wet!' His voice rose to a scream. 'It was blood—blood everywhere—and he with a knife in his heart.'

Foyle leaned over the table. 'Where's Ivan?—Russian, I suppose, by the name? He must be about the house somewhere.'

'I haven't seen him since he let the lady in,' faltered the butler.

The superintendent never answered. Bolt had silently disappeared. For five minutes silence reigned in the little room. Then the door was pushed open violently and Bolt entered like a stone propelled from a catapult.

'Ivan has gone—vanished!' he cried.

CHAPTER III

FOYLE caressed his chin with his well-manicured hand.

'H'm!' he said reflectively. 'Don't let's jump to conclusions too quickly, Mr Bolt. There's a doctor here, I suppose? Take this man to him, and when he's a bit calmer take a statement from him. I'll leave Ivan to you. Get some of the servants to give you a description of him, and 'phone it through to Flack at the Yard. Let him send it out as an "all station" message, and get in touch with the railway stations. The chap can't have got far. Detain on suspicion. No arrest. Hello, there's the bell. That's some of our people, I expect. All right, I'll answer. You get on with that.'

He had not raised his voice in giving his directions. He was as cool and matter-of-fact as a business man giving instructions to his secretary, yet he was throwing a net round London. Within five minutes of the time Bolt had gathered his description, the private telegraph that links Scotland Yard with all the police stations of London would be setting twenty thousand men on the alert for the missing servant. The great railway stations would be watched, and every policeman and detective wherever he might be stationed would know exactly the appearance of the man wanted, from the colour of his hair and his eyes to the pattern of his socks.

Foyle opened the door to a little cluster of grave-faced men. Sir Hilary Thornton, the assistant commissioner, was there; Professor Harding, an expert retained by the authorities, and a medical man whose scientific researches in connection with the Gould poisoning case had sent a man to the gallows, and whose aid had been most important in solving many murder mysteries; Grant of the finger-print department, a wizard in all matters relating to identification; a couple of men from his department bearing cameras, and lastly the senior officer of the Criminal Investigation Department, Green, and his assistant, Waverley.

Sir Hilary drew Foyle a little aside, and they conversed in low tones. Professor Harding, with a nod to the superintendent, had gone upstairs to where the divisional surgeon and another doctor were waiting with Lomont, the secretary of the murdered man, outside the door of the room where Robert Grell lay dead.

The doctors had done no more than ascertain he was dead, and Foyle himself had purposely not gone near the room until Harding had an opportunity of making his examinations.

'I shall take charge of this myself, if you do not mind, Sir Hilary,' Foyle was saying. 'Mainland is capable of looking after the routine work of the department, and in the case of a man of Mr Grell's importance—'

'That is what I should have suggested,' said Sir Hilary. 'We must get to the bottom of this at all costs. You know Mr Grell was to have been married to Lady Eileen Meredith at St Margaret's, Westminster, this morning. It's a bad business. Let's see what Harding's got to say.'

Their feet sank noiselessly into the thick carpet of the stairs as they moved towards the death-chamber. From an open doorway near the landing a flood of light issued.

'Very handy for anyone to get away,' commented Foyle. 'The stairs lead direct to the hall, and there are only two rooms to pass. This carpet would deaden footsteps too.'

They entered softly. Someone had turned all the lights on in the room, and it was bathed in brilliance.

A dying fire flickered in the grate; bookcases lined the red-papered walls, which were broken here and there by curios and sporting trophies gathered from many countries. There were a few etchings, which had evidently been chosen with the skill of a connoisseur.

Parallel with the window was a desk, scrupulously tidy. Half a dozen chairs were scattered about, and in a recess was a couch, over which the angular frock-coated figure of Professor Harding was bent. He looked up as the two men approached.

'It's clearly murder,' he said. 'He was probably killed between ten and eleven—stabbed through the heart. Curious weapon used too—look!'

He moved aside and for the first time Foyle got a view of the body. Robert Grell lay sprawled awkwardly on the couch, his face turned towards the wall, one leg trailing on the floor. A dark crimson stain soiled the white surface of his shirt, and one side of his dinner jacket was wringing wet. The dagger still remained in the wound, and it was that riveted Foyle's attention. He stepped back quickly to one of the men at the door.

'Send Mr Grant to me,' he ordered.

Returning to the body, he gently withdrew the knife, handling it with the most delicate care. 'I've never seen anything like this before,' he said. 'Queer thing, isn't it?'

It was a sheath knife with a blade of finely tempered steel about three inches long and as sharp as a razor. Its abnormality lay in a hilt of smooth white ivory set horizontally and not vertically to the blade, as is a rule with most knives.

Foyle carried it in the palm of his hand nearer to the light and squinted at it from various angles. One at least of the observers guessed his purpose. But the detective seemed dissatisfied.

'Can't see anything,' he grumbled peevishly. 'Ah, there you are, Grant. I want to see whether we can make anything of this. Let me have a little graphite, will you?'

The finger-print expert took an envelope from his pocket and handed it to the superintendent. From it Foyle scattered fine black powder on the hilt. A little cry of satisfaction came from his lips as he blew the stuff away in a little dark cloud. Those in the room crowded around.

Outlined in black against the white surface of the ivory were four finger-prints. The two centre ones were sharp and distinct, the outside prints were fainter and more blurred.

'By Jove, that's good!' exclaimed the professor.

Foyle rubbed his chin and handed the weapon to Grant without replying. 'Get one of your men to photograph those and have them enlarged. At any rate, it's something to go on with. It would be as well to compare 'em with the records, though I doubt whether that will be of much use.' He drew his watch from his pocket and glanced at it. 'Now, if you will excuse me, gentlemen, I should like to have the room to myself for a little while. And, Grant, send Green and the photographer up, and tell Waverley to act with Bolt in examining the servants.'

The room cleared. Harding lingered to exchange a few words with the superintendent.

'I can do nothing, Mr Foyle,' he said. 'From a medical point of view it is all straightforward. There can be no question about the time and cause of death. Good night—or rather, good morning.'

'Thank you, Mr Harding, good morning.'

His eyes were roving restlessly about the room, and he dictated the work the photographer was to do with scrupulous care. Half a dozen times a dazzling flash of magnesium powder lit up the place. Photographs of the room in sections were being taken. Then with a curt order to the photographer to return immediately to Scotland Yard and develop his negatives, he drew up a chair to the couch and began to go methodically through the pockets of the dead man.

Green stood by, a note-book in hand. Now and again Foyle dictated swiftly. He was a man who knew the value of order and system. Every step in the investigation of a crime is reduced to writing, collected, indexed, and filed together, so that the whole history of a case is instantly available at any time. He was carrying out the regular routine.

Only two things of any consequence rewarded his search—one was a note from Sir Ralph Fairfield confirming an appointment with Grell to dine at the St Jermyn's Club the previous evening; the other was a miniature set in diamonds of a girl, dark and black-haired, with an insolent piquant beauty.

'I've seen that face before somewhere,' mused the superintendent. 'Green, there's a "Who's Who" on the desk behind you. I want Sir Ralph Fairfield.'

Rapidly he scanned the score of lines of small type devoted to the baronet. They told him little that he had not known before. Fairfield was in his forty-third year, was the ninth baronet, and had great estates in Hampshire and Scotland. He was a traveller and a student. His town address was given as the Albany.

'You'd better go round to Fairfield's place, Green. Tell him what's happened and bring him here at once.'

As the chief inspector, a grim, silent man, left, Foyle turned again to his work. He began a careful search of the room, even rummaging among the litter in the waste-paper basket. But there was nothing else that might help to throw the faintest light on the tragedy.

A discreet knock on the door preceded Waverley's entrance with a report of the examination of everyone in the house. He had gathered little beyond the fact that Grell, when not concerned in social duties, was a man of irregular comings and goings, and that Ivan, his personal valet, was a man he had brought from St Petersburg, who spoke French but little English, and had consequently associated little with the other servants.

Foyle subsided into his chair with his forehead puckered into a series of little wrinkles. He rested his chin on his hand and gazed into vacancy. There might be a hundred solutions to the riddle. Where was the motive? Was it blackmail? Was it revenge? Was it jealousy? Was it robbery? Was it a political crime? Was it the work of a madman? Who was the mysterious veiled woman? Was she associated with the crime?

These and a hundred other questions beat insistently on his brain, and to none of them could he see the answer. He pictured the queer dagger, but flog his memory as he would he could not think where it might have been procured. In the morning he would set a score of men making inquiries at every place in London where such a thing was likely to have been obtained.

He was in the position of a man who might solve a puzzle by hard, painstaking experiment and inquiry, but rather hoped that some brilliant flash of inspiration or luck might give him the key that would fit it together at once. They rarely do come.

Once Lomont, Grell's secretary, knocked and entered with a question on his lips. Foyle waved him impatiently away.

'I will see you later on, Mr Lomont. I am too busy to see you now. Mr Waverley or Mr Bolt will see to you.'

The man vanished, and a moment or two later a discreet tap at the door heralded the return of Green, accompanied by Sir Ralph Fairfield.

The baronet's hand was cold as it met that of Foyle, and his haggard face was averted as though to avoid the searching gaze of the detective.

CHAPTER IV

FAIRFIELD, awakened from sleep by the news of the murder of his friend, had stared stupidly at the detective Foyle had sent to him.

'Grell killed!' he exclaimed. 'Why, he was with me last night. It is incredible—awful. Of course, I'll come at once—though I don't see what use I can be. What time was he murdered?'

'About ten o'clock. So far as we know you were the last person to see him alive—except the murderer,' said Green. 'Believe me, we're sorry to have to trouble you.'

The baronet's face had suddenly gone the colour of white paper. A sickening dread had suddenly swept over him. His hands trembled as he adjusted his overcoat. He remembered that he had assured Lady Eileen that Grell had been with him at the club from six till eleven. What complexion would that statement bear when it was exposed as a lie—in the light of the tragedy? His throat worked as he realised that he might even be suspected of the crime.

The ordinary person suddenly involved in the whirlpool of crime is always staggered. There is ever the feeling, conscious or unconscious: 'Why out of so many millions of people should this happen to *me*?' So it was with Sir Ralph Fairfield.

He pictured the agony in Eileen Meredith's eyes when she heard of the death of her lover, pictured her denunciation of his lie. The truth would only sound lame if he were to tell it. Who would believe it? Like a man stricken dumb he descended in the lift with Green, out into the wild night in a taxicab, his thoughts a chaos.

He was neither a coward nor a fool. He had known close acquaintance with sudden death before. But that was different. It had not happened so. He was incapable of connected thought. One thing only he was clear upon—he must see Eileen, tell her the truth and throw himself on her mercy. Meanwhile he would answer no questions until he had considered the matter quietly.

This was his state of mind when he shook hands with Foyle. He had schooled his voice, and it was in a quiet tone that he spoke.

'It's a horrible thing, this,' he said, twirling his hat between his long, nervous fingers.

Foyle was studying him closely. The movement of the hands was not lost upon him.

'Yes,' he agreed, stroking his chin. 'I asked you to come here because Mr Grell dined with you last night. Do you know if he left you to keep an appointment?'

'No—that is, it might have been so. He left me, and I understood he would be back. He did not return.'

'At what time?'

Fairfield hesitated a second before replying. Then, 'I haven't the remotest idea.'

The face of Foyle gave no indication of the surprise he felt. He did not press the question, but slid off to another.

'Do you know of any woman who was likely to visit him at that time of night?'

'Great heavens, no, man! Do you suspect a woman? He—' He checked himself, and looked curiously at the detective. 'Mr Grell was a friend of mine,' he went on more quietly.

'Things are bad enough as they are, but you know that he had influential friends both here and in America. They won't thank you, Mr Foyle, for trying to go into such things.'

Heldon Foyle's eyes lingered in quiet scrutiny on the other's face.

'I shall do what I consider to be my duty,' he said, his voice a little hard. 'Come, Sir Ralph, you will see I must do my best to bring the murderer of this man to justice. Had Mr Grell any relations?'

'I don't believe there's one in the wide world.'

'And you don't remember what time he left? Try, Sir Ralph. It is important. Before you came I sent a man to the club, and none of the servants recollects seeing either of you go. They say he was with you most of the evening. You can clear up this matter of time.'

'I don't remember what time he left me.'

The baronet's voice was hoarse and strained. Foyle rose and stood towering over him.

'You are lying,' he said deliberately.

Sir Ralph recoiled as though he had been struck in the face. A quick wave of crimson had mounted to his temples. Instinctively his hands clenched. Then regaining a little control of himself he wheeled about without a word. His hand was on the handle of the door when the superintendent's suave voice brought him to a halt.

'Oh, by the way, Sir Ralph, you might look at this before you go, and say whether you recognise it.'

He held his clenched hand out, and suddenly unclasped it to disclose the miniature set in diamonds.

Sir Ralph gave a start. 'By Jove, it's little Lola of Vienna!' he exclaimed. Then realised that he had been trapped. 'But I shall tell you nothing about her,' he snapped.

'Thank you, Sir Ralph,' said the other quietly.

'But this I think it right you should know,' went on Fairfield, standing with one hand still on the handle of the door: 'When

Grell was with me last night he showed me a pearl necklace, which he said he had bought as a wedding present for Lady Eileen Meredith. If you have not found it, it may give you some motive for the tragedy.'

'Ah!' said Foyle unemotionally.

CHAPTER V

DAY had long dawned ere Foyle and his staff had finished their work at the great house in Grosvenor Gardens. There had been much to do, for every person who might possibly throw a light on the tragedy had to be questioned and requestioned. The place had been thoroughly searched from attic to cellar, for letters or for the jewels that, if Sir Ralph Fairfield were right, were missing.

Much more there would be to do, but for the moment they could go no further. Foyle returned wearily to Scotland Yard to learn that of the finger-prints on the dagger two were too blurred to serve for purposes of identification. He ordered the miniature to be photographed, and held a short consultation with the assistant commissioner. The watch kept for Ivan had so far been without avail. In the corridor, early as it was, a dozen journalists were waiting. Foyle submitted good-humouredly to their questions as they grouped themselves about his room.

'Yes. Of course, I'll let you know all about it,' he protested. 'I'll have the facts typed out for you, and you can embroider them yourselves. There's a description of a man we'd like to get hold of—not necessarily the murderer, but he might be an important witness. Be sure and put that in.'

He always had an air of engaging candour when dealing with newspaper men. Sometimes they were useful, and he never failed to supply them with just as much information about a case as would in any event leak out. That saved them trouble and made them grateful. He went away now to have the bare details of the murder put into shape. When he returned he held the diamond-set miniature in his hand.

'This has been left at the Lost Property Office,' he declared unblushingly. 'It's pretty valuable, so they've put it into our hands to find the owner. Any of you boys know the lady?'

Some of them examined it with polite interest. They were more concerned with the murder of a famous man. Lost trinkets were small beer at such time. Only Jerrold of *The Wire* made any suggestion.

'Reminds me of that Russian princess woman who's been staying at the Palatial, only it's too young for her. What's her name?—Petrovska, I think.'

'Thanks,' said Foyle; 'it doesn't matter much. Ah, here's your stuff. Good-bye, boys, and don't worry me more than you can help. This thing is going to keep us pretty busy.'

He saw them out of the room and carefully closed the door. Sitting at his desk he lifted the receiver from the telephone.

'Get the Palatial Hotel,' he ordered. 'Hello! That the Palatial? Is the Princess Petrovska there? What? Left last night at ten o'clock? Did she say where she was going? No, I see. Good-bye.'

He scribbled a few words on a slip of paper, and touching the bell gave it to the man who answered. 'Send that to St Petersburg at once.'

It was a communication to the Chief of the Russian police, asking that inquiries should be made as to the antecedents of the Princess.

For the next three hours men were coming rapidly in and out of the superintendent's office, receiving instructions and making reports. Practically the whole of the six hundred men of the C.I.D. were engaged on the case, for there was no avenue of investigation so slender but that there might be something at the end of it. Neither Foyle nor his lieutenants were men to leave anything to chance. Green was seated opposite to him, discussing the progress they had made.

The superintendent leaned back wearily in his chair. Someone handed him a slim envelope. He tore it open and slowly studied the cipher in which the message was written. It read:

Silinsky, Chief of Police, St Petersburg.
To Foyle, Superintendent C.I.D., London.
Woman you mention formerly Lola Rachael, believed born Paris;
formerly on stage, Vienna; married Prince Petrovska, 1898.
Husband died suddenly 1900. Travels much.
No further particulars known.

Foyle stroked his chin gravely. 'Formerly Lola Rachael,' he murmured. 'And Sir Ralph recognised the miniature as little Lola of Vienna. She's worth looking after. We must find her, Green. What about this man Ivan?'

'No trace of him yet, sir, but I don't think he can give us the slip. He hadn't much time to get away. By the way, sir, what do you think of Sir Ralph?'

'I don't know. He's keeping something back for some reason. You'd better have him shadowed, Green. Go yourself, and take a good man with you. He mustn't be let out of sight night or day. I may tackle him again later on.'

'Very good, sir. Waverley's still at Grosvenor Gardens. Will you be going back there?'

'I don't know. I want to look through the records of the Convict Supervision Office for the last ten years. I have an idea that I may strike something.'

Green was too wise a man to ask questions of his chief. He slipped from the room. Half an hour later Foyle dashed out of the room hatless, and, picking up a taxicab, drove at top speed to Grosvenor Gardens. He was greeted at the door by Lomont.

'What is it?' he demanded, the excitement of the detective communicating itself to him. 'Have you carried the case any further?'

'I don't know,' replied the detective. 'I must see the body again. Come up with me.'

In the death-chamber he carefully locked the door. A heavy ink-well stood on the desk. He twisted up a piece of paper and dipped it in. Then, approaching the murdered man, he smeared the fingers of his right hand with the blackened paper and pressed them lightly on a piece of blotting paper. The secretary, in utter bewilderment, watched him compare the prints with a piece of paper he took from his pocket.

'What is it?' he repeated again.

'Mr Lomont,' replied the detective gravely, 'I wish I knew. Unless our whole system of identification is wrong—and that is incredible—that man who lies dead there is not Robert Grell.'

CHAPTER VI

LOMONT reeled dizzily, and his hand sought the support of the wall. To him Foyle's voice sounded unreal. He stared at the detective as though doubtful of his sanity. His life had been hitherto ordered, placid. That there were such things as crimes, murders, detectives, he knew. He had read of them in the newspapers. But hitherto they had only been names to him—something to make the paper more readable.

He was a thin-faced man of about thirty, with somewhat sallow cheeks on which there was now a hectic flush, a high-pitched forehead that seemed to have contracted into a perpetual frown, and colourless eyes. The son of a well-known barrister, he had tried his luck in the City after leaving Cambridge. In a few years the respectable income he had started with had dwindled under the drain of his speculations, and it was then that a friend had recommended him to Robert Grell, who was about to take up his residence in England. James Lomont had jumped at the chance, for the salary was respectable and would enable him to maintain a certain footing in society.

'Not Robert Grell!' he echoed incredulously.

Foyle fancied that there was some quality other than incredulity in the tone, but decided that he was mistaken. The young man's nerves were shaken up. So far as time would allow he had gathered all there was to know about him. Lomont had not escaped the network of inquiry that was being woven about all who had associated with Robert Grell.

No fewer than three chapters in a book the Criminal Investigation Department had commenced compiling were devoted to him. They lay with others neatly typed and indexed in Heldon Foyle's office.

One was his signed statement of events on the night of the tragedy. The last time he had seen Grell alive was at half-past six, when his employer had left for the St Jermyn's Club. He himself had gone to the Savoy Theatre, and, returning some time after eleven, had let himself in with his own key and gone straight to bed. He had only been aroused when the police took possession of the house. The third was headed: 'Inquiries as to career of, and corroboration of statements made by, James Lomont'.

The curtains had remained drawn, and only a dim light filtered through into the room. Foyle lifted a little green-shaded electric lamp from the table, and switched on the light so that it fell on the face of the dead man.

'Look,' he said, in a quiet voice, 'do you recognise your chief?'

The young man flung back his shoulders with a jerk, as though overcoming his own feelings, and approached the body with evident distaste. His hands, slender as a woman's, were tight-clenched, and his breath came and went in nervous spasms. For a moment he gazed, and then shook his head weakly.

'It is not,' he whispered with dry lips. 'There is an old scar across the temple. Mr Grell's face was not disfigured.' He stretched out a hand and clutched the superintendent nervously by the shoulder. 'Who is this man, Mr Foyle? What does it all mean? Where is Mr Grell?'

Foyle's hand had stolen to his chin and he rubbed it vigorously.

'I don't know what it means,' he confessed irritably. 'You know as much as I do now. This man is not Robert Grell, though he is astonishingly like him. Now, Mr Lomont, I rely on you not to breathe a word of this to a living soul until I give you permission. This secret must remain between our two selves for the time being.'

'Certainly.'

In spite of his air of candour, Heldon Foyle had not revealed all he knew. He left the house pondering deeply.

'You see, sir,' he explained to the Assistant Commissioner later, 'no one who knew Grell had seen the body closely. The butler had taken it for granted that it was his master. It was pure luck with me. In looking through the records in search of this woman Petrovska, I hit against the picture of Goldenburg. It was so like Grell that I went off at once to compare finger-prints. They tallied; and then young Lomont spoke of the scar. Though what Harry Goldenburg should be doing in Grell's house, with Grell's clothes, and with Grell's property in the pockets, is more than I can fathom.'

Sir Hilary Thornton drummed on his desk with his right hand.

'Isn't this the Goldenburg who engineered the South American gold mine swindle?' he asked.

'That's the man,' agreed Foyle, not without a note of rueful admiration. 'He'd got half-a-dozen of the best-known and richest peers in England to promise support, when we spoilt his game. No one would prosecute. He always had luck, had Goldenburg. He's been at the back of a score of big things, but we could never get legal proof against him. He was a cunning rascal—educated, plausible, reckless. Well, he's gone now, and he's given us as tough a nut to crack as ever he did while he was alive.'

'How did you get his finger-prints if he was never convicted?' asked Sir Hilary with interest.

Foyle looked his superior full in the face and smiled.

'I arrested him myself, on a charge of pocket-picking in Piccadilly,' he said. 'Of course, he never picked a pocket in his life—he was too big a crook for that. But we got a remand, and that gave us a chance to get his photograph and prints for the records. We offered no evidence on the second hearing. It was perhaps not strictly legal, but—' The superintendent's features relaxed into a smile. 'He never brought an action for malicious prosecution.'

'And about Grell? How do you propose to find him?'

Foyle drew his chair up to the table and scribbled busily for a few minutes on a sheet of paper. He carefully blotted it, and handed the result of his labours to Sir Hilary, who nodded approval as he read it.

'You think we shall catch one man by advertising for another?'

'I think it worth trying, sir,' retorted the superintendent curtly. 'The description and the photograph fit like a glove—and we shan't be giving anything away.'

As Heldon Foyle passed through the little back door leading to the courtyard of Scotland Yard an hour later, he stopped for an instant to study a poster that was being placed among the notices on the board in the door. It ran:

POLICE NOTICE.

———

£100 REWARD

HARRY GOLDENBURG, alias THE HON. RUPERT BAXTER,
MAX SMITH, JOHN BROOKS, etc.
WANTED FOR
MURDER.

———

DESCRIPTION.—Age, about 45; height, about 6 ft. 1 in.;
complexion, bronzed; square features; grey hair;
drooping grey moustache; upright carriage.

NOTE.—Henry Goldenburg has travelled extensively, and
is an American by birth, but his accent is almost
imperceptible. He speaks several languages, and
has resided in Paris, Madrid, and Rome.

_____

The above Reward will be paid to any person (other
than a member of any Police force in the United
Kingdom) who gives such information as will lead
to the apprehension of the above-named person.

The superintendent had wasted no time.

CHAPTER VII

THE first grey daylight had found Sir Ralph Fairfield pacing
his sitting-room with uneven strides, his hands clasped
behind his back, the stump of a cold cigar between his teeth.
His interview with Heldon Foyle had not been calculated to
calm him.

'I'm a fool—a fool,' he told himself. 'Why should they
suspect me? What have I to gain by Grell's death?'

It was the attitude of a man trying to convince himself.
There was one reason why he might be supposed to wish his
friend out of the way, but he dared not even shape the thought.
There was one person who might guess, and it was she whose
lips he hoped to seal. A quick dread came to him. Suppose
the police had already gone to her. The thought stung him
to action. He had not even removed his hat and coat since
his return from Grosvenor Gardens. He made his way to the
street and walked briskly along until he sighted a taxicab.

'507 Berkeley Square,' he told the driver.

It was a surprised footman who opened the door of the Duke of Burghley's house. Fairfield, at the man's look of astonishment, remembered that he was unshaven, and that his clothes had been thrown on haphazard. It was a queer thought to intrude at such a time. But he was usually a scrupulously dressed man, and the triviality worried him.

'Lady Eileen Meredith. I must see her at once,' he said peremptorily. 'Don't stand staring at me, man. You know me.'

The footman coughed apologetically.

'Yes, Sir Ralph. Lady Eileen is not up yet. If it is important I can get a maid to call her. Shall I tell his Grace?'

'No. It is of the utmost importance that I see her personally immediately.'

Sir Ralph breathed a sigh of relief as he was ushered into the cool morning room and the door closed behind him. At all events, the police had not seen her yet. He was first. That meant he would have to break the news to her. How would she take it?

'The poor little girl!' he muttered to himself. And then the door clicked.

Eileen Meredith stood there, a pink dressing-gown enveloping her graceful figure from shoulders to feet. There was questioning wonder in her grey eyes as she extended her hand, but no alarm. He almost wished there was. It would have made things easier.

'You, Sir Ralph?' she cried. 'What has brought you here so early? Has Bob repented of his bargain and sent you to call it off at the last moment?'

The man fumbled for words. Now that he was face to face with her the phrase he had so laboriously worked out to lead up to the news had deserted him. He pushed a chair towards her.

'Er—won't you sit down?' he said awkwardly.

He was striving for an opening. Both words and tone called the girl's direct attention to the haggard face, the feverish eyes. Her fears were alight on the instant. She regarded him with parted lips and gripped his arm impulsively.

'Something has happened!' she cried apprehensively. 'Why do you look like that? What is it?' Her voice rose and she tried to shake the silent man. 'Answer—why don't you answer? Is he ill—dead?'

Sir Ralph choked over his reply.

'He was killed last night—murdered.'

It was out at last. He had blundered clumsily, and he knew it. The colour drained from Eileen's face and she stood rigid as a statue for a moment. Then slowly she swayed forward. He stretched out his arms to prevent her from falling. She waved him aside dumbly and tottered to a couch. His directness had been more merciful than he had thought. She was stunned, dazed by her calamity. Her very silence frightened the man. She sat bolt upright, her hand resting limply in her lap and her dull eyes staring into vacancy. A tiny clock on the mantelpiece ticked loudly.

'Dead!' she whispered at last. There was no trace of unsteadiness in her voice and her eyes were dry. She spoke mechanically. 'And it is our wedding-day! Dead! Bob is dead?'

Her hair had fallen about her shoulders, and, beautiful in her grief, she inspired the man with almost supernatural awe. He had moved to the mantelpiece and, resting an arm upon it and one foot upon the fender, remained looking down upon her. He was waiting until the first numbness of the shock had passed. The little clock on the mantelpiece had ticked out ten minutes ere she spoke again. But her voice was pitched in more natural tones, and her face had regained something of its colour.

'How did it happen?'

Haltingly he gave such details as he knew. Her eyes were fixed on his face as he narrated his story. He hesitated as he referred to his telephone conversation with her. In her clear eyes he saw challenging scorn and stopped abruptly.

'You say that Bob asked you to lie to me?' she demanded.

'Not to you in particular. To anyone who rang up. I couldn't know whether he wished his instructions to apply to you.'

'No, no, of course not,' she interposed quickly, but with a tightening of the heart he recognised the bitterness of her tone. For all her soft daintiness, there was something of the tigress in Eileen Meredith.

The man she loved was dead. Well, she would have her vengeance—somehow, on someone. She was ready to suspect without thinking. And Sir Ralph Fairfield had laid himself open to suspicion.

'He was killed before eleven,' she went on remorselessly, 'and you told me he was in the club with you at that time.'

'You don't believe me.' He held out his arms to her imploringly, and then dropped them to his side. 'I give you my word that everything I have told you is true. Why should I lie now?'

She wheeled on him passionately.

'You ask me that?' she said tensely. 'You who thought he was in your way—that what you could not gain while he was living you might take when he was dead. Do you think your smooth-faced hypocrisy deceives me now? You pretended to accept your dismissal, pretended to be still my friend—and his.'

Her anger disconcerted the man more than her anguish had done. His breath caught sharply.

'You don't realise what you are saying,' he said, speaking calmly with an effort. 'Because I once loved you—love you still if you will—before ever Robert Grell came into your life, you hint an unthinkable thing.'

She crossed the room in a graceful swirl of draperies, and laid a finger on the bell. Her features were set. She was in no state to weigh the justice or injustice of the implied accusation she had made. And the man, for his part, felt his oppression brushed away by anger at her readiness to judge him.

'We shall see whether the police believe it unthinkable,' she said coldly.

A servant tapped discreetly and opened the door.

'Show this person out,' she said.

Sir Ralph bowed mechanically. There was nothing more to be said. He knew that in her present condition an appeal to her to suppress the story of the telephone message would be worse than useless. As he passed down the steps and into the street, a man sauntered idly a dozen yards behind him. And thirty yards behind that man was another whom the baronet might have recognised as Chief Detective-Inspector Green—had he seen him.

Within the house a girl, no longer upheld by the strength of passionate denunciation, had collapsed on a couch, a huddled heap of draperies, sobbing as though her heart would break.

CHAPTER VIII

IT was an hour after Fairfield had left her before Eileen Meredith's sobs died away in the deserted room. There was none to hear or see, and she gave way to her grief uncontrolled. Gradually the first shock passed. Her calmness came back to her, but she was a different woman to the vivacious, sunny girl who had looked forward to her wedding-day. Her face was set stonily, and in the grey depths of her eyes there lurked in place of laughter an implacable determination.

She had loved Robert Grell with the fierce, passionate devotion of a strong nature. The sudden news of his death had brought out the primitive woman bent on vengeance. It was no impulse of suddenly shattered nerves that had made her turn on Fairfield. To coldly analyse the facts for and against him was beyond her. She only thought of the man who had a possible motive for slaying her lover and had had a possible opportunity.

Yet none would have guessed the burning emotion that thrilled in her veins as she submitted to the ministrations of her maid. She had not even troubled to tell her father, although the elderly peer was her only near relative. Not until he was seated at breakfast did she inform him in level, passionless tones of what had happened. Even then she said nothing of her suspicions of Ralph Fairfield. But for her pale face she might have been speaking of something in which she was but slightly interested.

The Duke of Burghley dropped his knife and fork at her first words. As she finished, he stood over her and passed a hand tenderly around her.

'My poor, poor little girl,' he said. 'This is terrible. Fairfield ought to have seen me first. I must telephone for your aunt to come and stay here until we can get away.'

She shook her head a trifle impatiently.

'I don't want her, father. She cannot help me. I would rather be here alone with you. It would drive me mad to have sympathy showered on me. I want to see no one. I want to be left to myself.'

'But—my dear, I know it is a shock, but you cannot be allowed to brood—'

She rose abruptly from the table and put him from her.

'I shall not brood,' she said. 'I shall work. I am going to Scotland Yard to learn what they know.'

'Yes, yes, if you wish it,' he said soothingly. 'We will go at once. I will order the car now.'

'I would rather go alone, if you don't mind,' she said decisively, and the door closed behind her.

'She always was headstrong,' remarked the Duke of Burghley to the devilled kidneys, and stared moodily into the fire.

Since his wife had died he had always been governed by his impetuous, strong-willed daughter, and accepted the situation philosophically so long as he had his books and his club. He led a complacent life from which he was rarely stirred. But he was hit harder than he cared to admit by the way in which she accepted the tragedy. He wondered vaguely what he ought to do, and decided to consult Brown—Brown being the senior member of his firm of family solicitors.

In his room at Scotland Yard Superintendent Heldon Foyle, a cigar between his teeth, was studying the book which his staff was compiling. Already it formed a bulky volume of many hundred typewritten pages. Here were reports, signed statements, photographs, personal descriptions, facsimiles of finger-prints, telegrams, letters, surveyors' plans, notes—everything, important and unimportant, that might have a possible bearing on the case. The superintendent turned over the pages with a moistened forefinger, and made a note now and again on a writing-pad by his side.

'Puzzling cases are like a jig-saw puzzle,' he had once said. 'You juggle about with the facts until you find two or three that fit together. They give you the key, and you build the rest up round 'em. But it's no good trying to do it unless you've got your box of pieces complete.'

His box of pieces was not complete, and he knew it. Nevertheless, he could not resist trying to fit them together. But the announcement made by his clerk of the arrival of Lady Eileen Meredith came while he was still puzzling. She stood in the doorway, a dainty figure in furs, a heavy veil drawn over her face.

'Mr Foyle?' she asked hesitatingly.

He bowed and wheeled a big arm-chair near his desk.

'Yes. Won't you sit down, Lady Eileen? You have just missed one of our men. I sent him round to break the news to you. I need not tell you that we recognise how you must feel in these terrible circumstances. We shall trouble you as little as possible after you have answered a few questions.'

He was studying her shrewdly while he spoke, and her strange composure struck him at once. Even to her he had decided to say nothing of the identity of the murdered man. That could wait until he had had a better opportunity to judge her.

She sat down and rested her chin on one slim, gloved hand, her elbow on the desk.

'That's very good of you,' she said formally. And then broke direct into her mission. 'Have you found out anything, Mr Foyle?'

'It's rather early to say anything yet,' he hedged. 'Our inquiries are not completed.'

'There is no need for further inquiry. I can tell you who the murderer is.'

Superintendent Foyle coughed and idly shifted a piece of paper over the notes on his blotting-pad. His face was inscrutable. She could not tell whether her statement had startled him or not. For all the change in his expression she might have merely remarked that the weather was fine. Had it been anyone else he would have said that before the day was out he expected a dozen or more people to tell him that they knew the murderer—and that in each case the selection would be different. As it was he merely said with polite interest—

'Ah, that will save us a great deal of trouble. Who is it?'

'He is—I believe him to be Sir Ralph Fairfield.'

The superintendent's eyelids flickered curiously; otherwise he gave no sign of the quickening of his interest. He was a judge of men, and although Fairfield had rebuffed him he did not believe him to be a murderer. Still, one never knew. Those who kill are not cast in one mould. If Sir Ralph had slain Goldenburg in mistake for Grell, and Lady Eileen knew there must be a motive—for that motive he had to look no further than the beautiful, unsmiling face before him.

'You realise that you are making a very grave accusation, Lady Eileen?' he said. 'What reason should there be?'

She spoke rapidly, steadily, and he did not interrupt her. His pen rushed swiftly across the paper, taking down her words. They would presently be neatly typed and added to the book. When she paused, he replaced the pen tidily in its rack.

'This is what it comes to—that at eleven o'clock Sir Ralph said Mr Grell was with him. You say that you had refused an offer of marriage from Sir Ralph, and think that he murdered Mr Grell from jealousy. I may say that, though we know Sir Ralph was at his club for dinner and at eleven o'clock, we can find neither servants nor members who can say for certain that he was there at the time the murder was committed.'

She caught her breath. 'Then it was he!' she exclaimed eagerly. 'Bob had not another enemy in the world. You will arrest him.'

'Not yet,' Foyle retorted, and noted that her face fell. 'All this is only suspicion. We must have proof to satisfy a jury before we can do anything with a man in Sir Ralph's position. And now, if you don't mind, I should like to put a few other questions to you.'

When she left after half an hour, Foyle threw back his head with a jerk.

'A pleasant girl,' he commented. 'Seems wonderfully anxious to have Fairfield hanged. I suppose she was really infatuated with Grell. You never know how women are going to take things. I wonder if I can get a set of his finger-prints. That ought to settle the matter one way or the other, so far as he is concerned. But it won't clear up what Goldenburg was doing in Grell's place. I'll have to fix that somehow.'

CHAPTER IX

THE overmastering energy of Heldon Foyle was at once the envy and despair of his subordinates. There was a story that once he went without sleep for a week while unravelling the mystery of the robbery of the Countess of Enver's pearls. That was probably exaggerated, but he certainly spent no unnecessary time for rest or food when work was toward—and he saw also that his staff were urged to the limits of human endurance.

Having spent four hours sleeping in his clothes, he deemed that he had paid full courtesy to nature. He unlocked a drawer, picked out a deadly little automatic pistol, and dropped it into his jacket pocket. He rarely went armed, and had never fired a shot in his life, save at a target. But on certain occasions a pistol was useful to 'back a bluff'. And on the mission he had in mind he might need something. He felt in his breast-pocket to make certain that the enlarged photograph of the finger-prints found on the dagger were there, and sallied forth into the dusk.

In his own mind he had definitely decided on the immediately important points in the inquiry. There was Ivan, the missing servant, to be found, as also the Princess Petrovska. The police of a dozen countries were keeping a look-out for them. Then there was the knife with its quaint, horizontal hilt of ivory. Rigorous inquiry had failed to elicit its place of origin, yet so strange a weapon once seen would infallibly be recognised again. Finally, there was the question of Sir Ralph Fairfield.

The evening papers had seized avidly on a mystery after their own heart, and glaring contents-bills told of 'Millionaire Murdered on Wedding Eve. Strange Mystery'. But Foyle had already seen the papers. He held straight on for the Albany.

'Was Sir Ralph Fairfield in?' The question was superfluous, for he had already seen Chief Detective-Inspector Green standing outside apparently much interested in an evening paper. And Green would not have been there unless Sir Ralph were about.

Foyle was received coldly by the baronet, and his quick eyes noted a half-empty decanter on the table. Fairfield was palpably nervous and ill at ease. He was plainly distrustful of his visitor's purpose. The detective was apologetic and good-humoured.

'I have come to apologise for my rudeness at Grosvenor Gardens,' he began. 'I was worried, and you were, of course, upset. Now we are both more calm, I come to ask you if you would like to add anything to what you said. Of course, you'll be called to give evidence at the inquest, and it would make it easier for you as well as for us if we knew what you were going to say.'

Fairfield shrugged his shoulders. 'I have told you all you will learn from me,' he said quickly. 'I suppose you've seen Lady Eileen Meredith.'

'No.' The lie was prompt, but the superintendent salved his conscience with the thought that it was a necessary one. 'I don't know that she can tell us anything of value.'

An expression of relief flitted over the face of Grell's friend. After all, it was something to have the worst postponed. A man may face swift danger with debonair courage, may be undaunted by perils or emergencies of sport, of travel, of everyday life. But few innocent men can believe that a net is slowly closing round them which will end in the obloquy of the Central Criminal Court, or in a shameful death, without feeling something of the terror of the hunted. 'The terror of the law' is very real in such cases. Fairfield was no coward, but his nerves had begun to go under the strain of the suspense. It would have been different had he been able to do anything—to find relief in action. But he had to remain passively impotent.

'Well,' he said, 'I expect you're very busy, Mr Foyle. I don't want to keep you.'

The detective received the snub with an amiable smile. 'I won't force my company on you, Sir Ralph. If you will just dictate to me a description of the string of pearls that Grell showed you, I will go. Can you let me have a pen and some paper?'

Ungraciously enough Fairfield flung open a small inlaid writing-desk, and Foyle took down the description as though he really needed it. As he finished he held out the pen to Fairfield.

'Will you sign that, please? No, here.'

Their hands were almost touching. Foyle half rose and stumbled clumsily, clutching the other's wrist to save himself. The baronet's hand and fingers were pressed down heavily on the still wet writing. The detective recovered his balance and apologised profusely, at the same time picking up the sheet of paper.

'I don't know how I came to do that. I am very sorry. It's smudged the paper a bit, but that won't matter. It's still readable. Good-bye, Sir Ralph.'

So admirably had the accident been contrived that even Fairfield never suspected that it was anything but genuine. In a public telephone-box, a few hundred yards away, Heldon Foyle was examining the half-sheet of notepaper side by side with the photograph of the finger-prints on the dagger. A telephone-box is admirably constructed for the private examination of documents if one's back is towards the door and one is bent over the directory. Line by line Foyle traced 'laterals,' 'lakes,' and 'accidentals,' calling to his aid a magnifying glass from his waistcoat pocket.

When he emerged he was rubbing his chin vigorously. The prints were totally different. Sir Ralph Fairfield was not the murderer of the man so astoundingly like Robert Grell.

CHAPTER X

THE evidence of the finger-prints was entirely negative. Though Foyle believed that Fairfield was innocent, he never permitted himself to be swayed by his opinions into neglecting a possibility. It was still possible that the baronet might have been concerned in the crime even though they were someone else's prints on the dagger. At any rate Fairfield was suppressing something. It could do no harm to continue the watch that had been set upon him. So Foyle left Green and his companion to continue their unobtrusive vigil.

To justify his stay in the box—for he was artist enough to do things thoroughly even though it might be unnecessary—he lifted the receiver and put a call through to Scotland Yard.

'This is Foyle speaking,' he said when at last he had got the man he asked for. 'Is there anything fresh for me?'

'Nothing important, sir, except that Blake has found a curiosity dealer who says that the knife is one that must have come from South America. It is, he says, an unusual sort of Mexican dagger.'

'Oh. Is the man who says that to be relied on? He isn't just guessing? We can do all the guessing we want ourselves.'

'No, sir, we think he's all right. It's Marfield—one of the biggest men in the trade. By the way, sir, there's a lot of newspaper men been asking for you since you left. They want to know about Goldenburg.'

'So do I,' retorted the other. 'You'd better be strictly truthful with 'em, Mainland. Tell 'em you know no more than is on the reward bill. They won't believe you, anyway. You can say I've gone home to bed, and that there will be nothing more doing this evening. Good-bye.'

'A Mexican dagger,' he muttered to himself as he left the telephone-box. 'Now, if I were a story-book detective I should assume that the murderer was either a South American or had travelled in South America. It looked the kind of thing a woman might carry in her garter. And a veiled woman called on him that night'—he made a wry face. 'Foyle, my lad, you're assuming things. That way madness lies. The dagger might have been bought anywhere as a curiosity, and the veiled woman may have been a purely innocent caller.'

His meditations had brought him to a great restaurant off the Strand. He passed through the swing doors into the lavishly gilded dining-room, and selected a table somewhere near the centre. With the air of a man taking his ease after a strenuous day in the City, he ordered his dinner carefully, seeking the waiter's advice now and again. Then his eye roved carelessly over the throng of diners while he waited for his orders to be fulfilled. The apparently casual scrutiny lasted rather less than a minute. Then he shifted his seat so that he could see without effort the table where two men lingered over their liqueurs. A moment later one of the men noted the solitary figure of the detective.

He emptied his glass without haste and signalled to the waiter. Before that functionary had made out the bill Foyle had strolled over to the table, his face beaming, his hand outstretched.

'How are you, Eden?' he cried effusively. 'Who'd have thought of seeing you here! Business good? Still picking flowers?'

An expression of annoyance crossed the face of the slighter built of the two men, yet he shook hands readily.

'Why, it's Mr Foyle!' he exclaimed heartily. 'How are you? We were just going. Let me introduce Mr Maxwell.'

They called him the Garden of Eden at Scotland Yard—probably because the unwary might have thought him full of innocence. His smooth, bronzed boyish face showed ingenuousness and candour in every line. A glittering diamond pin adorned his necktie, a massive gold chain spanned his waistcoat, a gold ring with a single great ruby was on his finger. That was the only ostentation about him, and his quiet, well-cut clothes were in good taste.

Foyle acknowledged the introduction.

'From the colonies, I suppose, Mr Maxwell? I suppose Eden has told you he's just come over.' Eden surveyed the detective with wide-open, innocent blue eyes in which there dwelt hurt reproach. 'I hate to separate you, but I've got important business with him. Perhaps you'll meet another time.'

'Yes, you'll excuse me now, old man,' chimed in Eden blandly. 'Call for me at the Palatial at eleven tomorrow, and we'll make a day of it.'

Maxwell had no sooner accepted his dismissal than Foyle led the other over to his table. Eden walked with the manner of one uncertain what was about to happen.

'It is all right, Mr Foyle,' he protested eagerly. 'It is *all right*. I haven't touched him for a sou.'

Foyle began on the soup placidly.

'You're a joker, Jimmy,' he smiled. 'Don't get uneasy. I'm not going to carry you inside. Only you'll have to leave the Palatial tonight, Jimmy—tonight, do you understand? And if Maxwell turns up with a complaint against you there'll be pretty bad trouble. You'll be put out of temptation for good and all. There's such a thing as preventive detention in this country now, you know.'

The Garden of Eden looked pained.

'Truth, Mr Foyle, I haven't done a thing,' he declared earnestly. 'I'm trying the straight game now.'

Heldon Foyle wagged his head.

'And staying at the Palatial,' he smiled. 'Oh, Jimmy, Jimmy! I believe you, of course.' And he went on with his soup.

Suddenly he looked up. 'When did you last see Goldenburg?' he demanded curtly. 'No nonsense, mind, Jimmy.'

Eden's face had cleared. 'So that's the lay, is it?' he said with relief. 'I saw the bills out for him, and I don't mind helping you if I can, Mr Foyle. He was never what you'd call a proper pal, and I don't bear any malice, though you've just done me out of a cool five hundred. That mug who's just gone'—he jerked his head towards the door—'was going to follow my tip and back a horse that won't win tomorrow. That's a bit hard, isn't it, Mr Foyle?'

From his breast-pocket Foyle took a ten-pound note and slid it across the table. He followed Eden's meaning.

'Cough it up,' he advised.

The Garden of Eden took the note and thrust it into his trousers pocket.

'He was in Victoria Station, talking to a foreign-looking chap, on Wednesday night.' A look of astonishment crossed his face while he spoke. 'By the living jingo, there's the very man he was talking to coming in now.'

Foyle folded his serviette neatly and rose.

'Right, Jimmy. I'll talk to you later. Go to the Yard and wait till I come,' he said, and, walking swiftly across the room, thrust his arm through that of the new arrival.

'You are the man who used to be Mr Grell's valet,' he said quietly in French. 'I am a police officer, and you must come with me.'

CHAPTER XI

THE man tried to jerk himself free, but the detective's fingers closed tightly about his wrist.

'There is no use making a scene, my man,' he said, still speaking in French, his voice stern, but pitched in a low key. 'You are Ivan something-or-other, and you know of the murder of your master. So come along.'

'It's a mistake,' protested the other volubly in the same language. His words slurred into each other in his excitement. 'I am not the man you take me for. I am Pierre Bazarre, a jeweller of Paris, and I have my credentials. I will not submit to this abominable outrage. I know nothing of M. Grell; you shall not arrest me—'

Heldon Foyle cut him short. He had, without the appearance of force, quietly forced his prisoner outside the restaurant and signalled to a passing taxicab.

'I am not arresting you,' he said, ignoring the protestations of the other. 'I am going to detain you till you give a satisfactory explanation of your reason for leaving Mr Grell's house on the night of the murder.'

They were on the edge of the pavement close to the cab. Ivan with a quick oath wheeled inward, and struck savagely at the superintendent's face. Foyle's grip did not relax. He merely lowered his head, seemingly without haste, and, as the man swung forward with the momentum of the blow, jabbed with his own free hand at his body. So neatly was it done that passers-by saw nothing but an apparently drunken man collapse on the pavement in spite of the endeavours of his friend to hold him up.

The whole breath had been knocked out of Ivan's body by those two swift body-blows. Before he could recover, Foyle had lifted him bodily into the cab.

'King Street,' he said quietly to the driver, and sat down opposite to Ivan, alert and watchful.

'Sorry if I hurt you,' he apologised. 'It will be all right in a minute. It has only upset your wind a little. That will pass off.'

Ivan, his hands pressed tightly to the pit of his stomach, groaned. Presently he straightened himself up, and Foyle, calmly ignoring the assault, produced a cigar-case.

'Have a cigar? I've no doubt you'll be able to make things all right when we get to the station. There's nothing to worry about. You will just have a little talk with me, and as soon as one or two points are cleared up you'll be able to go.'

The case was struck angrily aside. Foyle smiled, and although his whole body was taut in anticipation of any fresh attempt at violence, he quietly struck a match and lit one himself.

'As you like,' he said imperturbably. 'They're good cigars. I have them sent over to me by a friend direct from Havana.'

All the while he was speaking he was scrutinising the man who had been Grell's valet with deliberate care. Ivan was sleek and well-groomed, with a dark face and prominent cheekbones that betrayed his Caucasian origin. The brows were drawn tightly in a surly frown; a heavy dark moustache hid the upper lip, and though the shoulders were sloping he was obviously a man of considerable physical strength.

Foyle felt that it was going to be no easy matter to win this man's confidence. Yet he was determined to do so. Beyond the fact that he had vanished when the murder was discovered, there was nothing so far to suggest that he was the actual culprit. Certain it was, however, that he must have knowledge of matters which would prove valuable. If he would volunteer the information, well and good. The detective did not wish to have to question him, for such a course, however advisable it might appear, could be made to assume an ugly look in the hands of the astute counsel, should the man be charged with the crime. Where by French or American methods a statement might have been extracted by bullying or by cross-examination, here it had to be extracted by diplomacy if possible.

Sullen and silent, Ivan alighted from the cab as it drew up under the blue lamp outside King Street police station. He passed arm-in-arm with Foyle up the steps. With a nod to the uniformed inspector in the outer office, the superintendent led him into the offices set apart for the divisional detachment of the Criminal Investigation Department. A broad-shouldered man with side whiskers, who was writing at a desk, looked up as they entered.

'Good morning, Mr Norman,' said Foyle. 'This gentleman wants to tell me something about the Grell case. Just give him a chair, will you, and send in a shorthand writer who understands French to take a statement.'

'I shall make no statement,' broke in the Russian angrily, speaking in French, but with a readiness that showed he was able to follow English. 'It's all a mistake—a mistake for which you will pay heavily.'

'Ah! that's just what I wish to get at. There seems to be a little confusion. Perhaps I have been over-zealous, but the fact is, Monsieur—er—Bazarre, you are wearing a false moustache, and that rather aroused my suspicions—see?'

His hand did not seem to move, yet a second later the heavy moustache had been torn from the man's face. He started to his feet with an exclamation. Foyle waved him back to his chair.

'I only wanted to feel sure that I was right. Now, monsieur, I want to make it clear that I have no right to ask you anything. If you wish to say anything, it will be taken down, and what action I take depends on what you say.'

Ivan scowled into the fire and preserved a stubborn silence. Whether he knew it or not, he held all the advantage. Unless he committed himself by some incautious word, there was little to implicate him in the murder. Suspicion there might be, but legal proof there was none. It would scarcely do to arrest him on such flimsy evidence. The Russian police had failed to trace his antecedents, and the Criminal Investigation Department were ignorant even of his surname. He had been known simply as Ivan at Grosvenor Gardens.

Foyle tried again, and this time his voice was silky and soft as ever as he uttered a plainer threat.

'I want to help you if I can. I don't want to have to charge you with the murder of Mr Grell.'

The warm blood surged crimson to Ivan's face. In an instant he was out of his chair and had leapt at the throat of the detective. So rapid, so unexpected was the movement that, although Heldon Foyle had not ceased his careful watchfulness, and although he writhed quickly aside, he was borne back by his assailant. The two crashed heavily to the floor. As they rolled over, struggling desperately, the grip upon the detective's throat grew ever tighter and tighter.

Half a dozen men had rushed into the room at the noise of the struggle, and strove vainly to tear the Russian from his hold. But he hung on with the tenacity of a mastiff. There was a ringing in Foyle's ear and a red blur before his eyes. With a superhuman effort he got his elbow under the Russian's chin and pressed it back sharply.

The grip relaxed ever so slightly, but it was enough. Instantly Foyle had wrested himself free, and Ivan was pinioned to the floor by the others.

'Handcuffs,' said the superintendent sharply.

Someone got a pair on the prisoner's wrists, and he was jerked none too gently to his feet. A couple of men still held him. At a word from Foyle the others had gone about their business, with the exception of Norman. The superintendent flicked the dust from his clothes, and picked something, which had fallen during the struggle, from the floor.

'You admit you are Ivan, then?' he said quietly.

The Russian showed his teeth in a beast-like snarl.

'Yes, I am Ivan,' he said. 'Make what you can of that, but you cannot have me hanged for the murder of Mr Grell—*and you know why.*'

'Because Mr Grell is not dead,' retorted the detective smoothly. 'Yes, I know that.'

He counted the rough-and-tumble but little against the fact that the Russian had now admitted that he knew it was not Grell's body that had been found in the study. Here was a starting-point at last.

'What I want now,' he went on slowly, 'is an explanation of how you came to have possession of these.'

He held up the thing he had picked from the floor. It was a case of blue Morocco leather, and as he opened it a magnificent string of pearls showed startlingly white against a dark background.

'These pearls were bought at Streeters' by Mr Grell as a wedding present to Lady Eileen Meredith,' he said. 'How do they come in your possession?'

'They were given to me by Mr Grell,' cried Ivan. The fierce passion that had made him attack Foyle on the hint of arrest seemed to have melted away.

Heldon Foyle's mask of a face showed no sign of the incredulity he felt. He made no comment, but ran his hands swiftly through the Russian's pockets, piling money, keys, watch, and other articles in a little heap on the table. Beyond a single letter there were no documents on the man. He scanned the missive quickly. It was an ordinary commonplace note from a jeweller in Paris, addressed to Ivan Abramovitch. This he placed aside.

'May as well have his finger-prints,' he said, and one of the officers present pressed Ivan's hands on a piece of inky tin, and then on a piece of paper. The superintendent glanced casually at the impression.

'All right,' he said. 'Take those handcuffs off. You may go, Mr Abramovitch.'

The Russian stood motionless, as though not understanding. Foyle wheeled about as though the whole matter had been dismissed from his mind, and caught Norman by the sleeve.

'Drop everything,' he said in a curt whisper. 'Take a couple of men and don't let that man out of your sight for an instant. I'll have you relieved from the Yard in an hour's time.'

'Aren't you going to charge him, sir?' asked the other in astonishment.

'Not likely,' said Foyle, with a laugh.

CHAPTER XII

HELDON FOYLE walked thoughtfully back to Scotland Yard, satisfied that the shadowing of Ivan Abramovitch was in competent hands. With the strong man's confidence in himself, he had no fears as to his decision to release the man. He was beginning to have a shadowy idea of the relation of pieces in his jig-saw puzzle. Ivan, he knew, ought to have been arrested if only for failing to give a satisfactory account of his possession of the pearl necklace. But the superintendent had, as he mentally phrased it, 'tied a string to him,' and it would not be his fault if nothing resulted.

It was well after midnight before he had finished his work at Scotland Yard. He had had a long interview with the Garden of Eden, in which promises were adroitly mingled with threats. In the result the 'bunco-steerer' had promised to keep his eyes and ears alert for news of anyone resembling Goldenburg. There was a string of other callers who had been discreetly sorted out by the superintendent's diplomatic lieutenants. Finally, he pulled out the book which dealt with the case, and with the aid of a typist added several more chapters. With a sigh of relief, he at last sauntered out into the cool, fresh midnight air.

Nine o'clock next morning saw him again in his office. Sir Hilary Thornton was his first caller. Foyle put aside his reports at his chief's opening question.

'Yes, we've taken every human precaution to preserve secrecy,' he replied. 'Everyone who knows that it is not Grell's body in the house has been pledged to hold his tongue. I have managed to get the inquest put back for three days, so that there will be no evidence of identification till then. That gives us a chance. And I've made out a confidential report to be sent to the Foreign Office, so that Grell's Government shan't get restive. Here are the latest reports, sir.'

The Assistant Commissioner bent over the sheaf of type-written documents for a little in complete absorption. As he came to the last sheet he gave a start of surprise.

'So you let this man Ivan go? Do you think that wise?'

'I'm fishing,' answered Foyle enigmatically. 'I couldn't have better bait than Ivan. There are three men sticking to him like limpets now, and a couple are keeping an eye on Sir Ralph Fairfield. I think that will be all right. Do you remember the Mighton Grange case? We knew there had been a murder, but couldn't do anything till we found the body. Dutful, the murderer, would have slid off to some place where there's no extradition, but for the fact that I had him arrested on a charge of being in the unlawful possession of a pickaxe handle. This affair is the converse of that. We can't afford to have Ivan under lock and key.'

Sir Hilary Thornton bit his lip and looked steadfastly at the scarlet geranium on the window-sill, as though in search of enlightenment.

'I believe I see,' he exclaimed after a pause. 'Ivan must have been something more than a valet. He's a superior type of man, and the conclusion to be drawn if he knows that Grell is alive—'

'Precisely,' interrupted the superintendent.

'Any result from the offer of a reward for Goldenburg?'

A flicker of amusement dwelt in Heldon Foyle's blue eyes. 'Yes. He has been seen by different people within an hour or two of each other in Glasgow, Southampton, Gloucester, Cherbourg, Plymouth, and Cardiff. Our information on that point is not precisely helpful. Of course, we've got the local police making inquiries in each case, but I don't anticipate they will find out much. Still, it will keep 'em amused.'

The necessity of a conference broke up further conversation. Gathered in the building were some thirty or forty departmental chiefs of the C.I.D., the picked men of their profession. Most of them were divisional detective inspectors who were in charge of districts, and some few were men who had special duties. They were ranged about tables in a lofty room, its green distempered walls hung with stiff photographs of living and retired officials. Men of all types were there, from the spruce, smartly groomed detectives of the West End to the burly, ill-dressed detectives of the East. Between them they spoke every known language. Here was Penny, who had specialised in forgeries; Brown, who knew every trick of coiners; Malby, the terror of race-course sharps; Menzies, who had as keen a scent for the gambling hell as a hound for a fox; Poole, who was intimate with the ways of railway thieves and shoplifters. Not one but thoroughly understood his profession, and knew where to look for his information.

Foyle took the chair, and a buzz of conversation became general. It was a business conference of experts. Views were exchanged on concrete problems; the movements of well-known criminals discussed. 'Velvet-fingered Ned' had disappeared from Islington and reappeared in Brixton. 'Tony' Smith was due out of prison. Mike O'Brien had patched up the peace with 'Yid' Foster, and when they got together—

So the talk went on, and so every district learned what was taking place in other districts. The superintendent sat silent for a while, listening. At last his smooth voice broke in.

'The man Ivan, whose description was circulated, is not to be touched now. Tell your men to let him alone if they come across him.'

There was a deep chorus, 'Very good, sir,' and Foyle, with a nod of dismissal, left the room. He stopped to make an inquiry in the clerk's office, and passing along the corridor unlocked a door and pressed a bell.

In under half an hour a big labourer, with corduroys tied about the knees, lurched unsteadily out of the Lost Property Office and passed into Whitehall. Rough, tousled hair, an unkempt moustache, and a day's growth of beard on the chin were details warranted to stand inspection. Heldon Foyle rarely used a disguise, but when he did he was careful that nothing should get out of order. Hair and moustache were his own, dyed and brushed cunningly. Yet, when he reeled against Green near the Albany, the inspector, who was an observant man, pushed him roughly aside with an anathema on his clumsiness.

'Didn't 'urt you, did it?' stormed the labourer aggressively. ''Course I look where I'm going.' Then in a lower tone: 'I'm Foyle. I got your telephone message. Anything moving now?'

'If you don't go away I shall call a constable.' Green had been quick to see his cue and spoke loudly. He went on rapidly. 'He hasn't stirred out. A post-office messenger has just gone in with a letter for him. I said I was expecting one, and got a glimpse at it.'

'All right, old pal. Don't get excited. You go home and tell the missus all about it,' retorted the labourer.

Green walked rapidly away, spoke a few words to a man who was standing on the other side of the road, deeply interested in a bookseller's window, and departed.

The superintendent felt in his pockets and produced a couple of boxes of matches. A constable strolled up, dignified and stern. A swift word in an undertone sent him away with burning cheeks.

In half an hour Foyle had sold a box of matches, for which he received sixpence with profuse thanks and inward disgust. If he sold his second box and still hung about, his loitering without excuse might attract undesirable attention. The contingency, however, did not arise, for a minute or two later Fairfield himself strolled into the street. Foyle rushed to open the door of a taxicab, which he hailed, but another tout was before him. Nevertheless, he heard the address.

'Grave Street, Whitechapel,' he murmured to himself, as the cab slipped away. 'Ivan has got to work.'

A short argument with a second cab-driver, who distrusted his appearance, was cut short by a deposit of five shillings as a guarantee of good faith, and the superintendent also began the journey. Behind him a third cab carried the man who had been so deeply interested in the bookseller's window.

CHAPTER XIII

GRAVE STREET, Whitechapel, is not a savoury neighbourhood. One may pass from end to end of its squalid length and hear scarce a word of English. Yiddish is the language most favoured by its cosmopolitan population, although one may hear now and again Polish, Russian, or German. In its barrack-like houses, rising sheer from the pavement, a chain of tenancy obtains, ranging from the actual householder to the tenant of half a room, who sublets corners of the meagre space on terms payable strictly in advance. A score of people will herd together in a room a few feet square, and never realise that they are cramped for space.

Here you will find petty thieves, versatile rascals ripe for any mischief, and sweated factory workers; here sallow-faced anarchists boldly denounce the existing order of things to their fellows and scheme the millennium. Slatternly women quarrel at the doors, and horse-flesh is a staple article of diet.

The neatly dressed Fairfield descending at the end of the street from his taxicab was as conspicuous among the unshaven idlers who hung about the pavements as the moon among the stars.

Sir Ralph picked his way towards a newspaper shop, his mind full of the message that had brought him to the spot. The letter delivered by the messenger had contained but a few words in printed characters.

'IF YOU WOULD LEARN THE TRUTH ABOUT THE MURDER IN GROSVENOR GARDENS, COME IMMEDIATELY TO NO.— GRAVE STREET.'

There was no signature, no clue to the identity of the writer. Fairfield had leapt at the chance to do something. Even if it were a hoax it would occupy his mind for a time, and take his thoughts away from the sinister shadow that overhung him. Somehow, however, he did not think it was a hoax.

The newspaper shop displayed the number given in the note on its grimy facia. The baronet, as he moved towards it, was unconscious of the slouching figure of the labourer, who had been selling matches near the Albany, a few paces behind him. His foot was on the threshold of the shop when a man, black-bearded and swarthy, pressed an envelope into his hand.

Foyle watched the incident and his pace quickened. Before Fairfield had time to do more than glance at the inscription of the envelope he was abreast. He lurched inward and his fingers snatched quickly at the note. The next instant he was running with long, even strides for the open of the main road.

It was barefaced robbery, of course, but he had not the inclination to stick at trifles. That the note had some bearing on the case he was investigating he felt certain. There was only one way to get it at once, and that was to steal. Anywhere else but in Grave Street he would have waited to face the matter out. Not that Grave Street would have frowned upon a theft, but that he would have been forced to reveal his identity, and Grave Street was not a healthy neighbourhood for solitary detectives.

Sir Ralph stood thunderstruck, but someone else acted. The black-bearded man had disappeared. From somewhere there were a couple of dull thuds like a hammer falling upon wood, and Foyle heard the whistle of bullets over his head.

'I'll get even for that,' he muttered between his teeth, but his headlong flight never slackened.

Behind him was a clatter of pursuing feet. Fairfield, recovering himself, had raised a cry and it was taken up.

'Stop thief! Hold him!'

He passed the man who had been so eagerly intent on the bookshop. The man made a clutch at him, missed and fell headlong right in the path of Fairfield, now a few paces behind. The baronet tripped over his body and was thrown violently to the ground.

Foyle made a mental note in favour of Detective-Sergeant Chambers, who had so adroitly intercepted the pursuit. As he came to the main road he slackened his pace to a sharp walk, and dived into an underground station. He breathed a sigh of relief as he passed down the steps to the platform.

He had anticipated trouble, but pistol-shots in broad daylight, even in Grave Street, had been outside his calculations. He had recognised the peculiar report of an automatic pistol. His adversaries, whoever they might be, were obviously very much in earnest. Pistol-shooting at detectives is not a commonplace pastime even with the most reckless of criminals. Foyle decided on another and early visit to Grave Street, and promised himself grimly that the target should be someone else, if it came to shooting again. He was in danger of losing his temper.

Not until he had got in the train did he open the note that was still between his fingers. He frowned as he read it.

'Curse it! This comes of acting on impulse. Why couldn't I have waited! I had the whole thing in my hands.'

The note said simply: *'I am alive. I must see you. Follow the man who gives you this note.—R. G.'*

Heldon Foyle had seen much of Robert Grell's writing during his search of the house in Grosvenor Gardens, and had no doubt that the note was his. His peace of mind was not increased by the reflection that had he waited and continued to shadow Fairfield he might have discovered the whereabouts of the missing diplomat. Now he had merely given notice as plainly as though he had shouted from the housetops that Fairfield was under observation. He had committed a blunder, and he did not forgive blunders easily, especially in himself.

Even a bath and a change into his normal clothing did not restore his equanimity. In his office he found Green, with a strange excitement in his usually stolid face.

'Hello, Mr Green. What's wrong?' he demanded.

The veteran chief detective-inspector pulled at his moustache.

'I don't know, sir, yet. You've come just in time. Waverley is missing.'

'Waverley missing! That's nonsense. He was put on to relieve Norman in shadowing Ivan Abramovitch.'

'He's missing,' repeated the other doggedly. 'Ivan went into a shop with an entrance in two streets, and the man who was assisting Waverley slipped round to the other side. He waited there an hour, and then went to look for Waverley.'

The superintendent gave a short, contemptuous laugh.

'Green, I guess you've been working too hard lately. You ought to apply for a fortnight's leave. Can't you see, Ivan came out and that Waverley never had time to give the tip to his man, but followed him straight away? There ought to have been three men on the job.'

Green drew himself up stiffly. Foyle had not recovered from the irritation caused by his own mistake, otherwise he would not have spoken as he did. Green was not the kind of man to hastily jump to conclusions.

'A third was not available when Waverley left,' he said. 'Here is why I say Waverley is missing. It came by messenger five minutes ago, addressed to you. As senior officer I opened it.'

Foyle took a typewritten sheet of paper from the other's hand. It read simply:

'DEAR MR. FOYLE,—You had better call your men off. We have got one of them safe, and hold him as a hostage for our own safety. If your people go on trying to make things unpleasant for us, things will get unpleasant for him. This is not melodrama, but brutal fact.'

There was no signature. Foyle's square jaw became set and grim. He had no doubt that the unknown writer fully meant the threat. He liked Waverley, yet the thought of the other's peril did not sway him for a moment. The man had fallen a victim to one of the risks of his profession.

'Do they expect us to back down?' asked the superintendent harshly. 'If Waverley has been fool enough to get himself in a fix, he must take his chance if we can't get him out. Let's have a look at this paper.'

He thrust his hand in a drawer, and, flinging a pinch of black powder on the letter, sifted it gingerly to and fro. In a few seconds four finger-prints stared out blackly from the white surface. They were at right angles to the type, and just beneath it. Foyle's face relaxed in a pleased smile.

'They've given us something that may help us, after all, Green,' he cried. 'Look here; these two middle ones are the prints on the dagger. Now let's see if we can learn anything from the typing.'

Half an hour later three men stood in a tiny room, darkened, save for a vivid patch of white on a screen a yard and a half square. Foyle and Green watched the screen intently as the third man inserted the slide in the powerful magic lantern. Magnified enormously, the typewritten characters stood out vividly black against the white.

'What do you make of it, Green?' asked the superintendent after a pause.

'Remington machine, latest pattern,' answered the other briefly. 'The letter "b" slightly battered, and the "o" out of alignment. Used by a beginner. There is double spacing between some of the lines and single in others. A capital "W" has been superimposed on a small one.'

'That's so,' agreed his superior thoughtfully. 'You might see if the Remington people can give us any help with that. If possible, get a list of all the people who have bought machines during this last six weeks. It's a long shot, but long shots sometimes come off. And if you come into my room I'll give you a pistol. It'll be as well for you to carry one while you're on this case. I was shot at myself, today.'

'Thank you, sir, I think I'll do without one,' said the other quietly. 'My two fists are good enough for me.'

'As you like,' agreed Foyle, and Green departed on his mission. When he returned, he walked into Foyle's room and laid a long list before his chief. The superintendent cast his forefinger slowly down it.

'October 14,' he read, 'Mr John Smith, c/o Israels, 404A Grave Street, Whitechapel.' He looked up into the stolid face of Green. 'That seems like it,' he went on. 'You and I will take a little trip this evening, Green. And I think you'd better have a pistol, after all.'

CHAPTER XIV

To all callers, relatives, friends, newspaper men, alike, Eileen Meredith denied herself resolutely. 'She has been rendered completely prostrate by the shock,' said the *Daily Wire* in the course of a highly coloured character sketch. Other statements, more or less true, with double and treble column photographs of herself, crept into other papers. Night and day a little cluster of journalists hung about, watching the front door, scanning every caller and questioning them when they were turned away. Now and again one would go to the door and make a hopeless attempt to see some member of the household.

But Eileen was not prostrate, in spite of the *Daily Wire*. She wanted to be alone with her thoughts. Her gay vivacity had deserted her, and she had become a sombre woman, with mouth set in rigid lines, and with a fierce intensity for vengeance, none the less implacable because she felt her impotence. In such unreasoning moods some women become dangerous.

She had curtly rejected her father's suggestion that she should see a doctor. Nor would she leave London to try and forget amid fresh surroundings.

'Here I will stay until Bob's murderer is punished,' she had said, and her white teeth had come together viciously.

A night and a day had passed since her interview with Heldon Foyle. Reflection had not convinced her that his cold reason was right. She had made up her mind that Fairfield was the murderer. Nothing could shake her from that conviction. Scotland Yard, she thought, was afraid of him because he was a man of position. The square-faced superintendent who had spoken so smoothly was probably trying to shield him. But she knew. She was certain. Suppose she told all she knew? Her slim hands clenched till the nails cut her flesh, as she determined that he should pay the price of his crime. There was another justice than the law. If the law failed her—

A medical man or a student of psychology might have found an analysis of her feelings interesting. She had reached the border-line of monomania, yet he would have been a daring man who would have called her absolutely insane. Except to Foyle she had said nothing of the feeling that obsessed her.

With cool deliberation she unlocked a drawer of her escritoire and picked out a dainty little ivory-butted revolver with polished barrel. It was very small—almost a toy. She broke it apart and pushed five cartridges into the chambers. With a furtive glance over her shoulder she placed it in her bosom, and then hastily returned to her chair by the fire and picked up a book. Her eyes skimmed the lines of type mechanically. She read nothing, although she turned the pages.

Presently she flung the book aside and, without ringing for a maid, dressed in an unobtrusive walking costume of deep black. She selected a heavy fur muff and transferred the pistol to its interior. Her fingers closed tightly over the butt. On her way to the door she was stopped by an apologetic footman.

'There's a lot of persons from the newspapers waiting out in the streets, Lady Eileen,' he said.

'Indeed!' Her voice was cold and hard.

'They might annoy you. They stop everyone who goes in or out.'

She answered shortly and stepped out through the door he held open. There was a quick stir among the reporters, and two of them hastily detached themselves and confronted her, hats in hand. She forced a smile.

'It's no use, gentlemen,' she said. 'I will not be interviewed.' She looked very dainty and pathetic as she spread out her hands in a helpless little gesture. 'Can I not appeal to your chivalry? You are besieging a house of mourning. And, please— please, I know what is in your minds—do not follow me.'

She had struck the right note. There was no attempt to break her down. With apologies the men withdrew. After all, they were gentlemen whose intrusion on a private grief was personally repugnant to them.

The girl reached Scotland Yard while Heldon Foyle was still in talk with Green. Her name at once procured her admission to him. She took no heed of the chair he offered, but remained standing, her serious grey eyes searching his face. He observed the high colour on her cheeks, and almost intuitively guessed that she was labouring under some impulse.

'Please do sit down,' he pleaded. 'You want to know how the case is progressing. I think we shall have some news for you by tomorrow. I hope it will be good.'

'You are about to make an arrest?'

The words came from her like a pistol-shot. A light shot into her eyes.

The detective shook his head. He had seen the look in her face once before on the face of a woman. That was at Las Palmas, in a dancing-hall, when a Portuguese girl had knifed a fickle lover with a dagger drawn from her stocking. Lady Eileen was scarce likely to carry a dagger in her stocking, but—his gaze lingered for a second on the muff, which she had not put aside. It was queer that she should not withdraw her hands.

'I don't say that. It depends on circumstances,' he said gently.

Her face clouded. 'I will swear that the man Fairfield killed him,' she cried passionately. 'You will let him get away—you and your red tape.'

He came and stood by her.

'Listen to me, Lady Eileen,' he said earnestly. 'Sir Ralph Fairfield did not kill Mr Grell. Of that I have proof. Will you not trust us and wait a little? You are doing Sir Ralph a great injustice by your suspicions.'

She laughed wildly, and flung herself away from him.

'You talk to me as though I were a schoolgirl,' she retorted. 'You can't throw dust in my eyes, Mr Foyle. He has bought you. You are going to let him go. I know! I know! But he shall not escape.'

The superintendent stroked his chin placidly. As if by accident he had placed himself between her and the door. He had already made up his mind what to do, but the situation demanded delicate handling.

'You will regret this when you are calmer,' he said mildly.

He was uncertain in his mind whether to tell the distraught girl that her lover was not dead—that the murdered man was a rogue whom probably she had not seen or heard of in her life. He balanced the arguments mentally pro and con, and decided that at all hazards he would preserve his secret for the present. She took a step towards the door. She had drawn herself up haughtily.

'Let me pass, please,' she demanded.

He did not move. 'Where are you going?' he asked. Her eyes met his steadily.

'I am going to Sir Ralph Fairfield—to wring a confession from him, if you must know,' she said. 'Let me pass, please.'

'I will let you pass after you have given me the pistol you are carrying in your muff,' he retorted, holding out his hand.

Then the tigress broke loose in the delicately brought-up, gently nurtured girl. She withdrew her right hand from her muff and Foyle struck quickly at her wrist. The pistol clattered to the floor and the man closed with her. It needed all his tremendous physical strength to lift her bodily by the waist and place her, screaming and striking wildly at his face with her clenched fists, in a chair. He held her there with one hand and lifted one of the half-dozen speaking-tubes behind his desk with the other.

In ten minutes Lady Eileen Meredith, in charge of a doctor and a motherly-looking matron hastily summoned from the adjoining police station in Cannon Row, was being taken back to her home in a state of semi-stupor. Foyle picked up the dainty little revolver from the floor and, jerking the cartridges out, placed it on the mantelpiece.

'You can never tell what a woman will do,' he said to himself. 'All the same, I think I have saved Ralph Fairfield's life today.'

CHAPTER XV

HELDON FOYLE was more deeply chagrined than he would have cared to admit by the disappearance of Waverley. It was not only that one of the most experienced men of the Criminal Investigation Department had fallen into a trap and so placed his colleagues in difficulties. The very audacity of the *coup* showed that the department was matched against no ordinary opponents. There is a limit even to the daring of the greatest professional criminals. If there were professionals acting in this business, reflected the superintendent, the idea was none of theirs. Besides, no professional would have written the letter threatening the Yard. That was no bluff—the finger-prints proved that. To hold a Scotland Yard man as a hostage was a game only to be played by those who had much at stake.

Only one man shared Heldon Foyle's confidence. That was Sir Hilary Thornton. To the Assistant Commissioner he talked freely.

'It's an ugly job for us, sir, there's no disguising that. Naturally, they count on us keeping our mouths shut about Waverley. It's lucky he's not a married man. If the story of the way he was bagged becomes public property we shall be a laughing-stock, even if we get him out of his trouble. And if we don't, the scandal will be something worse.'

'Yes. It's bad—bad,' agreed the Assistant Commissioner. 'The Press must not hear of this.'

'Trust me,' said Foyle grimly. 'The Press won't.'

'I don't like this affair of Lady Eileen Meredith,' went on Sir Hilary. 'After all, she has a good right to know the truth. Wouldn't it be better to let her know that Grell is alive?'

Foyle jingled some money in his trousers pocket.

'I hate it as much as you do, Sir Hilary. I can't take any chances, though. Grell knows we know he is alive. When he finds that this girl has not been told he may try to communicate with her, and then we may be able to lay hands on him and Ivan, and so clear up the mystery. There's another thing. As far as our inquiries through his solicitors and the bank go, he couldn't have had much ready cash on him. He'll try to get some sooner or later—probably through his friends. He's already tried to approach Fairfield.'

'I see,' agreed the other in the tone of a man not quite convinced. 'Now, when are you going down to Grave Street again? You'll want at least a dozen men.'

'There won't be any trouble at Grave Street,' answered Foyle with a smile; 'and if there is, Green and I will have to settle it. More men would only be in the way. Our first job is to get hold of Waverley.'

'But only two of you! Grave Street isn't exactly a nice place. If there is trouble—'

'We'll risk that, sir,' said Foyle, stiffening a trifle.

He went back to his own room and signed a few letters. Some words through a speaking-tube brought Green in, stolid, gloomy, imperturbable. The chief inspector accepted and lit a cigar. Through a cloud of smoke the two men talked for a while. They were going on a mission that might very easily result in death. No one would have guessed it from their talk, which, after half an hour of quiet, business-like conversation, drifted into desultory gossip and reminiscences.

'Sir Hilary wanted me to take a dozen men,' said Foyle. 'I told him the two of us would be plenty.'

'Quite enough, if we're to do anything,' agreed Green. 'I wouldn't be out of it for a thousand. Poor old Waverley and I have put in a lot of time together. I guess I owe him my life, if it comes to that.'

Foyle interjected a question. The chief inspector lifted his cigar tenderly from his lips.

'It was in the old garrotting days,' he said. 'Waverley and I were coming down the Tottenham Court Road a bit after midnight—just off Seven Dials. There were half-a-dozen men hanging about a corner, and one of them tiptoed after us with a pitch plaster—you'll remember they used to do the stuff up in sacking and pull it over your mouth from behind. I never noticed anything, but Waverley did. The man was just about to throw the thing over me when Waverley wheeled round and hit him clean across the face with a light cane he was carrying. The chap was knocked in the gutter and his pals came at us with a rush. A hansom driver shouted to us to leave the man in the roadway to him, and hanged if he didn't drive clean over him with the near-side wheel. That gave us our chance. We hopped into the cab and got away without staying to see if anyone was hurt. But if Waverley hadn't hit out when he did I'd have been a goner.'

'I had a funny thing happen to me once in the Tottenham Court Road,' said Foyle reminiscently. 'I was an inspector then and big Bill Sladen was working with me—he had a beautiful tenor voice, you will remember. We were after a couple of confidence men and had a man we were towing about to identify them. Well, we got 'em down to a saloon bar near the Oxford Street end, but I daren't go in because they knew me. It was a bitter cold night, with a cold wind and snow and sleet. So I stayed on the opposite side of the road and induced Bill to go over and sing "I am but a Poor

Blind Boy", in the hope that our birds would call him in and give him a drink. He hadn't been at it five minutes before a fiery, red-headed little potman had knocked him head over heels in the gutter and told him to go away. Bill could have broken the chap in two with his little finger, but he daren't do anything. He came over to me and I sent him back again. This time he did get invited inside. And there he stayed for a full hour, while the witness and I stood shivering and wet and miserable in the snow. We could hear him laughing and singing with the best of 'em. They wouldn't let him come away. It was not until I took all risks and marched in with the witness and arrested them that they tumbled to the fact that he wasn't a real street singer.' He glanced at his watch. 'You'd better go and have a rest, Green. Meet me here at half-past twelve. We'll take a taxi to Aldgate and walk up from there. And, by the way, here's a pistol. I needn't tell you not to use it unless you've got to.'

CHAPTER XVI

A BITTER wind was sweeping the Commercial Road, Whitechapel, as the two detectives, each well muffled up, descended from their cab and walked briskly eastwards. Save for a slouching wayfarer or two, shambling unsteadily along, and little groups gathered about the all-night coffee-stalls, the roads were deserted. Neither man had attempted any disguise. It was not necessary now.

As they turned into Grave Street they automatically walked in the centre of the roadway. There are some places where it is not healthy to walk at night on shadowed pavements. They moved without haste and without loitering, as men who know exactly what they have to do. From one of the darkened houses a woman's shrill scream issued full of rage and terror. It was followed by a man's loud, angry tones, the thud of blows, shrieks, curses, and brutal laughter. Then the silence dropped over everything again. The two men had apparently paid no heed. Even had they been inclined to play the part of knights-errant in what was not an uncommon episode in Grave Street, they knew that the woman who had been chastised would probably have been the first to turn on them.

There was a side entrance to 404A, which was the newspaper shop that Foyle had cause to remember. He struck the grimy panel sharply with his fist and waited. There was no reply. Again he knocked, and Green, unbuttoning his greatcoat, flung it off and laid it across his arm. He could drop it easily in case of an emergency. Still there was no answer to the knock.

'Luckily I swore out a search warrant,' muttered Foyle, and searched in his own pockets for something. It was a jemmy of finely tempered steel gracefully curved at one end. He inserted it in a crevice of the door and, leaning his weight upon it, obtained an irresistible leverage. There was a slight crack, and it swung inwards as the screws of the hasp drew. The two men stepped within and, closing the door, stood absolutely still for a matter of ten minutes. Not a sound betrayed that their burglarious entry had alarmed anyone.

Presently Green made a movement, and a vivid shaft of light from a pocket electric lamp played along the narrow uncarpeted passage. The superintendent gripped his jemmy tightly and turned towards the dirty stairs. Then the light vanished as quickly as it had flared up, and from above there came a sound of shuffling footsteps. Even Heldon Foyle, whom no one would have accused of nervousness, felt his heart beat a trifle more quickly. He knew that if he were as near the heart of the mystery as he believed any second might see shooting. Penned as he and his companion were in the narrow space of the passage barely three feet wide, a shot fired from above could scarcely miss.

Crouching low, he sprang up the narrow staircase in three bounds, making scarcely a sound. On the landing above he wound his arms tightly about the person whose movements he had heard and whispered a quick, tense command.

'Not a word, or it will be the worse for you. Let's have a light, Green.'

The prisoner kept very still, and Green flashed a light on his face. It was that of a man of forty or so, with pronounced Hebrew features. His greasy black hair was tangled in coarse curls, and a smooth black moustache ran across his upper lip. A pair of shifty eyes were fixed fearfully on Foyle, and the man murmured something in a guttural tongue.

'We are police officers. How many people are there in this house?' demanded Foyle sternly, in a low voice. 'You may as well answer in English. Quietly, now.'

He had released his hold round the Jew's waist, but stood with the jemmy dangling by his side and with ears cocked ready for any sound. Green had climbed the stairs and stood by his side.

Domiciliary visits are unfrequent in England, but the Jew was not certain enough to stand upon a legal technicality. As a matter of fact, the search warrant would have met the difficulty. He cringed before the two men, whose faces he could not see, for Green had thrown his wedge of light so that it showed up the man's sallow face and left all else in darkness.

'I do not know why you have come,' he answered, forming each word precisely. 'I have done nothing wrong. I am an honest newsagent. There is only my wife, daughter, son, lodger in house.'

'You are a receiver of stolen goods,' answered Foyle, something, it must be confessed, at a venture. 'Don't trouble to deny it, Mr Israels. We're not after you this time—not if you treat us fairly. What about this lodger of yours? Have you bought him a typewriter lately?'

'Yes—yes. I help you all I can,' protested the Jew, with an eagerness that deceived neither of the detectives. There is no class of liar so abysmal as the East-end criminal Jew. They will hold to a glib falsehood with a temerity that nothing can shake. If there is no necessity to lie, they lie—for practice, it is to be presumed. The best way to extract a truth is to make a direct assertion by the light of apparent knowledge and so sometimes obtain assent. Foyle knew the idiosyncrasies of the breed. Hence the threat in his demand.

'I bought a typewriter—yes,' went on Israels. 'I think he was honest. Didn't seem as though police after him.'

'Which room is he in?'

Israels jerked a thumb upwards. 'Next landing. Door on left,' he ejaculated nervously.

The superintendent pushed by the man. He knew that the critical moment had come. With his quick judgment of men he had summed up Mr Israels. Whatever the Jew's morals, it was evident that he had a wholesome respect for his own oily skin. He would not risk himself to save the neck of another man. Foyle's intentions were simple. He would steal quietly up the second flight of stairs, burst the door open if it were locked, and seize the man he was in search of in his sleep. But his plans were frustrated.

He had not taken two steps when a woman peeped from an adjoining room. He caught one glimpse of her in the semi-darkness with a police whistle at her lips. He sprang forward, and as he did so a shrill, ear-piercing blast rang out. Green was close behind him.

She shrieked as the detective tore the whistle from her, and he felt her slender figure entwine itself about him. Down he went, with his companion on top of him, and another woman's loud hysterical cries added to the pandemonium. Foyle picked himself up and, lifting the girl bodily, flung her without ceremony into the room from which she had emerged. From above a voice shouted something, and a knife whizzed downwards and struck quivering in the bare boards of the landing, grazing Green's shoulders.

All need for caution was gone now. Foyle had dropped his jemmy and his hand closed over his pistol. Only as a last resource would he use it, but if he had to—well, there could be no harm in having it handy. A door slammed as the two detectives climbed the second flight of stairs. Green flung himself against the one that had been indicated by Israels, and the flimsy fastening gave way under the shock of his thirteen stone. There was no one in the room. Savagely Heldon Foyle turned and caught the handle of a second door. It turned, and they entered the room, empty like the first, but with an open window looking out on a series of low roofs a dozen feet below. And over the roofs a shadowy figure of a man was clambering hurriedly. He could only dimly be seen.

Green clambered through on to the window-sill and dropped. He was unlucky. A projecting piece of wood caught his foot, and he staggered and lost time. Before he had recovered himself the fugitive was out of sight, and the sound of his progress had ceased. Foyle called to him to come back and, without waiting to see whether his orders were obeyed, made his way back again to the first-floor landing. Israels was still there, very white and shaky, as the superintendent struck a match.

'Where's that girl?' said the detective curtly. 'The one who gave the alarm.'

'My daughter? She thought you were burglars. She didn't know.'

'Where is she?'

Without waiting for a reply he entered the room whence she had emerged and, striking another match, applied it to a gas-bracket. A fat woman was sitting up in bed looking at him timorously. He paid no heed to her, but stooped to look under the bed. When he straightened himself Green had rejoined him.

'The girl gave us away,' exclaimed Foyle. 'Here, you, where is she gone?' He shook the woman roughly by the shoulder. 'Go to the bottom of the stairs, Green, and see that no one slips in or out. Take that chap outside down with you.'

'My daughter?' exclaimed the woman helplessly. 'She has gone to stay with her aunt. We are respectable people. You frightened her. We don't like the police coming here.'

'Highly respectable,' repeated Foyle under his breath. Aloud he said menacingly, 'We shall soon know whether you are respectable. Where does the girl's aunt live?'

'Twenty-two Shadwell Lane,' was the reply, glib and prompt.

Foyle looked for an instant penetratingly at her. Her eyes dropped. His hand went to his pocket and he calmly lighted a cigar. Then he went downstairs to where Green was on guard and politely apologised to Israels. Casually he repeated the question he had put to the woman. Yes, the Jew had seen his daughter go out. She said she was going to her aunt. Her aunt lived at 48 Sussex Street.

'I see,' said the superintendent quietly. 'The fact is, of course, that she is not your daughter, and that she has not gone to her aunt's. You are in an awkward corner, my man,' he went on, changing his tone and moving a step nearer. 'Better tell us the truth. Your wife has let me know something.'

As if mechanically, he was dangling a pair of shiny steel handcuffs in his fingers. Handcuffs seldom formed a part of his equipment, but tonight he had carried them with him on the off-chance that he might have to use them. The Jew shrank away, but the sight had proved effective.

'I'll tell all the truth,' he whined, with an outspreading gesture of his hands. 'I've done no wrong. You can't hurt me. She came here a day or two ago and paid five pounds for a week's lodging. I was to tell anyone who inquired that she was my daughter. She slept with my wife. What harm was there? I am poor. Five pounds isn't picked up like that every

day. The man came afterwards. He said he was a journalist
and asked me to buy him a typewriting machine. I asked no
questions. Why should I?'

His manner was that of a much-injured man. Foyle cut him
short now and again as he rambled on with a question. In half
an hour he felt that he had extracted a fair amount of truth,
mingled though it was with cunning lies. He guessed now that
the woman whom he had vaguely seen was she whose part in
the mystery of the house in Grosvenor Gardens had always
been shadowy and vague. She could be none other than Lola
Rachael, little Lola of Vienna, otherwise the Princess Petrovska.

CHAPTER XVII

THERE was nothing more to be done at Grave Street. Heldon
Foyle remained in the house while Green walked to the
chief divisional station, and in an hour or two the divisional
inspector with a couple of men arrived. Then Foyle saw to a
strict search of the house from top to bottom. Nothing there
was that seemed to possess any great importance as bearing
on the case. The man who had fled over the roof had used
a single room, apparently as bed-and sitting-room, so it was
to this place that the detectives devoted chief attention.

'He must have been sleeping in his clothes,' grumbled
Green. 'He hadn't time to dress. There's the typewriter the
note was written on.'

He sat down before a rickety table and, inserting a piece
of paper in the machine, slowly tapped out the alphabet, and
after a brief inspection passed the paper on to the superintendent, who scanned it casually, and was about to throw it
away when something gripped his attention.

'This looks queer,' he muttered, and held the paper up
slantingly away from the gas-jet in order to examine it by
what photographers call transmitted light.

IIis brows were drawn together tightly. The sheet of paper which Green had used was an ordinary piece of writing-paper. On its rough surface Foyle had noted a slight sheen, unusual enough to attract his attention. Even he would not have noticed it but for the angle in which he had happened first to look at it when he took it from Green. It might be an accidental fault in the manufacture of the paper. Yet, trivial as it seemed, it was unusual, and one of the chief assets in detective work is not to let the unusual go unexplained.

'It's the same typewriter. There can be no question of that,' said Green. 'You can see that the "b" is knocked about and the "o" is out of line.'

'That's all right,' said Foyle. 'I wasn't thinking of that. It looks to me as if there's some sympathetic writing on this.'

He held the paper so that the heat from the gas-jet warmed it. Every moment he expected that the heat would bring something to light on the paper. He gave a petulant exclamation as nothing happened, and his eyes roved over the table whence Green had taken the paper. He believed that he was not mistaken, that there was something written which could be brought to light if he knew how. He knew that there were chemicals that could be used for secret communications which could only be revealed by the use of other chemicals—a process something akin to development in photography. It was unlikely, if the user of the room had used some chemical agent, that he would have thought of destroying and concealing it. But there was nothing on the table that suggested itself to Foyle as having been used in the connection. Keenly he scrutinised the room, his well-manicured hand caressing his chin.

'Ah!' he exclaimed at last. He had noted a small bottle of gum arabic standing on the cast-iron mantelpiece.

Now, gum arabic can be used for a variety of purposes, and it has the merit of invisible ink of being made decipher-able by quite a simple process which minimises the risk of accidental disclosure. The superintendent held the paper to the gas again for a few minutes. Then from a corner of the room he collected a handful of dust—no difficult process, for it was long since the place had felt the purifying influence of a broom—and rubbed it hard on the rough surface of the paper. A jumble of letters stood out greyly on the surface. He looked at them hard, and Green, peeping over his shoulder, frowned.

'Cipher!' he exclaimed.

It was undoubtedly cipher, but whether a simple or abstruse one Foyle was in no position to judge. He had an elementary knowledge of the subject, but he had no intention of attempting to solve it by himself. There were always experts to whom appeal could be made. A successful detective, like a successful journalist, is a man who knows the value of special-ists—who knows where to go for the information he wants. That meaningless jumble of letters could only be juggled into sense by an expert. Foyle nevertheless scrutinised them closely, more as a matter of habit than of reading anything from them. They were:

UJQW. BJNT. FJ. UJM. FJTV. UIYIQL. SK. DQUQZOKKEYJPK. ANUJ. M.Q. NG. N. AYUQNQIX. IGZ. ANUJ. SIO. IGZ. SMPPN. RT. 12845 HGZVFSF.

'We'll let Jones have a go at that,' he said. 'Anything else now?'

Someone handed him the knife that had been thrown at him on the landing and a curious leather sheath that had been picked up near the bed. From the bottom of the sheath depended a leather tassel. Foyle looked it over and failed to discover any manufacturer's name. He slipped the weapon into his pocket with the mental reflection that it looked Greek. The search went on from attic to cellar, and profuse notes were taken of everything found, with its exact position. The elaborate trouble taken by these men to describe minutely in writing every little thing would have seemed absurd to anyone not versed in the ways of the Criminal Investigation Department. Yet nothing was done that was not necessary. An error of an inch in a measurement might make all the difference when the case came on for trial.

Foyle and Green left the house in charge of the divisional man. Already a description had been circulated of the man they had failed to surprise; but as neither had caught more than a glimpse of a shadowy figure in the darkness, they had had to rely on the descriptions given by Israels and his wife. And even if that estimable pair had really tried honestly to give a fair description of the man—which the detectives thought was extremely doubtful—there could be little hope that it was accurate. If the average man tries to describe the appearance of his most intimate friend and then asks a stranger to identify him, he will realise how misleading such descriptions may be even at the best of times. Yet the Criminal Investigation Department had to work with such material as they had.

Heldon Foyle was very silent as they trudged side by side out of Whitechapel into the silent City streets—for there are no taxicabs to be found in the East End at such hours. The case was developing; but though he was beginning to have a hazy glimpse into some of its workings, there was much that remained a mystery to him. His questionings of Israels had satisfied him that the man who had escaped was neither Grell nor Ivan. He could not blame himself for not effecting an arrest. Looking back over the night's events, he could not see that he could have taken further precaution. If he had taken more men the escape would have occurred just the same over the roofs, for he would still have felt it his duty to question Israels. He could not have foreseen that the ready-witted Lola was there, nor that she should have so ingeniously given the alarm. The luck had been against him.

Nevertheless he had gained an important fact. Lola was in London and was obviously acting in concert with Grell. It was easier to look for two persons than one. Sooner or later he would lay hands on them and solve the mystery of the murder. He clenched his fists resolutely as his thoughts carried him away. Meanwhile there was the cipher. If that could be de-coded it might be valuable.

Green's voice broke in upon his thoughts.

'We didn't find anything bearing on Waverley.'

'Waverley?' repeated Foyle. 'Oh yes, I had almost forgotten him.'

For an hour after they had reached Scotland Yard the superintendent laboured at his desk, collecting reports and writing fresh chapters in the book which held all the facts in relation to the crime, so far as he knew them. He slipped the result of his labours at last in an envelope and left them over to be dealt with by the inspector in charge of the Registry, which is a department that serves as official memory to Scotland Yard.

'That is all right,' he said, and stretched himself.

Someone knocked at the door. The handle turned and an erect man with his right arm carried in a black silk handkerchief improvised into a sling entered the room. It was Detective-Inspector Waverley.

CHAPTER XVIII

HELDON FOYLE was on his feet in a second, and he pushed a chair towards his subordinate. Detective-Inspector Waverley sat down and drummed nervously on his knees with the fingers of his left hand.

'Well, you've got back,' said the superintendent in a non-committal tone. 'We were beginning to wonder what had happened to you. I hope that arm of yours is not badly hurt. What has been the trouble?'

The inspector winced and sat bolt upright in his chair.

'I guess I was to blame, sir,' he said. 'I fell into a trap like a new-joined cabbage-boy. This man, Ivan Abramovitch, must have known that he was followed by a couple of us, so he threw off Taylor, who was with me, very simply, by going into a big outfitter's place in the City. I dodged round to a second entrance and, sure enough, he came out there. I couldn't get word to Taylor, so I picked him up, and a pretty dance he led me through a maze of alleys up the side of Petticoat Lane and round about by the Whitechapel Road. You will know the sort of neighbourhood it is there. Well, I suppose I must have got a bit careless, for in taking a narrow twist in one of those alleys someone dropped on me from behind. I hit out and yelled, but I didn't get a second chance, for my head was bumped hard down on the pavement and I went to sleep for good and plenty. There were a couple of men in it, for I could hear 'em talking before I became properly unconscious. They dragged me along, linking their arms in mine, and we got into a cab. I guess the driver thought I was drunk, and that they were my pals helping me home.

'When I came round my head was bandaged up, and I was in quite a decent little room, lying on a couch, with Mr Ivan Abramovitch sitting opposite to me. I couldn't give a guess where it was, for the window only looked out on a blank wall. I sat up, and he grinned at me.

'"I am a police officer," I said. "How did I get here?"

'"I brought you," he says with a grin. "You were taking too great an interest in my doings for my liking. Now I am going to take an interest in yours."

'At that I jumped for him and got a knife through my arm for my pains. After he'd sworn at me like a trooper in English, French, and Russian for about ten minutes he bandaged up the cut with his handkerchief, and told me if I made any more fuss I was in for trouble. Someone knocked at the door, but he ordered them off.

'"You won't get away from here alive without permission if I can help it," he said; "but if you do, you won't be able to identify anyone but myself. If you take it coolly there'll be no harm come to you."

'I tried to bluff a bit, but he just laughed. And then I stayed with him in the same room up to within an hour or two ago, when someone came into the house and he was summoned outside the door. They had an excited pow-wow, and I could hear a woman talking. Finally, the man came back and told me they'd determined to let me go. He put a handkerchief over my eyes, and after a while I was taken down into what I thought was a taxicab. I was turned out a quarter of an hour ago at the Blackfriars end of the Embankment.'

Foyle was by now striding up and down the office, his hands thrust deep in his trousers pockets. He paused long enough to blow down a speaking-tube and put a quick question.

'What was the number of the cab?'

'It had no police number. Its index mark was A.A. 4796.'

The superintendent drew from his pocket a little black book, such as is carried by every police officer in London. On the outside was inscribed in white letters: 'Metropolitan Police. Pocket Directory.' He turned over the pages until he found what he wanted. A messenger had pushed open the door.

'Southampton registration,' said the superintendent. 'Johns, get through on the 'phone to the Southampton police, and ask 'em to trace the owner of this car the moment the county council offices open.'

The messenger disappeared, and he turned on Waverley.

'The number's probably a false one—a board slipped over the real number, as they did in the Dalston case when some American toughs went through that jeweller a month or two back. We might as well look into it, though. These people are wily customers, or they wouldn't have kept you from seeing the rest of the gang. They tried to frighten us by threatening to make away with you. I think it likely that they found it rather a nuisance to look after you—especially when Green and I tumbled on to some of their people an hour ago. You haven't exactly covered yourself with glory, Waverley, but under the circumstances I shall take no disciplinary action. Now go and write out a full report, and then go home. The police surgeon will recommend what leave of absence you want to get over the stab in the arm. Good night—or rather, good morning.'

'Thank you, sir. Good morning, sir.'

Foyle never forgot discipline, which is as necessary, or more necessary within limits, in a detective service as in any other specialised business. To have sympathised with Waverley would have been bad policy. He had been made to feel that he had blundered in some way, and the feeling with which he had entered the room, that he was a martyr to duty, had vanished in the conviction that he was simply a fool.

Foyle lit a cigar and fell into a reverie that lasted perhaps ten minutes. He was glad that Waverley was safe, but a little disgusted that he had failed to baffle the precautions taken while he was a prisoner, and so have learnt something that might have been of value in the investigations. Presently he lifted the telephone receiver and ordered a taxicab from the all-night rank in Trafalgar Square. In a little while he was being whirled homeward.

Not till midday next day did he arrive at the Yard. A slip of paper was lying on his desk—the record of a telephone message from the Southampton police. It read:

'Halford, Chief Constable, Southampton, to Foyle, C.I.D., London.

Car No. A.A. 4796 belongs to Mr J. Price, The Grange, Lyndhurst.

Mr Price is an old resident in the neighbourhood and a man of means.

The car is a six-cylinder Napier.'

'As I thought,' commented Heldon Foyle thoughtfully, tearing the paper into little bits and dropping them into the waste-paper basket. 'The number was a false one. They knew that Waverley would have a look at the number. Oh, these people are cunning—cunning.'

Green found him, half an hour later, hard at work with the collection of typewritten sheets which formed the book of the case. Foyle was still juggling with his jig-saw puzzle, trying to fit fresh facts in their proper position to old facts.

'Well?' asked the superintendent abruptly.

Green read from a paper in his hand.

'Taylor, who is watching the Duke of Burghley's house in Berkeley Square, has just telephoned that a woman who corresponds to the description of Lola Rachael has just been admitted and is still there.'

Into Foyle's alert eyes there shot a gleam of interest.

'You don't say so?' he muttered. And then, more alertly, 'Is he still on the telephone? If so, tell him to detain her should she come out before I can get down. He must be as courteous as possible. We mustn't lose her now. And send a man down at once to bring Wills, the butler at Grosvenor Gardens, here. He's the only man who saw the veiled woman enter the house on the night of the murder.'

CHAPTER XIX

FROM behind the curtains of the sitting-room Eileen Meredith could see two men occasionally pass and re-pass the house. They did not go by often, but she knew that even if she could not see them they always held the house in view. They were not journalists—they were more sedate, older men. Nor did they molest anyone who entered or left the house. They merely exercised a quiet, unwearying, unobtrusive surveillance, and Eileen knew that Heldon Foyle had taken his own way of preventing her from seeing Sir Ralph Fairfield. She felt certain that were she to leave the house the men would follow her. She did not guess, however, that Foyle had intended them to give her an opportunity of discovering their presence. She would be the more unlikely to persist in her rash resolve if she knew it would be frustrated. Nor did she know that Fairfield was equally closely watched in all his comings and goings.

The hysterical outbreak that had been provoked by the superintendent's penetration of her doings when she had visited his office at Scotland Yard had been followed by hours of almost complete collapse. To her father enough had been told to make him hurriedly summon a specialist. The doctor explained.

'I have known similar cases follow a great shock. She is mentally unbalanced on one point. Unless anything occurs to excite her in connection with that, time will effect a cure. She must not be opposed in her wishes, and I would suggest that she be taken out of London and an effort made to distract her. Plenty of society, outdoor amusements—anything to occupy her mind.'

'I suggested that we should leave London,' said Lord Burghley gloomily. 'She refuses.'

'Then don't press her. Ask her friends to visit her, and don't let her leave the house except with a competent attendant.'

So it was that Eileen found herself practically a prisoner in her own home. She received the visitors invited by her father at first with a mechanical courtesy, but later on with an assumption of cheerfulness that deceived her father and even to more extent the doctor. She had begun to realise that she would never shake off the vigilance which surrounded her until she had convinced folk that she had regained her normal spirits. Her capabilities as an actress, which had won for her leading parts in many amateur plays, had never been taxed so hardly. But then she had invariably been cast for comedy. Now she felt she was playing tragedy. For night and day she never forgot. Always there was one thought hammering at her brain.

She withdrew into the room as a neat little motor-brougham halted at the door. In a little while Mrs Porter-Strangeways was announced. Reluctantly Eileen condescended to welcome the portly, middle-aged dame who was tacitly recognised as being the leader of American society in London. The girl smiled brightly as the woman rose to greet her with both arms outstretched.

'It is so good of you, dear Mrs Porter-Strangeways,' she exclaimed. 'I have only my friends to look forward to now.'

Mrs Porter-Strangeways indicated her companion by some subtle means of her own.

'You poor girl!' she exclaimed, throwing just the right reflection of sympathy into her not unmusical voice. 'I called before, but you were unfit to see anyone then. I took the liberty of bringing a friend to see you—the Princess Petrovska.'

The name conveyed nothing to Eileen. She knew not how the woman she faced was concerned in the tangle in which she herself was involved. She saw only a slim, beautifully dressed woman, whose age might have been somewhere between thirty and forty, and who still laid claim to a gipsy-like beauty. The dark eyes of the Princess dwelt upon the girl with a sort of well-bred curiosity. Mrs Porter-Strangeways imparted information in a swift whisper.

'A Russian title, I believe. Met her in Rome two years ago. She is a delightful woman—so bright and happy, though I believe, poor dear, she had a terrible time before her husband died. She called on me yesterday and asked me to bring her to see you. She's so interested in you. You don't mind?'

The quick thought that she was being made a show of caused a spasm to flicker across Eileen's face. Almost instantly she regained her composure, and for half an hour Mrs Porter-Strangeways prattled on. The other took little part in the conversation. Eileen could feel that the Princess was watching her closely under her cast-down eyelashes. The woman repelled and yet fascinated her. When the time came for leave-taking she found herself giving a pressing invitation to the other to call again. With a smile of satisfaction the Princess promised.

They had not been gone a quarter of an hour when the Princess was announced alone. Eileen, a little astonished, received her questioningly.

'I had to see you alone,' explained the older woman. 'I have something of importance to say to you—that's why I made Mrs Porter-Strangeways bring me. I feared that you would not see me otherwise.'

'To see me alone?' repeated Eileen, with the air of one completely mystified. Then, as the other nodded grimly, she closed the door of the room.

With a murmured 'Pardon me' the Princess walked across the room and turned the key. 'It will be better so,' she said. 'What I have to say must not be overheard. The life of a—someone may depend on secrecy.'

Eileen had begun to wonder if her strange visitor were mad. There was something, however, in her quiet, methodical manner that forbade the assumption. The Princess Petrovska had settled herself gracefully in a great arm-chair.

'No, I am not mad.' She answered the unspoken question. 'I am quite in my senses, I assure you. I have come to you with a message from one you think dead—from Robert Grell.'

The room reeled before Eileen's eyes. She clutched the mantelpiece with one hand to steady herself.

'From one I *think* dead!' she repeated. 'Bob *is* dead.' She gripped the other woman fiercely by the shoulder and almost shook her in the intensity of her emotion. 'He is dead, I tell you. What do you mean? I know he is dead. Do not lie to me. He is dead.'

The Princess Petrovska glanced gravely up into the strained features of the girl. Her own face was a mask.

'Calm yourself, Lady Eileen,' she said. 'You have been made the victim of a wicked deceit. He is not dead—but a man wonderfully like him is. I have come here at his request to relieve your mind.' She dropped her voice to a whisper. 'At the same time, he is in grave danger, and you can help him.'

The girl's hands dropped to her side, and she regarded her visitor helplessly. A new hope was beginning to steal into her heart, but her reason was all on the other side.

'He is dead,' she protested faintly. 'Fairfield killed him. Why should he hide if he is not dead? Why should he not come here himself? Why should he send you?'

'Don't be a fool,' retorted the other impatiently, and the impertinence of the words had the effect intended of bracing the half-fainting girl. 'He does not come because to do so would be madness—because if he showed himself he would be at once arrested by Scotland Yard detectives. They believe him to be the murderer of his double—a man named Goldenburg. There is a note he gave me for you.'

The letters danced before Eileen's eyes as she tore open the thin envelope and held what was undoubtedly Robert Grell's writing in her shaking hand. She was startled as never before in her life save when she heard of the murder. Slowly she read, the words biting into her brain:

> 'DEAREST,—Forgive me for not letting you know before that I am safe. I had no means of communicating with you with safety. The man who is dead was killed by no wish of mine. Yet I dared not run the risk of arrest. The bearer of this is an old friend of mine who will herself be in peril by delivering this. Trust her, and destroy this. She will tell you how to keep in touch with me.'

There was no signature. Mechanically Eileen tore the letter in two and dropped the fragments on the blazing fire. She felt the dark eyes of the Princess upon her as she did so. A spasm of jealousy swept across her at the thought that this woman should have been trusted, should have had the privilege of helping Grell rather than herself. She strove to push it aside as unworthy. He was alive. He was alive. The thought was dominant in her mind. She could have sung for very joy.

'Well?' asked the Princess.

'I don't understand,' said Eileen wearily. 'He does not explain. There is nothing clear in the note but that he is alive.'

'He dare say no more. We—that is—he's succeeded in evading the police so far. If by any chance that letter had fallen into their hands, it would have told them no more than they knew at present.'

'Where is he?' demanded Eileen. 'I must go to him.'

'No, that will never do. You would be followed. I will give any message for you. You can help, but not in that way. He is in need of money. Have you any of your own? Can you let him have, say, five hundred pounds at once?'

The girl reflected a moment.

'There is my jewellery,' she said at last. 'He—or you—can raise more than five hundred on that. Wait a moment.'

She left the room, and a smile flitted across the grave face of the Princess. A few moments later she returned with a little silver casket in her hands.

'And now,' she said, 'tell me what happened. Who killed this man Goldenburg?'

The Princess Petrovska gave a dainty little shrug.

'Mr Grell shall tell you that in his own fashion,' she said. 'Listen.'

For ten minutes she talked rapidly, now and again writing something on a slip of paper and showing it to Eileen. The girl nodded in comprehension, occasionally interjecting a question. At last the Princess rose.

'You fully understand?' she said.

'I fully understand,' echoed Eileen.

CHAPTER XX

HELDON FOYLE had been prepared to take any risk rather than allow the Princess Petrovska to escape him again. There was nothing against her but suspicion. It was for him to find evidence that might link her with the crime. It is in such things that the detective of actuality differs from the detective of fiction. The detective of fiction acts on moral certainties which would get the detective of real life into bad trouble. To arrest the Princess was out of the question; even to detain her might make matters awkward. Yet the superintendent had made up his mind to afford Wills the butler a sight of her at all costs. If Wills identified her it would be at least another link in the chain of evidence that was being forged.

He carried the butler in a taxicab with him to the nearest corner to the Duke of Burghley's house. A well-groomed man sauntered up to them and shook hands warmly with Foyle.

'She has not come out yet,' he said.

'Good,' exclaimed Foyle. 'Come on, Wills. You have a good look at this woman when she does come out, and stoop down and tie your shoe-lace if she's anything like the woman who visited Robert Grell on the night of the murder. Be careful now. Don't make any mistakes. If you identify her you'll probably have to swear to her in court.'

'But I never saw her face,' complained Wills helplessly. 'I told you I was not certain I'd know her again.'

He was palpably nervous and unwilling to play the prominent part that had been assigned to him. Foyle laughed reassuringly.

'Never mind. You have a look at her, old chap. You never know in these cases. You may remember her when you see her. Everyone walks differently, and you may spot her by that. It won't do any harm if you don't succeed.'

He led Wills to a spot a few paces away from the house, but out of view of anyone looking from the windows, and gave him instructions to remain where he was. He himself returned to the corner where Taylor, the detective-inspector who had greeted them when they drove up, was waiting. The other end of that side of the square was guarded by one of Taylor's assistants. Lola was trapped—if Foyle wished her to be trapped.

He beckoned to a uniformed constable who was pacing the other side of the road. The man nodded—detectives whatever their rank are never saluted—and took up his position a few paces away.

They had not long to wait. A taxicab whizzed up to the house, evidently summoned by telephone. Wills was staring as though fascinated at the slim, erect figure of the woman outlined on the steps of the house. He half stooped, then straightened himself up again. The superintendent muttered an oath under his breath and nodded to the loitering policeman. The constable immediately sprang into the roadway with arm outstretched, and the cab, which was just gathering way, was pulled up with a jerk. The blue uniform is more useful in some cases than the inconspicuous mufti of the C.I.D.

'Get hold of Wills and bring him after us to Malchester Row Police Station.' And, opening the door, he stepped within as the driver dropped in the clutch.

The Princess had half risen and gave a little cry of dismay at the intrusion. With grim, set face the detective adjusted his tall form to the limits of the cab and sat down beside her. His hand encircled her wrist, and he forced her back to the seat.

'I shouldn't try to open the door if I were you,' he said quietly. 'You might fall out.'

The woman dropped back and did some quick thinking. She had no difficulty in guessing who Foyle was, and she could scarcely have failed to see the staring figure of the butler as she left the Duke of Burghley's house. She fenced for time, doing the astonished, outraged, half-frightened innocent to perfection.

'What does this mean? How dare you molest me? Where are you taking me?'

The detective smiled easily as he answered in the formal words of C.I.D. custom: 'I am a police officer—perhaps I needn't tell you that—and I am taking you to Malchester Row Police Station.'

'To arrest me? You would dare? Do you know I am the Princess Petrovska? There is some mistake. I shall appeal to the Russian Ambassador. What do you say I have done? I am a friend of Lady Eileen Meredith, the daughter of the Duke of Burghley. She will tell you I have only just left her. You are confusing me with someone else.'

It was admirably done. The mixture of indignation and haughtiness might have imposed upon some people, and the threat of appeal to the Russian Ambassador had been very adroit. Heldon Foyle merely nodded.

'This is not arrest,' he replied. 'It is not even detention—unless you force me to it. I am inviting you to accompany me to give an account of your movements on the night that Harry Goldenburg was murdered. I will call your bluff, Lola, and we will call at the ambassador's if you like.'

She made a gesture with one hand, as of a fencer acknowledging a hit, and, turning her head, smiled sweetly into his face. Nevertheless, in spite of everything, she felt a little nervous. She had gone to see Eileen with her eyes not fully open to the risk she ran. Deftly used, newspapers have their uses. In supplying the story of the murder to the pressmen, Foyle had omitted all mention of the finding of the miniature. The woman had not known that Scotland Yard had a portrait of her, and had deemed it unlikely that she would be recognised by the watchers of the house. Although she had lived by her wits in many quarters of the world, she had hitherto avoided trouble with the police in England. She wondered how much Foyle knew. It was evidently of no use trying to impress him with the importance of her rank and connections. Princesses are cheap in Russia.

'You are Mr Heldon Foyle, of course,' she said. 'I have heard that you are very clever. I don't see what I can have had to do with the murder, even if I am Lola Rachael—which I admit.'

'We shall see. Can you prove where you were between ten o'clock, when you left the Palatial Hotel, and midnight on that date?'

She laughed merrily. 'You are not so clever as I thought,' she exclaimed. 'Do you think that I am a murderess? I went straight to an hotel near Charing Cross—the Splendid—and caught the nine o'clock boat train to Paris. It is easily proved.'

Foyle shifted to the seat opposite, so that he could see her face more easily.

'Then you don't deny that you visited Grosvenor Gardens that night, that you were admitted by Ivan Abramovitch, Grell's valet, and taken to his study?'

'Of course I do,' she retorted laughingly. 'If that's all you've got to go upon you may as well let me go now.'

'Very well. We shall see,' he answered.

The cab stopped at Malchester Row Police Station.

CHAPTER XXI

To the constable who opened the cab door Foyle gave quick instructions in a low voice. The Princess Petrovska found herself ushered into a plainly furnished waiting room, decorated with half-a-dozen photographic enlargements of the portraits of high police officials and a photogravure of 'Her Majesty the Baby.' There the policeman left her.

Foyle came to her a moment later. His couple of questions to the cabman as he paid him had not been fruitful. He had been ordered by the lady to drive to Waterloo Station. It was a fairly obvious ruse, which would have had the effect of effectually confusing her trail, for from there she might have taken train, tube, omnibus, tram, or cab again to about any point in London.

'I am sorry,' he apologised. 'We shall have to keep you here for an hour or two while your statements are verified.'

'I don't mind,' she countered lightly. 'It will be an amusing experience. I have never seen a police station before. Perhaps you would like to show me over while we're waiting, Mr Foyle.'

The superintendent was admiring her confidence a little ruefully. A pleasant-faced, buxom woman tapped at the door, and Lola eyed her with misgivings. Foyle's blue eyes were fixed on her face.

'I am afraid I must deny myself that pleasure,' he said suavely. 'There are other matters which will take up our time. First, I shall be obliged if you will let the matron here search you.'

The nonchalance of the Princess Petrovska had disappeared in a flash, and Foyle noted her quick change of countenance. She had recollected she was carrying Lady Eileen Meredith's jewels. They would inevitably be found, if she were searched. She was not so much worried by what explanation she could give as to what would be the result of a questioning of Eileen. Angrily defiant, she was on her feet in a flash.

'You have no right to search me. I am not under arrest,' she declared.

Foyle knew she was right. What he was doing was flagrantly unlawful unless he charged her with some offence. Yet there are times when it is necessary for a police officer to put a blind eye to the telescope and to do technically illegal things in order that justice may not be defeated. This he felt was one of the occasions. He ignored her protestations and left the room, closing the door after him. For a brief moment the woman forgot the breeding of the Princess Petrovska in the fiery passion of Lola the dancer. But if she meditated resistance, a second's reflection convinced her that it would be futile. The matron, for all her good-tempered face, was well developed muscularly, and did not seem the kind of woman to be trifled with. The Princess submitted with as good a grace as she could muster.

As the woman drew forth the casket of jewels Lola made one false move. She laid a slim-gloved hand on her arm.

'If you want to earn ten pounds you will give me that back,' she said softly.

The matron shook her head with so resolute an expression that the word 'twenty,' which trembled on the Princess Petrovska's lips, was never uttered. Gathering in her hands the articles she had found, she stepped outside. In three minutes her place was taken by Foyle. He quietly returned to her everything but the jewel case. This he held between his fingers. 'Where did you get this?' he demanded. His voice was keyed to the stern, official tone he knew so well how to assume.

She gripped the side of a chair tightly.

'What is that to do with you? It is mine. Give it to me.'

'Not unless you can prove it is yours. If you do not, I shall charge you with being in possession of property suspected to be stolen.'

She bit her lips until the blood came. Her face had become very pale. If the threat were meant seriously—and she could see no reason why it should not be—she was in an awkward predicament. Ordinarily she had ready resource, a fertile genius for invention. Now her wits seemed to have deserted her. Cudgel her brains as she would, she could see no way out of the difficulty. To boldly state that the jewels had been entrusted to her by Eileen would involve opening up a fresh line of inquiry for the C.I.D. men that might have disastrous results. Nor was there any person who might bear out a story invented on the spur of the moment.

'Well?' He spoke coldly.

'I refuse to tell you where I got them,' she retorted. 'You must do as you like.'

'Then it is my duty to warn you that anything you say may be used in evidence against you. You will be charged.' He opened the door and cried down the corridor, 'Reserve!' To the constable who answered he indicated the Princess by a nod. 'Take this woman to the detention room. She will be paraded for identification in half an hour.'

The detention room of a London police station is a compromise between the comparative luxury of a waiting-room and the harshness of a cell. Like a waiting-room it is furnished with chairs and tables, and like a cell its door is provided with a strong, self-acting lock. The Princess Petrovska gritted her teeth viciously as she was left alone, and paid no heed to the magazines and papers left on the table—a consideration for visitors that had not been discernible in the waiting-room.

Meanwhile, Foyle had set every available man of the divisional detachment of the C.I.D. busily at work. A couple had been sent to verify the account given by the woman of her movements on the night when the murder occurred. The remainder had been sent to bring in a score of women, the wives and daughters of inspectors and other senior officers.

Detective-Inspector Taylor had turned up with Wills, who was informed of the part he had to play.

'You say you couldn't recognise the woman who came out of Lord Burghley's house. Now we're going to give you another try. We don't want you to pick anyone out unless you're absolutely sure. Mind that.'

Some of the women who had been fetched in by the detectives were rejected by Foyle as being too unlike the Princess. He intended the identification test to be as fair as possible. The ten who finally took their places in the high-pitched charge room were as nearly like the Princess in build and dress as could be managed from the choice afforded. They stood in a row on the opposite side of the room from the steel-railed dock and the high desk. Then Lola was brought in. Her head was held high, and her lips curled superciliously as she took in the arrangements.

'Please choose a position among these ladies,' said Foyle urbanely. 'You may stand anywhere you like.'

There was an angry glitter in her dark eyes as she obeyed. She was not the sort of woman to risk a scene uselessly. Then Wills was brought in. Foyle put a formal question to him.

'Have you seen any of these ladies before? Don't be in a hurry to answer. Walk down the line and take a good look at each.'

Wills slowly carried out his instructions. As he reached the last woman he shook his head. Lola's eyes caught those of Foyle with a glance of malicious triumph. But the superintendent was not done yet.

'Walk round the room, if you please, ladies—from left to right. No, a little quicker. Now, Wills, see if you can recognise any of them by their walk.'

Three times they made the circuit of the room, while the butler darted nervous glances from one to the other.

'It's no good, sir,' he confessed at last. 'I don't know any of 'em.'

To Foyle the result was not unexpected. He had adopted the expedient as a forlorn chance of linking up the Princess with the crime. Now it had failed, he intended to try other measures. He dismissed Wills and the women with a nod of caution not to speak of the formality they had witnessed, and at a nod from him a uniformed inspector stood up by the high desk pen in hand.

'Do you charge this woman, Mr Foyle?' he asked.

Taylor had ranged up against her, and almost unconsciously she found herself standing by the desk facing the officer.

She searched the superintendent's inflexible face to see if it gave any sign of relenting. Foyle was calm, inscrutable, business-like. That was what had struck her from the moment she entered the police station—the cool, business-like fashion in which these men had dealt with the situation. There were no histrionics. They might have been clerks engaged in some monotonous work for all the emotion they evinced. They treated her as impersonally as though she was a bale of goods about which there was some dispute.

She was not a person easily daunted, but the atmosphere chilled her.

She reflected quickly that her refusal to explain the possession of the jewels was playing into Heldon Foyle's hands. He would guess that they were Eileen Meredith's—in any case, she could not stop him from seeing and questioning the girl. What advantage would it be to be placed under lock and key? Before the superintendent could reply she had made up her mind.

'One moment. I can explain how I got the jewels if I can see Mr Foyle alone.'

The inspector looked hesitatingly at the superintendent, who was stroking his chin with his hand. Foyle murmured an assent and led the way back to the detention room. The woman swung round to him quickly once they were alone.

'Those jewels were entrusted to me for a particular purpose by Lady Eileen Meredith,' she said peremptorily. 'That is all you have any right to know. You can easily ring her up and ask her. Do it at once and let me go.'

'Very well,' he said imperturbably. 'I shall keep you here until I have done so.'

But it was not to Berkeley Square that he telephoned from the privacy of the divisional C.I.D. offices. It was to Scotland Yard. Within five minutes Chief Inspector Green was setting out from the great red-brick building to see, first, the Duke of Burghley and, secondly, Lady Eileen Meredith. A full hour passed away, and Foyle received the result of the inquiries into Petrovska's movements. Her alibi was complete. In every particular her story of her movements had proved right.

Green, arriving at the police station with an agitated and puzzled nobleman and his solicitor, saw his chief for a few moments alone.

'She admits having handed over the jewels to Lola, but she won't say a word beyond that,' he said. 'She's as obstinate as a mule. I have told the Duke something of where we stand, and he has agreed to take the gems back without letting her know. It was a tough job, but I got him to see at last that the girl might be implicating herself. He says he's never heard of Petrovska.'

'H'm.' Foyle rubbed his chin vigorously. 'I'll have a talk with the old boy. See if you can get the Public Carriage Office to borrow us a taxicab, and get Poole to drive it slowly up and down this street. If she hails it when she goes out, well and good. If not, Bolt and you had better follow her, and the cab will come after you so that you can use it in emergency.'

Green had done his work with the Duke and the lawyer with tact. Foyle found his interview with them confined to evading questions that he had no wish to answer. He dismissed them at last with the jewels in the custody of the man of the law. Then he went straight to his prisoner.

'You can go,' he said abruptly. 'I shall ask you to be very careful, however, Princess. If you are wise you will leave England at once.'

'Why?' she asked, opening her blue eyes wide and gazing at him with blank astonishment.

His voice became silky.

'Because, my dear lady,' he said, 'I feel that your career in England may not be altogether without reproach. I shall try to find out a little more about it, and if I get a chance, I warn you frankly, I shall have you taken into custody. You are too mischievous to be allowed to run around loose.'

Her red lips parted in a scornful smile.

'Oh, you make me tired,' she retorted. 'Good-bye, Mr Foyle.'

'Pardon me,' he said, and thrusting a couple of fingers into his waistcoat pocket, fished out a piece of paper. 'Do you know this writing?'

She handed the piece of paper back to him with a shake of the head.

'No. I never saw it before,' she retorted, and passed out.
But Heldon Foyle had her finger-prints.

CHAPTER XXII

SIR HILARY THORNTON lifted his coat-tails to the cheerful blaze
as he stood with his back to the fireplace. Heldon Foyle,
with the book which he was giving his nights and days to
compiling on the desk in front of him, sat bolt upright in his
chair talking swiftly. He was giving an account of the progress
of the investigation. Now and again he ran a well-manicured
finger down the type-written index and turned the pages over
quickly to refer to a statement, a plan, or a photograph. Or
he would lift one of the speaking-tubes behind his desk and
send for some man who had been charged with some inquiry,
to question him on his report.

'These youngsters are all the same,' he complained queru-
lously. 'They will put flowers into their reports. It is always
a beast of a job to make 'em understand that we want a fact
plain and prompt. They can do it all right in the witness-
box, but when they get a pen in their hand they fancy they're
budding Shakespeares. The old hands know better.'

He passed from this outburst to particulars of what had
happened. The Assistant Commissioner listened gravely, now
and again interpolating a question or a suggestion. Foyle
rapidly ran over the case, emphasising his points with a tap
of his finger on the pile of papers.

'We're progressing a little, though not so fast as I'd like.
We know that Grell is alive, that he is in touch with Ivan
Abramovitch and Lola Rachael—or the Princess Petrovska, as
she calls herself. There is at least one other man in it—probably more. It's fairly certain that Grell knows who killed Harry
Goldenburg even if he didn't do it himself. Goldenburg was
apparently dressed in Grell's clothes before he was killed.

It is clear now that the clothes were his own with Grell's belongings put in the pockets. A Mexican dagger was used. That may be or may not be of importance. Grell has travelled in Mexico. We have eliminated Ivan and Sir Ralph Fairfield as the actual murderers. Nor do the Princess Petrovska's finger-prints agree. I had Bolt take the finger-prints of all the servants in the house, so that we are sure that none of them actually committed the crime. All this narrows the investigation. If we find Grell we are in a fair way to finding the author of the murder.'

Sir Hilary Thornton stroked his moustache doubtfully.

'That's all very well, Foyle, but Mr Grell is hardly the sort of man to commit murder. I gather that your suspicions point to him. Besides, where is the motive?'

'Every man is the sort of man to commit murder,' retorted the superintendent quickly. 'You can't class assassins. All murders must be looked upon as problems in psychology. Mind you, I don't say that Grell did have a hand in this murder. I am merely summing up the cold facts. Why should he disappear? Why should he mix himself up with the shady crew he is with—people who have twice tried to murder me, and who knocked out and kidnapped Waverley? If we find him, we shall find the murderer. That's why I wanted the description of Goldenburg sent out. It makes work—I've got two men out of town now working on statements made at Plymouth and Nottingham, which I feel sure will have no result, but it gives us a sporting chance to nail him if he tries to leave the country. Another line we're looking after is money. He's failed with Fairfield. Lola had a try with Lady Eileen Meredith, who handed over her jewels. We stepped in, bagged 'em, and gave 'em back to the Duke of Burghley. All this means he'll have to make some desperate try for cash soon.'

'In fact, it's check,' commented Sir Hilary, who was something of a chess-player. 'Now you're manœuvring for checkmate.'

'Precisely,' said Foyle. 'I've been trying, too, to get hold of something about Goldenburg. Neither we nor the American police have yet been able to connect him up with Grell. We're still trying, though. Sooner or later we shall get hold of something. And there's Lola. If we could have got Wills to identify her as the veiled woman, we should have had a very good excuse for arresting her in spite of her alibi. She's the sort of woman who would prepare an alibi. We've not got any proof that she knew Goldenburg. That's our great difficulty now—to link up the various persons and find how they've been associated with each other before. There's one thing, sir. I've managed to get the inquest adjourned for a month, so we shan't have to make any premature disclosures in evidence. The newspapers are still hanging about. They got wind that something was happening at Malchester Row, and there were a dozen or more men waiting for me when I came out, I told 'em that we'd been trying to identify a woman and had failed. They'd have known that anyway. They promised to be discreet. They're good chaps. It isn't like the old days. There was one man—Winters his name was—who came up to the Yard to see me once. He was told I was at Vine Street. He went down there and was told I hadn't been there.

'"Here's a piece of luck," he says to himself, and went back to his office. There he wrote up a couple of columns telling how the whole of the C.I.D. had lost trace of me. I came out of Bow Street, where I'd been giving evidence in a case, to see a big contents-bill staring me in the face:

FAMOUS
DETECTIVE
VANISHES

'Before I could buy a paper, another newspaper chap comes along. He stared at me as if I was a ghost.

'"Hallo!" he says. "Don't you know you're lost? Every pressman in London is looking for you."

'"Am I?" says I. "How?"

'Then it all came out. Since then I have been very careful in dealing with newspaper men.'

Sir Hilary laughed and nodded. 'Is there anything more?' he asked.

'Yes.' Foyle had grown grave once more. 'I handed over the cipher that we found at Grave Street to Jones, to see if he could make anything out of it. He's an expert at these kind of puzzles. Well, he's just reported that the thing is simple as it stands though in other circumstances it might be difficult. The translation runs:

'This will be the best method of communicating with E. M. if L. supplies her with key. Her 'phone number 12845 Gerrard.'

CHAPTER XXIII

UNLESS a case is elucidated within a day or two of the commission of an offence the first hot pursuit resolves itself into a dogged, wearisome but untiring watchfulness on the part of the C.I.D. A case is never abandoned while there remains a chance, however slight, of running a criminal to earth. And even when the detectives, like hounds baffled at a scent, are called off, there remains the gambler's element of luck. Even if the man who had original charge of the case should be dead when some new element re-opens an inquiry, the result of his work is always available, stored away in the Registry at Scotland Yard. There are statements, reports, conclusions—the case complete up to the moment he left it. The precaution is a useful one. A death-bed confession may implicate confederates, accomplices may quarrel, a jealous woman may give information. There have been unsolved mysteries, but no man may say when a crime is unsolvable.

Heldon Foyle had many avenues of information when it was a matter of ordinary professional crime. The old catchword, 'Honour among thieves,' was one he had little reason to believe in. There was always a trickle of information into headquarters by subterranean ways. The commonplaces of crime were effectively looked after. Murders are the exception in criminal investigation work, and while other crimes may be dealt with by certain predetermined if elastic rules, homicide had to be considered differently. Yet Foyle had cause to think that there might be little harm in setting to work the underground agencies which at first sight seemed to have little enough in common with the mystery of the rich Robert Grell. These spies and informers would try to cheat and trick him. Some of them might succeed. It would cost money, but money that might not be wasted.

Four of the five chief detective-inspectors who form the general staff of the C.I.D. were in the room, among them Wagnell, who had passed a quarter of a century in the East End and knew the lower grades of 'crooks' thoroughly, collectively, and individually.

Foyle shut the door.

'I wish some of you would pass the word among our people that we will pay pretty handsomely for anyone who puts us on to the gang mixed up in this Grell business. Word it differently to that. You'll know how to put it. You might get hold of Sheeny Foster, Wagnell, or Poodle Murphy, or Buck Taylor. They may be able to nose out something.'

'Buck was sent up for six months for jumping on his wife,' said Wagnell. 'I haven't seen Sheeny lately, but I'll try to get hold of him, and I'll have the word passed along.'

So, having made the first step in enlisting a new and formidable force of guerillas on the side of the law, Foyle went back to his office to revolve the problem in his brain once more.

His thoughts wandered to Sir Ralph Fairfield. Here was a man whose services would be invaluable if he could be persuaded to help. Grell knew him; trusted him. Foyle was a man who never neglected the remotest chances. He deemed it worth trying. True, so far as their encounters were concerned, Fairfield had not been encouraging. He would probably need delicate handling. Foyle wrote a note, scrutinised it rapidly, and, going out, gave it to a clerk to be sent at once by special messenger.

'Mr Heldon Foyle presents his compliments to Sir Ralph Fairfield and would be obliged if he could see him at his office at six o'clock this evening, or failing that, by an early appointment, on a matter of urgent importance.'

That was all it said: Foyle never wasted a word.

At five minutes past six that evening, Sir Ralph Fairfield was announced. He ignored the offer of a chair which was made by the superintendent, and stood with stony face a few paces from the door. Foyle was too wise to offer his hand. He knew it would not be accepted. He nodded affably.

'Good evening, Sir Ralph. I was hoping you would come. I would not have troubled you but that I felt you would like to know how we are getting on. You were a friend of Mr Grell's.'

'Well?' said Sir Ralph frigidly. 'I am here, Mr Foyle. Will you let me know what you want to say and have done with it?'

His manner was entirely antagonistic. There was still a lingering fear of arrest in his mind, but his attitude was in the main caused by the fact that he believed he had been suspected by the other. The superintendent partly guessed what was passing in his mind.

'I want your word first, Sir Ralph, that what I tell you shall not be spoken of by you to any living soul,' he said. 'Then I will tell you frankly and openly the whole history of our investigation, and you can decide whether you will help us or not. No—wait a moment. I know how loyal a friend you were of Robert Grell's, and it's in the light of that, that I am going to trust you. He is not dead. He is in hiding. It is for you to say whether you will help us to find him. If he is innocent he has nothing to fear.'

He was watching the other closely while he sprung the fact that Grell was alive upon him. He wanted to know whether it was really a surprise, whether in spite of the vigilance of the C.I.D. men Grell or his companions had managed to communicate with Fairfield. The baronet had opened his mouth to speak. A flicker of colour came and went in his pale cheeks, and he fingered his stick nervously. Then his jaw set, and he strode to where the superintendent was sitting and clutched him tightly by the arm.

'What's all this?' he demanded hoarsely. 'Do you mean to say Grell is not dead?'

'As far as I know he is as alive as you or I at this present minute,' said Foyle. 'If you want to hear about it all, give me your word and sit down. You're hurting my arm.'

'I beg your pardon,' said the baronet mechanically, and, stepping back, seated himself in a big arm-chair that flanked the desk. He passed his hand in a dazed fashion across his forehead and his composure came back to him. Staggering, incredible as the statement seemed, there was that in Foyle's quiet tones that gave it the stamp of truth.

'Of course, I'll give you my word,' he said.

Foyle was satisfied that the baronet knew nothing. There was a deeper policy behind the pledge he had exacted than that of preventing a leakage of confidence. Fairfield would not go behind his word. In that the superintendent had judged him accurately. But the pledge would also tie his hands should Grell or his companions eventually manage to communicate with him. Even if he decided not to help the police, he would find it difficult, without going behind his word, to assist the missing explorer.

From the beginning he traced the trend of the investigation, Fairfield leaning forward and listening attentively, his lips tight pressed. As Foyle brought out the points, the baronet now and again jerked his head in understanding. The detective slurred nothing, not even the accusation and resolve of the Lady Eileen Meredith. The baronet choked a little.

'You think she really meant to kill me?' He waved his hand impatiently as Foyle nodded. 'Never mind that. Go on. Go on.'

Foyle finished his recapitulation. Sir Ralph's eyes were fixed on a *Vanity Fair* cartoon of the Commissioner of Police hanging framed on the wall. He was trying to readjust his thoughts. From a man who believed himself under deadly suspicion he had suddenly become a confidant of Scotland Yard. He had been released of all fear for himself. And Bob Grell was alive after all; that, he reflected, was the queer thing. What did it mean? Where was the reason for this extraordinary tangle of complications? Grell always was deep, but, so far as his friend knew, he was a man strictly honourable. How had he come to be involved in an affair that looked so black against him? There was Eileen to be considered too. In spite of himself, he could readily believe the story of the pistol. She had believed him guilty of the murder. Her mood when last he saw her had been that of a woman who would stoop to anything to compass her vengeance. But she knew he was not guilty now. That might make a difference to his course of action. Should he throw in his lot with Foyle and assist in bringing Grell within the reach of the law?

'What do you say, Sir Ralph? Will you help us?'

Foyle's suave voice broke in upon the thread of his thoughts. He shook himself a little and met the detective's steady gaze.

'If I do, will it mean that you will arrest Grell for murder?'

The superintendent caressed his chin and hesitated a little before replying.

'I have been quite open with you, Sir Ralph. I don't know. As things are at present, it looks uncommonly as though he had a hand in it. He is the only person who can clear himself. While he remains in hiding everything looks black against him. We have managed to keep things quiet until the resumption of the inquest. When that takes place we shall not be able to maintain the confusion of identity. With things as they stand, the jury are practically certain to return a verdict of murder against him. If he is not guilty, his best chance is for us to find him. Understand me, Sir Ralph. If he is innocent you are doing him no service by refraining from helping us. Every day makes things blacker. If he is guilty—well, it is for you to judge whether you will shield a murderer even if he is your friend.'

To another person, Foyle would have used another method of persuasion, talking more but saying less. He had staked much on his estimate of the baronet's character, and awaited his reply with an anxiety of which his face gave no trace. Very rare were the occasions on which he had told so much of an unfinished investigation to another person, and that person not an official of Scotland Yard. Often he had feigned to open his heart with the same object—to win confidence by apparent confidence. The difference now was that he had given the facts without concealment or suppression.

Fairfield fingered his watch-chain, and the big office clock loudly ticked five minutes away.

'I will assist you as far as I can, but you must allow me to decide when to remain neutral,' he said at last.

'Agreed,' said Foyle, and the two shook hands on the bargain.

CHAPTER XXIV

DUTCH FRED changed his seat to one less conspicuous and farther up the tramcar. He felt that his luck was dead out, that life was a blank. And that Heldon Foyle of all men should have chosen that particular moment to board that particular tramcar had, as Fred would have expressed it, 'absolutely put the lid on.' Fred knew very well how to circumvent the precaution taken by order of the police that public vehicles should have the back of the seats filled in to prevent pocket-picking. Instead of sitting behind a victim, one sat by his side, with a 'stall' behind to pass the plunder to. A 'dip' of class—and Dutch Fred was an acknowledged master—never keeps his plunder on him for a single second longer than necessary. But with Foyle on the car it was too expensive to operate, especially single-handed. Therefore, Fred felt the world a dreary place.

He had boarded the car alone and without thought of plunder. Had it been in professional hours, he would have had at least one 'stall'—perhaps two—with him. As chance would have it, a portly business man, with a massive gold chain spanning his ample waist, had seated himself next the operator. And Fred had decided that the watch on the end of the cable was worth risking an experiment upon. Besides, the appearance of prosperity of the 'mug' spoke of a possible 'leather' stuffed with banknotes. Decidedly, even in the absence of a 'stall,' it was worth chancing. And then Foyle got on and spoilt it all. If anyone on the tramcar lost anything he would know who to blame.

For Heldon Foyle had spoiled one of the greatest coups that ever a crook had been on the verge of bringing off. Fred, immaculately clad, and with irreproachable references, had approached Greenfields, the Bond Street jewellers, with a formula for manufacturing gold. He had discovered the philosopher's stone. 'Of course, I don't want you to go into this until I've proved that it can actually be done,' he said airily. 'See there. I made that handful of gold-dust myself. You test it, and see that it's all right. Now, I'll sell you the secret of making that for £100,000. I don't want the money till I've given you a demonstration.'

So an arrangement was fixed up. The jewellers, with a faith that long experience had not destroyed, believed in Fred. Nevertheless, they took the precaution of calling in Foyle, then unknown to Fred save by name. In a little room in Clerkenwell the experiment took place. With ingenious candour, Fred prepared a crucible in front of his select audience after the various ingredients had been submitted to strict examination. Then he placed it on the fire, and stirred the contents occasionally. At last the process was finished, and at the bottom of the crucible was found a teaspoonful of undoubted gold-dust. Then, while Fred, with a broad smile of satisfaction, awaited comment, the detective, who had noted the strange fact that he had kept his gloves on while stirring the crucible, stepped up to him and deftly whipped one off. In the fingers were traces of gold-dust—enough to convict Fred and get him three years at the Old Bailey.

Out of the corner of his eyes, Fred watched the detective presently stand up and pass along the deck of the car towards him. The operator's face was bland, and he smiled with the consciousness of one who has nothing to hide as the superintendent sat down beside him.

'Hello, Mr Foyle! I am glad to see you,' he said, with a heartiness that he knew did not deceive the other. 'It's a long time since we met.'

The detective returned the greeting with a cheerfulness that was entirely unassumed.

'It's a piece of luck meeting you, Freddy,' he went on. 'But there, I always was lucky. You're just the man in the wide world I've been wanting to see.'

'What's on?' growled Freddy, with quick suspicion.

'Oh, you're all right,' the detective reassured him. 'I want you to help me. Let's get off at the next stopping-place and have a drink.'

His fears allayed, Freddy followed the detective off the car. They were professional enemies, it was true, but as a rule their relations were amicable. It was policy on both sides.

In the saloon bar of an adjacent public-house, Freddy unburdened himself fully and frankly while he sipped the mixed vermuth.

'I'm glad you struck me—on my word I am,' he said earnestly, while his active wits were wondering what the detective wanted. 'That bloke was carrying a red clock, and, though I was going for it, I had a feeling I should get into trouble. If you'd been a minute or two later, you'd—'

'Why talk of these unpleasant things, Freddy?' said Foyle, with a deprecatory wave of the hand. 'You know how I'd hate to have to do anything to disturb your peace of mind.' He drew him to a secluded corner of the lounge. 'Come over here. Now, listen. Do you know Goldenburg or any of his pals?'

Freddy started a little, and looked meditatively at the tips of his well-polished boots.

'The chap that did in Grell. I knew him a bit,' he said cautiously. 'He was in a different line, you know. Mostly works alone, too. I can't say that I know much about him. There's Charlie Eden, he was in with him once—I guess he's in town. And Red Ike, he knew him, too. Perhaps there's some more of the boys who had some does with him. But he always was a bit above us common crooks. I only went for big game once'—his gaze lingered on Foyle's ring—'and then it didn't come off.'

'Never mind about Eden. You keep your eyes skinned for Red Ike, or anyone else that knew Harry, and give me the office. It'll be worth your while. You can come to me if you're hard up. Have a shot at — and — and —' He named several public-houses which are known rendezvous for crooks of all classes. 'You see what you can pick up. And if ever you're in trouble, you'll know the wife and kid will be looked after.'

Freddy grinned cynically to hide a real appreciation. He knew that Foyle would do as he said. And in the criminal profession, however big the makings, there is very rarely anything like thrift. For a man who at any time might find himself doing five years, it was something to know that those left outside were in no danger of the workhouse. For even 'crooks' have human instincts at times.

'That's all right, Mr Foyle,' said Freddy. 'What you say goes. Who'll I ask for if you're not at your office?'

'You can talk to Mr Green.'

'Right oh!'

Freddy swung out into the dusk, whistling, for he had an assignment with his 'stalls' outside one of the big theatres. Foyle waited a few moments to let him get clear, and himself stepped into the street.

To the surprise and disgust of the rest of the 'mob,' Freddy early relinquished the evening's expedition, although his deft fingers had captured no more than a silver watch (hung deceptively on a gold chain, which he had left hanging), a woman's purse containing fifteen shillings in silver, and a pocket-book inside which were half-a-dozen letters. It was a poor hand, and Micky O'Brady, who was one of the 'stalls,' frankly expressed his disgust.

'What's the use of chucking it at this time o' night? It ain't nine o'clock yet. There's the lifts at the Tube that we haven't worked for weeks. 'Struth; what did you want to fetch us out for at all? The stuff you've got won't buy drinks.'

Freddy's lower jaw jutted out dangerously. He was a small man, but he had a hair-trigger temper. He always made a point to be unquestioned boss of his gang. Discipline had to be maintained at all costs.

'See here, Micky,' he said tensely. 'I've had enough tonight, and I'm going to give it a rest. So you'd better shut your face. I'm the man who's got the say, so here. You just bite on that.'

Micky, an Irish Cockney who had never been nearer Ireland than a professional visit to the Isle of Man, clenched his fists with an oath. He was a recent ally, and had not fully learned his position in Freddy's scheme of things. In just two minutes, he was sitting gasping on the pavement, trying to regain his wits after a tremendous punch in the solar plexus, while his fellow 'stall' was explaining to a constable that it was all an accident, and Freddy had quietly melted away in the direction of the Tube station.

The pickpocket never strained his luck, wherein he differed from the lower grade professors of his art. Common sense and superstition were both factors in his decision to suspend operations. He might as well spend his time, he decided, in trying to carry out Foyle's instructions. His intention took him to three public-houses as far apart as Islington, Blackfriars, and Whitechapel; at the latter place, in an ornate saloon bristling with gilt and glittering with mirrors, he found the man he wanted.

Leaning across the bar, exchanging sallies with a giggling barmaid, was a lean, sallow-complexioned man, whose rusty, reddish brown hair was sufficient justification for his nickname.

'Hello, Ike,' said the newcomer, adjusting himself to a high stool. 'How's things?'

'Hello, Dutch. Thought you got stuck the other side of the town. What are you going to have?'

Over the drinks they talked for a little on a variety of subjects—the weather, politics, trade—while the barmaid remained within hearing. Both were craftsmen in their particular line, and they spoke as equal to equal. Ike had made a specialty of getting cheque signatures for a little clique of clever forgers, and had his own ways of getting rid of his confederates' ingenuity. Nor was he above working side-lines if they promised profit, and in that respect, at least, he resembled Dutch Fred. His abilities in many directions had been recognised by Harry Goldenburg. It was not till they had gone over to a little table in a remote corner that Dutch Fred broached Goldenburg's name, in a tentative reference to the murder in Grosvenor Gardens.

'Funny thing you should speak about that,' commented Ike, glancing casually about to make certain that no one was within earshot. 'I hear that there's piles of stuff in that house, and there's only a butler and a man named Lomont, who was Grell's secretary, living there now to look after things. It would be easy to do a bust there.'

Fred's pulses jumped a little faster as he toyed with his glass. He knew something of Red Ike's methods, and felt certain that some proposal was coming. He could see the gratitude of Foyle taking some tangible form if he were able to bring this off. He had no scruples. Even if Ike suspected treachery after the event—well, he could look after himself.

'I don't know,' he said, shaking his head doubtfully. 'It isn't like a lonely suburban street.'

Ike grinned.

'I'm not a mug, am I? What do you say to walking in the front door, opening it with a key, and with the keys of the rest of the house in my "sky"? All I want is a straight man to keep doggo.'

'Criminy! Have you got the twirls?' he gasped. 'Where did you get 'em?'

'Never mind where they came from. I've got 'em. That's enough. More than that, I've got a lay-out of the house all marked out on paper, with every bit of stuff marked out where it ought to be. It's as easy as falling off a log.'

'Am I in it?' demanded Freddy.

'Why should I be telling you if you wasn't? You keep doggo outside if you like.'

More drinks were ordered, and Freddy came to business. 'What do I get?'

Ike let his chin rest meditatively on his slim fingers.

'Let's see. I cut in for a third, and I shall do all the work. I'll give you a quarter of that third. You won't have anything to do, except give me the office if anything goes wrong.'

''Struth!' Freddy was more hurt than indignant. 'You aren't going to Jew me down like that. Who else is in it?'

'Never mind who else is in it. I give you first chance, as a pal. You can take it or leave it.'

'Right, I'm on,' agreed Freddy.

CHAPTER XXV

THE compact between Heldon Foyle and Sir Ralph Fairfield had begun to bear fruit. For three days an advertisement had appeared in the personal column of the *Daily Wire*:

'Will R. G. communicate with R. F. Very anxious.'

Much thought had gone to the wording of the line. If Grell or any of his companions noticed it, Foyle felt certain that in some way or other an attempt would be made to get in touch with the baronet. He was fairly confident that the missing man needed money. He would probably not question how Fairfield knew that he was alive. If he rose to the bait there would be a catch of some sort. Whether Grell was the murderer or not, he held the key to the heart of the mystery. The superintendent emphasised this in a talk with Fairfield.

'It's a fair ruse. We're pretty certain he's hiding somewhere in London, and it's a big field unless we've got a starting-point. That's our trouble—finding a starting-point. In detective stories the hero always hits on it unerringly at once. There was one yarn in which the scratches on the back of a watch gave the clue to the temperament and history of its possessor. Now, that watch might have been borrowed or bought second-hand, or lost and restored at some time, and the marks made by anyone but its owner. That kind of subtlety is all right in print, but in real life it would put you on a false track in nineteen out of twenty cases. In ninety cases out of a hundred the obvious solution is the right one. In an investigation there may be coincidences of circumstantial evidence pointing in the wrong direction. But when you get first one coincidence, then a second, a third, and a fourth, you can be fairly sure you're on the right track. You don't add proof together. You multiply it. See here.'

He drew a piece of paper towards him and rapidly scribbled upon it.

One coincidence	= 0
Two coincidences	= 2
Three coincidences	= 6
Four coincidences	= 24
Five coincidences	= 120

'That's the kind of thing in terms of arithmetic. Now look at the parts in relation to each other. Grell leaves the club and gets you to lie about his absence. Coincidence number one. A man astonishingly like him is murdered in his study a short time afterwards. Coincidence number two. He is apparently dressed in Grell's clothes and has Grell's belongings in his pockets. Coincidence number three. Both Grell and his valet, Ivan Abramovitch, disappear. Coincidence number four. Ivan is found with the pearl necklace on him. Coincidence number five. Grell writes you a note, which I stole from you. Coincidence number six. You follow me? I could go on with other proofs. Grell *must* know who committed this murder, and if we get hold of him we shall know.'

'I see the point,' confessed Fairfield. 'All the same, I don't believe, even if he knows as you say, that he had a hand in it. This may be the hundredth case, you know, and there may be some satisfactory explanation of his actions.'

'I quite agree. Even cumulative proof may be destroyed. I can guess what you are half thinking. You believe that I've fastened my suspicions on Grell, and that I'm determined to go through with it right or wrong. That's a common mistake people fall into in regard to police functions. In fact, it doesn't matter a bit to a police official whether he gets a conviction or not—unless, of course, he neglects an important piece of proof through gross carelessness. All he has to do is to solve a problem and to place his answer before a magistrate, and then a judge and jury to decide whether he's right or wrong. No one but a fool would attempt to bolster up a wrong answer. In this case, too, you must remember that there are finger-prints. They cannot lie. If we get the right man—Grell or anyone else—there will be no question of doubt.'

Fairfield tapped a cigarette on the back of his left hand and rose.

'Well, even if you do draw Grell with that advertisement, I doubt if you'll get anything from him if he doesn't want to talk. I know the man, and he's hard to beat out of any decision that he makes up his mind to, as hard'—he bowed smilingly to the detective—'as you would be.'

'Thank you. If it were a question of Grell against Foyle I might have to go under. But it isn't. Behind me is the C.I.D., behind that the whole force, behind that the Home Secretary, and behind him the State. So you see the odds are on my side.'

A jerky buzz at the telephone behind the superintendent's desk interrupted any reply that Fairfield might have made. With a muttered 'Good-day', the baronet moved across the carpeted floor out of the room. As he closed the door Foyle put the receiver to his ear.

'Hello! Hello!. . . Yes, this is Foyle speaking. Oh yes, I know. . . . No, you'd better not tell me over the telephone. You can't come here. Somebody who knows you might see you. . . . Is it important?. . . All right. You'd better come to Lyon's tea-place in the Strand—the one nearest Trafalgar Square. I'll get Mr Green to go along and have a talk with you. Good-bye.'

Rubbing his hands together thoughtfully, the superintendent sent for Green. In a few moments the big figure of the chief inspector loomed in the doorway.

'Dutch Fred thinks he's got hold of something,' opened Foyle abruptly. 'I've told him to meet you at Lyon's in the Strand. I think he's all right, but don't let him have any money until you've tested his yarn.'

'Very good, sir,' said Green. 'I'll look into it.'

As he left, Foyle bent over his desk and, with the concentration that was one of his distinguishing traits, busied himself in a series of reports on a coining raid in Kensington, sent up to him by those concerned for his perusal. He had a theory that the efficiency of the battalion of detectives under him was not lessened by making his men tell him exactly how they were performing their work, both verbally and in writing. 'You may have brains, you may have intuition, you may have courage, but you'll never make a good detective without system,' he sometimes told young officers when they joined the staff of the C.I.D. There were things, of course, that could not be put in writing, but Foyle never invited his subordinates to act against the law. Such things have to be done at a man's own discretion without official sanction.

It was less than an hour when the chief inspector returned, portentously grave.

'Well?' demanded Foyle.

'The real goods,' said Green, who was obviously feeling pleased with himself. 'Your long shot has come off. They're falling short of money, for they've put Red Ike up to break into Grell's house and steal all the stuff in sight. Ike has asked Fred to give him a hand.'

A low whistle came from Foyle's lips. Why hadn't he thought of this? Discreetly done, with the help of a confederate—and apparently Grell had no lack of confederates—it would get over the money difficulty quite simply.

'Sit down, Green. Let's hear all about it,' he said, diving into his pocket for the inevitable cigar.

'It's all fixed up. Ike walks into the place with Grell's keys at eight o'clock tonight, while Freddy keeps watch outside—'

'And someone keeps an eye on Freddy, if I'm any judge. Go on. Who put Ike up to it?'

'He won't say. He's as tight as a drum about all that, according to Freddy. When we arrest him we must get something out of him.'

'I don't know,' said Foyle slowly. 'Ike's a queer bird. Dutch Fred will need to look after himself if ever he knows who gave the game away. Well now, let's fix up things. Is anyone keeping an eye on the place for Ike?'

'Freddy's supposed to be there.'

'And I guess that they've found out that Lomont and Wills will be out of the house tonight. You might find out for sure, Green. 'Phone Lomont, but don't stop 'em if they've made arrangements. It would simplify matters if we could get one or two of our own men in the house. We daren't do that, though.'

'Why not? If Freddy's keeping watch—'

'That's all right. It isn't Freddy I'm afraid of. There'll be someone else there. The people who put this game up are not going to trust a couple of crooks entirely. I think I'll take a stroll out that way myself about seven o'clock. We'd better have the place surrounded. I'll send for a section map of that part.'

A clerk brought the map, and Foyle's fingers described a wide, irregular circle, now and again halting at one spot where he wished a man to be placed.

'That ought to do,' said the superintendent when Green had finished taking a note of the various points. 'Pick out some good men, though I don't suppose they will have much to do. It's only a measure of precaution. You'd better be on hand yourself about half-past seven. If all goes well we shall get bigger game than Ike.'

CHAPTER XXVI

WITHIN the invisible cordon that Foyle had drawn about Grell's house in Grosvenor Gardens, Dutch Fred loitered, his keen,

ferret eyes wandering alertly over passers-by. Misgivings had
assailed him during a vigil that had lasted several hours. It was
all very well to be 'in with' the police; but suppose their plans
miscarried? Suppose Red Ike and his unknown friends got
to know that the 'double cross' was being put on them? Fred
fingered a heavy knuckle-duster in his pocket nervously. Man
to man, he was not afraid of Ike, but there were his friends.

The tall straight figure of Heldon Foyle, with coat collar
turned high up, had passed him once without sign of recognition and vanished in the enveloping shadow of the slight
fog that confused the night. Yet, though the superintendent
had apparently paid no heed, he was entirely alert, and he
had not failed to observe Freddy. What he wanted was to see
who else was in the street. He returned by a detour to an
hotel in the Buckingham Palace Road, outside which a big
motor-car was at rest, with a fairly complete mental picture
of three people who might be possible spies among those
he had passed.

The thickening fog was both an advantage and a disadvantage to the detectives—an advantage because it would force
any person watching on behalf of Grell and his associates
to keep within a reasonable distance of the house if Ike was
not to be lost sight of, and a disadvantage because it would
afford increased facilities for anyone to slip away.

To Green, seated in the motor-car, Foyle commented on
this fact.

'You'll have to have your breakdown rather closer to the
house than we thought,' he said. 'Give Ike a good chance
inside. You've got the duplicate key all right?'

'That's safe enough,' answered Green, tapping his pocket.
'If I don't see you after we've bagged him I'd better charge
him with housebreaking, I suppose?'

'Certainly. Now get along. It's a quarter to eight.'

The car moved silently forward and took the corner of
Grosvenor Gardens. Thirty paces beyond the spot where

Dutch Freddy was lighting a cigarette it came to a stop, while the chauffeur, dropping to the ground, rummaged fiercely with the interior. Green leaned back in the shadow, his eyes fixed on the steps leading to Grell's house. There was a sufficient air of plausibility about the whole accident to impress anyone but the most suspicious.

Heldon Foyle had entered the hotel, for he did not care to run the risk of frightening his quarry by showing himself again until it was necessary. But he kept a vigilant eye on the clock. Promptly as the hands touched ten minutes past eight he made his way once more to the corner of Grosvenor Gardens. A labourer, with corduroy trousers tied about the knee and a grimy, spotted blue handkerchief about his neck, approached him with unlit pipe and a request for a match.

'Red Ike's gone along,' he said, as Foyle supplied him. 'Nobody else has been hanging round except Freddy. The constable on the beat passed along just after Ike.'

The match was dropped in the gutter, and the superintendent, his face set grimly, moved slowly on. The labourer crossed to the other side of the road and followed. Foyle was quite near the house when Green walked up, accompanied by his chauffeur, and made quickly up the steps. Shadowy in the fog, the superintendent could see the dim outline of a constable's uniform. The man was peering anxiously at the doorway through which Green had gone.

'Well, my man,' said Foyle sharply, 'are you on duty here? Who are those people who have just gone in there?'

The policeman gave a barely perceptible start, and then took a pace forward.

'I—I believe they have no right there. I must go and see,' he said, but was brought up with a jerk as Foyle's hand clutched his wrist. The labourer who had wanted a light was coming across the road at a run and, though a little puzzled, had seized the constable's other hand.

'No, you don't,' said Foyle peremptorily. 'When you masquerade as a policeman again, my friend, make sure you have a letter of the right division on your collar. This district is B, not M. I am a police officer, and I shall arrest you on a charge of being concerned in an attempt at housebreaking. You'd better not make a fuss. Come on, Smithers. Let's get him into the car.'

The prisoner made no resistance. He seemed dazed. Once in the car, the detective took the precaution to handcuff him to his subordinate—right wrist to the officer's left wrist—for he did not know how long the wait for Green might be, and it seemed wisest not to run risks. Detectives rarely handcuff their prisoners unless travelling. It is conspicuous and unnecessary.

'Now we're more comfortable,' said Foyle, sinking into the cushions of the car. 'If you want to give any explanation before I formally charge you, you may. Only don't forget that anything you say may be used in evidence against you.'

'Is it an offence to go to a fancy-dress ball in a police officer's uniform?' asked the prisoner. 'Because if it is, I shall plead guilty.'

'You can make that defence if you like—if you think it will be believed,' retorted Foyle. 'It will be better for everyone if you tell the truth, though.'

The man lapsed into a surly, sullen silence, and the superintendent could feel that he was glaring at him in the darkness of the closed car. The other detective looked through the window.

'Here comes Mr Green, sir.'

Arm in arm and in amicable converse with Ike, the chief detective-inspector was approaching the car, with the chauffeur on the other side. Ike, it appeared, had been run to earth in the dining-room, and had surrendered at discretion. He had all the philosophy of the habitual thief who knows when the game is up. He grinned a little when he saw the handcuffed policeman in the car.

'Why, it's you, Mr Smith! Didn't you think I could be trusted for fair does over the stuff inside? You've fallen into it this time, and no blooming error. Where's Fred?'

'Fred who?' queried Foyle. 'Is there someone else in this job?'

But Red Ike was too old a bird to be deceived. Instinct, as well as reason, told him that he had been betrayed, and the absence of Fred but lent fuel to his suspicions.

'Aw—don't come it, Mr Foyle,' he said disgustedly, and added a picturesque flow of language, elaborating the steps he would take to get even with Dutch Fred when he had the opportunity. Not one of the detectives interrupted him. The more he talked the better, for he might drop something of value. Not until they drew up at the police station did his eloquence desert him. The superintendent descended first and gave a few instructions, while the *soi-disant* constable was taken to the cells. Ike found himself escorted upstairs into the C.I.D. office. Only Heldon Foyle and Green remained with him.

'Sit down and make yourself comfortable,' said the superintendent cheerfully. 'We want to have a little talk with you, Ike. Would you like a drink? Here, have a cigar.'

Red Ike's swift wits were on the alert. Never before had he known this kind of hospitality to be tendered in a police station to a man arrested red-handed. And although suspicious, he was nevertheless flattered. All criminals, whether at the top or bottom of their profession, are beset by vanity.

'A little out of your usual line this,' went on Foyle, watching his man intently. 'As neat a job as ever was spoiled by accident. Now you know, as well as I do, that we can't force you to talk. But it'll help us a bit if you tell us who you got those keys from, for instance.'

The office was small and plainly furnished, and Ike stared into the fire as he sipped his whisky, with placid face. That the interview was to be the English equivalent of the third degree, he knew not. There would be no bullying, only coaxing. Foyle was in a position where consummate tact was needed if he was to extract anything from the prisoner. He dared neither threaten nor promise. However helpful Ike might be, he would still have to submit the issue of guilt and punishment to a judge and jury. Ike, unlike Dutch Fred, had no relations, and if he had it was doubtful if any promise of consideration for them would move him.

'It's no good, Mr Foyle,' said Ike. 'The only man that was in this with me was Dutch Fred. You'd better go and get him, because I shall tell all about it in court. He gave me the keys.'

'Don't be a fool, Ike,' interposed Green.

The prisoner glanced from one to the other with cunning, twinkling eyes. He was too wary to say anything that may be used as evidence.

'I guess that it isn't bursting into the place that's put you two to work,' he said. 'You want to know something. If I could help you I s'pose you'd drop this case?'

Heldon Foyle shook his head resolutely.

'You know we can't do that in a case of felony. Mr Green will put in a good word for you at the trial. That's the farthest we can go to.'

Ike put down his empty glass. He believed he held the whip hand—that he had much to gain and nothing to lose by holding out for better terms. It was a false impression, though a natural one. Heldon Foyle had neither the power nor the inclination to drive a bargain that would permit Ike to go unscathed to renew his depredations on society.

'It's no good, guv'nor,' said Ike. 'If you want me to talk I'll do it—if you'll let me go.'

'Right.' Foyle rose abruptly. 'We'll let it go at that, Ike. You please yourself, of course. Mr Green, you'd better charge him now.'

He had passed out of the door, and his footsteps were dying away when Ike awoke to the fact that his attempt at bluff had failed. He raised his voice. 'Hi! Mr Foyle! Don't go yet. I'll cough up what I know. Come back.'

CHAPTER XXVII

A GRIM smile flickered under Chief Inspector Green's grey moustache as Heldon Foyle stepped briskly back into the room and closed the door. Ike met a stare of the superintendent's cold blue eyes squarely.

'You've got the bulge on me this time, guv'nor,' he admitted ruefully. 'I give you best. You're welcome to all I know—though that isn't much.'

Now that he was near attaining his end, Foyle had to steer a delicate course. The law very rightly insists that there shall be neither threat nor promise held out to any person who is accused of a crime. From the moment a police officer has made up his mind to arrest a man, he must not directly or indirectly induce a person to say anything that might prove his guilt—and a warning of the possible consequences is insisted upon even when a statement is volunteered. Otherwise admissions or evidence so obtained are ignored, and there is trouble for the police officer who obtained them. That is one of the reasons why detective work in England demands perhaps nicer skill than in most other countries.

Green had pulled a fountain pen from his pocket and adjusted a couple of sheets of official foolscap. Foyle remained standing.

'Don't let's have any misunderstanding,' he said. 'We're not making any promises except that the court will know you helped us in another case. If you choose to keep quiet we can't do a thing to you.'

'I know all about that,' said Ike, with a little shrug of his shoulders. 'You know I wouldn't squeal in an ordinary job. I'm no Dutch Freddy to give my pals away. I don't owe the chap anything who put me up to this. What do you want first?'

'Tell us all about it your own way. Where did you get the keys of the house?'

'Off that chap you raked in along of me. I was sitting in a little game of faro at a joint in the Commercial Road about a week ago, when this tough pulls me out and puts it up to me. I didn't much like it, but the chink who runs the show told me he was straight, and he offered me half—'

'You told Freddy you were only getting a third,' interposed Green.

'Did I?' Ike grinned cunningly. 'It must have been a slip of the tongue. Anyway, I said I'd chip in for half or nothing. He pow-wowed a bit, but at last he gave in. Funny thing about it was he wouldn't hear of keeping an eye open on the day we brought the job off. Said I must get a pal. Yet here he turns up as large as life all the time.'

The prisoner had hit on a point which had puzzled Foyle for a time, but light had already flashed upon him. In the ordinary course of things, a robbery at Grosvenor Gardens by two known criminal characters would not of necessity be associated with the murder. The third man was taking no chances of being identified as an associate.

'Anyway, I took the job on, and he handed me over the twirls and a lay-out of the house. He didn't tell me who was behind him. And I didn't ask too many questions. He called himself Mr Smith, and we met once or twice at the —.' He named a public-house in Leman Street, Whitechapel. 'That's where I was to have met him tonight with the stuff. Now you know all I know.'

'Not quite,' said Foyle quietly. 'What's the address of this gambling-joint where you first met him?'

Ike shook his head. 'Oh, play the game, guv'nor. You aren't going to have that raided after what I've done for you?'

'We'll see,' evaded Foyle. 'Where is it?'

Reluctantly, Ike gave the address. Green held out a pen to him and pointed to the bottom of the foolscap.

'Read that through and sign it if it's all right.'

The man appended a dashing signature, and with a cheerful 'Good night, Mr Foyle,' was ushered by a chief detective-inspector down to the charge-room. Heldon Foyle rested his elbows on the table and remained in deep thought, immobile as a statue. He roused himself with a start as Green returned.

'Both charged,' said the other laconically. 'The other chap refuses to give any account of himself. Refuses even to give a name. Seems to be a Yankee. I had his finger-prints taken. There was nothing on him to identify him.'

'Yankee, eh?' repeated Foyle. 'So is Grell. There won't be anyone in the finger-print department at this time of night. We'll go along and have a search by ourselves, I think. If we've not got him there, Pinkerton of the U. S. National Detective Agency is staying at the Cecil. We'll get him to have a look over our man and say whether he recognises him.'

'Very good, sir. There's one other thing. When I searched this man I found this. I don't know if you can make anything out of it. I can't.'

He handed across an envelope already torn open, addressed to 'The Advertisement Dept., The *Daily Wire*.' Within were two plain sheets of notepaper and a postal order. On one was written: 'Dear Sir, please insert the enclosed advts. in the personal column of your next issue.—John Jones.' On the other were two advertisements:

'R.F. You are closely watched. Don't forget 2315.
Don't forget 2315. G.'
'E. £27.14.5. Tomorrow. B.'

'Very curious,' commented Foyle. 'Copy them out carefully and have 'em sent to the paper. They can't do any harm. Now let's get along.'

The fog hung heavy over a muffled world as they walked down Victoria Street. Green, whose wits were a trifle less supple than those of his chief when imagination was required, put a question. Foyle answered absently. The mysterious advertisements were not altogether mysterious to him. He recalled the cipher that had been found at Grave Street, and decided that there was at least room for hope in that direction. Besides, there was at least one man now in custody who knew something of the mystery, and, even if he kept his lips locked indefinitely, there was a probable chance of a new line of inquiry opening when his identity was discovered. And even if finger-prints and Pinkerton failed to resolve that, there was still the resource of the newspapers. With a photograph scattered far and wide, the odds were in favour of someone recognising its subject.

As Foyle switched on the lights in the finger-print department, Green sat down at a table and with the aid of a magnifying-glass carefully scrutinised the prints which he carried on a sheet of paper. Ranged on one side of the room were high filing cabinets divided into pigeon-holes, numbered from 1 to 1024. In them were contained hundreds of thousands of finger-prints of those known to be criminals. It was for the detectives to find if among them were any identical with those of their prisoner.

The whole science of finger-prints for police purposes resolves itself into the problem of classification. It would be an impossible task to compare myriads of records each time. The system employed was absurdly simple to put into execution. In five minutes Green had the finger-prints of the two hands classified into 'loops' and 'whorls' and had made a rough note.

'W.L.W.L.L.
'L.W.W.L.W.'

That done, the remainder was purely a question of arithmetic. Each whorl was given an arbitrary number according to its position. A whorl occurring in the first pair counts 16 in the second, the third 4, the fourth 2, and the fifth 1. Thus Green's effort became:

$$\frac{16 - 4 - -}{- 8.4 - 1} = \frac{20}{13}$$

The figure one was added to both numerator and denominator, and Green at once went to the fourteenth pigeon-hole, in a row of the filing cabinet numbered 21. There, if anywhere, he would find the record that he sought. For a while he was busy carefully looking through the collection.

'Here it is,' he said at last and read: 'Charles J. Condit. American. No. 9781 Habitual Convicts' Registry.'

'Put 'em back,' said Foyle. 'We'll find his record in the Registry.'

The two detectives, uncertain as to where the regular staff kept the files of the number they wanted, were some little time in searching. It was Foyle who at last reached it from a top shelf and ran his eye over it from the photograph pasted in the top left-hand corner to the meagre details given below.

'This is our man right enough,' he said. 'American finger-prints and photograph supplied by the New York people when he took a trip to this country five years ago. Never convicted here. It says little about him. We'll have to cable over to learn what they know.'

'That gives us a chance for a remand,' remarked Green.

'Exactly. And in the meantime he may tell us something. A prisoner gets plenty of time for reflection when he's on remand.'

CHAPTER XXVIII

FIVE minutes after Big Ben had struck ten o'clock Heldon Foyle walked into his office to find Sir Ralph Fairfield striding up and down and glancing impatiently at the clock. He made no direct answer to the detective's salutation, but plunged at once into the object of his visit. 'Have you seen the *Wire* this morning?' he asked abruptly.

Foyle seated himself at his desk, imperturbable and unmoved.

'No,' he answered, 'but I know of the advertisement that brought you here. As a matter of fact, I sent it to the paper. I should have called on you if you hadn't come. Grell meant it for you, right enough.'

The significance of the detective's admission that he knew of the advertisement did not immediately strike Fairfield. He unfolded a copy of the *Daily Wire*.

'What do you make of the infernal thing?' he demanded. 'It's absolute Greek to me.'

With a letter selected from the pile of correspondence on his desk unopened in his hand, Heldon Foyle swung round and faced his questioner.

'It's simply a sighting shot, Sir Ralph,' he remarked quietly. 'Grell credits you with intelligence enough to remember that number later. Have you any knowledge of ciphers?'

'I have an elementary idea that to unravel them you work from the most frequently recurring letter; E, isn't it?'

'That's right,' said Foyle. 'But there are other ciphers where that system won't work. Mind you, I don't pose as an expert. If I had a cipher to unravel, I should go to a man who had specialised in them, exactly as I should go to a doctor on a medical question. Still, the advertisement today isn't a cipher. It means exactly what it says.'

'Thank you,' said Fairfield drily. 'I am now as wise as when I started.'

'Sorry,' murmured Foyle suavely. 'You'll be wiser presently. The thing isn't complete yet. If you'll excuse me a few minutes, I'll just run through my letters, and then, if you don't mind taking a little walk, we'll go and see Lady Eileen Meredith.'

Some formal reply rose to Fairfield's lips—he never knew what. The last time he had seen Eileen was fixed in his memory. Then she had practically denounced him as a murderer. Since then she had learnt that every shadow of suspicion had been cleared away from him. How would she receive him if he visited her unexpectedly with Foyle? Why did Foyle wish him to go? Perhaps, after all, there was nothing in it. He told himself fiercely that there was no reason why the meeting should embarrass him. Some day, sooner or later, they would have to meet. Why not now? He was hungry for a sight of her, and yet he was as nervous as a child at the thought of going to her.

The slamming of a drawer and the soft click of a key in the lock told that Foyle had finished. He picked up a copy of the *Daily Wire* and his hat and gloves.

'Now, Sir Ralph,' he said briskly, and together they descended the narrow flight of stone steps which leads to one of Scotland Yard's back doors. The detective was apparently in a talkative mood, and Fairfield got no chance to ask the questions that were filling his mind. In spite of himself he became interested in the flow of anecdotes which came from his companion's lips. There were few corners of the world, civilised or uncivilised, where the superintendent had not been in the course of his career. He had the gift of dramatic and humorous story-telling. He spoke of adventures in Buenos Aires, in South Africa, Russia, the United States, and a dozen other countries, of knife-thrusts and revolver shots, of sand-bagging and bludgeoning, without any suspicion of vaunting himself. The baronet made some comment.

'No,' said Foyle. 'Take it all round, a detective's life is more monotonous than exciting. It's taken me thirty years to collect the experiences I'm telling you about. Things always happen unexpectedly. Some of my narrowest squeaks have taken place in England, in the West End. Why, I was nearly shot in one of the best hotels by an officer sent over from the

United States to take charge of a man I had arrested. He was the sheriff of some small town and had a bit of a reputation as a gun-man, and had come over with the district attorney to escort the chap back. They did themselves well while they were here waiting to catch a boat back. One morning I strolled into the hotel, and who should run into me but the attorney with a face the colour of white paper.

"'That you, chief?' he gasps. "For God's sake don't go upstairs. —'s on the landing, blazing drunk and with his gun out. He's a dead shot.'

'Well, I could see that a Wild West sheriff was out of place in a decent hotel, so up I went. He had me covered like a flash, and I yelled out to him not to shoot.

"'Hello, chief," he says. "That's all right. Come right up. I won't do a thing. Just wait till I've plugged that cur of an attorney and we'll go and have a drink.'

'By this time I was up level with him. I daren't risk trying to get the revolver from him, for he was a quick shot, so I pushed my arm through his.

"'I haven't got much time, sheriff," says I. "Let's go and have a drink first, and you settle up with him afterwards.'

"'That's a bet," he says, and I led him down to the bar. I persuaded him to try a new drink of my own invention—its chief component was soda-water—and followed it up with strong hot coffee. Meanwhile I managed to get the gun away, on the pretext of admiring it. He was reluctant at first, telling me I could have it for keeps after he had finished that cur of an attorney. But I got it, and he was fairly sober by the time I left him.

'Then there was a sequel. I had warned the sheriff and the attorney, who had made up their differences, that the man they had got was a slippery customer to handle. However, they got him in the boat all right. When they got to New York I had a cable from the captain—a friend of mine. He said the prisoner had not only cleared off the ship by himself, but had carried away the hand-baggage of his escort.'

This reminiscence had brought them to Berkeley Square. Fairfield felt his heart thumping quickly although his face was impassive as the door was opened in response to Foyle's ring. She might be out; she might refuse to see them. Neither of the two alternatives happened. Within three minutes Eileen had descended to them in the drawing-room.

She stopped, a graceful figure in black, by the doorway, and gave a barely perceptible start as her eyes rested on the baronet. She bowed coldly.

'I did not know you were here, Sir Ralph. I understood Mr Foyle wished to see me.'

She was frigid and self-possessed. He had half expected some expression of apology for the wrong she had done him, but she entirely ignored that. But that Fairfield had himself well in hand he would have openly resented the snub inflicted on him. It was Foyle who answered.

'I brought Sir Ralph here. I thought his presence might be necessary.'

She moved across the room, and sank on a couch with a petulant frown.

'Well, I suppose you have some disagreeable business to transact. Let us get it over.'

The superintendent knew that he was dealing with a woman entirely on her guard. Her steady grey eyes were fixed on him closely, as though she could read his thoughts. He thought he could detect a slight twitching of the slender hands that rested idly on her lap.

'I want to know,' he said slowly, 'the meaning of the advertisement addressed to you by Robert Grell in this morning's *Daily Wire*.'

He could have sworn that his shot had hit, that she flinched a little as he spoke. But if so she showed no further sign. Instead, her face was all astonishment as she replied:

'I don't quite understand. What advertisement? I know nothing about Mr Grell since he left Grosvenor Gardens. Will you explain?'

Deliberately the superintendent took from his breast-pocket a copy of the *Daily Wire*, folded back at the personal column, and read:

'E. £27.14.5. Tomorrow. B.'

'That,' he said, 'is addressed to you. It is hardly worth while denying knowledge of it. It was found last night on a man arrested for attempted housebreaking at Mr Grell's house. I ordered that it be sent to the paper, together with another intended for the eye of Sir Ralph Fairfield.'

Her interest was plainly awakened.

'Then the other was for you!' she cried, turning to Fairfield. 'I wondered if—'

She paused with the realisation that she had admitted what she had a moment before denied. Foyle's foot pressed heavily on the toe of the baronet to warn him not to speak.

'Yes, it was for Sir Ralph,' he said. 'That is why I brought him here. It is you, though, who hold the key to this mystery. We know that you would have sent your jewels to Grell, that you are in communication with his friends. You are young, Lady Eileen, and don't realise that you are playing with fire. Your silence can do your lover no good—it may do him and yourself harm. You have been visited by the Princess Petrovska, an adventuress not fit to touch the hem of your skirt. You are already involved. Take the advice of a man old enough to be your father, and confide in us.'

She had risen, and her slim form towered over the seated detective. She seemed about to resent his words, but suddenly burst into a ripple of laughter.

'You would be offensive if you were not amusing, Mr Foyle. Don't you think my help would be a little superfluous, since you know so much?' she asked with a quietness that robbed the remark of some of its bitterness. 'I think you had better go now.'

'I am sorry,' said Foyle. 'You may regret that you did not take my advice.'

She herself held the door open for them to pass out. To the surprise of Fairfield, she held out her hand to him while ignoring the detective.

'Come back alone as soon as you can,' she whispered. 'I want to speak to you.'

Foyle had apparently neither heeded nor heard. Yet, as soon as they were out of eye-shot of the house, he turned to Fairfield.

'She asked you to go back?'

'Eh?' The baronet was startled. 'Yes. How did you know? Did you overhear her?'

'No, but I hoped she would when I took you there. That was the whole reason of our visit. I didn't expect to get her to say or admit anything.'

Fairfield came to an abrupt halt and gripped his companion by the arm.

'You intended— For what reason? How could you know?'

'Absolute common sense, my dear sir. That's all. Absolute common sense. If you are a chess-player, you know that the man who can foretell what move his opponent is going to make usually wins. Here, let's find a quiet Piccadilly tea-shop and I'll tell you all about it.'

There is no place which one may find more convenient for a quiet conversation than the London tea-shop before twelve in the morning. Over a cup of coffee in the deserted smoking-room Foyle spoke to the point.

'I did not tell you why I took you to see Lady Eileen, because I was afraid you might refuse. She has been antagonistic to you hitherto. The fact that Grell advertised you in somewhat the same manner as herself has given her the idea that, after all, you too might be trying to shield him. Naturally, she wants to be certain, in order that you may join forces.

That's why I prevented you saying anything. Now, if you go back to her you may tell her that I practically forced you to accompany me. You can win her confidence, and through her we may get on the right track.'

An angry flush mounted to Fairfield's temples.

'In short,' he said curtly, 'you want me to act as a spy on an unsuspecting girl. No, thanks. That's not in our bargain.'

He was genuinely angry at the proposal. The superintendent saw that he had been too blunt, and made haste to repair his error.

'Don't be in a hurry,' he protested. 'The girl, as I told her, is beginning to be mixed up in a dangerous business. This is the only way to extricate her. You may help her and Grell and us by doing as I ask. Consider it coolly, and you will see it is the best thing to do.'

Sir Ralph set down his cup and fingered his watch-chain. Foyle signalled the waitress, paid the bill, lit a cigar and waited.

'I'll have to think over it,' said Fairfield thoughtfully. 'Give me an hour or two.'

'Right you are,' agreed the detective heartily, and they made their way out into the street.

CHAPTER XXIX

IT was with mixed feelings that Fairfield yielded at last to Foyle's arguments and returned to see Eileen Meredith. To his consent he had attached the condition that he was to be allowed to use his own judgment as to how much of the interview he should communicate to the detective, and with this Foyle had to be content.

The baronet found the girl waiting for him, her face alight with eagerness. She was in her own boudoir, luxuriously ensconced in a big arm-chair, and she smiled brightly at him—such a smile as he had not seen since before the murder. He obeyed her invitation to sit down.

'You wanted to see me alone,' he said.

She nodded. 'Yes, I want to know if we are allies—or enemies. I know I have treated you abominably, but I was driven half mad by the thought that Bob was dead. Now we are working together—are we not?'

He made a little gesture with his hands, helplessly as one at a loss.

'In so far as we both wish to get Grell out of his difficulty— and I wish I knew what that was—yes,' he replied. 'I don't believe him to be a murderer, but why does he remain in hiding? He is not the sort of man to do foolish things, and that is foolish on the face of it. He has some strong reason for being out of the way. Can you explain?'

She pulled her chair closer to him, and laid one slim hand on his.

'I cannot explain—I can only trust. He looked to us to help him. I know that he wants money, for he sent a friend to tell me. I had none, but I gave her my jewels. Detectives were watching her, and they, with the connivance of my father, took them from her. Now, you, his most intimate friend, must help him. He has given you the key to the cipher which will appear, and then, I suppose, he will tell you how to get it to him.'

She had apparently taken it for granted that the baronet was with her in whole-souled devotion to her lover. His fingers beat a tattoo on his knee.

'So that advertisement was the key to a cipher? Do you know when I shall get a message?'

'I shall get one tomorrow. You—who knows?'

'Then you can tell me how to read it?'

She hesitated a moment, finger on chin. Then, animated by a quick resolve, she moved to a little inlaid desk and unlocked a drawer. She returned with a piece of paper in her hand.

'What was the number mentioned in your advertisement?'

'2315.'

For a little the only sound in the room was the scratching of pencil on paper. At last she finished, and handed the result to him. He wrinkled his brows as he studied it.

THIS IS THE KEY

2315 23 152 315

VKJX KV UMG NFD

'The bottom line is the top one turned into cipher,' she explained. 'The middle line is the key number. In the first word you take the second letter from T, the third from H, the first from I, and so on. It is a cipher that cannot be unravelled without the key number. H becomes K once and M once.'

'I see.' The simplicity of it at once dawned on him. 'That was what Foyle meant when he said that some ciphers could not be solved by the recurring E,' he said unthinkingly.

She had risen and flung away from him in quick revulsion. One glance at her face told him what he had done.

'You spy!' There was stinging scorn in her tone. 'You have talked it over with Foyle, and that man knows all. You are here to worm out what I know in order to betray your friend. Oh, don't trouble to lie'—as he would have spoken—'I can see your object. And I nearly fell into the trap.'

The man was not without dignity, as he stood a little white but steady. 'You may call me what you like,' he said in a low voice. 'Spy, if you will. Believe me or not, I have acted for the best, for you and for Grell. You once called me a murderer—with what justification you now know. Are you so ready to judge hastily again?'

If he had hoped to move her from her gust of passion, he quickly learned his mistake. Her lips curled in contempt, and, drawing her skirts aside as she passed him as though a touch might contaminate her, she swept to the doorway. For one instant she stood posed.

'You call yourself a spy. It is a good name. For a police spy there is no room in this house.'

With that she was gone. The man had flushed under the biting contempt in her voice and words, and now stood for a little with hands tightly clenched, gazing after her. He felt that, from her point of view at least, there was some truth in her words. He was—whatever his motives— a police spy. And yet he was but concerned to clear up the horrible tangle in which his friend and the girl had become involved.

He did not know that he was watched from behind the curtains as he walked blindly into the street. Eileen, with lips firmly set and face tense, was concealed behind curtains. No sooner had he gone than she hurriedly dressed herself and ordered an electric brougham. She had come to believe that her lover's safety depended on her actions that day. Foyle knew the secret of the cipher, and Grell's advertisement told her that he intended communicating something to her by that method the next day. At all costs she must prevent him betraying himself.

Only one course occurred to her. She must go to the office of the *Daily Wire* and prevent his advertisement from appearing. How she was to do it she had not the slightest idea. That she left for later reflection.

The car rolled smoothly towards Fleet Street, but no inspiration came to her. She alighted at the advertisement office, with its plate glass and gilded letters, and was attended by an obsequious clerk. Outwardly calm, but with her heart beating quickly beneath her furs, she put her inquiry to a sleek-haired clerk. He was polite but firm. It was quite possible that such an advertisement as she mentioned had been sent for insertion the following day, and again it might not. In any case he was forbidden to give any information. It would be quite out of the question to stop any advertisement unless she held the receipt.

'But if the advertisement has not already been given in, can you give a note to whoever brings it?' she asked, in a flash of inspiration.

'Yes, that could be done.' She tore off her glove, and with slim, nervous fingers wrote hurriedly. The sleek clerk supplied her with an envelope, and as she placed her message in it and handed it to him she felt it was a forlorn hope. There was only one other way of outwitting the detectives. Should Grell give any address in his message, she must reach him early in the morning before the police could act. A couple of questions elicited the fact that the paper would be on sale by four the next morning. That would mean another journey to Fleet Street, for the ordinary newsagents' shops would not be open at that time. The brougham turned about and began the homeward journey.

A respectably dressed working man, who had apparently been absorbed in a page of advertisements of situations vacant displayed on a slab in the window, slouched into the office, and a man bareheaded and wearing a frock-coat moved briskly forward, apparently to attend to him. Yet it was more than coincidence that they met at a deserted end of the counter.

'That was Lady Eileen Meredith,' said the workman, in a quick, low voice. 'What did she want?'

'She's guessed that we know the cipher,' retorted the other. 'She gave a letter to be handed over to whoever brings the advertisement. Here is what she says.' He pulled the letter which Eileen had written five minutes before from its envelope: '"The police know the cipher. Be very cautious. R. F. is acting with them." I'll telephone to Mr Foyle at once. You had better stay outside.'

The second man went back to the pavement and resumed his study of the advertisement board, but a close observer might have seen that his eyes wandered past it now and again to the persons inside the office. Half an hour went by. Then the frock-coated man inside took a silk hat from a peg and placed it on his head. Simultaneously a woman went out. A dozen paces behind her went the workman, and a dozen paces behind him the frock-coated man.

Heldon Foyle had selected his subordinates well for their work. Acting on the policy of leaving nothing to chance, he had taken a hint from the advertisement addressed to Eileen, and had the office watched from the time it opened. It was simple to get the manager's permission to place one man within, and to get him to direct the clerks to pass through his hands all cipher advertisements for the personal column. If the advertisement came through the post, their time would be thrown away. If it was delivered by hand, there was a chance of learning whence it had been dispatched. The intervention of Lady Eileen was an accident that could not have been foreseen. In that matter luck had played into Foyle's hands.

CHAPTER XXX

BETWEEN Berkeley Square and Scotland Yard, Fairfield consumed ten cigarettes in sharp jerky puffs. Yet he was scarcely conscious of lighting one. Indeed, as he climbed the wide flight of steps at the main entrance, it seemed as though no palpable interval of time had elapsed since he had been practically turned out of her father's house by Eileen Meredith.

Heldon Foyle put away the bundle of documents that contained the history of the case as the baronet was announced, and waved his visitor to a chair.

'Well?' he asked.

Fairfield shrugged his shoulders. 'A nice mess you've got me into,' he complained. 'Why didn't you tell me you knew the secret of the cipher?'

The detective's face was full of ingenuous surprise as he answered:

'Didn't I? I thought I made it perfectly clear to you. I am sorry that you misunderstood. I should have made it plainer. What has gone wrong?'

Sir Ralph made an impatient gesture. 'Oh, what's the use of talking nonsense? You did not tell me that you knew the cipher, and as a consequence Lady Eileen now knows that you know.'

The superintendent gave no indication of the chagrin with which the news filled him. His features were perfectly expressionless. A part of his plans had failed from excess of caution. He did not need Fairfield to tell him what had happened. He could make a fairly accurate guess as to the manner in which he had been unwittingly betrayed. His thoughts turned at once to the question of what the girl would do. If he had judged her right, she would try to warn Grell. Either she knew his address or not, but it was unlikely that she did, as they were communicating in cipher. The obvious thing for her to do was to try to stop the advertisement. There was, however, little he could do. He had men on duty in Berkeley Square and in Fleet Street. He would soon hear of any new developments.

'That's a pity,' he said reflectively. 'It may mean a re-arrangement of our plans. And believe me, Sir Ralph, I badly regret now that I did not go into fuller details with you. What happened?'

Stumblingly, Sir Ralph recapitulated the scene at Berkeley Square, giving even the epithets by which the girl had addressed him. Foyle tapped lightly on his desk with the end of a penholder. The event had been as he thought. He looked Sir Ralph straight in the eye.

'She told you that you were a spy—that I had used you as a tool,' he said sharply. 'You have been hurt by her words. I don't want you to feel that you are anything but a free agent, or to do anything that you consider dishonourable. But I must know whether you are still willing to act with us, or whether you wish to stand aside.'

Fairfield threw the stump of cigarette viciously into the fire.

'I am acting with you, of course,' he answered sullenly, 'though I wish you to ask for my help only when it is absolutely necessary. What I complain of is, that I have not been frankly treated, and that I have been placed in an invidious position with Lady Eileen. You must remember that I have feelings, and that it is not pleasant to be told one is acting as a spy, especially by—by an old friend. You know, Mr Foyle, that I have only been wishful to serve those I have known.'

There was something pathetic in his endeavour to justify his actions to himself. Foyle murmured a sympathetic, 'I understand—yes, yes, I know,' and then became thoughtful.

'After all,' he said at last, 'this does not make us so very badly off. You are openly on our side now, Sir Ralph, so there can be no fear of your again being accused of acting in an underhand manner. There is nothing more to be done at the moment. I will keep you posted as to any steps we are taking.'

'Very well. Good morning, Mr Foyle.'

The baronet was gone. The superintendent resumed his perusal of documents. He felt some little compunction at what had happened. Yet it was his business to clear up the mystery, and to use what instruments came to his hand, so long as the law was not violated. There is a code of etiquette in detective work in which the first and most important rule is: 'Take advantage of every chance of bringing a criminal to justice.' In using Fairfield as an instrument, Foyle was merely following that code.

In a little, Foyle had finished and sent for Green. The chief inspector came with a report.

'A woman brought the advertisement to Fleet Street, sir,' he said. 'Blake has just telephoned up that he and Lambert are keeping her under observation. He 'phoned earlier that Lady Eileen Meredith had been there.'

'Yes, I suppose so. What does the advertisement say?'

'He couldn't tell me on the 'phone. He had to hurry away to look after the woman. It is being sent up by taxicab.'

'That's good. By the way, Green, keep half-a-dozen men handy, and be about yourself.'

'Very good, sir. Is there anything on?'

'I don't quite know. We may have to go out in a hurry. I'll tell you after we have deciphered the advertisement.'

CHAPTER XXXI

IT was with an eagerness sternly suppressed that Heldon Foyle took from a messenger the note which he knew contained Grell's advertisement. Although outwardly he was the least emotional of men, he always worked at high tension in the investigation of a case. No astronomer could discover a new comet, no scientist a new element with greater delight than that which animated the square-faced detective while he was working on a case.

He drew out the sheet of paper gingerly between his finger-nails, and tested it with graphite. Eight or nine finger-prints, some blurred, some plain, appeared black against the white surface, and he gave an ejaculation of annoyance.

'The fools! I warned them to handle it carefully. Now they've been and mixed the whole lot up.'

He blew down one of the half-dozen speaking tubes hanging at the side of his desk, and gave a curt order. When Green appeared he was engrossed in copying the advertisement on to a writing-pad. He laid down his pen after a while.

'That you, Green? Send this up to Grant, and ask him to have it photographed. See if he can pick out any of the prints as being in the records or bearing on the case. Somebody's been pawing this all over, and the prints are probably spoilt.

It's been printed out, too, so there isn't much chance of identifying the writing. Anyhow, we'll have a look more closely at it when the finger-print people have done.'

He bent once more to his desk with the copy of the cipher. He knew the key, and it was not necessary to resort to an expert. By the time the chief inspector came back he had a neatly copied translation on his pad.

'Listen to this, Green,' he said.

'"E. M. Am now safe on board a barge moored below Tower Bridge, where no one will think of looking for me. Have good friends but little money, owing to action of police. Trust, little girl, you still believe in my innocence, although things seem against me. There are reasons why I should not be questioned. Shall try to embark before the mast in some outward bound vessel. Crews will not be scrutinised so sharply as passengers. There are those who will let you know my movements. Fear the police may tamper with your correspondence, but later on when hue and cry has died down will let you know all."'

The two detectives looked at each other.

'A barge below Tower Bridge,' repeated Green, with something like admiration. 'That was a good shot. He might have stayed there till doomsday without our hitting on him, or anyone taking any notice of him.'

'I don't know,' said Foyle. 'A newcomer on the river would attract attention. These watermen know each other. There's only one way that I can see in which he would avoid being talked about. He is a watchman.'

'You're right, sir,' agreed the other emphatically. 'This is a matter where Wrington of the Thames Division will be able to help us. Hope we can find him at Wapping. Shall I ring through?'

'There's no hurry for a minute or two,' said Foyle. 'Let's get the hang of the thing right. There's probably some hundreds of barges below Tower Bridge. It will be as well to keep a close eye on the docks and shipping offices. You see, he asserts his innocence.'

'H'm,' commented Green, with an intonation that meant much. 'He says, too, that there are reasons why he shouldn't be questioned.'

'Well, we shall see. There had better be an all-station message about the docks. Send two or three men down to Tilbury to watch outgoing boats there. We shan't need any other men from here. Wrington's staff know the river, and will get on best with them. I don't want to leave here until Blake lets us know more about the woman who left the advertisement. That gives us another possible clue.'

It was some time before Wrington, the divisional detective-inspector at the head of the detective staff of the Thames Division, could be found, for like other branches of the C.I.D. he and his men did their work systematically, and usually left their office at nine o'clock only to return at six. At length, however, he was found at a wharfinger's office, where there had arisen some question of a missing case of condensed milk. Within half an hour he was at Scotland Yard.

A tall man with tired grey eyes, about the corners of which were tiny wrinkles, with a weather-beaten face and grey moustache, he aimed to look something like a riverside tradesman. There was a meekness in his manner and speech that deceived people who did not know his reputation. He spoke five languages fluently, and two more indifferently. Along the banks of the thirty-five-mile stretch of river for which he was responsible he had waged incessant warfare on thieves and receivers for thirty years, till now practically all serious crime had disappeared.

He it was who, a dozen years before, had fought hand to hand with a naked and greased river thief armed with a knife, in a swaying boat under Blackfriars Bridge; he, too, solved the mystery of a man found dead in the Thames who had been identified by a woman as her husband—a dare-devil adventurer and unscrupulous blackmailer, who was declared by a doctor and a coroner's jury to have been murdered. Step by step he had traced it all out, from the moment when a seaman on a vessel moored at one of the wharves had taken a fancy to bathe, and being unable to swim had fastened a line round his waist and jumped overboard. He had neglected to make the end on board properly fast and was swept away by the current. The rope had twirled round him, and as the body swelled became fixed. A blow on the head from the propeller of a tug completed a maze of circumstantial evidence which might have served as an excuse to most men for giving up the problem. Yet Wrington had solved it, and the record, which had never seen the light of publicity, was hidden in the archives of the service.

This was the man Foyle had now called in. He stood, with stooping shoulders, nervously twisting his shabby hat, apparently ill at ease. His nervousness dropped from him like a garment, however, when he spoke. Foyle made clear to him the purport of the excursion they were to embark on.

'Very good, sir,' he said. 'If you think the man you want is on the river, we will find him. I guess, as you say, he's got a job as a watchman. He's probably had to get somebody to buy a barge, for they don't give these jobs without some kind of reference.'

'A reference could easily have been forged. But that doesn't matter. How soon can you get your men together?'

'An hour—perhaps two. They're scattered all over the place. I sent out to fetch 'em before I left Wapping.'

'Three or four will be enough. With Green and yourself and myself we should be able to tackle anything. Have a launch and a motor-boat at Westminster Bridge Pier in a couple of hours' time. If you can borrow them off someone, so that they don't look like police craft, so much the better.'

'I can do it, sir.'

'Good. In two hours' time, then.'

And Heldon Foyle turned away, dismissing the subject from his mind. Green had gone upstairs to find how Grant of the

Finger-print Department had progressed in his scrutiny of the finger-prints on the advertisement. He found his specialist colleague with a big enlargement of the paper on which the advertisement had been written mounted on paste-board, and propped up in front of him, side by side with an enlargement of the prints found on the dagger.

'Any luck?' asked Green.

Grant shifted his magnifying glass to another angle and grunted.

'Can't tell yet,' he said irritably. 'I've only just started. Go away.'

'Sorry I spoke, old chap,' said the other. 'Don't shoot; I'm going.'

Grant rested his chin on one elbow and stared sourly at the intruder.

'Great heavens!' he said. 'Isn't it enough to have two of my men ill when there are four hundred prints to classify, to have three newspaper reporters and a party of American sociological researchers down on me in one day, without—'

But Green had fled to the more tranquil quarters on the first floor.

'Mr Foyle asking for you, sir,' said the clerk.

He pulled open the door of the superintendent's room. Foyle had got his hat and coat on.

'Blake's wired that the woman has taken a ticket for Liverpool,' he said. 'He's gone on the same train. Now that's settled, let's see if we can't hurry Wrington up.'

CHAPTER XXXII

IN the corner of the first-class carriage farthest away from the platform, the Princess Petrovska sat with her hands on her lap and a rug round her knees, glancing idly from under her long eyelashes at the people thronging the Euston departure platform. Her eyes rested incuriously now and again upon a couple of men who stood in conversation by a pile of luggage some distance away, but within eyeshot of the compartment.

She had some vague recollection of having seen one of the men before, and though she remained apparently languidly interested in the business of the platform, she was racking her brains to think who he was or where she had seen him. It was recently, she was certain. Suddenly she leaned forward, and her smooth brow contracted in a frown. Yes—she was nearly certain. He had an overcoat and a silk hat on now, but when she last saw him he had been a bare-headed, frock-coated clerk in the advertisement office of the *Daily Wire*. The frown disappeared and she dropped back. But behind the placid face an alert brain was working. Had the man followed her, or was it a mere coincidence? Was he a detective? With an effort of will she stilled the apprehension in her breast. Her confidence reasserted itself. Even if he were a detective, what had she to fear? She had merely delivered a cipher advertisement over the counter. It was unlikely that it would be read by others than the person for whom it was intended. Even if it were, there was nothing in it to incriminate her.

Her lips parted in a contemptuous smile.

'I don't believe he is a detective at all,' she murmured.

All doubts on the subject, however, were set at rest as the express began to glide out of the station. As though taken unawares by its departure, the man hastily shook hands with his friend and sprinted for the train, swinging himself into the woman's compartment with a gasp of relief.

'Phew,' he said. 'A narrow shave that,' and then, as if realising the sex of his companion, 'I—I beg your pardon. I hope the carriage is not reserved. If so, I will change.'

She smiled winningly at him.

'No, don't disturb yourself, I beg. It would be a pity after all the trouble you have taken—to catch the train.'

Detective-Inspector Blake was not by any means dull. His immobile features gave no sign that he was half inclined to believe the woman was gibing him. 'Now, what the devil does she mean by that?' he said, under his breath. He bowed in acknowledgment of her courtesy, and drawing a paper from his pocket unfolded it.

'And how is the charming Mr Foyle?' said the Princess, speaking with a soft drawl. 'I do hope he is still well.'

This time Blake was taken unawares. He dropped the paper as though it were red-hot, and the woman laughed. A moment later he was ashamed of himself. She had trapped him into a tacit admission that he was a detective. A surprised denial of acquaintance with Mr Foyle might have ended in an apology on her part for a mistake. Well, it was too late now.

'So you are a colleague of Mr Foyle's?' she went on, and though her voice was soft there was a trace of mockery in it. 'He is charmingly considerate to send you to look after me. I was desolated to think that I should have to take such a long journey by myself.'

'The pleasure is mine,' said Blake, falling in quickly with the atmosphere she had set. Nevertheless, he was not quite easy. He recalled the troubles that had beset Waverley, and half regretted that he had not brought his companion on the train with him.

'Smoke, if you like,' she said, with a gracious wave of her hand. 'I know you are dying to do so. Then we can talk. Do you know, I have long wished to have a talk with a real detective. Your work must be so fascinating.'

He took a cigarette case slowly from his pocket, and dangled it in his hand. He had never before seen the Princess, but he was certain of her identity.

'Indeed,' he said grimly. 'I thought you had met Mr Foyle. In fact, I believe that he afforded you some opportunity of seeing a portion of the workings of our police system. Do you smoke? May I offer you a cigarette?'

She selected one daintily.

'Thank you. But that was different. I don't think it quite nice of you to refer to it. It was all a mistake. Mr Foyle will tell you so, if you ask him. Do detectives often make mistakes?'

Her air of refreshing innocence tickled Blake. He laughed.

'Sometimes,' he admitted. 'I made a mistake just now in coming on this train alone.'

She laughed musically in pure amusement.

'I believe the man is afraid of me,' she said, addressing the ceiling. Then more directly, 'Why, what harm could a poor creature like myself do to a great stalwart man like you? I should have thought you'd greater sense.'

'Common sense is my strong point,' he parried.

'And therefore you are afraid,' she laughed. 'Come—Mr—Mr—'

'Smith—John Smith.'

'Mr John Smith, then. It's a good English name. I shan't do you any harm. But if you like to lose sight of me when we reach Liverpool—'

'Well?'

'It would be worth £50 to you.'

He shook his head. 'I am afraid, Princess, you have a very poor opinion of the London police. Besides, I told you just now that common sense was my strong point.'

She shrugged her shoulders for answer. The train droned on. They had lunch together and chatted on like old friends. It was when they had returned to their own compartment, and the train was nearing Liverpool, that Blake found his cigarettes had run short. The Princess produced a daintily-jewelled enamelled case.

'Won't you try one of mine?' she asked. 'That is, if you care for Egyptian.'

He took one. What harm would there be in a cigarette? Yet, in half an hour's time, when the train slowed into Lime Street

Station, the Princess descended to the platform alone. In his corner of the compartment Blake slumbered stertorously.

CHAPTER XXXIII

HELDON FOYLE and Chief Inspector Green paced to and fro along Westminster Pier watching a couple of motor-boats as they swung across the eddies to meet them. A bitter wind had chopped the incoming tide into a quite respectable imitation of a rough sea. There were three men in each boat. Wrington at the tiller in one, Jones, his lieutenant, steering the other.

'It's going to be a cold job,' commented Foyle, as he turned up his coat collar and stamped heavily on the frosty boards.

'Ay,' agreed Green. Then, without moving his head: 'There's that chap Jerrold of the *Wire* behind us. Has he got any idea of what we're on?'

Foyle wheeled sharply, and confronted a thin-faced, sallow-complexioned man with a wisp of black hair creeping from under his hat, and with sharp, penetrating, humorous eyes. Jerrold was one of the most resourceful of the 'crime investigators' of Fleet Street, and, while he had often helped the police, he could be a dangerous ally at times. He started with well-affected surprise as Foyle greeted him.

'Well, I never! How are you, Mr Foyle? And you, Mr Green? What are you doing down here?'

'For the matter of that, what are you doing?' asked the superintendent, who had made a shrewd guess that he and his companion had been seen from the Embankment, and that Jerrold, scenting something afoot, had descended to wait an opportunity. But Jerrold was ready.

'Me?' he retorted. 'Oh, I'm writing a story about Westminster Bridge. Cracks have developed in the pier. Is it safe? You know the kind of thing.'

'Yes, I know,' agreed Foyle, with a smile and a glance at the waiting boats. 'Well, it's nice weather. Green and I are just going off with Wrington. There's some question of increasing the river staff, and we've got to go into it.'

Jerrold nodded as gravely as though he quite accepted the explanation. In fact, Foyle, shrewd as he was, could not feel certain that he had. The journalist took a casual glance about the wide stretch of water, and with an unconscious gesture that had become habitual with him flung back the lock of hair that dangled over his right eyebrow.

'Got a minute to spare?' he asked. 'A rather quaint thing happened at our office. You know they're excavating the foundations for a big hotel in Piccadilly? Well, on Monday a couple of burly navvies, carrying a big paper parcel, came up to the *Wire* office and Brashton saw them.

'"Me an' my mate 'ere,' says the spokesman, "'ave been employed on those works in Piccadilly, and we made an interesting discovery today. Seeing as the *Wire* is an enterprising paper an' pays for news, we thought as 'ow we'd come along.'

'"Always glad to pay for information if we use it," says Brashton.

'"We'll leave it to you," says the spokesman, undoing the parcel. "Look at this."

'Inside the wrappings was a battered but full-sized human skeleton. Brashton was a bit staggered, but put a few more questions to the men, and they went away. He forgot all about the skeleton till M'Gregor, the news editor, happened in. Mac's hair stood on end, and he pointed at the skeleton with a long forefinger.

'"What's that?" he demanded.

'Brashton looked up from some copy he was writing. "That," he said calmly. "Oh, that's not necessarily for publication; it's just a guarantee of good faith." And he explained.

'Mac was horror-struck. He stared at Brashton as though he had taken leave of his senses.

"'Good God, man," he cried, "why did you let them leave it here? It might have died of the plague or something." And, stepping back into the corridor, he yelled for a boy. "Take that thing away," he ordered. "Get rid of it. Put it in the furnace."

'Well, they took it down and cremated it. Today, a fine, old, crusty police sergeant rolled up to the office. He wanted to see someone, he said, about the find of a body in Piccadilly.

'Brashton received him suavely. "Very good of you to come, sergeant," he said. "We're always grateful for any information about matters of interest."

'The sergeant fidgeted with his helmet. "That's all right, sir," he said. "As a matter of fact, though, I've come to you for information this time. You see, I'm a coroner's officer, and we've got to hold an inquest, but we ain't got no body to hold it on!"

'For a moment Brashton was flabbergasted, but he recovered himself almost immediately. "I'm very sorry," he apologised, "but the fact is, although we had the skeleton here it has—er—been mislaid."

'That coroner's officer,' went on Jerrold gravely, 'is now looking over the excavations to see if it's possible to find a few odds and ends to hold the inquest on. But I see Mr Green's getting impatient. Don't let me keep you.'

The boats had been brought up to the quay and, as the detectives stepped aboard, slipped downstream, hugging the Embankment. Foyle turned a speculative eye on the pier they had just quitted. A steam launch had just brought up, but Jerrold had vanished. The superintendent swore softly.

'So that's why he kept us talking,' he said. 'He suspects something, and wanted to keep us till he could send for a boat himself. We shall be a regular procession if we don't stop that.' He leaned over and spoke to Green in the second boat. Immediately it slackened speed, and as the launch came alongside the chief inspector swung deftly aboard.

'Where's Mr Jerrold?' he demanded of the man at the wheel.

'Who's he?' was the gruff response.

'Come, you know who he is well enough. He's the man who's borrowed or hired this craft, and he got on board just now. I want to speak to him. If he has ordered you to follow us, let me tell you that I am a police officer, and shall be justified in arresting you for obstructing me in the execution of my duty if you are not careful.'

'Hello, Mr Green. Threatening the skipper? What's wrong?' said the equable voice of Jerrold, emerging with cigarette between his teeth through the sliding door of the saloon.

The detective swung round upon him angrily. 'This isn't the game, Mr Jerrold. We can't have you following us like this.'

The journalist gave a shrug. 'Really? Do you object to me having a blow on the river? Because I'm going on, in any case. I can't help it if you're going the same way.'

Green was helpless, and he knew it. Although he raged inwardly, he knew that it would be unwise to arrest the journalist, though such a course might be justified. Apart from the bad feeling such procedure might create, there was the difficulty of establishing a case without disclosing the object of their journey. It was a dilemma where diplomacy might with advantage be employed. He smiled at the reporter.

'Mr Jerrold, can't we settle this without quarrelling? We're on a queer job, and you might spoil it all by hanging around. Leave us to it, and if there's anything fit for publication you shall have first pull. Don't ask me anything else and I'll promise you that.'

'Honour?' queried Jerrold.

'Honour,' repeated Green.

'Right you are. Slip off and we'll go back. Ring me up at the office.'

The steam launch wheeled about as Green took his place in his own boat. Both men were satisfied. Each knew that the other would not go back on his word. The chief inspector's boat caught up with that which carried Foyle and Wrington just below Waterloo Bridge. They were threading the tiers of barges moored on the southern side. The group of detectives, with eyes ceaselessly watchful, passed comments in a low voice. They were not hopeful of finding their quarry yet. The search was merely one of precaution. Now and again one of the boats stopped and a man clambered aboard a barge, dropping back in a few minutes with a shake of the head. Foyle and Green left all this to the river men. They knew the work.

But, swift as they were, they made slow progress. Foyle glanced uneasily at his watch. It was already growing dusk, and the lights on the bridges were reflected in fantastic shapes from the dark waters. The superintendent spoke in a low voice to Wrington, who jerked his head in sharp assent.

'You're right, sir. If we take the likely one now we can leave the others till we've finished. We'll get on. Let her out, boys.'

The two boats leapt forward, unobtrusively stealing a course in the shadow of the barges. It was delicate work in the gathering darkness, for many times a lighter swinging at its moorings threatened to crush them; but always they avoided the danger, though to the untrained faculties of Foyle it seemed that the margin of safety was no more than the breadth of a knife blade.

At London Bridge they crossed to the northern side, and here the real hunt began. Wrington signalled for the lights to be put out, and they stole forward, two black blotches on the dark water. Once they narrowly escaped running down a Customs' patrol boat, and voices cursed them with vigour out of the gloom. Again, as they were about to pass under a mooring rope, someone yelled to Foyle to duck. The warning came too late, and he would have been swept into the water but that a ready knife severed the rope. Then there was a halt for a little, while the barge was secured again.

'There's a new caretaker on a tier of barges just above Tower Bridge,' whispered Wrington tensely. 'We'll try there first. Keep your voice low if you want to speak, sir. Sound travels a long way on the water. Ah, there it is.'

Foyle had got good eyesight, but he could make out nothing but a smudge where Wrington pointed—a smudge emphasised by a tiny point of twinkling light. The two motor-boats slowed down and approached, as it were, on tiptoe one on either side of the vessel. As they came nearer a barge took shape at the head of a long string.

'Stop her,' ordered Wrington. 'Now, sir, will you board her with me? Get ready.'

As they lurched against the sides of the craft the two leapt aboard. Green and Jones had come up from the other side. The superintendent gave a whispered order, and the other three ranged themselves around a small deck cabin, while he thrust open the door and entered. It was quite dark within, and a smell of stale tobacco smoke met his nostrils.

He stood still and lit a match, holding himself in readiness for anything. A figure was dozing in a chair at the other side of the cabin. Foyle crossed stealthily and quietly encircled the man around the waist, pressing his arms to his side with all his strength. The man, suddenly awakened, struggled vigorously.

'Keep still,' ordered Foyle, doggedly maintaining his hold. 'Hi, Green, Wrington! Give me a hand here, will you?'

CHAPTER XXXIV

POWERFUL as he was and with his prisoner at a disadvantage, Foyle found it all he could do to maintain his hold until his companions broke through to his help. Even then it was no easy task, and the fight raged over the tiny cabin with the police hanging on to their prisoner like dogs to a wounded bear. No one spoke a word; there was only the quick panting of struggling men, the shuffling of their footsteps, and now and again a sharp crash as some piece of furniture overturned.

Their very numbers handicapped the police in that confined space. Hands sometimes tore at Foyle, sometimes at the prisoner. The superintendent hung on with the tenacity of a bulldog, until a sudden lurch against the side brought his head sharply in contact with the boarding. Half dazed, he involuntarily relaxed his grip. The prisoner tore himself away and struck out viciously. A man fell heavily. For the fraction of a second a shadowy figure was indistinctly outlined in the doorway. Almost simultaneously Foyle, Green, and Wrington flung themselves in pursuit. They were too late. A soft splash told that the man had taken the only possible avenue of escape.

'Look lively with those boats. He's gone overboard,' yelled Wrington. 'Light up and get close in to the bank.'

With the alacrity of men well used to sudden emergencies those detectives in the boats were at work on the word. One darted to cut off retreat to the northern bank, though the forbidding parapet of the Tower made it impossible for any man to land for a hundred yards or more. The other cruised cautiously among the strings of barges, watching for any attempt to land on one of them.

The superintendent had dashed to the stern of the barge and dropped into a small dinghy tethered there. At his word the others came running, and with Wrington at the oars they also crept about in determined search.

'It's hopeless,' growled Green, in an undertone. 'On a night like this we might as well look for a needle in a haystack.'

'We won't give up yet, anyway,' retorted Foyle, and there was an unwonted irritability in his tone. 'We've mucked it badly enough, but I'm not going to fling it up while there's a sporting chance of finding him. Do you think he'll be able to swim across the river, Wrington?'

'It would need a good man to do it in his clothes. The tide's running pretty strong. More likely he's let himself drop down below the bridge, and will try to pull himself aboard one of these craft.'

Heldon Foyle rubbed his chin. Every moment their chances of catching the fugitive lessened. In the darkness, which the lights from the bridge and from adjacent boats only made more involved, there was little hope of finding the man they wanted. He had not been seen from the moment of the first plunge, and there were a score of places on which he might have taken refuge, and where, now that he was warned, he could dodge the searchers. He might have committed suicide, it was true, but somehow Foyle did not think that likely.

For two hours the search continued, and then Foyle, chilled to the bone, decided that it was hopeless. Wrington hailed the other boats, and the detectives returned to the barge. A light thrown into the tiny cabin disclosed amid the disorder an open kit-bag full of linen. Green pulled out the top shirt and felt its texture between thumb and finger. Then he pointed to the name of a West-end maker on the collar.

'Yes, it's hardly the kind of thing a barge watchman would wear,' commented Foyle. 'We'd better take the bag along, and you can go through it at your leisure. The laundry marks will tell whose they are. You had better stop here, Wrington, and take charge. Find out whom the barge belongs to, and make what inquiries you can. Better have it thoroughly searched, and report to me in the morning. Use your discretion in detaining anyone who comes aboard.'

One of the motor-boats took Foyle and Green back to Scotland Yard. Both were glum and silent: Foyle because his plan had miscarried at the very moment that he had reached the keystone of the problem; Green because it was his natural habit. It was easy enough to realise now that the whole question was one of light. Had someone thought to strike a match while the struggle was going on there would have been no confusion, and the man would have been unable to get away.

Nor did the news that awaited Foyle at his office tend to make him more pleased with the progress of the investigation.

A telephone message had come through from the chief of the Liverpool detective force:

'Man found drugged in first-class compartment of express from London, bears warrant card and other documents identifying him as Inspector Robert Blake, C.I.D., London. Is now under care of our surgeon, and has not yet recovered consciousness. In no danger. He travelled from London with a woman fashionably dressed, dark hair, dark blue eyes. Am now endeavouring to find her. Can you suggest any steps we can take?'

Foyle banged his fist viciously on his desk. 'There! We're not the only people who have made blunders today, Green. Look at that. Wire to them a full description of this woman Petrovska, and tell 'em to detain her if they come across her. We charge her with administering a noxious drug, and that'll hold her safe till we get the business cleared up. If she's trying to slip out of the country, they're pretty safe to get her in one of the liners. Wire over our men at Liverpool to the same effect.'

Green slipped away. In a little he returned with a slip of paper in his hand. 'Wire's gone to Liverpool. I've drafted this out for Mr Jerrold, if you'll just look at it. I promised him he should know anything there was to tell.'

The sheet of paper read:

'In connection with the investigation into the murder of Mr Robert Grell, Superintendent Heldon Foyle, accompanied by Chief Detective-Inspector Green, Divisional Detective-Inspector Wrington, and other detectives, examined the body of a man found in the river, whom it was supposed might be the man Goldenburg, for whom search is being made. The police are of the opinion that the drowned man is not Goldenburg.'

A light of amusement twinkled in Foyle's blue eyes.

'Don't you think he'll discover that to be a deliberate lie, Mr Green?'

'Well,' said Green doggedly, 'we can't tell him what has happened, and we've got to satisfy him somehow. I promised to let him know something, and it's true that a body has been found. I asked Wrington. And it's true that it's not Goldenburg.'

'Oh, all right, let it go. You'd better arrange the laundry inquiry first thing in the morning. Now let me alone. I want to think.'

CHAPTER XXXV

SIR HILARY THORNTON had come to Heldon Foyle's stock-taking. The superintendent, with a mass of papers on the desk in front of him, talked swiftly, now and again referring to the typewritten index of reports and statements in order to verify some point. The Assistant Commissioner occasionally interpolated some question, but for the most part he remained gravely silent. Foyle recapitulated the events of the preceding day.

'It was sheer foolishness, Sir Hilary,' he admitted bitterly. 'If we hadn't blundered Grell would have been in our hands now. As it is, we have to begin the search for him all over again.'

Through the open window came the rumble of a motor-omnibus used by the police to test applicants for licences. Thornton swung the window close.

'You still think that Grell had a hand in it?'

'I'm never positive, Sir Hilary, when it is a question of circumstantial evidence. But there can be no question that if he is not guilty himself he knows who is. I am so certain that I had a schedule of witnesses made out for the Treasury. Here they are.'

He selected a sheet of paper and passed it to the other. Thornton read it and handed it back without comment.

'There are gaps in it, of course,' went on Foyle. 'As a matter of evidence, though, practically all we want is to identify the finger-prints. They of themselves would determine the investigation. But we can't tell whether they are Grell's or not until we get hold of him. We've identified the linen found in the bag on the barge as having been bought for Grell, but there is no name or initials on the bag itself. I have not yet heard from Wrington. He may have something further to report. About Goldenburg. I got Pinkerton's to look into his career in America. They have discovered that five years ago he was in San Francisco for three months, and at that time he was apparently well supplied with money. Grell arrived there a month before he left, and they left the city within a day of each other.'

'A coincidence.'

'It may be or may not. Grell's movements were pretty well chronicled in the American Press at that time, and it is at any rate conceivable that Goldenburg went there with the express intention of meeting him. More than that, Grell was staying at the Waldorf Astoria in New York two years ago. Goldenburg went straight there from India—which he had made too hot to hold him—stayed at the same hotel, and left within three days for Cape Town. Why should he go to Cape Town *via* New York? I may be right or wrong in the opinion I have formed, but at any rate we have established a point of contact between the two men.'

'There is something in that,' agreed Sir Hilary, with a jerky nod of the head.

'More than that, on the New York visit Goldenburg was accompanied by a woman whose description in every particular corresponds with that of the Princess Petrovska—though she called herself the Hon. Katherine Balton. There is material enough in that information, Sir Hilary, to draw a number of conclusions from. At any rate, they go to confirm my opinions at present. I know very well that there is sometimes smoke without fire, but my experience is that you can usually safely lay odds that there is a fire somewhere when you do see smoke.'

The elliptic form of speech was sometimes adopted by Heldon Foyle in discussing affairs with one whose alertness of brain he could depend upon. Thornton twisted his grey moustache and his eye twinkled appreciatively.

'That's all right,' he said. 'But how do you account for Grell finding people ready to his hand in London to help him disappear at the very moment he needs them? There are several people mixed up in it, we know; but how is it that they are all loyal to him? We know that criminals will not keep faith with each other unless there is some strong inducement. How do you account for it?'

'There may be a dozen reasons. Purely as an hypothesis, Grell may have a hold on these people by threatening them with exposure for some crime they have committed. Self-interest is the finest incentive I know to silence.'

'All the same, it's queer,' said Sir Hilary, with a little frown. 'What do you propose to do?'

Heldon Foyle's lips became dogged. 'Break 'em up piece-meal as we lay our hands on 'em now. We've got one—the man we roped in with Red Ike. He's as tight as an oyster; but while we've got him he can't do anything to help his pals. Then there's the Princess. She's as slippery as an eel; but if the Liverpool people can get hold of her we may reckon she'll be kept safe for a few weeks on the charge of drugging Blake. Then there's Ivan Abramovitch. We may be able to lay our fingers on him. If there's any more in this business I don't know 'em; but every one of the gang we take means so much less help for Grell.'

A discreet knock at the door heralded the entrance of a messenger, who laid an envelope on the table and silently disappeared.

'Western Union,' muttered the superintendent. 'This may be something else from Pinkerton's, Sir Hilary. Don't go yet.'

And, tearing open the envelope, he crossed the room and pulled down a code-book. In a little he had deciphered the cable. 'We're getting closer,' he said. 'Pinkerton's have got hold of "Billy the Scribe", who identified the photograph of the dagger with which the murder was committed as one that he believes was in the possession of Henry Goldenburg when he last saw him. That may be fancy or invention, or it may be important. Hello! what is it?'

It was Green who had interrupted the conference. 'Lady Eileen Meredith, sir—Machin reports that she left her home at five this morning, walked to Charing Cross Station, bought a copy of the *Daily Wire*, looked hurriedly through it, and then worked out something on a small notebook. Then she returned home, and came out again in half an hour's time and went to Waterloo Bridge floating station. There she asked to see one of the detective branch, and they referred her to headquarters at Wapping after nine this morning. Machin says he had no chance to telephone through before. She has not gone to Wapping,' he added, as he saw the eyes of his chief seek the clock. 'She went straight back home and has not come out since.'

A low whistle came from between Foyle's teeth and his eyes met Thornton's. 'She knew the advertisement was to appear in the *Daily Wire*, and she got up early to warn Grell that we know, in case he should give an address. She did not discover a little paragraph of Mr Green's invention till after she returned home, and then her curiosity was stirred, and she hoped, by going to Waterloo, to find a subordinate detective whom she might pump. What do you think, Green?'

'I agree with you, sir. She'll turn up here later, I shouldn't wonder.'

Sir Hilary Thornton strode to the door, returning the greeting of Wrington, whom he passed as he retired. The river man was evidently pleased with himself. Foyle took a place in front of the fire and waited.

'Had a cold night?' he queried.

'Been too busy to think about it, sir,' he chuckled. 'We discovered that the owners of the barge engaged the man who gave the name of Floyd on the written recommendation of a firm of steamship agents—that, by the way, was forged, for the agents deny all knowledge of the man. He was supposed to have been an American sailor. Once or twice he has been visited on the boat by a couple of men who pulled up in a dinghy hired from Blackfriars. The regular waterman hardly ever caught a glimpse of him—he never showed himself by day. This morning a letter was sent aboard addressed to James Floyd, Esq. I never opened it, thinking perhaps you might prefer to do so. We searched the barge from end to end, and Jones is outside with a bag of different things you might like to see. What I thought most important, however, was this.'

He dipped his hand in his jacket pocket and, withdrawing a small package wrapped in newspaper, carefully unfolded it. Something fell with a tinkle on Foyle's desk.

'By the living jingo!' ejaculated Green. 'It's the sheath of the dagger!'

The superintendent picked up the thing—a small sheath of bright steel with, on the outside, a screw manipulating a catch by which it might be fastened to a belt. He handled it delicately from the ends.

'I believe you're right,' he said. 'Now, what about the letter?'

CHAPTER XXXVI

THE motive of the actions taken that day by Eileen Meredith had been accurately diagnosed by Heldon Foyle. She had returned to her home after her visit to the police at Waterloo Bridge in a state of the keenest uncertainty. Not for an instant did she credit the paragraph referring to the dead body. The police had been able to read the cipher message from Grell, and she assumed correctly enough that they had been more successful than herself in obtaining an early glimpse of the advertisement. What, then, had become of her note of warning?

She was half reclining in a big easy-chair, her arms resting on the broad ledges, her fists tightly clenched. Her train of thought led her to alarming conclusions. If the police had been watching—and that now occurred to her as having been an obvious step—they must not only have seen her note, but they might have secured and questioned the person who brought the advertisement. And if so, might not Robert Grell's hiding-place have been betrayed? Her heartbeats became unsteady. What if the visit of the detectives down the river had been not to identify a drowned corpse, but a living prisoner? Suppose Grell were already in their hands?

She jumped to her feet. The watch on her wrist spoke to quarter to eleven. Her reflections had occupied many hours. She was already dressed in a brown walking costume, and she had not even removed her hat since she returned. In answer to her summons a maid appeared with a cup of coffee and a couple of biscuits on a tray. That reminded her that she had not eaten since she had risen. She drank the coffee and ate the biscuits, while waiting for the brougham she had ordered. Within a quarter of an hour she was on her way to Scotland Yard.

In the circular hall, entered through swing-doors from the wide steps of the main entrance, a uniformed policeman hurried forward to take her card. Through the big windows she could see beneath her the surging life of the Embankment and the smooth traffic of the river. Had the river given up its secret? The constable returned, and she was ushered along a grey and green corridor to Foyle's room. He had his overcoat on, and his hat and stick lay on the table. He smiled a polite welcome at her, and she strove to read his genial face without success. For her there was something of humiliation in the situation. She, who had taken pains to be offensive on the last occasion that they had met, was now dependent upon his good-nature for the information she wanted.

'What can I do for you, Lady Eileen?' he asked with grave courtesy.

She had dropped into a chair and her grey eyes met his, half defiant, half entreating. She answered with quick directness, 'You can tell me what has happened to Mr Grell.'

He opened his hands in a gesture of surprised expostulation. 'My dear young lady! I only wish we knew.'

Her foot tattooed impatiently on the floor. 'Please don't treat me as if I were a child, Mr Foyle. Something has happened since yesterday morning. I demand to know what it is.'

Foyle was invariably gentle with women, and her insistent dignity rather amused than angered him. 'Since you demand it,' he said suavely, laying a scarcely perceptible stress on the word demand, 'I will tell you. As the result of certain information, observation has been kept on Lady Eileen Meredith. She was followed yesterday to the advertisement offices of the *Daily Wire*, where she made inquiries respecting a certain cipher advertisement which was to appear in that paper. Failing to obtain what she wanted, she left a note warning someone in the following terms: "The police know the cipher. Be very cautious. R. F. is acting with them."'

An angry flush swept across the girl's pale cheeks. 'I know you have set your spies about me,' she said scornfully. 'I did not come here to ask you that. What—'

'One moment. Let me finish. This morning Lady Eileen rose at an unfashionable hour—about four, to be exact—and went out to obtain a copy of the *Daily Wire*. Having deciphered the advertisement, and finding that it afforded no direct clue to Grell's whereabouts, she returned home and there came across a paragraph—which I will confess was inspired in this office—that set her wondering whether, after all, her lover was safe. She went out again—this time to Waterloo Bridge police station—and there made some inquiries—'

Eileen had got to her feet. She was plainly angry. 'I don't want to know how effective your spying on a harmless woman can be.'

'I am glad you admit it is effective,' he answered quickly. 'I wanted to bring that home to you. You cannot or will not understand in how perilous a situation you may find yourself if you go on playing with fire. There is no one else who has fuller sympathy with you or greater understanding of your feelings than I. Therefore I warn you. Do you know that merely on what you have done and are doing I should, were I certain that Grell was guilty, be justified in having you arrested as an accessory after the fact?' His voice became very grave. 'If your conduct has not hampered this investigation, Lady Eileen, it has not been for want of effort. Take the warning of a man who wishes you well. For neither your position nor your friends will save you if ever you stand in my way. I shall do my duty, whatever the consequences.'

She was more impressed by his words and his tone than she would have cared to admit. But except that her face became a shade paler, she gave no indication that the warning touched her. Foyle had picked up his hat and stick.

'You have not found him, then?' she cried. 'Can it be doing you any harm to say what has happened?'

'We have not found Grell—yet,' he answered. 'We found where he had been hiding, but he got away.'

A sigh of relief came from between her lips. She scarcely noticed the abruptness with which he ended the interview, and returned his bow almost with cordiality. Foyle only stayed long enough to thrust a few papers into the safe, and then followed her out. Two resounding smacks called his attention to the landing of the private stairs, where Chief Detective-Inspector Green was struggling in the embrace of a stout, matronly woman, while a half-suppressed snigger came from a passing clerk.

Green, his solemn face crimson, pushed the woman gently away from him towards a girl and a young man who were apparently waiting for her. 'There, there; that will do. Let us know if everything does all right. Won't keep you a moment, sir,' and he disappeared along the corridor.

When he returned he had recovered something of his usual impassivity. But he could not be oblivious to the twinkle in Foyle's eyes. 'Women are the very devil,' he said as if in answer. 'There's no knowing what they'll do. Now, the young girl there wanted to run away with a man of fifty, who is already a married man. So her mother—the old lady you saw kissing me—brought her up here, evidently under the impression that we can do anything. I took the girl into my room and gave her some good advice, telling her she had much better marry the young man you saw—they had been engaged, and quarrelled—and I told of some cases like her own that had come under my own knowledge. She wept a bit, admitted I was right, and then suddenly flung herself on top of me and started hugging and kissing me. I got her outside, told her mother that the matter was all right, when I'm blessed if she didn't try it on too. That was just as you came out. You may have noticed that I side-stepped warily round the young man.'

'Be careful, Green. Is she a widow?' laughed Foyle. And then, more seriously: 'How far is it to this place? Our man may be out when we get there.'

'Shall we leave it till tonight, sir? It will be more certain then.'

'No, we'll chance it. Let's have a look at the letter.' He fished a note out of his pocket and paused to read it through, carefully replacing it in its envelope as he finished.

It was the letter that had been addressed to Floyd on the barge *Flowery Land*. It read:

'DEAR MR. FLOYD,—I have tried to carry out your instructions, but luck has been against me, as I have to be very careful. It has been easy enough to buy the seamen's discharges that you require, but I have been unable to see Lola since she took the advertisement today, so do not know if she has managed to raise money. I believe I am fairly safe here, and my friends are to be relied upon, though they are much occupied with the gambling and the smoke, so there is not much quietness. If you write, address me as Mackirty, 146 Smike Street, Shadwell.'

It had needed little penetration to identify the writer of the note as Ivan, and to guess that he had taken refuge in a gambling and opium den. Indeed, this latter fact was soon verified by a telephone appeal to the detective-inspector in charge of the district, who declared that he was only waiting for sufficient proof of the character of the house before making a raid. Foyle had promptly ordered the place to be discreetly surrounded, but that no steps were to be taken until his arrival. He had conceived an admiration for Ivan's cunning in the matter, for there was no place where a fugitive could be more certain of having the intrusion of strangers more carefully guarded against than a gambling-house.

He was willing to forego a conviction against the keepers of the place rather than miss an opportunity of securing Ivan. For cautious steps are always necessary in proceeding against such places. It is so easy to transform a game of baccarat, faro, or fantan into an innocent game of bridge or whist with a few innocent spectators, and to hide all gambling instruments between the time the police knock and the time they effect an entry. Then, however positive the officers may be, they have no legal proof, unless one of their number has been previously introduced as a 'punter,' and to do that would require time.

Smike Street at one time had been a street of some pretensions. Even now, in comparison with the neighbourhood in which it was set, it maintained an air of genteel respectability, and its gloomy three-storeyed houses had in many cases no more than one family to a floor. It was, however, one of those back streets of the East End which are never deserted, for its adult inhabitants plied trades which took them abroad at all hours—market porters, street hawkers, factory workers, dock labourers, seamen, all trades jostled here. One or two of the houses bore a sign, 'Hotel for Men Only.'

It was at the corner that Foyle and Green were joined by the divisional detective-inspector, and the three swung into the deserted saloon bar of a shabby public-house which afforded a better opportunity for unobtrusive conversation than the street. Leaving the glass of ale he ordered untouched upon the counter, the superintendent rapidly learned all steps that had been taken.

'It's a corner house on this side,' said the local man, 'kept by an old scoundrel of a Chinaman calling himself Li Foo, and a man who was a bit of a bruiser in San Francisco at one time—a chap called Keller. He looks after the faro game in a back room on the first floor, while the chink runs the black smoke upstairs on the stop storey. They're the bosses, but there's three under-dogs, and the place is kept going night and day.'

Foyle grunted. 'How long have you known this? Couldn't you have dropped on 'em before?'

The other made a deprecatory gesture with his hands. 'They're cunning. The show had been running three months before we got wind of it. That was about a month ago, and we've tried every trick in the bag to get one of our men inside. There's no chance of rushing the place on a warrant either, because both front and back doors are double, and only one man is allowed to go in at a time. They won't open to two or more. Before we could get the doors down there'd not be a thing left in the place as evidence.'

A gleam of temper showed in Foyle's blue eyes. 'That's all very well, Mr Penny. It won't do to tell me that you've known of this place for a month and that it is still carried on. Why didn't you let a man try single-handed? With the door once open he could force his way in.'

'I couldn't send a man on a job like that,' protested the other. 'Why, you don't know the place. They'd murder him before we could get at him.'

He flinched away from Foyle as though afraid his superior would strike him. For the superintendent's hands were clenched and his eyes were blazing. Yet when he spoke it was with dangerous quietness.

'A man of your experience ought to know by now that it's his business to take risks. If you'd made up your mind there was no other way of obtaining evidence you should have sent a man in. Never mind that now. Take your orders from Mr Green for the day. Green, I'll be back in an hour. I'm going into that place. Act according to your own discretion if you think I'm in difficulties.'

CHAPTER XXXVII

THE game of faro is one that makes no strenuous demands on the skill of the players. It is chance pure and simple, and therein lies its fascination. While baccarat or chemin-de-fer are almost invariably games to be most in favour when the police raid a gambling-house in the West End, at the other side of the town it is invariably discovered that faro holds first place in the affections of gamblers. In its simplest form it is merely betting on the turn of each card throughout a pack.

Although it was broad daylight, the room in which the operations took place was shuttered and had the blinds drawn. A three-light gaselier beat down on a big table in the centre of the room, round three sides of which were ranged a dozen or fifteen men eagerly intent on the operations of the banker. A heavy-jowled man with overhanging black eyebrows, he was seated in a half-circle cut into the centre of one side of the table. In front of him was a bright steel box sufficiently large to contain a pack of cards with the face of the top card discernible at an opening at the top. The cards were pressed upwards in the box by springs, and at the side a narrow opening allowed the operator to push the cards out one at a time, thus disclosing the faces of those underneath and deciding the bets. On each side of the box were the discarded winning and losing cards, and on the dealer's left a tray which served the purpose of a till in receiving or paying out money. A cloth with painted representations of the thirteen cards of a suit was pinned to the table nearest to the players, and they placed stakes on the cards they fancied would next be disclosed. Twice the box would click out cards amid a dead silence. Those who had staked out money on the first card disclosed won, those who had staked on the second lost.

There was often dead silence while the turn was being made, save for the click of a marker shown on the wall and guarded by a thick-set little man with red hair, fierce eyes, and an enormous chest. But directly afterwards babel would break out, to be sternly quelled by the heavy-jowled man.

'I 'ad set on sa nine,' . . . 'Say, that king was coppered,' . . . 'I ought ter have split it.'

The jargons of all the world met and crossed at such time. It was rarely that there arose a serious quarrel, for Keller and his myrmidons had a swift way of dealing with malcontents. When a man became troublesome, the fierce-eyed little marker with the big chest would tap him on the shoulder.

'That's enough, you,' he would say menacingly.

If the warning were not sufficient the left hand of the little man would drop to his jacket pocket, and when it emerged it would be decorated with a heavy brass knuckle-duster. It took but one blow to make a man lose all interest in the game, and thereafter he would be handed over to the tender mercies of 'Jim,' a giant of a door-keeper, who after dark would drop him into the street at some convenient moment, with a savage warning to keep his mouth shut lest a worse thing befall him.

This was the place Heldon Foyle had made up his mind to enter single-handed—a place in which the precautions against surprise were so complete that every article which could be identified as a gambling implement was made of material which could be readily burnt, or soluble at a temperature lower than that of boiling water. A big saucepan was continually simmering on the fire, so that the implements could be dropped in it at a second's notice.

But Heldon Foyle had hopes. At the worst he could only fail. He returned to Scotland Yard and shut himself up for twenty minutes in the make-up room. When he reached Smike Street again he was no longer the spruce, upright, well-dressed official. A grimy cap covered tousled hair. His face was strained, his eyes bloodshot and his moustache combed out raggedly. A set of greasy mechanic's overalls had been drawn over his own clothes. He walked uncertainly.

Green and the local inspector saw him reel past the public-house in which they still remained, as affording an excuse to be near the spot, and reel up Smike Street. Towards the end he appeared confused and gravely inspected several houses before approaching the gambling-joint. He rapped on the door with his knuckles, ignoring both the knocker and the bell. It opened a few inches wide, enough for the scowling face of Jim the door-keeper to appear in the aperture.

Supporting himself with one hand on the door-post, Foyle leered amiably at the Cerberus. 'Hello, old sport, I want t'come in. Open the door, can't you?'

'Git out of it, you drunken swab. You don't live here,' said Jim, taking stock of the drunken intruder and coming to a quick decision.

The door slammed. Foyle beat a tattoo on the panels with his hands, swaying perilously to and fro the while. Again the door opened the cautious six inches, and Jim's face was not pleasant to look on as he swore at the disturber.

'Tha'ss allri', ol' sport,' hiccoughed Foyle. 'I want to come in. A Bill Reid tol' me if I wanted—hic—game I was to come here. You know ol' Bill Reid'—this almost pleadingly—'he'll tell you I'm allri', eh?'

The door-keeper of the gaming-house holds an onerous responsibility. On him depends the safety of the gamblers from interference by the representatives of law and order. Jim's suspicions were lulled by Foyle's quite obvious drunkenness. Nevertheless, a drunken man who had apparently been told of the place was a danger so long as he remained clamouring for admittance on the step. Jim tried tact.

'There's nothing doing now,' he explained. 'You go away and come back tonight. It'll be a good game then.'

'Tha'ss a lie,' said Foyle, with an assumption of drunken gravity. 'Old Bill Reid he says to me, he says—'

But Jim had lost the remainder of his small stock of patience. He jerked the door again in Foyle's face, pulled off the chain and leapt out, his intention of throwing the other into the street and so ending the argument once for all written on every line of his stalwart figure.

That was his programme. But Foyle had also his programme. He had got the door open. All that remained between him and the entrance was the muscular figure of Jim. He suddenly became sober. The door-keeper's hand grasping at his collar clutched empty air. The detective's head dropped. Jim was met half-way by a short charge and Foyle's shoulder caught him in the chest. Both men were forced by the momentum of the charge back through the open door and fell in a heap just within.

At ordinary times the two would have been fairly evenly matched. Both were big men, though the door-keeper had slightly the advantage in size. He had, however, been taken by surprise and received no opportunity to utter more than a stifled oath before his breath was taken away. Inside the house Foyle stood on no ceremony in order to silence his opponent before those within could be alarmed. He had fallen on top of Jim. Pressing down on him with head and knee, he swung his right fist twice. Jim gave a grunt and his head rocked loosely on his neck. He had, in the vernacular of the ring, been put to sleep.

The effects of a knockout blow, however deftly administered, do not last long. The detective's first move was to close the street door, leaving the bolts and chains undone, so that it was fastened merely by the catches of the Yale locks. Then he whipped a handkerchief about the unconscious man's mouth, and silently dragging him to a sitting posture, handcuffed his wrists beneath his knees, so that he was trussed in the position schoolboys adopt for cock-fighting. He surveyed his handiwork critically, and, a new idea occurring to him, unlaced the man's boots, and, taking them off, tied the laces round the ankles. That would prevent the man rattling his boots on the floor when he came to, and so have given the alarm.

The inner door had been left open by Jim, a lucky circumstance for Foyle, as otherwise he would have been at a loss, for it was of stout oak and he must have made considerable noise in forcing it. Yet he did not make any attempt to soften his footsteps as he climbed the stairs. He hoped to be taken as an ordinary client long enough, at any rate, to discover the whereabouts of Ivan. Once that was achieved he was reckless as to his identity becoming known.

He needed no guide to the right door, for the clink of money and the exclamations of many voices guided him. He threw it open and entered the faro room with quiet assurance. Beyond a quick glance from Keller no one took any notice of him. They took it for granted that Jim had gone into his *bona-fides* and that he was 'square'.

He took up a position at the end of the table nearest the door, and apparently watched the game before staking. In reality he was studying the faces of the players. He was uncertain whether he would find Ivan there, but he had calculated that the Russian would at least be watching, if not taking a hand, if only as a means of passing the time during his voluntary imprisonment. And he was right. Seated at the table two or three paces away was the Russian, lost to all save the turn of the card.

Foyle bent over and staked a coin. At the same moment Ivan's eyes met his in puzzled recognition. There was a crash and the gambler sprang up, overturning the chair. His hand was outstretched, the finger pointing at the detective.

'That man—how did he get in here?' he cried, with something like alarm.

CHAPTER XXXVIII

FOR a second or a trifle more a dead silence followed Ivan's denunciation. Heldon Foyle backed towards the door, dragging with him a chair which he had clutched with some idea of using it as a shield should there be a rush. There arose an angry snarl among the gamblers, for with them suspicion was quick. A rush of crimson had swept across Ivan's face at the first alarm. He ejaculated something excitedly in Russian, and then went on in English:

'He is a police officer. I know him. It is the man Foyle of Scotland Yard.'

At the mention of the word police the hubble died down a little. Heldon Foyle, leaning quietly on the back of the chair, took advantage of the lull.

'Yes, I am a police officer,' he admitted confidently. 'The place is surrounded. It will pay you to behave yourselves—you over there, put that knife away, do you hear?'

The order was sharp and authoritative, and the Greek in whose hand the detective had caught the gleam of steel thrust it back hastily into the sheath at his belt. There were men there who would have thought little of murder, and Foyle knew that once they were roused to fighting-pitch he stood little chance. At the first sign of flinching on his part they would be on him like a pack of wolves. He held them for the moment only, as a lion-tamer holds his beasts under control—by fearless domineering assumption of authority. They were like a flock of sheep. Only two men he feared—Ivan and Keller. Both were men above the average intelligence, and both had more reason to fear the law than the others. If either of them took the initiative he might be placed in an ugly position. He felt for his whistle while they remained inactive, uncertain.

'Let's teach the dog a lesson,' hissed a venomous voice—that of Keller. 'He's trying to bluff us.'

'Boot him, boys,' incited Ivan, edging forward and so creating a movement towards the detective.

Heldon Foyle put his whistle between his teeth and gripped the heavy chair with both hands. As the rush came he blew the whistle three times in the peculiar arrangement of long and short blasts that is the special police call, and swung the chair down with all his force on the leading man. It was Keller. The gaming-house keeper dropped, stunned, and the detective swept the chair sideways and so forced a clear space about himself. Again the whistle thrilled out, and Ivan dodging sideways seized one of the legs of Foyle's unwieldy weapon. Menacing faces besieged the detective on all sides. Other hands assisted the Russian to hold the chair. And still no help came. Once the door opened and the wrinkled leathern face of a Chinaman protruded through the slit, took in the scene with quick understanding and disappeared. That was all the notice taken of the row by the habitués of the opium den on the high floor. The two or three clients who were stretched on the low couches were either entirely under the influence of the drug or too listless to worry about anything short of an earthquake—if even that would have aroused them.

It was with small hope that the superintendent sounded his whistle again. A heavy blow on the face laid open his cheek, and he saw the little red-headed man who had slipped on his heavy brass knuckle-duster dodge back into the crowd. He relinquished his hold of the chair and defended himself with his hands. He carried a pistol in his pocket, but, imbued with the traditions of the London police, he would not use a lethal weapon save in the last extremity. Inch by inch he sidled along the wall, fighting all the while until he reached the corner. Here the crowd could only come at him from the front.

A knife was thrown and a bottle crashed against his shoulder. The crisis had come. He dropped his guard and his hand closed over his pistol. Those nearest to him recoiled as the muzzle was thrust into their faces.

'He daren't shoot,' insisted a voice which Foyle recognised as that of Ivan.

In fact, the gibe was partly true. The detective had himself well in hand, and he knew that even though he were justified, a wounded man would lead to an inquiry which at the very least would prevent his going on with the Grell investigation for some time. But to let the taunt pass would invite disaster. He dropped the weapon to his thigh, forefinger extended along the barrel to help his aim, and pressed the trigger with his second finger twice. The reports were deafening in the confined space of the room, and one man put his hand to his head with a sharp cry. He need not have disturbed himself, for the bullets had passed over him and were buried in the opposite wall.

'We'll see whether I daren't fire,' said Foyle grimly. 'Come on. Who'd like to be the first?'

There was no answer to his challenge, for from below came the sound of a crash and the quick tread of many men racing up the stairs. One or two of the gamblers turned white, and Foyle felt the tension of his nerves relax. Half-a-dozen men, headed by Green and Penny, were rushing into the room.

A little gurgling laugh burst from the superintendent, and he waved his hand about the room. 'You see, Penny, it could be done, single-handed. That is Ivan over there. Take good care of him, Green. Keller is that man knocked out down there.' And, swaying, he crashed forward to the floor in a dead faint.

When he came round he was lying on a couch with his injured face and shoulder neatly bandaged. There were only two other persons in the room, Green and one of the local detectives, who were systematically making an inventory of everything in the room. The superintendent struggled to a sitting position and the movement brought Green to his side.

'Hello, Green,' said the superintendent cheerfully. 'You've got 'em all away, I see. How long have I been lying here?'

'Matter of half an hour. It's only a case of loss of blood, I think. You must have been bleeding for some time before we broke in on the tea-party. We put some first-aid bandages on.'

'I'm all right,' said Foyle, rising stiffly. 'What happened? You were a deuce of a time answering my whistle.'

'We tried the wrong door first, and it's my belief that nothing short of dynamite would move it. It's steel-lined, and with all the bolts pushed home we stood no chance. We gave it up after a while and tried the other. Luckily that was not bolted.'

'I know. I left it like that purposely.'

'Well, we didn't know. By that time we got thirty uniform men down here, and they followed us up. Once we got the door down and found the chap you'd trussed behind it, we had no trouble worth mentioning except with Master Ivan, who fought like a wild cat. We got the cuffs on him at last, but even then it took four men to get him away. Penny is down at the station waiting till you come before charging 'em. What is it to be? Attempt to murder?'

'No, I don't think we can get a conviction on that,' answered Foyle. 'There's plenty up against them—unlawful wounding, assaulting a police officer in the execution of his duty, frequenting a gaming-house, and, of course, Ivan could be charged with the Waverley affair if we find it necessary now. I see you've started running over the house.'

'Only just started. We are waiting for the divisional surgeon to see to you and three men who are sleeping like logs in the opium-joint upstairs. The Chinaman seems to have vanished—at any rate, he can't be found. It's just about time this place was broken up. Keller took no chances with the bank.' He picked up the faro-box. 'Now, in the States this kind of thing would not go. It's a two-card needle-tell swindle.'

'That's done with fifty-four cards to the pack, isn't it?' asked Foyle indifferently, handling the box. 'I've seen something like it before. The dealer is warned of the approach of duplicate cards by a tiny needle-point jumping out of one side of the box.'

'That's it.'

'Well, all that will have to be explained when the case comes on for trial. I'm more interested in Ivan just now. It's something to have him under lock and key. I'll leave you here to handle the remainder of the business and get down to the station. No—I'll not wait for the doctor. I feel perfectly fit now.'

In spite of his assertion the superintendent felt a little dizzy when he reached the open air. A big crowd filled the street, and a dozen reporters who had been held sternly at bay by the constables on duty at the gambling-house pounced on him determinedly. He laughingly waved them aside, but they would not be denied, and while they walked at his side gave a succinct account of what had happened, omitting all reference to Ivan Abramovitch.

'New thing for you to come all the way to the East End to take charge of a gambling raid, isn't it?' asked Jerrold, the *Wire* man, in a tone that told of a shrewd suspicion of something underlying.

'Oh, it's been an experience,' said Foyle lightly, indicating his bandaged head. 'I've told you everything I know now, boys. If there's anything else you can use, I'll have it at the Yard presently. So long.'

The journalists melted away, and Foyle presently found himself in a dingy back street where the local police station was situated. Here also a crowd of men and women had gathered, and the reserve men at the door were repelling eager women who, not knowing who had been taken in the raid, feared that their husbands might be included and were anxious to know the worst; for news of that kind spreads rapidly.

A motor-car standing without told the superintendent of Sir Hilary Thornton's presence. And the Assistant Commissioner was the first person he saw as he entered the place. Thornton came forward with hand outstretched.

'Thank God, Foyle! We had a rumour at the Yard that you had been badly hurt. I see you've been knocked about a bit. What made you take a hand yourself down here? Couldn't you leave a raid to be carried out by the local folk?'

'I didn't come down here specially for that reason,' smiled the superintendent. 'I wanted to get hold of Ivan Abramovitch, and everything else was purely incidental.'

'They're waiting for you to settle who shall be charged with what,' said Thornton. 'Be as quick as you can, and I'll wait and give you a lift back in the car. I'll not be happy till I've heard all about this.'

The two passed into the charge-room, where Penny was in conversation with the superintendent of the division. In reply to a question, he thought for a little.

'We've got eighteen men in all, sir,' he answered. 'It would have been fifty if we'd been able to bring our coup off at night.'

'Very well. Have 'em all in except Abramovitch and Keller. I will pick out those I want charged with assault, or who I think were mixed up with Keller. The remainder might be let out on bail after you have verified their addresses.'

The prisoners were ushered into the room, a shame-faced, sullen, dispirited gang now. Penny and a clerk passed along the line, taking their names, while Foyle scrutinised their faces. Finally, the superintendent touched four men on the shoulder one after the other. One was Jim, the door-keeper; another the red-haired man with the big chest; the third and fourth two men who had been prominent in the attack. Penny put a tick against their names, and the whole of the prisoners, many of whom had broken into voluble protest and appeal, were taken back to the cells. Foyle had determined to leave the business of charging them to Green and Penny.

CHAPTER XXXIX

SOMETHING of the chagrin caused to Heldon Foyle by the escape of the man on the barge had vanished with the success of his operations in Smike Street. If his frontal attack had failed, he had at least achieved something by his flank movement. The break-up of the gambling-den, too, was something. Altogether he felt that his injuries were a cheap price to pay for what had been achieved.

In bare detail he related the sequence of events to Sir Hilary Thornton, who, with a gloved hand jerking at his grey moustache, listened with only an occasional observation.

The inevitable crowd of journalists, who had been warned by telephone from their colleagues at Smike Street, were jumbled in a tiny, tiny waiting-room when Foyle and his superior reached headquarters. The superintendent, having changed his attire, made it his first business to satisfy their clamorous demands by dictating a brief and discreet account of the raid, to be typed and handed out to them, then with a head that ached intolerably he forced himself to do some clear thinking.

With the dossier of the case before him, he read and re-read all that had been gathered by his men and himself

since that night when he had been called from his sleep
to find Harry Goldenburg dead. Was there some point he
had overlooked? He knew how fatal it was in the work of
criminal investigation to take anything for granted. Although
the main work of the explorer was now focused on Grell, it
was not entirely certain that he was the murderer. Indeed,
strange as his proceedings had been, there might be some
explanation that would account for them. It might be that
after Grell was found the whole investigation would have
to begin again with the scent grown cold. Stranger things
had happened.

The superintendent dropped his papers wearily into a
drawer and turned the key. His speculations were unprofit-
able. He turned over in his brain his plans for running down
Grell. Of the people who had been assisting him to evade
capture three were out of the way for the time being. Ivan
Abramovitch and Condit were safely under lock and key.
The Princess Petrovska was out of London, and there was a
fair margin of assumption that she was located somewhere in
Liverpool, where the local police were assisting the Scotland
Yard men. It was hardly possible that she would double back,
even if she evaded their rigorous search. With the detectives
on duty at the London termini reinforced and on strict watch,
her chances of doing so were very slim.

With three of his friends out of touch, and hampered by
want of money, Grell would have to seek a fresh refuge. The
chief result of Foyle's actions had been to make any steps he
might take more difficult. That was all. It was still possible
for him to dodge the pursuit.

The evening papers with the story of the raid were already
upon the streets. What would be the effect upon Grell's plans
when he learned that Ivan had been captured? In the case
of an ordinary criminal, Heldon Foyle might have forecasted
what would happen with a fair degree of certainty. But Grell
was not an ordinary criminal, even if he were a criminal at

all. If he could gain a hint of the possible intentions of the fugitive he might be able to meet them.

There was a vague chance that either Ivan Abramovitch or Condit might be induced to volunteer a statement, although the possibility was remote. In America or France there would have been ways of forcing them to speak. In England it was impossible.

With a yawn Foyle relinquished his efforts, and his head dropped forward on his desk. In a little he was fast asleep. He was roused by a light touch on the shoulder. Green had returned.

'Hello!' said the superintendent. 'I must have dozed off. How have you got on?'

Green adjusted his long body to the comfort of an arm-chair. 'We found the Chinaman. He'd climbed through a trap-door on to the roof. We went over the house with a tooth-comb, both before and after I'd had a little talk with Keller. It seems that both he and his partner the Chinaman had known the man for some time before they gave him a room. They're old hands at the game and won't talk too much. He went out very occasionally, and mostly at night. We found nothing bearing on the murder, but plenty to show that Keller and his pal were running a pretty hot shop.'

'H'm! Could you dig anything out of any of the others? There was the door-keeper.'

'No. Tight as oysters, all except those who don't know anything. Ivan has a fit of the sulks. He's called in Mordix to help him fix up his defence.'

The superintendent was rubbing his chin. 'Mordix isn't too scrupulous. I think we'll hold over the charge of abduction for the time being until we see how things look. Nobody hurt much, I suppose?'

The saturnine features of the inspector wrinkled into as near a grin as they were capable of. 'Some of them are rather sore, but the doctor thinks they can all appear in court tomorrow.'

Foyle stretched himself and rose. 'Right. We won't worry any further about it for the moment. I'm feeling that the best thing for me is a good night's rest. You'd better go home and do the same. Good night.'

CHAPTER XL

A NOTE came to Sir Ralph Fairfield while he was lingering over his breakfast, and the first sight of the writing, even before he broke open the envelope, caused a thrill to run through him.

'You must see me at once,' said the well-remembered writing imperatively. 'Urgent, urgent!'

The paper trembled in Fairfield's hands, and it was only the reminder of the servant that the messenger was waiting that brought him sharply out of his daze.

'Yes, yes. Show him in. And, Roberts, while I am engaged I don't want to be disturbed by anybody or anything. Don't forget that.'

If Roberts had not been so well trained it was possible that he might have shown surprise at his master's order. For through the door he held open there shambled an ungainly figure of a man, hunchbacked, with a week's growth of beard about his chin, and wearing heavy, patched boots, corduroys, a shabby jacket and a bright blue muffler. His cap he twisted nervously in gnarled, dirty hands as he stood waiting just inside the room till he was certain that the servant had retired out of hearing.

Then, with a swift movement, he locked the door, straightened himself out, and strode with outstretched hand to where Fairfield stood, stony-faced and impassive. The baronet deliberately put his hands behind him, and the other halted suddenly.

'Fairfield!'

Then it was that the impassivity of Sir Ralph vanished. He gripped his visitor by the arm, almost shaking him in a gust of quick, nervous passion.

'You fool—you damned fool! Why have you come here? If they catch you, you will be hanged. Do you know that? For all I know the place is watched. They may have seen you come in. Perhaps the place is surrounded now.'

'I'll risk it,' said the other coolly, drawing a chair up to the table. 'I've got to risk something. But I don't think they saw me come in. I don't think they'll catch me, and if they do I don't think they'll hang me. What do you think of that, Fairfield?'

There was the old languid mockery in his voice, but his friend, looking at him closely, could see that the face had become a trifle thinner, that beneath the dirt that begrimed it there were haggard traces that betrayed worry and sleep-lessness. Fairfield had thought much of Robert Grell lately, but he had never dreamed that the hunted man would come to him—come to him in broad daylight, without a word of warning. Did Grell know that he was in touch with the police? Had he come, a driven, desperate man, to fling reproaches at the friend who had joined in the hunt? That was unlikely. Grell, murderer or not, was not that type. He did nothing without a reason. He was, Fairfield reflected, a murderer—a murderer who had not dared stay to face the consequences of his deed. That surely severed all claims, whatever their old friendship might have been.

'What do you want?' he asked, with a hard note in his voice. 'Why have you come to me?'

The man in the chair lifted his shoulders.

'That is fairly obvious. I want you to do what, if our situations were reversed, I would do for you. I want money. If you can get me a few hundreds I shall be all right.'

A spasm contracted Fairfield's face for a second. He had not asked for explanations. Grell had volunteered none. It seemed as though he were taking for granted the assumption that he was guilty of the murder. Surely an innocent man would have been eager to assert his innocence at the first opportunity. When Sir Ralph answered, it was slowly, as though he were weighing each word that he spoke. 'I would be willing enough to help a friend—you know that, Grell. But why you should think I would lift a finger to help you evade justice I fail to see. I know enough of the law to know that I should become an accessory to the fact.'

'You really think I killed that man?' The words came quick and sharp, like a pistol shot. 'I thought you had known me long enough—'

'Words,' interrupted Fairfield bitterly. 'All words. You were the last man I should have thought capable of such a thing; but all the facts are against you. Need I go over them? Let me tell you that if ever a jury knows what Scotland Yard knows and you stand in the dock, no earthly power can save you. If that crime is on your conscience it seems to rest lightly enough.'

Grell stood up and rested one hand lightly on the sleeve of his companion. 'Fairfield, old chap,' he said earnestly, 'we have been through enough together to prove to you that I am not a coward. I swear on my honour that I had nothing to do with that man's death—though I have had reason enough to wish him dead, God knows. Do you think it is fear for myself that has driven me into hiding?'

Fairfield shook his head impatiently, and shaking himself clear paced quickly up and down the room. 'That's all very well, Grell,' he said more mildly, 'but it is hardly convincing in the face of facts. You disappear immediately after the murder, having got me to lie to cover your retreat, and the next I hear from you is when you want money. It's too thin. If I were you I should go now. For the sake of old times I will say nothing about your visit here, but to help you by any other means—no. If you had no hand in that murder, come out like a man and make a fight for it. I will back you up.'

'Thanks.' There was a dry bitterness in Grell's tone that did not escape Sir Ralph. 'I couldn't have got better advice if I'd gone to Scotland Yard itself.' His voice changed to a certain quality of harshness. 'Look here, Fairfield. Suppose I do know something about this business; suppose I know who Harry Goldenburg was, and how and why he was killed; suppose I had stayed while inquiries were being made, then I should either have to have betrayed a friend or taken the burden on my own shoulders; suppose I say I was honest that night when I asked you to conceal my absence from the St Jermyn's Club; that I did nothing which I would not do over again'—he banged his fist on the table and his eyes glowed fiercely—'I tell you I have had no choice in this matter. Even you, who know me as well as any man, do not know what I had been through until that man lay dead. Since then I have suffered hell. The police have been at my heels ever since. I carried little enough money away with me, and I dared not attempt to change a cheque while I was thought to be dead.' He drew a gold watch from his pocket. 'I dare not even pawn this, for even the pawnbrokers are watched. They stopped all my efforts to raise money in other directions, and have isolated me from my friends. I have fifteen shillings left, and yet since they routed me out of cover the day before yesterday I have not dared get a lodging for fear that I might arouse suspicion. I slept on the Embankment last night.'

He paused, breathless from his own vehemence. Fairfield had seen him in moments of danger, yet never had he seen him so roused out of himself. He could see one of the sinewy hands actually trembling, and that alone was proof enough of the violence of the hunted man's emotion. He went to a side table, and pouring out a generous dose of brandy from a decanter, squirted a little soda-water in it and handed it to Grell. But his face was still hard and set.

'Drink that,' he said. And then, as the other obeyed: 'It is no use fencing with the question, Grell. If you want me to help you you will have to give some explanation. I am not going to dip my hands in this business blindly. Don't think it's a matter of you and I simply. This concerns Eileen.'

Grell put down his empty glass and stared into the other's eyes. 'Ah yes, Eileen,' he said quietly. 'What about her?'

'This,' Fairfield spoke tensely, 'that if you are guilty you have ruined her life; if you are innocent and cannot prove it you might as well be guilty. I'll not conceal from you that I have given Scotland Yard some measure of assistance in trying to find you. Do you know why? Because I judged you to be a man. Because I thought that if put to it you might prove your innocence or take the only course that could spare her the degradation of seeing the man she loved convicted as a murderer.'

A grim unmirthful smile parted Robert Grell's lips. He understood well enough what was meant. 'You always were a good friend, Fairfield,' he retorted. 'Perhaps you have a revolver you could lend me.'

'Will you use it if I do?' burst impulsively from Fairfield's white lips. He was sincere in his suggestion. To his mind there was only one escape from the predicament in which his friend found himself. Anything was preferable, in his mind, to the open scandal of public trial.

'Don't be a fool,' said Grell, making a gesture as though waving the subject aside. 'I shall not commit suicide—at any rate, while I've got a fighting chance. Let's get to the point. Will you lend me some money?'

The clear-cut face of Fairfield had gone very pale. When he answered it was with dry lips and almost in a whisper.

'Not a farthing.' And then with more emphasis—'Not a farthing.'

A mist was before his eyes. The lock of the door clicked and Grell shambled out. For ten minutes or more Ralph Fairfield remained, his fingers twitching at the buttons of his waistcoat. A revulsion of feeling had come. Had he done right? Was Grell's course the wisest, after all? How had his own feelings towards Eileen influenced him in his decision not to help the man who had been his friend?

He resolved to try to shake the matter from his mind, and his hand sought the bell-push. Twice he rang without receiving any reply, and he flung open the door and called imperatively:

'Roberts!'

Still his man failed to answer. He walked quickly through all the rooms that constituted his apartments. There was no trace of the missing servant. A quick suspicion tugged at his brain, and he wondered why he had not thought of it before. Of course, Roberts knew Grell, but the disguise of the explorer was not absolutely impenetrable. In spite of his clothes, his missing moustache, and his tousled hair dyed black, Fairfield had known him. Why not the servant? And if Roberts had recognised him and was missing—

Fairfield began to hurriedly put on an overcoat.

CHAPTER XLI

THE police court proceedings in connection with the gambling-joint in Smike Street had opened satisfactorily so far as the police were concerned. All the prisoners but the principals and those involved in the attack on Heldon Foyle had been subjected to small fines, and were, as the legal phrase goes, 'bound over.' The remainder had been remanded for a week at the request of the prosecuting solicitor, a half-hearted request for bail being refused.

For the first time since he had attained the rank of superintendent, Foyle himself had gone into the witness-box. That was unavoidable, as he was the only man who could give direct evidence of the character of the house. Hitherto he had arranged so that the court work fell on his subordinates while he gave his attention to organisation and administrative detail; for the giving of evidence is only the end of the work of a detective. There are men behind the scenes in most cases that come into the criminal courts who are never told off, happenings never referred to. They are summed up in the phrase 'Acting on information received, I—' The business of a detective is to secure his prisoner and give evidence, not to tell how it was done.

'Still no news from Liverpool,' said the superintendent as he left the court with Green. 'I begin to wish I'd sent you down there. That woman has got the knack of vanishing.'

'Yes,' agreed his lieutenant, producing a well-worn brier and pressing the tobacco down with a horny thumb. 'And yet people think we've got an easy job. Lola knows her business, and I'm open to bet she'll not be found before she wants to be found.'

Foyle chuckled at this enunciation of rank heresy. Only a veteran of Green's experience would have dared question the ability of Scotland Yard to maintain a scent once picked up. The superintendent did not take the pessimism too seriously. In theory it is not difficult for one person to disappear among forty millions, but to remain hidden indefinitely, in the face of a vigorous, sustained search by men trained to their business is not so simple in practice.

'You've got a habit of looking on the worst side of things,' he laughed. 'I've never known us want anyone we knew badly but what we got 'em at last. Besides, Blake's down there, and he's a good man. He's got a personal interest in running her down now.'

'H'm,' commented Green, in the tone of one not entirely convinced, and lapsed into a stolid silence which would have irritated some men, but merely amused the superintendent.

They separated at the door of Foyle's room at headquarters, and an impatient detective-sergeant, whose duty it was to weed out callers, promptly headed Heldon Foyle off.

'A man's been waiting to see you, sir,' he said. 'He refused to give his name, but said he had some important information which he would only give to you personally. He wouldn't hear of seeing anyone else.'

'Yes, of course. They've all got important information, and they all want to see me personally—or else the Commissioner. Well, where is he, Shapton? Show him in.'

'I can't. He's gone, sir. He'd been waiting here half an hour or so when he was taken away by Sir Ralph Fairfield.'

If he had not been trained to school his feelings, Heldon Foyle might have started. As it was, he picked up a pen and toyed idly with it. The man, who had a fair idea that his news was of importance, was a little disappointed.

'I see,' said the superintendent. 'What happened?'

'Why, Sir Ralph asked to see you and was shown into the waiting-room with the other man. They both seemed a bit upset, and the first chap's jaw dropped. "So you are here," says Sir Ralph, a bit angrily. "Yes, sir," says the other, and he had become sulky. "This is my man," says Sir Ralph to me, "and I would like a word with him alone, if you don't mind." Of course, I left 'em alone. In a quarter of an hour they came out, and Sir Ralph told me that there had been a little misunderstanding—that neither of them wished to see you after all.'

'Thank you, Shapton,' said the superintendent, resting his chin on his hand. 'Ask Mr Green if he can spare a moment, will you?'

In the interval that elapsed before the chief inspector came, Foyle did some quick thinking. Criminal investigation is always full of unexpected developments, and this seemed to him to offer possibilities. It was clear to him that a man had come to Scotland Yard to give some information, and that Fairfield had followed post-haste to shut the man's mouth. For the moment he put aside all speculation as to the baronet's motive. The question was, who was the man he had taken away? Who would be likely to know something? It must be someone intimately associated with the baronet, someone who probably lived with him. There was only one man—his servant.

The line of reasoning became clear. What would a servant know which he would recognise as of obvious importance?

Fairfield might have received a letter from Grell, but if he did not wish to let the police know of it, he would scarcely have been careless enough to leave it where his man might have obtained access to it. The second solution was more probable. Suppose Grell had paid a visit to Fairfield and the man had recognised him?

Foyle was not led away by theories. He knew that the most ingenious deductions often led to failure. But in this case he had nothing to lose by putting the matter to the test. He had not taken off his hat or coat, and when Green came in he was ready to put his plan into execution. In a few words he told what had happened and his conclusions.

'What I want you to do, Green, is to ring up Fairfield and get him out of the way on some pretext. Keep him here till I come back. I'm going to have a talk with that servant. If you can't get him on the 'phone, you'll have to go round and get him out somehow. I want a good man whom he doesn't know to come to the Albany with me. Give me a chance to get there before you ring up.'

'Very good, sir. Maxwell is free. I'll tell him you want him.'

In a quarter of an hour Maxwell, an unobtrusive, well-dressed man, had taken up his station and was casually loitering where he could see all who entered or emerged from the Albany. Foyle himself was out of view, but he had a fine sight of his subordinate. Ten minutes elapsed. The well-dressed detective dropped the stick he was listlessly swinging between his fingers, and Foyle knew that Sir Ralph had risen to the bait. It remained to be found out whether the servant was still in the chambers.

Waiting just long enough for Fairfield to get a reasonable distance away, Foyle was whirled up in the lift to the baronet's rooms. His first pressure on the bell remained unanswered, but at a second and longer ring he was confronted by the upright figure of Roberts. The servant gave a little gasp of astonishment as he saw his visitor.

'Sir Ralph is out, sir,' he stammered.

'Yes, I know,' said the detective pleasantly. 'I did not come here to see Sir Ralph, but to see you. You know who I am. Let me in, won't you?'

He pushed his way into the place and entered the sitting-room, Roberts following closely behind him. The man was evidently very nervous. Foyle sat down.

'Now, my man, you needn't feel nervous. Your master won't be back yet awhile. You came to my office to see me this morning, and left before I got back. I've come to see what this important information you've got for me is.'

Roberts shifted his weight from one foot to the other and rubbed his hands together nervously. His eyes never met the superintendent's. 'It's all a mistake,' he asserted unsteadily. 'I—I—'

'That won't do, my man,' said Foyle brusquely. 'You know something which it is important I should know. Sir Ralph has told you to keep your mouth shut. But you're going to tell me before either of us leaves this room. I want you to speak now. Never mind about thinking of a lie.'

His blunt manner had its effect. Roberts drew himself together. 'Right, sir, I'll tell you what I came about. You're a gentleman and won't see me a loser. Sir Ralph, he promised to look after me if I kept my mouth shut.'

It is no part of a detective's duty to allow personal feelings to interfere with his business. Foyle's contempt for a man who was ready to bargain to betray his master's confidence was sunk in his content at so easily obtaining his ends. 'That will be all right,' he answered. 'You'll be paid according to the value of your information.'

'Then it's this, sir,' blurted out Roberts. 'Mr Grell, whom you thought was murdered, is not dead. He came here an hour or two ago, and was in with Sir Ralph for quite a time.'

'Oh.' The detective smiled incredulously, and snapping open his cigar-case selected a smoke, nipped off the end, and deliberately struck a match. 'You've got hold of some cock-and-bull idea. I suppose you've deceived yourself with some fancied resemblance.'

'It was Mr Grell himself, I tell you,' averred the servant earnestly. 'Don't I know him well enough? He was roughly dressed and had shaved off his moustache, but I'm certain of it. He came up by the lift as large as life with a note for Sir Ralph. I didn't notice him much at first, because I thought he was a street messenger. But when Sir Ralph told me to bring him in I had a good look at him. I knew I had seen him before, but the change in him threw me off for a while. It was only after I left him with Sir Ralph that it came on me like a shot. I knew that there was a reward out in connection with the murder, and I came on to you at once. If you had been in I should have told you all this then, but Sir Ralph came after me and promised to pay me well to keep my tongue between my teeth. But right is right, sir, and I hope you'll do what you can for me. For I'll take my dying oath that the man I saw here was Mr Grell.'

With calm, expressionless face Foyle listened. His inferences were justified. It would be necessary to keep Roberts from gossiping, and for that reason it was policy to discount the importance of his information. The detective puffed a cloud of smoke to the ceiling.

'You seem pretty sure of yourself. I think you've made a mistake, but we'll go into the thing fully and you'll get whatever your information is worth. How long was this chap in with your master?'

'I don't know. I didn't see him come out. He had been in there about ten minutes when I started out to see you.'

'Right. Now I'm going to wait here till your master comes back. You can deny that I have questioned you, or that you have told me anything, if you like. I shan't give you away. Where's the telephone?'

With a little breath of relief the servant conducted Foyle to an inner room and pointed out the instrument. A few seconds sufficed to put the superintendent in communication with Green, and in a quick, low-voiced conversation he was told what device had been practised to keep Sir Ralph away.

'I'll let him go now, then?' said Green, and his superior assented.

When Sir Ralph Fairfield returned to his chambers, he found Heldon Foyle seated before the fire engrossed in a paper and with his feet stretched out to the cheerful blaze.

'Good morning, Sir Ralph,' said the detective, rising. 'I just dropped in as I was near here to tell you how things were progressing, and to see if you'd got any news.'

CHAPTER XLII

BUT that his breath came a little faster, Fairfield gave no sign of the perturbation that Heldon Foyle's presence caused him. That the summons to Scotland Yard had been a pretext to get him out of the way was now obvious. The only question was whether Roberts had divulged anything to the detective during his absence.

It was quite impossible to allow Grell's visit to him to be used in the investigation. That was not in the bargain with Foyle. Innocent or guilty, his friend had trusted him, and to use that trust to hound him down would savour of treachery. There was no doubt that Foyle knew something. He wondered how much.

He returned his visitor's greeting. 'Always glad to see you, Mr Foyle, though I'm afraid there's nothing fresh so far as I am concerned. I see my man's made you comfortable. There's been a mistake somewhere. I've been to Scotland Yard waiting for you.'

His head was in the shadow and Foyle could not see his face. He could not be sure whether the words were a challenge, and made a little gesture with his hand.

'That's a pity,' he said. 'Things have got muddled up somehow. However, now we're here it's all right. By the way, we narrowly missed laying our hands on Grell an hour or two ago.'

Although he was staring placidly into the fire he did not fail to note the quick start that the baronet gave. And it was not a feigned start. Fairfield could not understand this indirect method of attack.

'What!' he stammered. 'You nearly arrested him?'

'It was touch and go,' said Foyle languidly. 'Some of our men got on his trail and followed him until he reached here. They never saw him come out.'

'Do you mean to say that Grell has been here—here today?' demanded Fairfield, putting as bold a face on the matter as was possible.

'I do,' said Foyle quietly.

'Without my knowledge?'

Heldon Foyle shook his head, and thrusting his hands into his jacket pockets faced the baronet squarely. 'That's what I want to know. Was it without your knowledge, Sir Ralph?'

Fairfield met that searching gaze unflinchingly. There was a touch of hauteur in his tone when he replied, 'Do you suggest that I am hiding him?'

Had Foyle not been sure of his facts the manner of the baronet might have convinced him that he was in error. As it was, he ignored the evasion. It was essential to know whether the fugitive had been supplied with any money and whether he had given any indication of his plans. 'I feel quite certain that you have had a talk with him lately,' he said. 'I thought you were going to do what you could to help us clear up this mystery. Why deny a fact that is plain?'

Sir Ralph clenched his teeth. It was clear that Foyle was certain of his ground; that it was no use any longer trying to throw dust in his eyes. 'Well?' he demanded icily. 'I suppose I am not entirely a spy at your disposal, Mr Foyle. I am like most men, I have my limits. I prefer to remain master of my own actions.'

'I should be the last to dispute it,' said Foyle, with a slight bow, 'or to take advantage of the good-nature that has led you to assist us hitherto. Of course you could not foresee that Grell would come to you, and you naturally do not want to take advantage of his confidence. But we already know of his visit, so there is no breach of trust there. All I ask is that you should simplify the matter by telling me what occurred at your interview. Perhaps you have forgotten, Sir Ralph, that there is a punishment for assisting a man to escape—by lending him money or otherwise. That is merely for information. It is not a threat.'

'Thank you,' said the other. 'It would make no difference to me whether it was a threat or not.' He remained in thought for a moment. The fact that Grell had entered the place and apparently got clear away had led him to believe that the police knew nothing of the visit, that the only risk of the interview being disclosed lay with Roberts. If the detectives had really been close on the heels of the fugitive, as Foyle said, it could do no harm to admit the truth. His promise to say nothing could hardly be considered to cover the contingency. 'Has Roberts been talking to you?' he asked abruptly.

'Roberts?' repeated the superintendent, with a puzzled frown. 'Oh, of course, he's your servant. I asked him one or two questions, but he didn't seem to understand me.'

The answer was so quick, so naturally given, that any suspicion that remained in Fairfield's mind was lulled. He shrugged his shoulders. 'Well, for what it is worth, I don't mind admitting that Grell did come to see me. All he wanted was money. He is frightfully hard up, and apparently the operations of your people have harassed him dreadfully.'

'Did you let him have any money?'

Fairfield shook his head. 'No; I absolutely refused unless he would come out of concealment and try to justify himself.

With that he went. He was here less than twenty minutes or half an hour.'

The detective played with his watch-chain. 'Yes, yes. I don't see that you could have done anything else. I suppose you made no suggestion to him?'

'In what way?'

Gently stroking his chin, Foyle answered in a soft voice, 'The other day a man came to see me. He was a man of high social standing and had fallen into the clutches of a gang of blackmailers. He wanted us to take action, but he absolutely refused to go into the witness-box to give evidence. I pressed him, pointing out that that was the only way in which we could bring home anything against them. "It will ruin me," he declared. "Is there no other way it can be put a stop to?" I replied that we were helpless. "What can I do?" he cried. "Is the thing they accuse you of true?" I asked. He flushed and admitted that it was. "Well," I said, "if you ask my advice as a man and not as an official, I should meet with an accident." But he would not take my advice,' he concluded, with a keen glance at the baronet, on whom the parable was not lost.

'I did suggest that way out,' admitted the baronet reluctantly. 'He wouldn't hear of it. And Grell is not a coward.'

'He gave no hint of where he was going when he left you?'

'Not the slightest.'

Foyle picked up his hat. There was nothing more of value to be gained by prolonging the interview. 'I am very much obliged to you, Sir Ralph,' he said. 'Perhaps you will keep in touch with me in case anything arises. Good morning.'

Long ago Foyle had made up his mind as to the probable course that would be taken by Robert Grell. The man was evidently driven into a corner, or he would scarcely have taken the enormous risk of going to see Ralph Fairfield. There remained two things, the detective reasoned, which he might now do. Penniless and without help, he might try to plunge back into the obscurity of underground London, or he might try some other friend or acquaintance. But every person he confided in would increase his risk. Fairfield was his closest friend, and yet he had declined to lift a finger. Would he go to men he was less intimate with—or would he endeavour in person to enlist the aid of the woman he was to marry?

No one knew better than Heldon Foyle the danger of jumping to conclusions. Inferences, however clever, however sound they may seem when they are drawn, are apt to lead one astray. The detective who habitually used the deductive method would spend a great deal of his time exploring blind alleys. Yet Foyle, with the unostentatious Maxwell at his right hand, hurried in the direction of Berkeley Square with a hope that his theory might not be ill-founded.

A little distance away from the Duke of Burghley's house he crossed the road and spoke to a cabman who was lounging on the seat of his motionless vehicle. Curiously enough, the constables patrolling the beat did not order that particular cabman away to a rank, although he had been there for several hours, creating a technical obstruction.

'Have you seen a man call over the road lately?' asked the superintendent.

'No, sir,' answered the cabman alertly. 'The only person has been a messenger-boy with a note for Lady Eileen Meredith. He told me it had been handed in at the district messenger office at Victoria. Lady Eileen came out shortly afterwards and walked away in the direction of Piccadilly. Phillips has gone after her.'

'Right. Report to the Yard directly she returns, and keep a sharp look-out.'

'Very good, sir,' said the cab-driver, and Foyle turned away to mount the steps of the house. The footman who answered the door replied that both his Grace and the Lady Eileen were out. He could not say when they would return. The superintendent tapped the step impatiently with the tip of his well-polished American boot, and his brow puckered. Finally he produced a card.

'I think I had better wait,' he said. 'My business is important.' That procured his admission into the house, but he had no idea of waiting in idleness in one of the reception-rooms. Eileen had received a note which had taken her out—he shrewdly suspected that it was from Grell. It was conceivable, though it was not probable, that she might have left it about. It was for him to learn the contents of that note if possible. 'Look here, old chap,' he said, with an assumption of familiarity that flattered the frigid footman, 'I want to see Lady Eileen directly she comes in, and I don't want to be announced.' He winked as though from one man of the world to another. 'You understand, don't you?'

The footman grinned knowingly as he thrilled all over with the knowledge that the Scotland Yard man was making a confidant of him. It was one of Foyle's ways always to attach as many people as he could to his object. He had an extensive acquaintance with waiters and hotel hall-porters.

'Yes, sir, I think I can arrange that,' said the footman. 'I can put you in her own sitting-room, and she'll most likely go straight there when she comes back.'

'That's the ticket,' said Foyle. 'I like a man who's got brains.' A sovereign changed hands. 'Now, if you ever hear anything, perhaps you'll let me know. Drop into my office when you're by and have a chat and a cigar.'

'I will that, sir,' said the man. 'Thank you, sir.'

Heldon Foyle was left alone in the room. He sat quite still for a little, but his eyes were busy. At last he rose and aimlessly paced the floor once or twice. In the grate a dull fire was burning, and a few fragments of blackened paper lay on the dying coals. Here and there a word stood out in a mouldy grey against a black background. Foyle did not touch the paper till he had read:

'. . . both . . . minent . . . sufficient money to . . . ade for . . . Petrov . . . guesse . . . fear . . . timately exposure must come. If . . . open cheque . . . ther . . . gold, and bring . . . God's sake . . . desperate.'

Foyle's lips puckered into a whistle as he transferred the words to his pocket-book. He dared not touch the fragments till he had done so, and every moment he feared that some draught might destroy the whole thing. His keen professional instincts were saddened by the impossibility of saving what might be an important piece of evidence. Under favourable circumstances there might have been some chance of retrieving and preserving it by blocking the chimney to prevent a draught and then carefully sticking the burnt fragments with gum on to transparent paper. But that method was impossible. Foyle tried gingerly to rescue the fragments, but a burst of flame frustrated him, and a moment later they were destroyed.

An ejaculation of annoyance escaped his lips, and he turned to the dainty little desk at another portion of the room. It was locked, but that was a matter of little consequence. Like most detectives, Foyle carried a bunch of keys rather larger than are to be found in the possession of the ordinary man, and the fourth that he tried fitted.

The neat interior slab of the desk was clear and tidy. One or two letters of no consequence reposed in an inside drawer, and these the superintendent replaced. A footstep outside caused him hurriedly but noiselessly to close the desk and resume his seat, sitting idly with crossed legs. But the interrupter passed, and he returned to the desk. From a recess he drew out a cheque-book and examined the counterfoils of the used cheques with interest. The last counterfoil was blank.

'Ah!' he muttered, with a jerky little nod of satisfaction, and turned his attention to the blotting-pad. A few minutes' close inspection and he drew the top sheet away and, rolling it up, placed it in the breast-pocket of his overcoat. Again he closed the desk and glanced at his watch. A touch at the bell summoned the footman.

'I don't think I'll wait, after all,' said Foyle. 'Time's getting on, and I've several things to attend to.'

'Shall I tell Lady Eileen you called, sir?'

'Oh yes, certainly. Tell her I'll call back about six this evening.'

In deep thought Heldon Foyle sauntered away from the house, and Maxwell joined him as they turned a corner. The superintendent said nothing till they reached Piccadilly. Then he tore a sheet of note-paper from his pocket-book and handed it to his companion.

'Cut along up to the Metropolitan and Provincial Bank, Maxwell. A cheque, No. A834,076 for £200, signed Burghley, has been presented this morning. Find out who cashed it and how it was paid. If there were any notes, get their numbers and come straight on to me at the Yard.'

The superintendent swung himself on to a passing motor-bus and selected a seat on top, with his brain still revolving the events of the morning. Once he took out a pencil and drafted a description of Grell's appearance and dress as Roberts had seen him. As a matter of course, he intended that to be telegraphed and telephoned to his men all over London. It was as well not to neglect any precaution.

He was passing through the little back door which leads to the quarters of the C.I.D. when he came face to face with a young man bearing all the appearance of a clerk who was just passing out. 'Hello, Phillips!' he exclaimed. 'You've been after Lady Eileen, haven't you? What luck did you have?'

'I've just reported to Mr Green, sir,' was the answer. 'She walked to the Metropolitan and Provincial Bank and took a taxi when she came out. I followed in another cab, but my man punctured a tyre in the Strand and I missed her.'

Foyle frowned and gripped the man's arm. 'Come upstairs with me and tell me all about it. What number was her taxi?'

'County Council LD 6132, police 28,293. Mr Green has got the name of the driver from the Public Carriage Department, and I was just going out to see if I could get hold of him.'

'Right; you get along, then. And don't forget that if you miss people like that again, accident or no accident, there'll be trouble.'

Green was waiting for his chief. A question elicited the steps he had taken to get hold of the driver of the cab, from whom some account of Lady Eileen's movements might be expected. An all-station message had been flashed out, asking that the cab, wherever it was sighted, should be sent, unless still carrying a passenger, to Scotland Yard. There was little chance of the driver neglecting to obey the summons.

'It's unlucky that our man failed to keep her in sight,' said Foyle. 'I'll bet a hundred to one that she's arranged to meet Grell somewhere. However, there's nothing to do now but to wait. Just look here, Green. Here is something I picked out of the lady's fire. Help me and we'll see if we can reconstruct the entire message.'

He laid his pocket-book containing the string of disconnected words on the desk as he spoke. The two bent over them.

CHAPTER XLIII

THERE is no person in London easier to find than a cab-driver whose number is known, for the supervision of the Public Carriage Department is exhaustive. Yet, even so, it was some hours before the man Foyle sought was reported as being on his way to Scotland Yard.

He came at last, wonder and a little alarm in his face as he was brought into the room where the superintendent and Green sat. There are many rules the infringement of which will imperil a licence, and he was not quite sure that he might not have broken one.

Foyle motioned for the door to be shut. 'So you're the cab-driver we're looking for, are you?' he said. 'You're William White?'

'Yes, sir,' answered the man. 'That's my name.'

'All right, White. There's nothing to be alarmed about. You picked up a lady outside the Metropolitan and Provincial Bank this morning. Just sit down and tell us where you took her.'

'Oh, that is it?' said White, relieved to find that it was merely an inquiry and not an offence that he was called upon to answer for. 'Yes, sir. I did pick up a lady there. I took her along to the General Post Office, and waited while she went in. Then—'

'Wait a minute,' interrupted Foyle. 'How long was she in there?'

'Ten minutes as near as a touch, according to the way the taximeter jumped while I was waiting. When she came out she asked me if I could take her to Kingston. I said yes. And she told me to stop on the Surrey side of Putney Bridge, because she expected to pick up a friend, sir. Well, he was waiting there for us—'

'What kind of a looking man was he?'

'A tough sort of customer. Dressed like a labouring chap. I thought it was a queer go, but it wasn't none of my business, and ladies take queer fancies at times. She didn't say nothing to him that I could hear, but just leaned out of the window and beckoned. He jumped in and off we went. We stopped at a tailor's shop in Kingston, and the man went in while the lady stayed in the cab.'

'What was the name of the shop?'

'I didn't notice. I could show it to anyone, though, if I went there again.'

'Very well. Go on,' said Foyle curtly.

'Well, in a matter of a couple of minutes out comes the chap again and spoke to the lady. She got out and paid me off. He went back into the shop and she walked away down the street.'

'And that's the last you saw of them, I suppose?' asked the superintendent, with his left hand rubbing vigorously at his chin.

White shook his head. 'No, sir. I went away and had a bit of grub before coming back. As I passed Kingston railway station, I saw the lady standing by a big motor-car, talking to the man seated at the wheel. I thought at first it was the chap I had driven down, but I could see it wasn't when I got a closer look at him. He was better dressed and held himself straighter.'

'Ah! Could you describe him? Did you notice the number of the car?'

The driver scratched his head. 'A sort of ordinary-looking man, sir. I didn't take much stock of him. The car was A 1245—a big brown thing with an open body.'

'Right you are, White,' said Foyle with a nod of dismissal. 'That will do for now. You go down and wait in the yard with your cab, and we'll get someone to go with you to Kingston. And keep your mouth shut about what you've told us.'

When the door closed behind the man, his eyes met those of the chief detective-inspector. 'You'll have to go to Kingston, Green. It's a hot scent there. You've got the numbers of the notes that Maxwell got from the bank. Find out if any of them were changed at the tailor's. They've taken precautions to blind the trail. What I think happened is, that she telephoned from the General Post Office to some motor-car firm to send a car from London to Kingston railway station, under the impression that it would be less risky. He went into the tailor's place to arrange for a change of clothes, and she dismissed the taxi as a measure of precaution. It was a piece of luck that the man noticed the motor-car, but we can't be absolutely certain of the number he gave. He had no particular reason to remember it. Anyway, I'll send it out to the county police, and ask them to keep their eyes open. Meanwhile, I'll set some men to work to see if any of the big garages have sent a car to Kingston, and get the number verified. If you 'phone me when you get down there, I'll let you know how things stand.'

Green had his hand on the handle of the door, but suddenly something occurred to him. 'Do you think she's gone with him, sir?'

Heldon Foyle made a little gesture of dissent. 'I don't think it likely. It would double the danger of identification. But we can soon find if she's gone back to her home. I told Taylor, who is watching in Berkeley Square, to report when she returned.' He touched a bell and put a question to the man who entered.

'Yes, sir,' was the reply. 'He rang up half an hour ago. You told me I wasn't to disturb you. He reported Lady Eileen Meredith had just gone in.'

'There you are, then, Green,' said Foyle. 'That point's settled. You get along. I wish I could come with you, but it won't do for me to leave London just now, and goodness knows where you may have to finish up. Good-bye and good luck.'

When Green had gone, Foyle gave a few instructions to cover the points that had arisen, and walked to Sir Hilary Thornton's room. The Assistant Commissioner looked up and proffered a cigar. 'Think of the angels,' he said. 'I was just wondering how things were going.'

'Things are straightening out a bit,' said the superintendent. 'It's been a busy day, and it's not over yet.' And, puffing a ring of smoke into the air, he told in bare, unadorned fashion the events of the day. 'It has been a narrow thing for Grell,' he concluded. 'Even now, I fancy we shall get him. Green's as tenacious as a bull-dog when he's got something to take hold of.'

With his hands thrust deep in his trousers pockets, Sir Hilary strode to and fro across the room. 'It's time we got a bit forward,' he said. 'The adjourned inquest will come on again soon, and we shan't be able to keep the question of identity up our sleeves any longer.'

'There's a week yet,' answered Foyle. 'I don't think it will much matter what is revealed then.'

The Assistant Commissioner came to a halt. 'You're not a man to be over-confident, Foyle,' he explained. 'Do you feel pretty certain of having Grell under arrest by that time? I've not interfered with you hitherto, but for heaven's sake be careful. It won't do to make a mistake—especially with a man of Grell's standing.'

Heldon Foyle lifted his shoulders deprecatingly. 'It all depends upon an idea I have, sir. I am willing to take all responsibility.'

'You're still convinced that Grell is guilty?'

'I am convinced that he knows all about the murder,' answered Foyle ambiguously. 'With the help of Pinkerton's, I've traced his history back for the last twenty-five years. He's had his hands in some queer episodes in his time before he became a millionaire. There are gaps which we can't fill up, of course, but we're pretty complete. There was one thing in his favour. Although he's known toughs in all corners of the world, he's never been mixed up in any dirty business. And as he's carried out one or two political missions for the United States, I suppose he's had to know some of these people. Tomorrow or the next day, I expect to have the records of both Ivan Abramovitch and Condit. It will all help, though the bearing on the murder is perhaps indirect.'

'You're talking in parables, like a detective out of a book,' said Thornton, with a peevishness that his covering smile could not entirely conceal. 'But I know you'll have your own way when you don't want to be too precise. How do you regard the burnt paper? Is it important?'

'It would have been if I could have saved it,' said the detective regretfully. 'As it is, it's of no use as evidence in a court, for it only rests on my word. I keep pegging away at it, but I'm not certain that I can fill it out as it should be. But you never know your luck in our trade. I remember a case of forgery once. The counterfoil of a tradesman's paying-in book showed £100 with which he was not credited in the books of the bank. The cashier was confident that his initials in blue pencil on the counterfoil were genuine. Yet he was equally certain that he had not received the money. The tradesman was certain that he had sent the money. There it was. I was at a dead end. One day, I noticed a little stationer's store near the tradesman's office. In the window were some blue pencils. I walked in and bought something, and casually remarked that I shouldn't have thought there was much demand for those pencils. "Oh, schoolboys buy 'em," said the old woman who served me. "There's old —s' son over the way. He buys half a dozen at a time." Well, off I went to the grammar school that the boy was attending, and had a talk with one of the masters. He admitted that the lad was exceptionally clever at drawing. I was beginning to see my way, so had the boy called out of his class into a private room. "Now, tell me, my boy," I said, "what did you do with the money you stole from your father on such and such a date?" The bluff worked. He turned pale, and then admitted that he had forged the initials, taken the money, and gone on a joy-jaunt for a week while he was supposed to be staying with an aunt. There was the luck of the idea coming in my head through looking at those pencils.'

'Have you been looking at blue pencils today?' asked Thornton with interest.

'Something of the kind,' admitted Foyle, with a smile, and before he could be questioned further had vanished.

He had said nothing of the blotting-paper incident, for there were times when he wished to keep his own counsel even within the precincts of Scotland Yard itself. He did not wish to pin himself down until he was sure. In his own room, he unlocked the big safe that stood between the two windows, and taking out the roll he had abstracted from Lady Eileen's desk, surveyed it with a whimsical smile playing about the corners of his mouth. Once he held it to the mirror, and the word 'Burghley' was plainly reflected.

'That ought to do,' he murmured to himself, and, replacing it in the safe, swung the heavy door to.

The jig-saw puzzle to which he had likened criminal investigations was not so jumbled as it had been. One or two bits of the picture were beginning to stick together, though there were others that did not seem to have any points of junction. Foyle pulled out the dossier of the case, and again went over the evidence that had been collected. He knew it practically by heart, but one could never be too certain that nothing had been overlooked. He was so engaged when Mr Fred Trevelyan was announced.

'Fred Trevelyan? Who is he?' he asked mechanically, his brain still striving with the problem he wished to elucidate.

'That's the name he gave, sir,' answered the clerk, who ranked as a detective-sergeant. 'I should call him Dutch Fred.'

'Oh, I was wandering. Send him in.'

There was nothing of the popular conception of the criminal about Freddy as he swaggered into the room, bearing a glossy silk hat of the latest fashionable shape on one arm. His morning coat was of faultless cut. His trousers were creased with precision. Grey spats covered his well-shone boots.

Foyle shook hands with him, and his blue eyes twinkled humorously. 'On the war-path, I see, Freddy. Sit down. What's the game? Going to the big fight?'

The last remark was made with an object. Professional boxing attracts perhaps a larger number of the criminal fraternity than any other sport, except, possibly, horse-racing. In many cases, it is purely and simply love of the game that attracts. There is no ulterior motive. But in the case of Freddy, and men in his line, there was always the chance of combining pleasure with profit. The hint was not lost on the pick-pocket. A hurt expression crossed his face.

'No, Mr Foyle,' he declared earnestly. 'I don't take any interest in boxing. I just called in to put you wise to something as I was passing.'

'That's very nice of you, Freddy. What was it?'

The pick-pocket dropped his voice. 'It's about Harry Goldenburg,' he said. 'I saw him today.'

Foyle beat a tattoo on his desk with his fingers. 'That so?' he said listlessly. 'Out on the Portsmouth Road, I suppose?'

Dutch Fred sat up with a start. 'Yes,' he agreed, 'just outside Kingston. How did you know?'

'Just a guess,' laughed the superintendent. 'Well, what about it? Did you speak to him?'

'I didn't have a chance,' retorted Freddy. 'I was in a little run-about with a pal when he came scooting by hell-for-leather. We only got a glimpse of him, and if he noticed us he made no sign. I thought you'd like to know, that's all. It was an open car, brown colour. I couldn't see the number for dust; it was A something.'

'Well, we know all that,' said Foyle. 'All the same, Freddy, I am glad you dropped in: I won't forget it.'

'Right oh, Mr Foyle. Good evening.' And the pick-pocket swaggered out, while Foyle thoughtfully stowed away his papers.

Someone brought in a cup of tea and some biscuits, and his watch showed him that it was a quarter to five. He had promised to call on Lady Eileen about six o'clock, and his mind dwelt on the potentialities of the interview as he lingered over his frugal meal. He had just poured out his second cup, when the telephone buzzer behind him jarred.

'A call from Liverpool, sir,' said the man in the private exchange. 'Mr Blake wants you. Shall I put him through?'

A few minutes elapsed before Foyle heard the voice of the man who had been outwitted by the Princess Petrovska. 'Is that Mr Foyle? This is Blake speaking. We've got on the track of the lady again. She'd been staying at a boarding-house pretending she was a member of a theatrical company. A local man spotted her and came back to fetch me to make certain of her identity. But she must have got wind of it somehow, for she's hired a motor and slipped off. We're after her now. She's only got half an hour's start, and we've wired to have the main roads watched. I expect we'll have her in an hour or two.'

The superintendent coughed. 'Get along then, Blake. And don't smoke when you're on the job this time. Good-bye.'

He replaced the receiver and returned to his neglected cup of tea. Things were evidently stirring. Was it altogether chance, he wondered, that Petrovska had chosen the day to make a move? Strange coincidences did happen at times, yet there was a possibility that her movements were correlated to those of Grell. Had the two managed to communicate? Well, at any rate he could rely on Blake and his assistants to find out whether she had received letters or messages. The matter was out of his hands, and it was not his habit to worry about affairs which he could not influence.

CHAPTER XLIV

THAT Heldon Foyle had come so closely on the heels of Grell's message was something of a shock to Eileen. She had not supposed that the detectives would be so quickly again on the trail. Her heart beat a little quicker, but her face gave no sign as she drew off her gloves while the footman told her of the superintendent's call at six.

When she was alone she sat with her long, slender hands gripping the arms of her chair, her grey eyes reflecting the light of the fire as she stared abstractedly into its depths. That she had done her utmost to help Grell escape she did not regret; she rather triumphed in the fact. Foyle could know nothing of that—at the worst he could only suspect. Her precautions had been too complete. She was confident that she and Grell were the only two people who knew of the day's happenings. In any case, she argued to herself, it was better to see Foyle. She had come to respect his acumen, and fear he might draw an inference not too far from the truth if she denied him an interview. Besides, she asked herself, what had she to fear? Grell was safely away, and she could trust not to betray herself.

At six o'clock to the minute a footman—whose wooden face gave no indication of the fact that a moment before he had confidently informed Foyle in a stage whisper, 'She seemed pretty cheerful when she came in, sir—been sitting all alone since'—brought her a card. Then Foyle was ushered in—calm and unruffled as though he were merely making a social call. She returned his bow frigidly.

'I hope you will not consider my call inconvenient, Lady Eileen,' he said suavely. 'I considered it of importance that I should see you as soon as possible.'

She crossed her knees and regarded him composedly. 'I am sorry I was out when you called this morning. Had I known, I should have waited for you.'

The detective admired the manner in which the girl carried off a difficult situation. She spoke quite indifferently, and yet he knew that she was entirely on her guard. He smoothed the top of his hat with his hand.

'Sometimes an appointment with one's bankers is a thing one can't put off,' he said blandly.

A tiny spot of colour burned in each of her cheeks and she flashed one quick look at the detective. This was an attack in flank which she had not expected. 'My bankers?' she lied instantly, 'I have not been to my bankers'.'

'I beg your pardon,' he said, his voice keyed to a curious inflection. 'I was under the impression that you had—that, in fact, you changed a cheque for £200 made payable to bearer.'

She tried to hide a new feeling of alarm under a smile. 'Well, and if I did?' she challenged. 'That is, of course, my private business, Mr Foyle. You surely haven't come to cross-examine me on my habits of personal extravagance?'

'Partly,' he countered. 'Shall we be plain with one another?'

She rose and stood with one arm resting on the mantelpiece, looking down on him. 'By all means let us be plain. I am only a girl and I cannot altogether follow the subtleties of your work.'

'We are not such dreadful people really,' he smiled. 'We try to do unpleasant work as little unpleasantly as possible. As you say, you are only a girl, and although perhaps uncommonly clever, you are—if you will pardon me—a little apt to let your impulses outreach your reason. More than once I have tried to advise you as I would my own daughter. Well, now, here is some more advice—for what it is worth. Tell me exactly what you did between the time you went out this morning and the time you came in—whom you saw and where you went. Will you do that?'

The tick of a small clock on the mantelpiece was loud. Eileen contemplated the tips of her boots with interest. Then a little ripple of laughter shook her. 'You are a dreadfully suspicious man. If it interests you, then, you can have it. I went to the bank, and from there took a cab to my dressmaker's, where I paid a bill and was fitted for a new gown. I went on and did some shopping at various places. Shall I write out an exact account for you?'

If it had been the detective's design to entrap her into a series of falsehoods he might easily have done so. But there was no object in pursuing that course. He met her ingenuous gaze with a little lift of his shoulders. 'This is mere foolishness, Lady Eileen. I want to give you the opportunity of stating frankly what occurred from the moment you got Robert Grell's letter this morning. You know this story of the dressmaker would fall to pieces the instant we started making inquiries to verify it.'

'So I'm on my defence, then?' she said abruptly. He nodded and watched closely the changing expression of her features. 'I have done nothing that gives you any right to question me,' she went on defiantly. 'And I am not going to submit to any more questions. Good morning. Can you find your own way out?'

She caught at her skirt with one hand and with her chin tilted high in the air would have withdrawn haughtily from the room. She was afraid that his shrewd, persistent questioning and persuasion might end in eliciting from her more unguarded admissions. He had reached the door before her, however, and stood leaning with his back against it and his legs crossed and his arms folded. She stopped sharply and he divined her intention.

'I shouldn't touch the bell if I were you,' he said peremptorily. 'It will be better for both of us if I say what I have got to say alone.'

The decision in his tone stopped her as her hand was halfway to the bell-push. She paused irresolute, and at last her hand dropped at her side. Foyle moved to her, laid a gentle hand on her shoulder and half forced her to a seat. After all, with all her beauty and her wits she was but a wayward child. Her eyes questioned him and her lips quivered a little.

'Now,' he said sternly. 'Tell me if your father signed the cheque you cashed, or whether you put his signature to it yourself?'

Her lips moved dumbly and the room seemed to quiver around her. Finely as she had held herself in control hitherto, she was now thoroughly unnerved. She covered her face with her hands, and her frail figure shook with dry sobs. Foyle waited patiently for the outburst to pass. Suddenly she sprang to her feet and faced him with clenched hands.

'Yes, I did sign it,' she blazed. 'My father was out, and I wanted the money at once. He will not mind—he would have given it to me had he been here.'

He checked her with a deprecating movement of his hand. 'Don't excite yourself, please,' he said soothingly. 'I felt bound to let you see there was a serious reason why I should press you to give an account of your movements today. Sit down quietly for a moment.'

He waited patiently while she resumed her seat. He had foreseen that while she was on her guard he was unlikely either by threats or coaxing to induce her to speak. The hint of forgery had been deliberately intended to throw her off her balance. She could not know that her blotting-pad had betrayed that and more. Nor could she know that without the evidence of her father and the bank officials—neither of which was likely to be willingly given in the circumstances—she was not amenable to a criminal charge. 'Will you tell me now why you were so anxious to obtain that money—why you could not wait for an hour or two until your father returned? Don't hurry yourself. Think. Remember that I shall be able to check what you say.'

'I—I—' She choked and gulped as if swallowing something.

'Will it help you if I tell you that two of the notes which were given in exchange for the cheque were changed at a tailor's shop at Kingston, where a rough-looking man bought an overcoat and a suit of clothes?'

'You—know—that?' she gasped, the words coming slowly one by one from her lips. The accuracy of his knowledge, and the swiftness with which it must have been gained both astonished and astounded her.

'I know that,' he repeated. 'And I know more. I know, for instance, that Mr Grell went to Sir Ralph Fairfield before applying to you. Did he tell you that?' He waited, but she made no answer. 'I know too that he has left London. You know where he is making for. Where is it?'

Slowly she shook her head. 'I can't tell you,' she cried vehemently. 'You cannot force me to. He is an innocent man. You know he is. You can expose me—tell all the world that I have been guilty of forgery if you like—you will not get me to lift a finger to hound him to his death.'

Foyle had failed. He knew it was of little use pushing the matter further. He picked up his hat and gloves and mechanically passed a hand over his forehead. But there was one thing that had to be done before he left. 'I will not trouble you any further now,' he said in a level voice. 'I may take it you will tell your father of the—the banking episode. That will relieve me of a rather painful task.'

'I will tell him,' she said dully.

'Then good evening, Lady Eileen.'

'Good evening.'

The superintendent drew on his gloves as he passed out of the street door. 'She knows her own mind, that girl,' he said to himself. 'She won't give away a thing. Either she's very much in love with him, or—'

He rounded the corner into Berkeley Street.

CHAPTER XLV

THE first part of the commission given by Heldon Foyle to Chief Detective-Inspector Green was simple to execute and cost him no effort of ingenuity. A straight drive through into Kingston, a call at the tailor's shop where Grell had re-fitted himself with clothes, and a few minutes' conversation with the assistant who had served him, gave him all the facts concerning the appearance of the man he was following.

'I'd better take these two notes away,' he said, beginning to fold up the flimsies. 'I shall want you to keep a note of the numbers, in case you are called upon to give evidence.'

The tailor scratched his head doubtfully, and cast a glance on a policeman passing slowly on the other side of the street. He was beginning to suspect the tall stranger who asserted he was a police officer, and so calmly appropriated money. He was wondering whether, after all, it might not be an ingenious scheme of robbery. He had heard of such things, and the composure of the detective did not comfort him. Green had given no proof of his identity beyond his bare word.

With some mumbled excuse the tailor stepped to the door and beckoned to the policeman. With much volubility he explained the situation and his suspicions. The constable listened gravely. He was very young to his duties, and remembered the cautions that had been given him not to accept anyone's word where actions were suspicious.

'He didn't show you a warrant-card, did he?' he asked. 'All right, Mr Jones, you leave this to me.' And he marched importantly into the shop.

Green, who had just lit a well-worn brier pipe, and was waiting for the assistant to return in order to pay him the value of the notes, smiled grimly at the apparition of the constable in uniform. He guessed exactly what had happened.

'This is the man?' asked the police officer. The tailor nodded, and he went on, addressing Green, 'What's this about you taking money and pretending to be a police officer?' He had produced an official notebook and looked very important as he loomed in the doorway, gazing sternly at the detective. 'Don't answer any questions unless you want to. You know I shall have to take anything you say down in writing, and it may be used as evidence against you.'

The situation had a piquant humour that tickled Green. The constable was strictly within his duty, as he had been called in, but the pomposity of his manner betokened that he was very, very young in the service. In a deliberate silence the detective felt in his pocket for a warrant-card that would clear up the mistake. A moment later he was wildly searching in all his pockets without success. For the first time in a lifetime in the service he must have been careless enough to leave it at home.

He flourished a number of envelopes inscribed 'Chief Detective-Inspector Green, New Scotland Yard, S.W.,' but the knowing look of the young constable was emphasised by the cock of the eyebrows. Green never carried official documents except when he was obliged to.

'That won't do, old chap,' said the constable, in the manner of one well used to the ways of the criminal fraternity. 'You don't come that on me. You might have written those envelopes yourself. You'll have to come along.'

If the letters had failed to impress him, Green felt certain that his visiting-card would be of little use. Since he had decided to visit the police station in any case, it did not much matter. It was humiliating, in a way, but it did not much matter.

'All right, my man,' he said authoritatively. 'I'll see the station officer. Send for a cab.'

'Cool hand, isn't it?' whispered the policeman to the tailor. 'See how he's dropped trying to pull off his bluff on me. Just hop out and see if you can find a cab. I'll keep an eye on him.'

So it was that a high official of the Criminal Investigation Department reached an outlying police station under the conduct of a young constable whose swelling pride was soon reduced to abject misery as the divisional detective-inspector, who was leaning on a high desk and chatting with a station-sergeant, sprang forward to greet the suspect.

'They 'phoned through from headquarters for me to meet you here, sir. There's one or two messages come through for you.'

The constable's jaw dropped. 'Is this man—this gentleman from the Yard?' he gasped.

The local man stared from Green to the policeman, and from the policeman to Green. Some notion of what had happened began to occur to him. 'What the blazes—' he began, but the chief inspector cut him short.

'That's all right,' he said. 'I was careless enough to come out without a warrant-card, and this young man has made a little mistake. Don't you worry about it, my lad. Only, next time, don't put so much zeal into a doubtful case. Cut along back to your beat and give that chap this.' Some sovereigns chinked. 'Now, Mr Malley, I'll be glad to have those messages, and to put a call through to Mr Foyle.'

He followed Malley into an inner room, and the local man handed him a couple of messages which had been telephoned to Scotland Yard by the county police, and one sent by Foyle immediately after his interview with Dutch Fred, giving amplified particulars of the car. Green made his report over the telephone and then, replacing the receiver, turned to Malley. 'This last message shows he's got a good start. He passed through Haslemere an hour ago. Can you get away yourself, or have you got a good man you can lend me?'

'That's all arranged, sir,' was the answer. 'Mr Foyle said that I was to go with you if you wanted me.'

'Right. We'll have to rake out a good car somewhere. You see to that. We'll pick up any fresh news at the county police station at Haslemere. This man may have been stopped by now.'

Malley was already speaking into the telephone. He paused for a moment. 'Will a chauffeur be necessary, sir? I could drive, if you liked.'

'So much the better. Tell 'em to hustle the car along here. It'll be just as well to have plenty of petrol.'

A matter of ten minutes or a quarter of an hour before the motor-car was at the police station. Malley slipped into the driver's seat, and Green coiled up his long body by his side. With a jerk they started, and in a little were out on the broad Portsmouth road, while a thin, penetrating rain was powdering the windscreen. Presently Malley increased the speed and, though it was well outside the legal limit, Green made no remonstrance.

Stolid and unimaginative as he might seem to casual acquaintance, the chief inspector usually worked with tremendous enthusiasm and doggedness. As Foyle had said, he was as tenacious as a bull-dog. He was determined to catch Grell, if human wit and perseverance could do it. And he chafed to think that the start had been so long.

Dusk had fallen before they entered Haslemere, pausing only to ask their way to the local police headquarters. Short as the run had been, they were both chilled to the bone, and their overcoats were sodden with rain. There was no thought of a halt, however. A man ran bare-headed out of the police station door as though he had been waiting for them.

'Mr Green?' he asked.

'That's my name,' answered the chief inspector.

'Your people have been on the 'phone to us, and so have the Hampshire Constabulary at Petersfield. Nothing has been seen of the car you want since it passed through here, apparently on the way to Petersfield. We didn't know you wanted it held up till too late, but one of our bicycle patrols remembered having seen it go by. Ten minutes later, we got word. Both Petersfield and Midhurst have had men out waiting for it. No luck at all. It seems to have vanished clean off the face of the earth. You'll probably meet some of our bicycle patrols if you're going on. We've been searching the by-roads.'

Green bit back an expletive. The prospect of a night's search in the wet and wind and rain did not appeal to him. There seemed no help for it, however. 'Much obliged,' he said. 'We'll watch for your men. Drive on, Mr Malley.' And they slipped forward into the gloom.

'There's too much of the needle in a haystack business about this to suit my taste,' he complained when once they were clear of the town. 'That car might have taken anyone of fifty side-turnings. Anyway, we'll go on to Petersfield and see whether they've had any luck. Slow down a bit. There's not much object in speed now.'

Presently their big acetylene lights picked out a caped policeman standing in the centre of the roadway, his arm upraised for them to halt. They could see his bicycle resting on the grass. As they stopped, he advanced and, glancing at the number on the bonnet, scrutinised the two detectives sharply.

'It's all right, constable,' said Malley. 'We're not the people you're looking for. We're from London, and we're looking for the same man.'

The policeman, satisfied, stepped back with a clumsy salute and a 'Beg pardon, gentlemen,' and once more they were off. Ten minutes later, another cyclist, pedalling furiously, rode into the zone of light cast by their head-lamps. A hail brought him to a stop, and Green put a question, explaining who he was.

'We've found it, sir,' exclaimed the man excitedly. 'It's in a lane at the other side of the little village called Dalehurst, a mile farther up. It had been run into a ditch and left there. There's no sign of the man who was in it. I'm just riding in to report. There's a sergeant looking after it.'

'Never mind about reporting, yet,' said Green. 'You come back with us and show us where this car is. I'll take all responsibility.'

They travelled on at a pace that permitted the cyclist to keep alongside, and presently, turning sharply to the right, picked their way along a narrow roadway which, overgrown with grass and flanked by densely-wooded country, was as desolate and lonely a spot as could be conceived. The car bumped and swayed over ruts and hummocks, and Green touched his companion's sleeve to bid him stop.

'We shall get on quicker and safer if we walk,' he said, and dropped stiffly to the ground. Malley followed suit, and swung his arms vigorously about his body to restore some degree of warmth to his cramped frame.

'We'll carry one of the headlights with us,' said Green. 'Faith, it's muddy.'

Their boots made a soft, squelching noise as they tramped on under black shadows of the trees for a hundred yards. The track of the previous car was embedded plain on the soft earth. And here and there were footmarks recently made which the three avoided confusing, on Green's order, by keeping to the side of the roadway. The wheelmarks ended abruptly round a slight bend, where they came upon the car itself. It was tilted at an acute angle, with its leading front wheel embedded in the low ditch. All the lights had been extinguished, and the rear of the car, with the number, was picked out in high relief against the dark background by the acetylene light carried by Malley.

'Who's that?' growled a husky voice, and a police-sergeant stepped into the section of light.

'It's all right, sergeant,' said the man who had acted as guide to the detectives. 'It's only two gentlemen from London who are engaged on the case. I met them and brought them along.'

The chief inspector had taken the lamp from Malley and was throwing its light on the ground around the car. Then he stepped into the car itself and began a minute inspection of rugs and cushions. The search was only a matter of habit, and it revealed nothing. He stepped down and pointed to some footprints. 'Anyone been here but you two men?' he asked. 'Here, both of you, press your right feet here. That's it.' He contemplated the marks with careful deliberation for a while, and then, stepping wide, followed a series of footmarks leading up the lane.

'Our gentleman walked pretty fast,' observed Green. 'See how plain the heel and toe marks come out, while the rest of the impression is blurred. Hello! what's this?'

The road had terminated abruptly in a bridle-path leading apparently to the interior of the wood, and the footprints had become more and more indistinct with the transition to ground covered with fallen leaves. They had failed entirely as Green spoke, and he flung the light about in an effort to pick them up again. Then something met his eye on a spike of blackthorn, and he carefully picked off a thread of brown cloth. 'We're done for tonight, I'm afraid,' he said. 'He's gone off the track and got into the wood. We'll get back, Malley, and try to find a room or somewhere to sleep near here. Then we can turn out with daylight. But first of all we must 'phone to the Yard. By the way, sergeant, do you know whose estate we're on?'

'I'm not quite sure,' growled the officer. 'It used to be Colonel Sawford's, but I believe he sold it to that man who was killed in London a little while back. Grell was his name, wasn't it?'

'Really? Thank you, sergeant. Come on, Malley. Perhaps we can find the village post office and use the 'phone.'

CHAPTER XLVI

IT was to Heldon Foyle's own house, and not to Scotland Yard, that Green telephoned eventually. Clad in a bright blue dressing-gown, the superintendent listened, with a few non-committal interjections, until his lieutenant had finished.

'On his own land, eh?' he said at last. 'What do you make of it, Green? Is it genuine, or has he done it just to throw us off, and doubled back on his trail? It looks as if he intended us to find that motor-car.'

Green disagreed. 'It's a deserted, blind road made for wood-cutters years ago. It was only a chance that a constabulary sergeant found it. He may have left it there for the time being, relying on coming back to hide it properly out of sight. And this is an ideal place for anyone to keep close. It would take a thousand men to search the wood anything like thoroughly.'

'There's some sort of house on the estate, I suppose?' demanded Foyle.

'Yes, I've not been up to it, but I'm told it's a big, rambling old place called Dalehurst Grange, approached through sloping meadows and backing on to the woods. It would be easy for a man to see anyone in the house coming from the front and slip away into the undergrowth. Malley's gone up to have a look at the place. We'll need a search warrant to go over the place, but I don't think it'll be any good.'

'Nor I,' agreed Foyle. 'It'll have to be done some other way. You've asked the county constabulary to make inquiries and to watch the railway stations round about, of course? All right. You run things on your own discretion, and if you or Malley see me just shut your eyes. Now give me your address and report to the Yard as usual.'

The superintendent lit a cigar after he had replaced the receiver, and thoughtfully toasted his slippered feet before the fire. Presently he rose, turned over the leaves of a time-table, and discovering that Dalehurst possessed no railway station, discarded it in favour of a gazetteer. From that he found that the village was four miles from Deepnook, and the time-table again consulted showed him that he could reach the latter place in a couple of hours from Waterloo.

Before he went to bed that night he packed the kit-bag that had accompanied him in most of his wanderings all over the globe. Other things than clothes found a place in its depths, among them a jemmy, some putty, and a glazier's diamond. The superintendent had an idea that they might be more effective than a search warrant.

Yet, as he turned the key, he realised that the energy and the efforts of both himself and Green might be wasted. There was a possibility that it was a blind trail—that Grell had contrived the whole thing as a blind, and had slipped out of the net that had been drawn for the brown motor-car. The thought induced Foyle to telephone through to headquarters to order a fresh warning to be wired through to the police at all the ports. He believed in leaving as little as possible to chance.

The night staff was still on duty when he reached Scotland Yard the next morning. The detective-inspector in charge stared at a corpulent man clad in a Norfolk jacket, knicker-bockers of brown tweed, whose heavy boots clanged along the corridor. The hair, moustache, and eyebrows of the intruder were a shiny black, and a little trimming with scissors and a judicious use of a comb and brush had altered the appear-ance of the superintendent's face as completely as the clothes had altered his figure.

He was no believer in stage disguises. False beards and wigs were liable to go wrong at critical moments. He nodded reas-suringly to the inspector and placed his kit-bag on the floor.

'It's all right, I'm Foyle right enough. I'm thinking of a change of air for a day or two,' was all the explanation he vouchsafed. 'I want to just run through my letters and catch the nine-ten train from Waterloo. I'll leave a note over for Mr Mainland, who'll take charge while I'm away.'

He went methodically through the heavy morning's corre-spondence, pencilling a few notes here and there on the letters, and sorting them into baskets ranged on the table as he finished. Precisely at a quarter to nine he touched a bell, and gave a few brief instructions. Then, carrying his bag, he descended the flight of steps at the front entrance and walked briskly along the Embankment. As he crossed the footway of Hungerford Bridge, a biting wind swept up the river and he shivered, warmly clad though he was. One of his own men passed without recognising him, and the superintendent smiled to himself.

There were five minutes to spare when he sank into the corner seat of a smoking compartment, and composed himself with a couple of morning papers for the journey. But he read very little. There was much to occupy his mind, and as the train slipped out of Waterloo station he tossed the periodicals aside, crossed his knees, blew a cloud of smoke into the air, and with a little gold pencil made a few notes on a visiting-card. London slipped away, and an aeroplane flying low came into his line of vision as they passed Weybridge. The open pasture meadows gave place to more wooded country, and he placed his pencil back in his pocket as they ran into Deepnook.

A solitary porter shuffled forward to take his bag. Foyle handed it over. 'Is there a good hotel in this place?' he asked.

'There's the Anchor, sir,' answered the porter. 'It's a rare good place, an' they say as 'ow Lord Nelson stayed there once. They aren't very busy at this time of the year. Only one or two motorists stopping there.'

'What's good enough for Nelson is good enough for me. Is it far, or can you carry that bag there?'

The porter hastened to reassure the gentleman. It was a bare three minutes' walk. Might he ask if the gentleman was staying long?

Foyle wasn't sure. It depended on how he liked the country and on the weather. 'By the way,' he went on, with an air of one faintly curious, 'didn't Mr Grell, who was murdered in London, have some property this way? Dalehurst Grange or something? I suppose you never saw him?'

'That I 'ave,' asserted the porter, eager to associate himself, however remotely, with the tragedy. 'I've seen him time and again. He always used this station when he came down from London—though that wasn't often, worse luck. He was a nice sort of gentleman, though some of the folks down here pretended that 'e was not what you'd call in proper society, because he was an American. But I always found 'im generous and free-'anded. And to think of 'im being done to death! My missus says she's afraid to go to bed afore I go off duty now. It was a great shock to us, that murder.'

He spoke with a solemn shake of the head, as though he lived in daily dread of assassination himself. 'You see the last train through, I suppose?' asked Foyle irrelevantly.

'Yes, sir. The ten-nine up. As I was saying, what with these 'ere murders and things—'

'Have they shut the Grange up, or is there still someone living there?'

'Well, they got rid of most of the servants. I believe there's still a 'ousekeeper there and a maid, as well as a gardener. I remember when Mr Grell first took over the place, Bill Ellis— 'e's the blacksmith—ses to me—' He entered into lengthy reminiscence, to which Foyle only paid casual heed. He had learned what he wanted to know. Grell, if he had left the neighbourhood the preceding night, had not done so from Deepnook, where he would have infallibly been recognised.

The porter was still talking when they passed under the branching arms of the giant chestnut that shaded the courtyard of one of the prettiest of the old coaching inns of England. Foyle slipped a shilling into his guide's hand, and registered himself as 'Alfred Frampton—London.'

Local gossip is often of service to the man who knows how to lead it into the right channels. The superintendent decided that an hour or two might be profitably wasted in the lounge, where half-a-dozen men were sitting at a small table before a huge, open fireplace. He ordered a drink and sat a little apart, relying on their provincial curiosity to presently drag him into the conversation. By the time the lunch he had ordered for one o'clock was ready, his habit of handling men had stood him in good stead. 'Mr Frampton of London' had paid for drinks, told half-a-dozen good stories, laughed at a score of bad ones, asked many innocent questions, and deftly given the impression that he was a London business man in search of a few weeks' rest from overstrain. Moreover, he had gained some knowledge of the lay of the country and acquaintances who might be useful. One never knew.

The afternoon saw him tramping through the picturesque countryside, with its dropping hills and wooded valleys. He moved as one careless of time, whose only object was to see the country. Once he stayed to talk with a stone-breaker by the side of the wood; once he led a farmer's restive horse and trap by a traction engine. On both occasions he contrived to drop a good deal of information about himself, and his reasons for being in that part of the country. That it was false was little matter. The best way to stop local gossip is to feed it. A mysterious, quiet stranger would be speculated about, the amiable business man from London with a love of chat was quite unlikely to arouse suspicions.

Sooner or later Grell, if he were in the neighbourhood, would learn of the presence of Green and Malley. His attention would be concentrated on what they were doing. Foyle, acting independently, was looking for an opening to attack from the rear. He had a great opinion of Grell's capacity for getting out of awkward situations. He sauntered through Dalehurst, stopping at a little general store to buy some tobacco and gather more gossip. The village shop invariably focuses village gossip. A garrulous old dame talked at large with the affable stranger, and when the superintendent emerged he was certain that Chief Inspector Green and those acting with him had succeeded in maintaining an adequate discretion in regard to the events of the preceding night.

As Foyle passed on, he observed a man hurrying towards him and recognised Malley. Abruptly the superintendent turned his back and, leaning his arms upon a low stone wall, seemed lost in contemplation of a little churchyard. When the divisional inspector had passed on, Foyle resumed his walk.

It cost him some little trouble to find the road in which the motor-car had been left derelict. The sodden earth still retained wheel tracks, and it needed but a glance to show that the car had been removed but a few hours before. He walked on till he came to the place where Green had found the strip of brown cloth, which was fairly plain to find, for the footsteps of Green and the other police officers when they followed the trail ceased there as Grell's had done.

Here he drew a small pocket-compass from his waistcoat pocket, and pressing a spring released the needle. As it came to rest he thrust aside the hazel bushes and plunged in among the undergrowth. Now and again he consulted the compass as he walked leisurely forward, wet branches brushing his face and whipping at his clothes. For the brief portion of the way a keeper's path facilitated his progress, but at last he was forced to abandon this and return to the wilder portion of the wood. He was making a detour which he hoped would lead him to the back of Dalehurst Grange.

At last he could see a clear space ahead of him, and in a little, sinking on his knees on a bank, was peering downhill to an old-fashioned, Jacobean manor-house, from whose chimney smoke was lazily wreathing upward. Between him and the house a meadow sloped for a hundred yards, and the back of the house was bounded by an irregular orchard.

'Pity I didn't think to bring a pair of field-glasses,' muttered Foyle, as his eyes swept the place. 'I can't tell how those mullioned windows are protected. Well, I may as well make myself comfortable, I suppose.'

A little search rewarded him with a great oak tree, and in the fork of a branch twenty feet high he found an easy seat from which he could watch the house without any great risk of being seen himself. Immobile as a statue, he remained till long after dusk had fallen and a steady light appeared at one of the windows. It was, in fact, ten o'clock, and the light had disappeared when he dropped quietly to earth and, with quick footsteps, began to cross the meadow to the orchard.

Under the fruit trees the detective moved slower and held his stick before him, softly tapping the ground as though he were blind. He had not taken half-a-dozen steps before the stick touched something stretched about a foot from the ground. Stooping, he groped in the darkness.

'A cord,' he muttered. 'Now I wonder if that is merely a precaution against burglars or—' and, stepping over the obstacle, he went on cautiously feeling his way. Twice more he found cords stretched across the grass, so that an unwary intruder might be tripped up, but his caution enabled him to avoid them.

The walls of the house loomed before him. He stepped to the nearest window and tested it. It was fastened tightly, nor could he see inside. Foyle had no taste for the haphazard, and would have liked to be certain of the run of the house. But one window was as good as another in the circumstances. He worked deftly with a glazier's diamond for a while, and at last removing one of the diamond panes of glass thrust his hand through and undid the latch. The window swung open, and the superintendent sat down on the grass underneath and swiftly unlaced his boots.

In another two minutes he was inside the house, and pulling an electric torch from the capacious pocket of his Norfolk jacket, he swept a thin wedge of light about the room. It was furnished as a sitting-room, but there was no reason for examining it minutely. Foyle pulled open the door and moved into a thickly carpeted corridor, which made his stockinged feet almost unnecessary.

Door after door he opened and noiselessly examined with the aid of his single beam of light. By the time he had come to a finely carved, old oak staircase, he had a rough idea of the plan of the house as far as the ground floor was concerned. The upper floors demanded more caution, for there the servants might be sleeping.

The first door that Foyle tried after the landing was locked. Pressing his ear to the keyhole, he could hear the deep, regular breathing of someone within. Twice he tried keys without success. At the third attempt the bolt of the lock gave. He pushed the door back and there was a crash as a chair which had been wedged behind it was flung to the floor.

A woman shrieked, and Foyle drew back into the shadow of the landing, cursing his luck. Then there came the sound of rapid footsteps. The superintendent drew himself together, and his muscles grew taut as a man came running. A light blazed up as the man passed through the doorway. Foyle caught one glimpse of a square-faced man fully dressed and acted rapidly. He dashed forward and his hand twined itself round the other's wrist.

'Mr Robert Grell, I believe,' he said suavely.

CHAPTER XLVII

WHEN Heldon Foyle leapt forward, his whole body had been keyed for a struggle. Whatever resources Grell might have in the house the detective stood alone, so far as he knew. It was possible that Green might have arranged to have the place watched, but, on the other hand, it was unlikely that he would do more than have the roads patrolled and the railway station warned. To have watched the Grange so effectively that no one could get away from it would have taken a score or more of men, and even so the position would have made it impossible for them to have remained hidden.

All this Foyle reckoned on. He had hoped to find Grell and to catch him unawares, perhaps asleep. That project had failed, and when the man had replied to the woman's scream, Foyle had deemed the boldest course the safest. Grell had wrenched himself round, the fist of his free hand clenched, but he made no attempt to strike. An elderly woman sat up in bed, surprise and terror in her face. Just behind Foyle stood two maids in their night attire, shivering partly with cold, partly with fright, their eyes wide open.

'That is my name,' answered Grell, speaking as quietly as Foyle himself. 'I can guess who you are. If you will wait just a moment while I assure these women that there is no need for alarm I will come down and talk with you. You had better go to sleep again, Mrs Ellis. And you girls get back to bed. This is a friend of mine.'

The maids retired reluctantly and Foyle linked his arm affectionately in that of Grell. The alarm in the housekeeper's face did not abate.

'But who—who is he?' demanded Mrs Ellis, extending a quivering finger in the direction of the superintendent.

Grell lifted his shoulders. 'Mrs Ellis is my housekeeper here,' he explained to Foyle. 'The maids didn't know I was in the place. It's all right, Mrs Ellis. I'll just have a chat with this gentleman. Don't you worry.'

He closed the door as he spoke. Foyle's right hand was resting in his jacket pocket. 'I may as well tell you, Mr Grell,' he said, 'that I am armed. If you make any attempt at resistance—'

'You will not dare to shoot,' ejaculated Grell smilingly. 'Oh, I know. We're in England, not in the backwoods. Come downstairs and have a drink. I don't want you to arrest me until we've had a talk. By the way, may I ask your name?'

Despite himself the superintendent laughed. If Grell was a murderer he certainly had coolness. But there might be some trick in the wind. He was keenly on the alert.

'Foyle is my name,' he answered—'Superintendent Foyle. I am afraid I shall have to refuse that drink, and as for the talk, I may presently determine to arrest you, so anything you say may be used as evidence. Of course you know that.'

'Yes, I know that. No objection to my having a drink, I suppose, even if you won't join me?'

'Sorry to seem ungracious, but even that I can't allow.'

'Ah. Afraid of poison, I suppose. Just as you like. Well, here we are. If you will let go my arm I assure you I will neither attack you nor try to escape. Then we can sit down comfortably.'

They had entered a room whose walls were lined with books and pictures, apparently the library. Foyle shook his head at the other's request. Of course it might be all right, but the man was a suspected murderer. He would accept no man's word in such a case. 'I am afraid it is impossible, Mr Grell,' he said gently. 'I am anxious not to seem harsh, but you see I am alone with you and my duty. . . . If, however, you will allow me, I have a pair of handcuffs.'

Wide as his experience had been he could not recall a notable arrest taking place in this way. He had fallen in with Grell's mood for many reasons, but he chuckled to himself as he made the polite suggestion of handcuffs. Grell did not seem to mind. His self-possession was wonderful. Foyle reflected that it might be reaction—the man was possibly glad the tension was over.

'By all means, if it will make you easier,' he said. Foyle slipped the steel circlets on his wrists, not with the swift click that is sometimes written of, but with deliberate care that they should fit securely, but not too tightly. The juggling feat of snapping a pair of handcuffs instantly on a man is beyond most members of the C.I.D.

Grell selected a chair and Foyle, watchful as a cat, sat by him. 'May I ask what you intend to do now?' queried the former.

'Wait till daylight and then send one of the maids with a message to the nearest police station,' replied Foyle. 'Would you like a cigar? I can recommend these.'

He proffered his case and Grell took one. He held it between his fingers with a whimsical smile. 'Do you mind cutting it and giving me a light?' he asked. 'It's rather awkward with these—er—ornaments.'

The superintendent did as he was requested and Grell puffed luxuriously. Foyle remained silent. Although he was aching to put questions, he dared not. 'Do you really think that I killed Harry Goldenburg?' asked Grell suddenly.

'I don't know,' confessed the superintendent non-committally. 'I think you may have.'

'Yes. That's a pity,' said Grell, lifting his cigar to his mouth. 'This affair must have cost you a great deal of trouble, Mr Foyle. And it's all wasted, because, of course, I had nothing to do with it.'

'I want to know,' said Foyle, a bit of American vernacular that came from his lips unconsciously.

'Tell me why you never announced that I was alive?' asked Grell. 'You'll have to do it, you know.'

'Well, there's no harm in admitting now that one idea was to make you think that we were deceived, and so to throw you off your guard.'

'And it did until you got hold of Ivan. Well, you've made a mistake this time, Mr Foyle. There were finger-prints on the dagger with which Goldenburg was killed, eh?'

Foyle inclined his head. His blue eyes were alight with interest which he made no effort to conceal. He half guessed what was coming, but he found Grell's ways disconcerting and could form no certain judgment. Certainly Grell did not behave like a guilty man—that is, a man guilty of murder. But neither did he behave like an innocent man. He was too totally unconcerned with the gravity of his position.

'Yes, there were finger-prints,' he said. 'I have a photograph of them in my pocket if you would like them compared now.'

'With mine? That's what I was about to suggest. You'll find some writing-paper and ink in the desk behind you. I suppose they will do.'

The prisoner smiled as he saw Foyle carefully shift his chair to guard against any sudden rush, before turning his back. He was a moment preparing the materials and then placed a blank sheet of paper on a little table in front of Grell. 'Will you kindly hold out your hands?' he said. As Grell did so he smeared the tips of the fingers of the right hand with ink. 'Now press your fingers lightly but firmly on the paper. Thank you.'

He brought a little standard lamp closer, and under its rays studied the two sets of prints closely. He did not need a magnifying-glass to see that none of Grell's finger-marks agreed with the two that were clear on the dagger. Grell leaned back in his chair as though the matter were one of complete indifference to him.

'Does that satisfy you, Mr Foyle?' he asked at last.

The superintendent nodded as their eyes met. 'It satisfies me that you did not actually kill the man,' he said steadily. 'I'll own I'm not surprised at that. I believe if you had killed him you would have been man enough to have stayed and faced the consequences. You will observe that I have not formally arrested you yet. But I do believe that you know all about the crime—that you were perhaps an eye-witness.'

For the first time during the interview Robert Grell lost hold of his self-control. His fists clenched and the steel of the handcuffs bit deep into his wrists as he momentarily forgot that he was handcuffed. There was a meaning in Foyle's tone that he could not fail to understand. He caught at his breath once or twice and his temples flamed scarlet.

'Speak plainly now!' he cried hoarsely. 'What are you hinting at?'

Slowly Heldon Foyle began to tear the sheet of paper bearing Grell's finger-marks into minute fragments. He was calm, inscrutable. 'I thought I made myself clear,' he replied. 'To make it plainer I will ask you if a man, famous, rich, and with an honourable reputation, flies on the eve of his wedding-day, assisted by his valet, hides himself in a low part of London, and associates with doubtful characters, whose friends abduct and drug police officers, who uses, in short, every effort to avoid or to hamper justice—has not some strong reason for his actions? Is it not plausible to suppose that he is an accessory either before or after the fact?'

Grell sighed as if in relief, and, stooping, picked up his cigar, which had fallen on the carpet. He had recovered his calm. 'You are a better judge of evidence than I am,' he said unemotionally. 'Personally, I don't think the facts you have mentioned would convict me of anything but eccentricity. Who is this Harry Goldenburg, anyway? Beyond the fact that he's my double I know nothing of him. That's certainly a coincidence, but why on earth I should conceal anything I know is beyond me.'

'You're talking nonsense, Mr Grell, and you know it,' said Foyle, with a weary little gesture. 'There's too much to be explained away by coincidence. We know who Harry Goldenburg was, and that there was a strong motive for your wishing him out of the way.' He leaned over a little table and his face was close to Grell's. 'You can only delay, you cannot prevent justice by keeping your mouth shut.'

The firm lines of Grell's mouth grew obstinate. 'I shall stick to my story,' he said. And then, with a return to his former flippancy of manner, 'You're a clever man, Mr Foyle. I never realised till you and your men were on my heels how hard a time a professional criminal must have. Even now I am not clear how you knew I was down here. When I found the police in charge of the motor-car I had left I thought they were merely guarding it as a derelict. I did not guess that you knew I had escaped from London in it.'

'A mere question of organisation,' said Foyle. 'As a matter of fact, we know most of your movements from the time you left Sir Ralph Fairfield's flat to the moment you separated from Lady Eileen at Kingston. By the way, she made some money over to you. You may care to know that that was got by forgery.'

Surprise had leapt into Grell's face as the superintendent drily recounted his movements. It was succeeded by a flash of fury at the last words. 'Be careful, sir,' he said tensely. 'You need not lie to me.'

'It is the simple truth. Lady Eileen got a note from you asking for money. She had none, and her father was out, so she signed a cheque in his name and cashed it personally.'

Grell's face had become grey and he buried it in his hands. His shoulders shook and Foyle could understand how hardly he had been hit. To have had to appeal to the girl for monetary help was bad enough. To find that she had committed a crime to help him was to add an anguish to his feelings that he had not known before. Somewhere in the house a clock struck midnight, the slow, deep strokes reverberating heavily.

'She did *that*—for me!' said Grell, lifting his head, haggard and wan. Then, as a thought occurred to him, 'She is not under arrest?'

'No. I had her word that she would inform her father.'

Grell made no answer. He stared moodily in front of him. The superintendent had no desire to break in on his reverie. He walked across the room, picked up a magazine, and sat down, again facing his prisoner, while he idly turned over the pages. Presently Grell's head drooped forward.

He was asleep.

CHAPTER XLVIII

THE hours dragged wearily with Foyle. The soft breathing of the sleeping man as he rested with his head pillowed on his arms was the only sound that broke the stillness of the night. The superintendent himself dared not sleep. He tried to read, but the magazines failed to interest him. He got up and quietly strolled about the room, examining the bookcases with incurious interest.

His thoughts were busy. Apart from all the other facts, Grell's manner was more than sufficient confirmation of the fact that he was holding something back—something vital to the success of the investigation. The superintendent had a very shrewd idea of his reasons. Grell was a strong man—a man likely to hold to his own line at all costs. He had already proved that no personal considerations would move him.

The superintendent reviewed the situation impartially, his brow furrowed, his lips tight pressed together. He was as certain as though he held the other's signed confession that Robert Grell had it in his power to say who killed Goldenburg. How would he break through his silence? For, come what might, he felt that Grell's place was rather in the witness-box than in the dock. That he preferred the dock was proof of the strength of the motive which actuated him. No amount of persuasion, Foyle knew, would make him open his lips. Disgrace by the fear of a public trial had failed to move him. If he was to be induced to tell his secret it must be by strategy.

Heldon Foyle held his own code of ethics in his profession. In his own mind he held that all things which were legal were permissible in facilitating the ends of justice. Grell could, if he were so minded, give sworn evidence on what Foyle could only suspect. Grimly the superintendent resolved that in a contest of will he would win.

A gentle tap at the door broke his train of reflection, and the white face of the housekeeper peered in. Her eyes rested first on the sleeping man, but his attitude concealed the handcuffs. She turned a half-frightened glance on Foyle.

'Excuse me, sir. I couldn't sleep, so I dressed, and thought I would look in to see if Mr Grell or you would like anything. Perhaps a cup of coffee—'

'No, thank you,' said the superintendent. 'By the way, now you're here you'll perhaps tell me whether you expected Mr Grell's arrival. Didn't you think he was dead?'

She advanced a little into the room, closing the door behind her. 'That I did, sir,' she answered timorously. 'I couldn't make it out when I got his telegram from Liverpool. It gave me a shock.'

'From Liverpool?' repeated Foyle slowly. 'So he sent a wire from Liverpool, did he? Would you mind if I had a look at it?'

He could see the hesitation in her face and went on: 'See here, Mrs Ellis, there has been a murder, though, fortunately,

Mr Grell was not the victim. I am interested in the matter, and you will be acting in his interests if you show it to me.'

'I don't know what to do, I'm sure,' quavered the woman irresolutely. 'I was supposed to have burnt it. Hadn't I better wake him up, and then he can let you look if he likes?'

A strong hand pushed her back as she would have endeavoured to rouse Grell. 'I shouldn't worry him if I were you,' said Foyle. 'You may take it that I have a right to see that message.'

He spoke authoritatively. Her hand fumbled beneath her apron and she produced a buff-coloured envelope. The detective took out and unfolded the wire. He read:

'Mrs Ellis, Dalehurst Grange, Dalehurst.—There has been mistake of identity. Am safe and well. Shall be down this evening, but time uncertain. Please have room ready. Let no one know you have heard from me. Burn this.—R. G.'

The detective refolded the telegram and placed it in his waistcoat pocket. His mind dwelt more on the significance of its dispatch from Liverpool than on the message itself. The Princess had been at Liverpool. It was a plausible presumption that she had sent the wire and that she therefore must have been in touch with Grell.

'Yes, I guess you must have been a bit startled when you got that,' he said. 'Did Mr Grell give any explanation when he came?'

'Yes, in a way. He got here an hour or two after it came and must have let himself in with his own key. He walked in on me while I was doing some sewing in my own sitting-room. He said that the police had asked him to keep out of the way, because if it was known that he was alive it might hamper them. He told me not even to let the maids know that he was here, and he came straight up to this room and locked himself in. I had made a bed ready, but he has slept on the couch over there.' She nodded towards a big settee under the window. 'He said the bedroom might do for a lady friend he was expecting who might arrive at any moment. He told me, too, that it might be necessary to leave suddenly.'

The old lady had, it was evident, made a good guess at the identity of her questioner or she would not have answered so freely, in spite of the detective's authoritative manner. Foyle put one or two further questions to her and then dismissed her with a quiet word of thanks. He began to see that he had struck harder than he knew when he had descended on the house in the guise of a burglar. Dalehurst Grange was, of course, a rendezvous, and the Princess Petrovska was on her way to join Grell. The superintendent rubbed his hands together as he thought of the surprise in store for her.

Dawn was breaking over the woods when Robert Grell woke with a shiver. He stood up and stretched himself. 'Good morning, Mr Foyle,' he said genially. 'I'm afraid I dropped off, but I've had rather a wearying time lately. Now, what's the programme? I suppose a bath is out of the question, or'—with a glance at his fettered hands—'even a wash may be dangerous. Faith, you don't believe in running risks!'

Foyle smiled in response to the banter. 'Only a fool runs risks when there's nothing to be gained. But I'm prepared to run one if you like to fall in with a plan I've thought out. You're not under arrest yet. You needn't be if you care to undertake to give evidence when the inquest is resumed. For you are at present the only person who can clear up the whole thing. Mind you, it would depend on what came out at the inquest whether we should then arrest you. I can give no guarantee about it. But if you accept, all that will be necessary is to quarter a couple of my men with you for the time being.'

Grell walked to the window and stared out upon the wooded country. Presently he wheeled upon the superintendent with a short laugh. 'My dear man,' he cried, 'you will harp on that one point. I appreciate your offer of comparative liberty, but if I accepted I should do so under false pretences, because my evidence will be that I know nothing.'

'You can't stop my knowing the truth,' answered Foyle equably. 'Sooner or later I shall be able to prove it. And if you persist it will make things much more unpleasant for you.'

The other said nothing for a while. A struggle was taking place in his mind that was indicated with a nervous twitching of the fingers. His shoulders were bent and his head bowed. Foyle waited patiently. Outside a bird started a 'jig-jig-jig—br-brr' that set the teeth on edge. The trees, stirred by a newly sprung up breeze, rustled uneasily.

'No, it's no good,' said Grell at last. 'I know nothing.'

The detective rubbed his chin thoughtfully. 'Will you tell me if you had any visitors on the evening of the murder?' he inquired, blandly ignoring the other's refusal. He noticed a quick flash of surprise pass over Grell's countenance and drew his own conclusions. Swiftly a new thought came to him. 'Did Goldenburg come to you alone?'

The prisoner remained silent, and Foyle knew that he was considering the advisability of answering. 'I don't see why you shouldn't know that, if you want to. He came with a friend of mine. She left shortly afterwards.'

'She?' Foyle seized on the word. 'It was a woman, then?'

Grell bit his lip. He had said more than he meant to. The superintendent frowned thoughtfully, and his active brain was beginning to see things more clearly. It was a full five minutes before he spoke again as one making an assertion rather than asking a question.

'That would be Lola, of course.' His blue eyes met Grell's frown with an ingenuous stare. 'This is beginning to get clearer, Mr Grell. Goldenburg was blackmailing you, eh? Maybe he had letters which you wouldn't have liked Lady Eileen to see—what?'

An ejaculation came from Grell. The detective directed his gaze to a picture opposite him, and continued, as though thinking aloud:

'Now I come to think of it, was Goldenburg a relative of yours? The likeness is amazing. Well, suppose, for the sake of argument, he was. And Lola—where does Lola stand? Was it to her, by any chance, that the letters were directed? Was she merely a friend, or did she stand in closer relationship to either of you?'

Grell yawned ostentatiously, but although Foyle had been apparently looking away from him he had followed the effect on the other's face of every one of the seemingly casual questions he had put.

'I am afraid I am boring you. It's a bad habit, thinking aloud.'

'It does seem futile,' agreed Grell. 'You surely have little need to exercise yourself about these things.'

'Ah, you think so? I am beginning to think that something more is necessary. It may be—of course, this is only for the sake of illustration—that the dagger was handled by someone after the murder had occurred. However, let the subject drop. Perhaps your housekeeper will get us some breakfast while one of the girls runs into Dalehurst.'

While waiting for a reply, he rang the bell and gave some directions, with a note to the housekeeper. The breakfast that she ultimately served up was a credit to her skill as a cook. Both men ate with an appetite that the unusual nature of the situation did not destroy, though Grell found the handcuffs troublesome.

The superintendent laid down his knife with a sigh of content.

The sound of a motor-car horn was borne faintly in upon them. In a few minutes the housekeeper ushered Green and Malley into the room. The chief inspector returned Foyle's greetings and flung his heavy overcoat on to a chair. His eyes wandered over the prisoner with a little pardonable curiosity. Grell bore the inspection with a smile.

'I congratulate you, sir,' said Green. 'We'll have the thing fairly straightened out in a day or two now.'

'I hope so,' said Foyle. 'Mr Malley, will you stay with this gentleman for five minutes? I want to speak to you in another room, Green.'

He led the way to the little sitting-room, through the window of which he had effected an entrance. A look of comprehension spread over Green's face as he noticed the missing diamond pane. 'Malley told me he passed you in the village yesterday. You got our man quicker than I should have thought possible in the circumstances. How did he take it?'

The superintendent gave a brief recapitulation of the steps he had taken since he left London. Green rubbed his grizzled head and followed the recital with keen appreciation. It did not occur to him to feel hurt that Foyle had acted independently.

'As a matter of fact,' he said, 'I've got a search-warrant in my pocket, and we were coming over this house today. I didn't anticipate much profit, because he could have easily slipped away into the woods. I got the county constabulary to put a cordon of patrols round about, and hoped to drive him into their hands. But it was a slim chance. However, we've got him now.'

'Yes, we've got him now,' agreed Foyle. 'There only remains the Petrovska woman, and we'll have her today. Listen.'

He told of what he had learned from the housekeeper, and they discussed the probabilities of the woman reaching Dalehurst Grange. If she managed to escape Blake and the other detectives who were hot-foot on her trail there was little doubt but that she would walk blindly into a trap. That she had not already reached the Grange and departed Foyle was satisfied, although she had had ample time to travel from Liverpool. As Green phrased it, 'she might almost have walked it.' But the exigencies of the pursuit might have brought about delay if she attempted to confuse her track. If Foyle had been able to get in touch with Blake he would have called him off in order to let her proceed unfettered. That could not be done.

'She'll not dream anything's wrong here if we're careful,' said Green. 'Will you wait for her, or shall I?'

'This is up to you, Green. I'll leave you. You might have had Malley, but I can't drive the car myself, and I want to get back to town. Do you think you'll be able to manage alone?'

'I think so,' said the chief inspector confidently.

'I'll get the local superintendent to send up a couple of plain-clothes men as we pass. You'll bring her straight back to town.'

'Ay!'

In a quarter of an hour all preparations were finished. Malley was in the driving-seat of the car. Foyle and Grell sat in the tonneau, and it was no coincidence that the right hand of the prisoner and the left hand of the detective were hidden beneath the rug which covered their knees. For Foyle had handcuffed his man to himself. It was merely a matter of travelling precaution. The superintendent did not believe that Grell would attempt to escape, but there was no excuse for giving him any temptation. Anyway, it did no harm.

'You'll charge him with the murder directly you reach town, I suppose?' whispered Green, standing by the step of the car.

'Murder?' repeated Foyle. 'Grell did not commit the murder. I shall detain him a day before making any charge against him at all. Drive on, Malley. See you later, Green.'

The car whizzed away. Chief Inspector Green stood bare-headed in front of the house, scratching his head, and with a look of bewilderment on his face.

CHAPTER XLIX

It is permissible in certain circumstances for the police to detain a suspect, without making any charge, for a period of not more than twenty-four hours. Heldon Foyle had taken advantage of this to hold Grell while he tried to draw further together the tangled threads of the investigation.

He had changed out of his tweeds and, once more the spick-and-span man about town, he sat down in his office with an order that he was to be informed the moment that Sir Hilary Thornton returned. Meanwhile, he occupied himself with a work of composition. It was necessary to break gently to the public the fact that Robert Grell was not dead. But it had to be done in the right way. He could not altogether see what evidence might have to be offered at the inquest, but he was sure the newspapers would label it 'sensational.' He wanted to prepare, at any rate, for the revelation of the dead man's identity. That there was no possibility of avoiding, but it could be rendered less startling if it did not come suddenly. And beyond the public interest in the case Foyle had another reason for the publication of his effort. He worked steadily and made three drafts before he had completed his task. Two of them he tore up, and the third he read over carefully, making one or two alterations.

'When the inquest in reference to the Grosvenor Gardens murder is resumed it is understood that evidence of a remarkable nature will be brought forward by the police. Inquiries made by the C.I.D. have placed it beyond all doubt that the crime was not a planned one, and evidence is still being collected against a suspected person.

'A man for whom a rigorous search has been made by the police has been found in a Sussex village by Scotland Yard officers, acting in conjunction with the county constabulary. He was taken to Malchester Row police station, where he has been detained. It is understood that he refuses to give any account of the circumstances in which he took to flight.

'On inquiry at Scotland Yard yesterday, a representative of this journal was informed that the officers engaged on the case expect to be in a position to clear up the mystery in the course of the next few days.'

'That ought to do,' he muttered, as he blew down a speaking-tube. To the detective-inspector who came in response to his summons he handed the paper. 'Have fifty copies of that made, and bring me one. Put someone to 'phone through to all the journalists on the list, asking 'em to call here at half-past six tonight. They're each to have a copy of that.'

There was guile in Foyle's fixing of the time. He knew that the paragraph would be a bombshell in Fleet Street, and did not want it to explode prematurely. At half-past six all the evening papers would have ceased publication for the day. At half-past six, too, he would take good care to be far away from the hordes of Press men, hungry for details, who would strive to find more information from the hints given. At that time they were likely to find any person wiser than themselves, and he had seen to it that there should be no indiscretion at Malchester Row.

'Sir Hilary just come in, sir,' said someone, opening the door just wide enough to permit a head to be thrust within; but before Foyle could move the Assistant Commissioner himself walked in.

'One moment, Sir Hilary,' said the superintendent, and dashed out, to return again almost immediately. 'I just wanted to make certain that we shouldn't be disturbed. There's a lot to tell you. Things have been happening.'

'So I gather,' said the other, settling himself in the arm-chair. 'You've got Grell, I hear. What's the next move? Do his finger-prints agree?'

'They do not. He is not the murderer, but he won't say who is. The next move is, that I intend that to go in all the morning papers.'

He placed in Thornton's hand a copy of the typewritten paragraph, and the Assistant Commissioner read it slowly through. 'I don't quite follow,' he said as he handed it back. 'It hints that Grell will be charged with the murder.'

'Exactly. It is intended to convey that impression. To tell you the truth, I have a piece of evidence of which I have not spoken to you before. It indicates a person possibly guilty whom we must not neglect. If she is guilty—which I half doubt—that paragraph may help us to get at the missing evidence.'

His voice sank to a whisper and he leaned forward with arms outspread over his desk. As he spoke, Thornton's voice changed. He leapt to his feet and brought his fist down vehemently on the desk.

'I don't believe it, man!' he cried. 'I don't believe it! It's incredible. You've made a mistake. It can't be. Why, you've believed it was Grell yourself all along. If you've made a mistake then, why not now?'

Foyle's chin became a trifle aggressive. Thornton's astonishment was natural, but the superintendent did not like the appearance of lack of confidence. His blue eyes were alight. 'You can draw your own inference from the facts, Sir Hilary,' he said coldly. 'I am clear in my mind. I have done nothing, because I want to make the evidence as to motive indisputable. Should I find I am wrong I shall, of course, write out my resignation.'

Thornton was not usually an impulsive man. He had recovered himself immediately upon his outburst and was once more calm and self-possessed.

'Don't be offended, Foyle,' he said, more mildly. 'I beg your pardon. It was just a bit startling at first. We've been associated too long for misunderstanding. I'll back you up, and there's not going to be any talk of resignations.'

'Thank you, Sir Hilary,' said the superintendent, entirely mollified. Going to the big safe he unlocked it and took something from the shelf which he handed to the Assistant Commissioner. The two bent over it.

It was nearly two hours before the two concluded their task. Sir Hilary, his hands clasped behind his back, walked in deep thought back to his own room. Heldon Foyle put on his hat and coat and ordered a taxi.

'Brixton Prison,' he said to the driver.

CHAPTER L

THERE are many people who pass Brixton Prison everyday who have no conception of its whereabouts. The main entrance is tucked away a hundred yards or so down an unobtrusive turning off Brixton Hill. Within a little gate-house inside the barred gates a principal warder sits on duty.

Although Foyle was tolerably well known to the prison officials, the usual formalities had to be gone through, and he was kept outside till a note he had pencilled was sent up and replied to by the governor. Then, conducted by a warder, he was taken over the flagged courtyard and through long corridors to the remand side of the prison.

Another warder opened one of the heavy cell doors, and a man seated on a low bed looked up with a frown of recognition. The superintendent remained standing by the doorway. 'Sorry to trouble you, Abramovitch,' he said briskly. 'I just wanted to have a little talk with you.'

Ivan rose and deliberately turned his back. 'You must go to my solicitor if you have any questions to ask,' he said sullenly.

Heldon Foyle seated himself at the end of the bed and nursed his stick. 'That wouldn't be of much use, would it?' he asked smilingly. 'What I want to speak to you about has nothing to do with the present charge against you. Mr Grell is in our hands now, and in the circumstances I thought you might care to know it.'

The valet wheeled about and thrust his face close to the immobile face of the detective.

'You've arrested Mr Grell?' he cried. 'Are you lying?'

'I am not lying. He is in custody and may be charged unless you like to clear him.'

Ivan took a couple of short steps. His lips were firmly pressed together. The detective watched him narrowly as he came to an abrupt halt.

'You think I can clear him?' he said slowly. 'You are wrong.'

'But you know he never committed the murder?' The words came sharp as a pistol shot. Ivan never answered, and Foyle went on: 'You have done all you could to help him escape us. Now we have got him you can only help him by telling the truth. There was some strong motive to induce you to take all the risks you have done. What is at the back of it?'

Ivan studied his questioner suspiciously. Foyle made haste to dispel what was at the back of his mind. 'You had reason for refusing to speak before,' he insisted. 'I'm not blaming you. Consider the thing fairly as it stands now and you'll see that you best serve your master by perfect frankness. I'm not trying to trap you. You may trust me.'

The scowl on the face of the valet faded and his sloping shoulders squared a little.

'You are right. Secrecy can no longer do good,' he said. 'I will tell you what I know.'

He sat down by Foyle's side and went on: 'I was always what you English call a bad egg. I broke with my family many years ago—it doesn't matter who they were—and left Russia to become an adventurer at large. In the years that followed I was everything everywhere—seaman, barber, waiter, soldier, and gambling-house cheat. I wasn't particular how I picked up a living nor where it led me. All that won't interest you. I was operator in a gambling-joint at San Francisco when I first met Goldenburg, though I knew him by reputation. He came to our place now and again, and we were on speaking terms. After that Grell came and I mistook him for the other man. That was how we first became acquainted.'

'That would be almost five years ago?' interposed Foyle quietly.

'Just about that. They never came together, by the way, and Grell always called himself Mr Johnson. His own name would have been too well known. Well, one night, or rather one morning, he had been winning pretty heavily. He must have had close upon four or five thousand dollars in notes on him. At the time I didn't attach any significance to the fact that two or three of the worst toughs at the table went out shortly after him. I followed about five minutes later to get a breath of air, and came on the gang in a narrow, deserted street, just as they brought Grell down with a sandbag. It was no business of mine and ordinarily I should have walked away, but that I'd had a little difference with one of the gang earlier in the day, so I sailed in with a gun, broke 'em up, and helped Grell to his hotel. He came round before I left him, and I told him my name, and he gave me five hundred dollars, telling me to look to him if ever I was in trouble.

'Well, next day I was fired from my job. I could guess that the people whose game I'd spoilt were at the bottom of it, but that didn't worry me much. I had a bit of money and I came back to Europe—London, Paris, Vienna, Rome— everywhere but Russia. I lived sometimes by my wits, sometimes by any odd job I could turn my hand to. My father and mother had both died, and my only living relative was my sister, a girl of eighteen, living in St Petersburg. From her I heard occasionally.'

A spasm crossed his face as though some painful recollection had been brought to his mind, and he passed a handkerchief across his brow, which had suddenly become wet with perspiration.

'It was through her that I again met Grell,' he resumed, speaking more slowly. 'She was alone and practically unprotected. She wrote to me that a certain high official had been paying her unwelcome attentions, but I suspected nothing till I one day learned that she had been arrested for a political offence—she, who never knew the meaning of the word politics. I knew what that meant. . . . At the time I was in straits myself, for fortune had not been kind at the cards. This was in Vienna. I was staring out of my window in a kind of daze when I saw a man pass in a motor-car. It was Grell—the man whom I had known as Johnson.

'In desperation I sought him out—it was easy enough to find where he was staying—and told him my story. I asked him to loan me money, because I knew that I might have to bribe officials. He offered to do more—to accompany me to St Petersburg and use all his influence on behalf of my sister.

'It was at his suggestion that I travelled as his valet. My appearance had altered since I was last in Russia, but difficulties might have arisen. We travelled night and day, but we were too late. The girl who had never harmed a single person in her white life was dead—killed by the hardships to which she had been subjected. I—I—'

He covered his eyes with his hands for a moment, and Foyle waited patiently. Ivan controlled himself with an effort. 'Grell advised me to come away, but I was determined to stay for a while. I had work to do. I told him nothing, but steadily I sought for the man who had killed her as surely as though he had plunged a dagger in her heart. I found him at last—'

'Wait a moment,' interjected Foyle quickly. 'I want to know nothing of that; that has nothing to do with me.' He had guessed what work it was that the hot-blooded Russian had remained to do. No man is bound to incriminate himself.

'It was through Grell that I got away scot-free. No one suspected the valet of so well-known a man. He asked no questions, though I could tell that he knew what—what I knew. He risked much to shield me, although never a word passed between us. Could I do less when it came to my turn? I came back to England with him, and I remained his personal servant. I kept my distance from the other servants.'

'In fact, you pretended to have little acquaintance with English?' interrupted Foyle.

Ivan nodded. 'That was so. On the nights when I was free, I wandered about London and picked up a few old acquaintances, among them being Charlie Condit. I shan't tell what I knew about him, but it was enough to keep him civil, and later on he did what I told him.

'On the night that the murder occurred, I happened to be in the hall about nine or a little after, when I saw a man and a woman through the shaded glass standing on the steps outside. I opened the door before they could ring. For the moment I thought the man was Mr Grell, but a second later I recognised Goldenburg. He did not remember me. The woman, too, I knew at once. I had met her occasionally in different cities of Europe. It was the Princess Petrovska. Goldenburg spoke of an appointment and showed me a note from Mr Grell directing that the bearer should be shown to the study to await his arrival.

'That was enough for me. I showed them up and left them. I did not hear Mr Grell return, but about ten o'clock he rang for me and met me at the door of his study. He told me that he was expecting a lady, and if she called she was to be brought straight up; and he said the other people were just going. Almost immediately after he told me she came. Wills was going to the door, but I was in front, and I showed her up.'

Foyle shifted his position a little. 'Who was she?' he asked.

'I couldn't see her face; she wore a heavy veil.'

'All right; go on.'

'I knocked at the door of the study, but no one replied. She pushed by me and entered, closing the door after her. I went away to my own room. Whatever was taking place was no business of mine. I must have dozed off in my chair, for when I was awakened by Mr Grell shaking me by the shoulder, he was white and quite collected.

'"Ivan," he said, "there's been murder. Come with me. Don't speak, and tread softly."

'I followed him into the study. All the lights were out, and before turning them up he locked the door. As he turned the switch I could see the body lying on the couch, and drew back. "Who is it?" I asked.

'"Goldenburg," he replied. And after a pause: "He was a relative of mine. I have killed him. You must help me to get away, Ivan."

'He seemed profoundly moved and yet held himself strongly in hand. One thing I noticed. Although he said he had done it, his hands and clothes were spotless. And yet there had been much blood about the room. I said nothing of that, and he quickly began to turn things out of his pockets. Both he and the dead man were in evening dress, and he hastily transferred all his property to the dead man's pockets, taking what Goldenburg possessed. He picked up the sheath of the dagger from the floor. It was one he had bought in South America.

'"It will give us a chance to get well clear if they think that this is my body," he explained. "Go and pack a bag, Ivan."

'When I got back with the bag, he had finished. He put on a hat and overcoat and we went out, walked to Victoria Station, and from there took a taxicab to Charing Cross. From there we walked to an all-night Turkish bath establishment, and that gave us an opportunity to change into some rough tweeds that I'd shoved in the bag. In the morning we went to the East End and fixed up rooms with some people I knew of. We had come away without any money, but Grell somehow managed to get in touch with the Princess Petrovska, with whom, apparently, he had some arrangement. She had, it seems, booked through to Paris from Charing Cross, but instead of getting on the boat at Folkestone had returned by the next train and taken quiet lodgings at Kennington. That was to put you on a false track in case of accidents.'

Foyle smiled a little ruefully. 'So that was how it was done,' he remarked.

'We were determined to get out of the country, but the reward bill with a description of Goldenburg that pictured Grell stopped us trying ordinary methods. It was necessary to raise money, and I, recklessly enough I suppose, went out with the pearls which Mr Grell had entrusted to me, in the hope of meeting a jeweller, with whom I had a casual acquaintance, at the restaurant, when you fell in with me. The jeweller's letter which you found on me was, by the way, a forgery.

'When you seized me I was taken by surprise. When I was allowed to go, after you had told me that the dead man was not Grell, I felt certain that you would have me followed. Your men were very clever, and I could not shake 'em off at first. I was determined to go to any length to protect Grell, so I went into an outfitter's where there was a public telephone, and put a call to a place where I was sure to find Condit. I fixed up with him to wait for the man who was shadowing me, and I led him down to Whitechapel. It was simple enough for Condit to drop on him from behind, and then the two of us knocked him senseless, got him into a cab, and carried him away to Smike Street—to the place which you raided.

'Mr Grell knew nothing about that incident till it was over. He was staying in Grave Street at the time, and the idea occurred to me of holding your man as a hostage. We meanwhile contrived to send a note to Sir Ralph Fairfield. In case of accidents, I was to meet him in Grave Street and lead him round about till I was certain he was not followed.'

'Then you were the black-bearded man who fired at me!' exclaimed Foyle. 'I might have guessed it.'

'And so you were the navvy!' said Ivan. 'I didn't know that, but I at once made up my mind it was dangerous to meddle with Fairfield if he was watched. I gave him the slip, went back to Mr Grell, and typed out a note to you. You got it?'

'Yes. I got it. Where did the paper you used come from?'

Ivan's brow contracted into a frown of deep thought. 'I forget—no—I got it from Mr Grell. He tore off a half-sheet from a letter.'

Foyle was thinking of the finger-prints he had found on that notepaper. Ivan plunged again into his narrative. 'After that the Princess came, and Condit. She had fixed up an arrangement with the people living in the house that they were to declare her their daughter if inquiries were made. I don't know if she slept there after, but she did that night. We worked out a cipher in order to attempt to communicate secretly with either Sir Ralph Fairfield or Lady Eileen Meredith. As I have said, the lack of money was our trouble, and we had to get some—somehow. Condit went away, and I persuaded Mr Grell to go with him and spend the night at a gambling-joint in Smike Street. I remained. You see, we guessed you might want to examine the house, but we weren't certain. We were right. As you know, I only got away over the roofs just in time, and the Princess slipped away while you were engaged.

'After that it was a game of hide-and-seek. We decided that it was too dangerous to keep your detective a prisoner, and sent him back in a motor-car we hired. It was easy enough to make a false number to slip over the real one, so that it couldn't be traced.

'It was my idea after that that Mr Grell should become a watchman on the river until we could get away by embarking before the mast. We tried the advertisement method of communication and failed.

'The Princess undertook to see Lady Eileen—with what result you know. You know all that has happened since. I do not regret what I have done. If the killing of you or any other man would have saved Grell, I would not have hesitated.'

'Thanks,' said Foyle drily. 'You had a good try more than once. Now, are you willing to have your statement taken down by a shorthand writer—so far as it refers to events in London?'

'I'll repeat it when you like,' answered Ivan, squaring his shoulders. 'Now you say that you want to prove Mr Grell's innocent I have nothing to hide. For I am certain that he is innocent.'

'Tell me one other thing,' said the superintendent. 'What is the association between Petrovska and Grell? Why should she have taken part in this business?'

Ivan spread out his white hands. 'That you must find out either from Mr Grell or her. I don't know.'

Foyle drew out his watch. 'All right, Ivan. I'll see you again shortly. Meanwhile, I'll send someone along to get your statement. I don't think you'll regret having decided to speak. Good-bye.'

CHAPTER LI

BOTH Sir Hilary Thornton and Chief Inspector Green were waiting for Heldon Foyle when he returned to his office. The superintendent darted a question at the chief inspector as he flung off his overcoat.

'Yes, sir,' answered Green. 'She's at Malchester Row now. There was no trouble at all. She came up to the Grange at half-past three, in a car, and asked the maid who answered the door for Mrs Ellis. The girl showed her into a sitting-room, acting on my instructions, and I walked in on her and told her I should detain her. She was angry at first, but in a moment or two she laughed, and asked if Mr Grell was taken. That was all there was to it. I brought her back straight away by train. She seemed to treat it as a joke, but never a word about the case did she utter.'

'And how did you get on, Foyle?' demanded the Assistant Commissioner.

The superintendent plumped into a chair. 'I am sending a man up to get a statement from Ivan,' he said. 'There's much to be said for that Russian if his story is true—and I couldn't see any holes in it.'

He related particulars of the interview that had taken place in the cell. Neither Thornton nor Green spoke till he had finished. The Assistant Commissioner smoothed his moustache, Green rubbed his head.

'Then Grell admitted the murder to Ivan?' said the latter, turning a puzzled face to Foyle. 'You told me he was not the murderer.'

'Nor was he,' answered the superintendent. 'According to Ivan, there was no blood on his clothes or on his hands a few minutes after Goldenburg was killed.'

'Well, this beats all,' exclaimed Green. 'I'm hanged if I understand!'

Foyle lowered his voice to a whisper, and Green's saturnine face became a study as he listened. He gave a little gasp. 'It lies between the three of them,' said Foyle. 'I am inclined to believe that we have been rather wrong in our first impressions of the finger-prints. But it never does to take chances. Suppose you go and take charge at Berkeley Square. There are four men there already. Lady Eileen has certainly had something to do with this, and we don't want to lose sight of her.'

Green went off, his lips puckered into a whistle. Thornton gave a shrug. 'And now?' he said. 'It seems to me rather a deadlock if Mr Grell and the Princess remain obstinate.'

'Yes,' agreed Foyle. 'It's one of those cases in which it is a pity we're not allowed to adopt the French method of confrontation. Still, there's a shot in the locker yet. Perhaps you might care to come along with me and see Grell now. These disclosures of Ivan's make a difference, and rather bear out a suspicion I've had since I talked with Grell.'

The Assistant Commissioner agreed, and in a little they were walking to Malchester Row police station. The office of Bolt, the divisional detective-inspector, was empty, and with an order that they were not to be disturbed, Foyle and his chief entered the room. Under the escort of a uniformed inspector, Grell was brought in. The superintendent closed and locked the door, Grell moving stiffly aside to allow him to do so.

'Do you know Sir Hilary Thornton?' asked Foyle suavely.

Grell bowed. The Assistant Commissioner extended his hand. 'How do you do, Mr Grell? I should have been glad to have met you under happier circumstances, but I assure you that the respect in which I have always held you is not lessened by this unfortunate business.'

The prisoner shook hands doubtfully and his eyes flashed a questioning look upon Foyle. The superintendent's face was blandly unconscious of the effect of the Assistant Commissioner's remark, although the words had been rehearsed and revised a dozen times during their walk to the police station. But he had to do with a man as astute and ready as himself.

'That's very good of you, I'm sure,' said Grell, and a smile illumined his face as he added: 'Though I don't know why this matter should increase your respect.'

'Don't you?' said Foyle, laying stress on his words and eyeing the other meaningly. 'Suppose it is because since I left you this morning, Ivan Abramovitch has made a full statement to me?'

A little apprehensive shudder swept through Grell's frame. His lips opened to say something, but he checked himself suddenly. 'What's that to do with me?' he demanded quietly.

'A great deal, if it's true, as I know it to be. Now, Mr Grell, you are not obliged to answer any questions unless you like—you know that—but I warn you that your failing to do so cannot prevent us arresting the guilty person. We know you are innocent—though whether you may be charged as an accessory after the fact or not is another question. What do you say?'

The prisoner had leaned his arm on the table. His fists were clenched until the finger-nails bit into the flesh.

'If you've made up your minds, so much the better for me,' he said with a half laugh. 'Who have you fixed your suspicions on?'

It was clear that he had doggedly set himself to avoid affording them any help. His chin was as fixed as that of Foyle himself. The strong wills of the two men had crossed. The superintendent felt all his fighting qualities rise. He was determined to break down the other's wall of imperturbability. He accepted Grell's silence as a challenge.

Thornton's gentle, cultured voice broke in. 'We are only anxious to spare you as much as possible. You are a prominent man, and though you must be brought in, it will serve no purpose to increase what will create enough scandal.'

'I fear you are wasting your time, gentlemen,' said Grell, stretching himself wearily. 'Won't it cut this short if I admit that I killed Goldenburg? I will sign a confession if it will please you.'

The eyes of Thornton and Foyle met for a second. There was a meaning look in the superintendent's, as who should say, 'I told you so.' Then he took from his breast-pocket a piece of paper, which he unfolded as he smiled amiably at Grell.

'That is childlike. Your finger-prints prove it is false. Perhaps you will tell us what underlies this note that you sent to Lady Eileen Meredith the day you left London.'

He read:

'We are both in imminent danger unless I can procure sufficient money to help me evade the search that is being made for me. If I am arrested, I fear ultimately exposure must come. If you have no other way of obtaining money, will you try to get an open cheque from your father? You could cash it yourself for notes and gold and bring it to me. For God's sake do what you can. I am desperate.'

He read it swiftly, as though certain of the accuracy of the words. As a matter of fact, he was not. He had pieced together the broken words and phrases that he had taken from the burning paper in Eileen Meredith's room as well as he could. In filling up some of the gaps he might have been preposterously wrong.

'Where did you get that?' demanded Grell. 'Eileen told me she had burnt it.'

His words were an admission that the note was practically correct. Foyle placed it carefully back in his pocket, while Grell stared at the opal shade of the electric light.

'She did burn it,' he answered. 'I chanced to be able to retrieve the message. I feel certain that, however dire your necessity, you would not have written to her in that strain unless you had some strong reason. Who did you mean when you said "both in imminent danger"?'

'Ivan and myself, of course.'

'Ivan was under arrest at that time. Nothing could avert the danger from him. And you say that you feared exposure if you were arrested. That, of course, meant that you would be unable to keep shielding the person you are shielding?'

A dangerous fury blazed in Grell's eyes—the fury of some splendid animal trapped and tormented yet unable to escape from its tormentors. He glared savagely at the superintendent.

'I am shielding no one,' he declared.

'You can, of course, make any answer you like. Suppose we go on to another point which perhaps you will have no objection to clearing up now. We have Harry Goldenburg's record. We know he had been blackmailing you, and we know that he was your brother. No; sit still. He was your brother, was he not?'

'My half-brother. How did you know that? How did you know he was blackmailing me?' Grell spoke tensely.

'Oh, simply enough. The likeness was one thing, and a hint I got from Ivan that he was a relative confirmed me in an opinion I had already formed by another fact—which I observed when I saw you at Dalehurst—that you had a similar walk. You will remember, I asked you if he was a relative, but you would not answer. The supposition that you were being blackmailed was borne out by inquiries made for us by Pinkerton's, which proved that Goldenburg had visited you several times and that he was always in funds after he left you, however low he might be before. I think it is a fair inference.'

'Quite fair.' Grell's face was a little drawn, but he spoke quietly. 'You are quite correct, Mr Foyle. As you know so much, there can be little harm in enlightening you on that part of the story. I take it that you treat it as confidential.'

'Unless it becomes necessary to use it for official purposes, as evidence or otherwise,' said Thornton before the super-intendent could reply. 'We cannot give an absolute pledge.'

CHAPTER LII

'VERY WELL; I am content with that.' The prisoner nursed his chin in his cupped hands and stared unseeingly at the distempered walls. 'It began years ago, on a little farm in New Hampshire. That was my father's place. He died when I was six or seven, and my mother married again. The man was the father of Harry Goldenburg. I was eight years old when Harry was born. Four years later, my mother died, and when I was sixteen I ran away from home. You will know something of my career since then: the newspapers have repeated it often enough—office-boy, journalist, traveller, stockbroker, politician. I was still young when I became a fairly well-known man. In the meantime I had not seen nor heard anything of my brother except that he had left the village when my stepfather died.

'In Vienna some years ago I became intimate with Lola Rachael—the woman you know as the Princess Petrovska. She was a dancer then and had hosts of admirers among the young men about town. As a matter of plain fact, I believe she was employed by the Russian Government for its own purposes. But of that I was never certain. Anyway she entangled me. And I believe she really had an affection for me. It was during that time that I was fool enough to write her letters—letters which she kept.

'Eventually I went back to the United States. I became a state senator and became involved in politics. One day I was in my hotel in Washington when I received a visit from my brother Harry Goldenburg. I was in a way glad to see him, although he was practically a stranger. He impressed me favourably—perhaps the fact that we were so alike physically had as much to do with it as his suave ways and gentle manners. Even at the time I believe he was suspected by the police of being an astute swindler. Of that, of course, I was ignorant. He told me a story of a mail order business he had established in Chicago which was doing great things, but which was hampered for lack of capital. Well, to cut the story short, I lent him five thousand dollars. A month later, he wrote to me for two thousand, and got it. A few weeks after that I read of a great fraud engineered in Central America and there was a three-column portrait in the paper of the man at the bottom of it—my brother. That opened my eyes. When next he came to me—he was audacious enough to do it within the year—I charged him with living by fraud. He laughed in my face and admitted it. When I threatened to call in the police, he merely shrugged his shoulders and asked what I thought of a flaming headline in the press:

'BROTHER OF SENATOR GRELL HELD FOR BIG FRAUDS.'

'I could see it all just as he painted it. My political career was very dear to me just then. Such a thing would have killed it. I knew if I exposed him he was capable of carrying out his threat. However, I told him to get out of the place before I threw him out of the window. He could see I was losing my temper and took a little pistol from his pocket—a Derringer.

"'I have a number of letters which you sent to a lady in Vienna," he said. "I know many newspapers which would offer me a good price for 'em."

'I think it was perhaps fortunate for me that he held the pistol—or I might have done something I should afterwards have regretted. He flung a letter face upwards on the table. It was one of those I had written to Lola Rachael. If he had the rest of the correspondence—and he swore that he had—it would have been deadly in the hands of an unscrupulous political opponent. As you know, electioneering in the States is rather different from what it is here. I was fool enough to pay him money on his promise to suppress them. He would not sell them outright.

'That was the beginning. After that I never had a secure moment unless I was away on an exploring expedition. The moment I reappeared in civilisation my brother would seek me out. He was cunning enough to press me only to the verge of endurance. He could judge exactly how much I would stand. At last, however, I resolved not to yield another penny to his extortions. I cut loose from all my affairs in the United States and came to England. I thought I could fight him when I had reduced the stakes. I found after all that I had increased them, for I met Eileen—Lady Eileen Meredith.'

He paused. Neither of his two hearers said anything. An injudicious remark might break the thread of his thoughts.

'When I became engaged to her,' Grell resumed, 'I knew that it would not be long before Goldenburg would see his chance. I set to work to find Lola, and discovered her as the Princess Petrovska. Then for the first time I learned that she had married Goldenburg—but she admitted that any affection she held for him had long since faded. They had parted a few weeks after the marriage—which they both seemed to regard somewhat cynically—and she had resumed her first husband's name. She admitted that she had helped him to blackmail me, but apparently she herself had handled little enough of the loot. She was vicious enough about it. I gave her a cheque and induced her to come to London. I had it in mind to stop this blackmail before I was married.

'As I expected, Goldenburg was not long in scenting profit. He descended on me ravenously. I told him that I would pay him ten thousand pounds if he would put all the letters he possessed in my hands but that I would not otherwise buy his silence. He could see that I was in earnest, and asked for time to consider. I gave him till the night before my wedding. I said nothing of the Princess Petrovska. I knew that they would meet. One cannot be too scrupulous in dealing with a scoundrel, and she had her instructions—to steal the letters from him if necessary, while pretending that she was only anxious to join forces with him in looting me.

'But all her efforts went for nothing. He recognised the value of her co-operation in the circumstances, but would give her no hint of the place where he had concealed the letters. Time drew on. You will know enough of her to recognise Lola as a clever, resolute woman. She made up her mind to accompany Goldenburg to his appointment with me as a last resort. It was to keep that appointment that I left Ralph Fairfield at the club the night before the wedding—the night of the murder.'

He breathed heavily. Thornton picked up a piece of paper and crumpled it nervously between his lean hands. Foyle, eager and alert, was leaning forward, anxious not to miss a word. A great deal of what had been obscure was being cleared up. But so far nothing that Grell had said but could be interpreted as a motive—and a singularly strong one—which might in other circumstances weave a hangman's rope about his own neck.

'You did not want anyone to know that you were absent from the club,' remarked Foyle. 'Why?'

'That was merely a matter of precaution. I wanted my interview with Goldenburg to be secret. I had given Goldenburg a note which would ensure his being shown to my study and I was purposely a bit late for the appointment. I wanted to give the Princess Petrovska all the opportunities possible. But when I reached there it was clear to me that she had failed. He had not brought the letters with him. I got rid of the woman, and Goldenburg and I quarrelled. Then it was that I killed him.'

'And what of the other woman?' asked the superintendent.

'What other woman?'

'The veiled woman who was shown up to you by Ivan.'

'There was no other woman,' said Grell, his lips tightening. 'I have told you as much as I intend to.'

'Just as you like. I believe you have told the truth up to a point, Mr Grell. It is fair to assume that a blackmailer of Goldenburg's calibre would have taken precautions lest you should fail to comply with his demands. Doesn't it appear a fair assumption that he might have taken steps to arrange the presence of the person most interested, next to yourself? He probably never mentioned that he had done so until it was too late for you to stop her. I mean Lady Eileen Meredith.'

The table crashed to the floor as Grell, the last remnants of his self-restraint gone, leapt to his feet. Sir Hilary Thornton sprang between the two men. Foyle also had risen, and though his face was impassive the blue eyes were sparkling and his fists were clenched.

'You liar!' raved Grell. 'How dare you bring her name into it!'

'This excitement will not advance matters,' said Foyle placidly. 'Sit down for a little, Mr Grell. You cannot prevent the inevitable.'

The tense muscles of the prisoner relaxed and a shivering fit shook him from head to foot. He could see the blow that he had striven to avert falling while he stood impotent. He had taken every risk, made every sacrifice man could make, to turn it aside. Now he had been told that he had failed. It was not easy to admit defeat. His debonair courage had gone.

Sir Hilary Thornton laid a hand gently on his shoulder. 'My dear Mr Grell,' he said, 'I don't want to use the ordinary cant about duty and all the rest of it. We may sympathise with you—personally, I admire the attitude you have taken, though perhaps I shouldn't say it—but our own feelings do not matter the toss of a button. Nothing you can do or say will swerve us from what we judge to be the interests of justice.'

'Let me alone for a little while,' answered Grell dully; 'I want to think.'

They sent him back to the detention-room where, with a constable seated opposite to him, he was to spend the night. Foyle rested one arm on the mantelpiece and kicked the fire viciously into a blaze.

'Ours is an ungrateful business, Sir Hilary,' he grumbled, 'but I've never come across a man who put so many difficulties in the way of being saved from the gallows as Mr Robert Grell.'

Thornton took a long breath that was almost a sigh. 'Poor chap,' he said reflectively. 'Poor chap!' And then, after an interval, 'Poor girl! Couldn't you have dropped a hint, Foyle?'

The introduction of sentiment into business was a folly that Heldon Foyle seldom permitted himself. With a shrug he pulled himself together. He shook his head. 'We've got to be more certain yet. I daren't tell him too much—for my idea may prove to be wrong. You must remember that it was undoubtedly Eileen Meredith's finger-prints on the dagger. At present it is only surmise of mine how they got there. Finding the prints on her blotting-pad, which I showed you, corresponded with those on the dagger you gave me, was one of the biggest surprises of my life. But we may clear it up now.'

'H'm,' said Thornton. 'Well, we shall have to look sharp.'

A thought struck Foyle. He stood rigid as a statue for a

moment, and then slapped his knee with sudden energy, 'By God! I believe I've got it!' he exclaimed, and jumped for the telephone.

'Put me through to the Yard. . . . Hello! I want Mr Grant. . . . That you, Grant? . . . About the Grosvenor Gardens case. Tell me. Might the finger-prints on the dagger have been caused by someone withdrawing it and replacing it after the murder had been committed? Would the second handling have obliterated first prints? . . . Blurred them. I see. But if the person who first handled the dagger wore gloves? Thanks. That's what I wanted to know.'

He replaced the receiver and turned triumphantly on Thornton. 'That bears out my idea, Sir Hilary. Will you excuse me while I see if Bolt's on the premises?'

Without waiting for a reply, he darted from the room. The Assistant Commissioner's brow puckered and he thoughtfully replaced the upset furniture. By the time he had finished Foyle had returned.

'Just caught him,' he said. 'I've sent him to collect all the men he can find to make some fresh inquiries.'

'I'm a little bewildered,' confessed Thornton, jingling some money in his trousers' pockets and turning blankly upon the superintendent. 'Do you think you'll be able to do it—to bring this crime home to the Princess Petrovska?'

'I think I can,' replied the superintendent. 'I was a blind ass not to see it earlier. Lola's alibi—which is proved to be false, if what Grell and Abramovitch say is true—helped to blind me. I was thrown off, too, by the finger-prints on the blotting-pad, which corresponded to those on the dagger, and also to those on the typewritten warning which Ivan sent me. The only plausible motive for Grell's actions, if he was not guilty himself—and that we are fairly certain of—was his desire to shield someone else. There could be only one person for whom he was willing to make such a sacrifice— Lady Eileen Meredith.'

'Yes, I understand that. But the finger-prints on the warning?'

'They puzzled me for a while. But that was made clear when I talked to Ivan. He had typed it on the blank half-sheet of a letter given to him by Grell. That letter—it is only an assumption of mine—was one that had been written to Grell by Lady Eileen. That clears that point.'

'Still, I don't see how you have anything against Lola more than you had before.'

'There is this. The weak link in the chain of evidence against Lady Eileen Meredith was the lack of motive. That was why I did not have her arrested immediately I found that it was her finger-prints upon the dagger. The strongest point against the Princess is the motive. She was married to Goldenburg, but was not on the best of terms with him. She was bought by Grell to play the part of Delilah to the blackmailer. My theory is this—bear in mind that it is only a theory at the moment. Grell, for some reason, left her alone with Goldenburg in his study. There was a quarrel, and she stabbed him. It must have been all over in a few seconds, and there was no outcry. You will remember that the body was found on a couch in a recess, and you may have noted that curtains could be drawn across to shield it from the rest of the room. Petrovska may have drawn the curtains and slipped away before Grell returned. She is a woman of nerve and would at once set about manufacturing an alibi.'

'All this is very ingenious, Foyle,' remarked Thornton, 'but I don't know that it sounds altogether convincing to me.'

'It is pure surmise, Sir Hilary. Its chief merit is that it fits the facts. Of course, Lady Eileen may be the murderess after all. I am only working out an alternative. To carry it on a bit further. When Lady Eileen came, Ivan showed her up to the room. No one answered his knock. She went in and shut the door after her. It is my idea that there was no one in there when she discovered the dead man. She was dumbfounded at first, and probably the body being in the shade did not permit her to see the face clearly. She placed her hand on the hilt of the dagger, intending to withdraw it, but could not bring herself to use the necessary force.'

'Why didn't she call out?' demanded Thornton. 'It seems to me—'

'There is no accounting for actions arising out of sudden emotions. Lady Eileen Meredith is as extraordinary a woman in her way as the Princess Petrovska in hers. She had found a man murdered in her lover's study—and she may have had a shrewd idea of the reason why she was summoned there. You follow me? Probably as she stood there, hesitating what to do, Grell returned. I think it likely that he stood by the door, took in the situation quietly, and stole away with the impression that she had killed Goldenburg. If she was bending over the dead man, that was what he might naturally think.

'It is likely that he would make up his mind in an instant. To him the fact that she had raised no outcry would be significant of her guilt. She, let us suppose, stole away, having made no attempt to examine the body closely and not daring to summon anyone, for fear that Grell should prove to be the murderer. He watched her go, already determined to destroy the scent by taking the blame on his own shoulders.

'By the time she reached her own home reflection had shown her that there was one possible chance that Grell might not be guilty. She rang up the St Jermyn's Club and asked for him. Fairfield answered, declaring that his friend was in the club, but busy—too busy to talk to the girl he was to marry next day, mark you. It is idle to suppose that she did not appreciate the excuse as a flimsy one—one manufactured perhaps for the purpose of an alibi. She must have gone to bed filled with foreboding.

'All this is hypothesis. I am supposing that she never closely inspected the features of the dead man. The next morning she is informed that Grell was the victim. At once the lie that Fairfield told her assumed a new aspect. She denounced him as the murderer. She dared not say that she was the first to discover the body, for that would have meant revealing that she knew he was being blackmailed.

'Then the Princess Petrovska paid her a visit and told her that Grell was not dead but in hiding. There was nothing for it, in default of any explanation, but to revert to the thought that he was the murderer. She went to extreme lengths to help him—even to forgery. She believes him guilty still; he believes her guilty.'

'But Petrovska?' objected Thornton.

'I was coming to that. She is a clever woman. When Grell got in touch with her the following day she may have had many reasons for assisting him. She most likely had a shrewd idea of the situation and resolved to profit by it to avert suspicion. While Grell was suspected she would be safe. But it may have occurred to her that if we laid our hands on him and he told us anything, we might get on her track. Suppose that to be so, it is not difficult to see why she should take a prominent part in assisting him. She would still have a certain amount of money, for he paid her to come to England, and she, as we know, would stand at nothing.'

'It all sounds very interesting,' commented the Assistant Commissioner, 'but it looks to me as though it may be a tough proposition to get evidence bearing it out.'

Foyle pulled out his watch. 'My idea may all tumble to pieces as soon as a test is applied. I can't pretend to be infallible. But we can try. I am going back to Scotland Yard now, sir. It is ten o'clock. I expect to be at it all night. Are you coming back?'

'No, I don't think I can be of any assistance to you. I shall be glad if your theory does come out all right this time. The alternative suspicions are horrible. Good night, Mr Foyle.'

CHAPTER LIII

WITH his mind revolving the strength and weakness of his theory, Heldon Foyle returned to Scotland Yard. He paused for a moment at the door of the night-inspector's room.

'Anything for me, Slack?' he asked. 'Has Mr Bolt come in? Ah, there you are, Bolt. Come down to my room.' He led the way down the green corridor, the divisional inspector following.

'Well?' asked the superintendent sharply, as he seated himself in his office.

'I have seen the manager, a hall-porter and a chamber-maid at the Palatial, sir. They repeat what they said in their statements before. The Princess left the hotel at about ten o'clock. No one can fix the time precisely, but it was certainly not before ten. She made up her mind very suddenly, the manager tells me.'

Foyle was rummaging with some papers. 'Thanks very much, Bolt. Stand by in case I want you. Tell Slack if he hears from Mr Green to ask him to leave things and come up to me.'

He concentrated himself on the neat bundle of documents in front of him, and gave his mind with complete detachment to the study of several of them. The investigation had narrowed itself. Whoever was guilty was in his hands. The choice lay between Robert Grell, Lady Eileen Meredith, and the Princess Petrovska.

The reconstruction of the crime for the benefit of the Assistant Commissioner, Foyle had purposely made provisional, but he was becoming more than ever convinced in his own mind that, in spite of appearances, Lola was the person at the bottom of the matter. She had left the Palatial about ten. If, he argued, she had left Grosvenor Gardens immediately after the murder it would have been possible for her to get to the Palatial by that time and to immediately make arrangements to leave. But for all that his intuition told him he was right, he could see no way of fixing the guilt on her.

He placed the dossier back in a drawer and, lighting a cigar, paced up and down the room puffing furiously. Half an hour after midnight Green came in.

'Yes, it's worth trying,' soliloquised Foyle aloud.

'What is, sir?' asked the chief inspector, stopping with his hand on the door-handle.

'Ah, Green. I was just thinking aloud. Everything all right in Berkeley Square?'

'Everything quiet, sir.'

'Well, things have been happening since I last saw you. I want your opinion. Sit down and listen to this.'

Green selected a comfortable arm-chair by the desk, while the superintendent went over his interview with Grell. The chief inspector made no comments until the story was finished. Then he sat in silent thought for a while.

'I've got faith in your idea, sir,' he admitted at last. 'It's likely to be right as anything. But I am doubtful if we shall be able to get any admission from the Princess.'

'One never knows,' retorted Foyle. 'She's not under arrest yet—only detained. We're entitled to ask her questions to see if she can clear herself. But our best chance is to take her off her guard. We might go along and wake her out of her sleep now and chance it.'

The Princess Petrovska had been allotted a couch in the matron's room of Malchester Row police station, partly to spare her the ignominy of a cell, partly to ensure that she should be under constant supervision. Her sleep was troubled, and she woke with a start when the matron roused her.

'You must dress at once. Some gentlemen are waiting to see you.'

'Waiting to see me? Who are they?' she asked. Her nerves were still quivering, but her voice was steady and her face composed.

The matron had received her instructions. 'I don't know who they are,' she replied, in a tone that did not invite further questioning.

Lola, for all her iron will, found her mind dealing with all sorts of possibilities as she dressed herself mechanically. It was not for nothing that Foyle had chosen that hour for his visit. The sudden summons at such an hour, amid unusual surroundings and the speculation as to what it would be for, had upset the woman's balance.

She was taken by the matron into the same room where Grell had been questioned an hour before. Foyle and Green sat at the table and, to her imagination, there was something of judges in their attitude. A chair had been placed at the other side of the table facing them, and the lights were so arranged that while her face would be fully illuminated, theirs would remain in the shadow.

'Sit down, will you,' said Foyle suavely, when the matron had gone, closing the door behind her. 'We're sorry to trouble you at this hour, but matters of urgency have arisen.'

She strove to read their faces as she seated herself, but the light baffled her. 'I am quite at your disposal, Mr Foyle,' she said, hiding her uneasiness under an appearance of flippancy. 'What do you want?'

The superintendent balanced a pen between his fingers. 'Mr Green has already explained that you are not under arrest,' he said, in a quiet, cold voice. 'We are detaining you. Whether you will be the subject of a grave charge depends upon your answers to the questions we shall put to you. You must clearly understand, however, that you are not bound to answer.'

'That sounds serious,' she laughed. 'Go on, Mr Foyle. Put your questions.'

'Very well. Do you still deny that you visited Mr Grell's house on the night that the murder took place? I think it fair to tell you that we have had statements both from Ivan Abramovitch and Mr Grell that you were there.'

He eyed her sternly. She made an expressive gesture with her white hands, and her rings sparkled in the electric light. 'I'll not dispute it in the circumstances.'

'You went there with Harry Goldenburg, your husband, in connection with a scheme of blackmail he had conceived.

You were to get certain letters from him for Mr Grell if you could?'

She bowed. 'You are correct, as usual.'

'Mr Grell left the room for some reason, and during his absence you had an altercation with Goldenburg.'

One slender hand resting on the table opened and clenched. She contemplated her finger-nails absently. 'Oh, no,' she said blandly. 'We were always on the most amicable terms.'

Foyle leaned over the table, his face set and stern, and gripped her tightly by the wrist. 'Do you realise,' he demanded, and his voice was fierce, almost theatrical in its intensity, 'that you left your finger-prints on the hilt of the dagger with which you killed that man—indisputable evidence that will convict you?'

She shuddered away from him, but his hand-grip bruised the flesh of her wrist as he held her more tightly. He had timed his denunciation well. The strain she had put on herself to meet the situation snapped with the sudden shock. For a brief second she lost her head. She struggled wildly to release herself. His blue eyes, alight with apparent passion, blazed into hers as though he could read her soul.

'I never left finger-prints,' she exclaimed wildly. 'I wore gloves. . . . Oh, my God!'

The superintendent's hand opened. The storm of passion on his face died down. The woman, now with a full realisation of what her panic had done, was staring at him in an ecstasy of terror. Green was writing furiously.

It was Foyle who broke the stillness that followed. 'That will do, I think,' he said in an ordinary tone of voice, as though resuming a dropped conversation. 'Have you got that down, Green? Mrs Goldenburg'—he gave her her real name—'you will be charged with the wilful murder of your husband. It is my duty to warn you that anything you say may be taken down in writing and used as evidence against you.'

A hysterical laugh came from the woman's lips. She flung her hands above her head and went down in a heap, while shriek after shriek of wild, uncanny laughter echoed in the room.

CHAPTER LIV

THE blaze of electric lights under their opal shades in Heldon Foyle's office became dim before the growing of the dawn. The superintendent, a cigar between his lips, was working methodically over half-a-dozen piles of papers. At the other side of the table Green puffed furiously at an old brier as he compiled from the documents Foyle handed him a fresh list of witnesses and their statements to be submitted to the Treasury solicitors.

All night the two men had toiled without consciousness of fatigue. Their jigsaw puzzle was at last righting itself. The fragments of the picture had begun to shape clearly. Their efforts had at last been justified. That alone would be their reward. The trial would show little of the labour that the case had cost—only the result. The hard labour of many scores of men would never be handled outside the walls of Scotland Yard. They had nothing to do with the guilt or innocence of the Princess Petrovska. When the case was handed over to the Treasury it would be entirely straightened out, and it would be for them to present the simple issue to the judge and jury at the Old Bailey.

Foyle flung away the remnant of his cigar, and drew out his watch. It was nine o'clock. Sir Hilary Thornton, who had heard of the woman's confession by telephone, might be expected at any moment.

'That ought to do, Green,' said the superintendent, as he strung tape round the discarded bundles with which they had been working. 'We'll have the lady brought up at the afternoon sitting of the court. That'll give us time to talk it over with the people from the Treasury. Yes, what is it?'

A man had tapped and opened the door. Before he could reply, a slim figure pushed by him. Green rose to his feet and hastily pushed his pipe into his pocket. Foyle raised his eyebrows and stood up more slowly. Lady Eileen Meredith confronted them with wild eyes and pallid face. She swayed a trifle, and the chief inspector with a quick movement placed his arm round her waist and helped her to a chair.

'You are not well, Lady Eileen,' said Foyle, slipping to her side. 'Shall I do something?—send for a doctor?'

She waved a slim hand in an impatient negative. 'I—I shall be all right in a minute,' she gasped. Her throat worked. 'I wanted to see you, Mr Foyle. I wanted to tell you—to tell you—'

Her voice trailed away in piteous indecision. Heldon Foyle whispered a few words to Green, who nodded and passed out. The superintendent took a small decanter from a cupboard, poured something into a glass, and added some water.

'Drink this,' he said sympathetically. 'You will feel better afterwards. That's right. Now, you wanted to tell me something.'

A little colour returned to the girl's pale cheeks. Her hands opened and shut convulsively.

'The paper—this morning!' she exclaimed incoherently. 'It said—it said—'

Foyle rubbed his chin. 'It said that we had detained a man in Sussex,' he said encouragingly.

She pulled herself together a little, but her whole form was trembling. 'It was Mr Grell?' she asked eagerly.

He inclined his head in assent. 'Yes, it was Mr Grell.'

Her face dropped to her hands and her frame shook. But when she raised her head she was dry-eyed. The emotion that possessed her was too deep for tears. She gazed in a kind of stupor at the immobile face of the detective.

'You have made a ghastly mistake,' she said, and her voice was level and dull. 'Mr Grell had nothing to do with the murder. I killed that man. I have come here today to give myself up.'

A twinkle of amusement shot into the blue eyes of Heldon Foyle. The girl, oblivious to all save the misery that enwrapped her, noticed nothing of his amusement. But his next words aroused her.

'That's curious,' he said slowly, 'very curious. You are the third person to confess to the murder. Really, I don't believe you can all be guilty.'

She stared at him in dumb amazement. Her tortured mind was slow to accept a new idea. 'The third!' she echoed mechanically.

'Yes, the third. The others are Mr Robert Grell and the woman you know as the Princess Petrovska, who in our police jargon would be described as *alias* Lola Rachael, *alias* Lola Goldenburg.' He smiled down at her as she turned her bewildered face towards him. 'So you see, there is no great need to alarm yourself. The mystery is all but cleared up. If you will permit me, my dear young lady, I should like to congratulate you.'

'But—but—' She struggled for words.

Foyle seated himself, and picking up a pen beat a regular tattoo on his blotting-pad. He went on, unheeding the girl's interruption.

'I won't deny that if you had told me you killed Harry Goldenburg a day or two ago, I might have believed you, and it might have made things awkward. But there is now no question of that. We know now that it was neither you nor Mr Grell. If you had told us the real facts at first so far as you were concerned, it would have simplified matters. However, there is no reason why you shouldn't do so now.'

The warm blood had suffused her cheeks. She had risen from her seat, unable at first to comprehend the full meaning of it all. 'I cannot understand,' she exclaimed.

'You will presently. Now, if you don't mind, sit down quietly, and tell me in your own way exactly what happened on the night this man was killed. Take your own time. I shall not interrupt.'

A lurking fear at the back of the girl's mind that he was trying by some subtle means to entrap her into an admission that would implicate Grell disappeared. He dropped his pen. She searched the square face, but could see nothing behind the mask of smiling good nature. Her own curiosity was alight, but she sternly suppressed it.

'You know about the letter?' she asked. 'The letter I got from Goldenburg?'

He shook his head. 'Assume that I know nothing. Begin at the beginning.'

'Well, that was the beginning. I did not know it was from Goldenburg then, for it was unsigned, and both the address and the note itself were in typewriting. It was delivered by an express messenger. It said that the writer had something of importance affecting my future happiness to say to me, and that I could learn what it was by calling at Mr Grell's house about ten. The writer advised me to keep my visit as secret as possible.'

'Ah! What time did you get the note?'

'I am not quite sure. It was about half-past nine or quarter to ten.'

'Very neatly timed to prevent you making inquiries beforehand. Go on.'

'I was perhaps a little frightened and the note piqued my curiosity. The quickest way to learn what was wrong seemed to me to follow the writer's instructions. I went to Grosvenor Gardens, where I was apparently expected, for a man-servant let me in and took me to Mr Grell's study. I walked in by myself, not permitting him to announce me. The room was in semi-darkness, but I could make out a figure on a couch at the other end of the room. I walked over to it. The face was in shadow, and not until I was quite close could I see the stain on the shirt front. It took me a few moments to realise that the man was dead.

'Then I wanted to scream, to call out for help, but I could not. It was all too terrible—horrible—like a ghastly dream.

Gradually my wits and my senses returned to me. It came into my mind like a flash that the letter I had received hinted at blackmail. I could not see the dead man's face.'

Her voice died away and she looked a little hesitatingly at the superintendent. He nodded encouragingly.

'Don't be afraid, Lady Eileen. You had found a dead man in Mr Grell's house—a man whom you suspected of blackmailing your fiancé. You not unnaturally thought that he had been killed by Mr Grell.'

'Yes.' She was speaking in a lower key now. 'I feared that Mr Grell in an excess of passion had killed him. What was I to think?' She made a gesture of helplessness with her hands. 'My brain was in a whirl, but I seemed to see things clearly enough. I dared not raise an alarm, for I recognised that my evidence as far as it went would be deadly against the man I loved. I laid my hand on the dagger to withdraw it, but at that moment I heard the door behind me open and close quickly. I turned, but not sharply enough to see who the intruder was.

'Then the idea came to me that I must get quietly out of the place. So far as I knew I was the only person who could guess that Mr Grell had been blackmailed and so supply a motive for the crime. I slipped downstairs and went home. You will understand my state of mind. At about eleven o'clock I thought of a possible chance of speaking to Mr Grell. I rang up his club. Sir Ralph Fairfield answered. He assured me that Mr Grell had been there all the evening, but was too busy to speak to me. I was unspeakably relieved.

'Then in the morning, he, Sir Ralph Fairfield, came to see me. I partly guessed his mission, but the full shock came when he told me that it was Mr Grell who was murdered. I think I must have been mad at the time. I said nothing about my own discovery—if Mr Grell had been blackmailed, I did not want any details to come out. Besides, it seemed obvious to me that Fairfield had said Grell was at the club in order to shield himself.' She flushed slightly. 'I knew Sir Ralph loved me. I thought he was guilty and—and denounced him.

'I continued to believe that until the Princess Petrovska came to me with a note from Mr Grell bidding me trust her. I gave her my jewels, and she told me he could communicate with me by cipher. I returned to my first idea that he had killed Goldenburg—the Princess told me the murdered man's name—rather than submit to blackmail. I determined to do all I could to help him, for, murderer or not, I loved him—I loved him. You know how our attempt to communicate by cipher failed.

'A day or two ago he sent me a note—a mysterious note—saying we were both in danger. I could not understand that part of it, but it was clear he wanted money. I could not get it except by putting my father's name to a cheque. You know all about that. I took a taxicab and arranged to meet him at Putney.'

'You went to the General Post Office before that,' interposed Foyle.

'Yes, I wanted to order a motor-car to meet us at Kingston. I thought it safer to do it from a public-call office so as to leave as little trace as possible. I picked Mr Grell up at Putney, and gave him the money. Neither of us referred directly to the murder during the journey. He told me that he was making for his place in Sussex, and should there make a plan for getting out of the country. He argued that the less I knew of details the better.'

'A reasonable feeling, under the circumstances,' murmured Foyle. And then, with a smile, 'Your finger-prints on the dagger have been partly responsible for a lot of bother, Lady Eileen. If you had followed my advice at first—but it's no use harping on that. You have believed Mr Grell to be the murderer, I suppose, and made your own confession to shield him. I don't know that I oughtn't to congratulate you both, for he has certainly made enormous sacrifices, and taken enormous risks to shield you.'

'To shield *me*?' Her astonishment was palpable.

'To shield you. He had at least as much reason—if you'll forgive me saying so—to believe you guilty as you had to think he was a murderer. It was he—if my guess is correct—who opened the door while you were stooping over the murdered man. He must have jumped to the conclusion that you had at that moment killed the man, and took his own way of diverting suspicion from you. That is the only explanation that appears plausible to me.'

A new light of happiness was in her grey eyes, and she smiled. The direct common sense of the detective had brought home to her the motive for the portion of the mystery that until that moment had perplexed her. Robert Grell had laid down everything for her sake. And she had never thought—never dreamed. . . . The voice of Foyle, apparently distant and far away, broke in on her thoughts.

'I have sent for Mr Grell. He will be here shortly. There is still some light that he may be disposed to throw on the affair—now. Meanwhile, if you do not object, I should like to have the statement you have just made put in writing. I will have a shorthand writer in and place this room at your disposal.'

She murmured some words of assent and he disappeared. In a few minutes he returned with one of the junior men of the C.I.D., who carried a reporter's notebook in one hand and a pencil in the other.

Heldon Foyle strolled away to Sir Hilary Thornton's room. The Assistant Commissioner was just hanging up his overcoat. He turned quickly and held out his hand to the superintendent.

'Congratulations, Foyle. I hear it's all plain sailing now. Come and tell me all about it.'

CHAPTER LV

FOR ten minutes the two heads of the detective service of London were in conference. Then there was an interruption.

The door was pulled open without any preliminary knock, and Chief-Inspector Green strode swiftly in, with Robert Grell at his heels. Both men were plainly stirred by some suppressed excitement. Green laid a note down in front of Foyle.

'Petrovska has killed herself,' he exclaimed. 'The matron found her poisoned in her cell, a minute or so after I reached Malchester Row. There was poison in one of her rings. She left this letter addressed to you.'

'Ah!' There was no betrayal of astonishment or any other emotion in the superintendent's tone. He fingered the letter carelessly. 'Won't you sit down, Mr Grell? No doubt you'll excuse us for a moment. Sit down, Green.'

He tore open the letter and glanced over the neat, delicate handwriting. Thornton was leaning eagerly across the table. 'A confession?' he asked.

'Yes—a confession,' he replied. 'Shall I read it aloud?' His eyes rested for an instant on Robert Grell. 'You may care to hear it,' he added.

'Go on,' said Thornton.

Foyle spread the sheets on the table in front of him and began to read in a steady, expressionless tone.

'Heldon Foyle, Esq., Superintendent, C.I.D., New Scotland Yard, S.W.—

'Sir,—It would be futile, after what happened this morning, to dispute any longer the correctness of the conclusions you have come to. I killed Harry Goldenburg, and there is no need for any cant about repentance. He deserved all he got. As for myself, I was fool enough to step into a trap, and there is only one way out. I ought to have beaten you, but as I failed, it may interest you to know the bare facts.

'Goldenburg was, as you guessed, my husband, though it was long since we had lived together. Before I met him, however, I had become acquainted with Mr Grell—I think it was in Vienna. I was on the stage there, and had a circle of admirers, of whom he became one. Whether you believe it or not, I assure you, on the word of a dying woman, there was nothing harmful in our intimacy. But letters passed, and his I kept.

'He disappeared out of my life after a while, and ultimately I met Goldenburg. We were both living on our wits. I, of course, could not fail to be struck by his astonishing likeness to Mr Grell, and he told me eventually of their relationship. There is no use beating about the bush. Other people than Grell had written to me in the old days, and I had my own methods of forcing them to keep me silent. In plain words, a great part of my living was by blackmail, but I naturally acted very delicately. Harry Goldenburg wormed his way into my confidence, and it occurred to me that such a man would be an invaluable ally.

'We worked together for a while—I forgot to say we had been married—and I entrusted him with all the letters I had—including Grell's. Even the keenest woman will be a fool sometimes. You will guess what happened. He saw no need to share his plunder with me, and he left me. There was no open quarrel, but I determined that some day I would get even. But on the few occasions we met afterwards I preserved a friendly attitude. I even helped him in certain affairs.

'Then there came the time when Mr Grell sought me out and paid me to attempt to recover his letters. I jumped at the chance, for apart from the money it seemed a fine opportunity to score off Goldenburg. I hadn't much difficulty in getting in touch with him when he reached London. He thought—and I encouraged the thought—that, like himself, I had been attracted here by the prospect of bleeding Grell on the eve of his marriage. I proposed a business partnership, and he, probably laughing in his sleeve, agreed. He had no intention of paying me my share, but he thought I might be useful in case the threat of publishing the letters might not be enough.

'But I never got the letters, although I used every means that occurred to me. I even suggested that he should entrust them to me so that I might try to extort money by their means from Lady Eileen Meredith. He would have none of it. I changed my ground and arranged to accompany him on what was to be the final decisive interview with Grell on his wedding eve.

'I said little during the preliminary talk. Both men were firm. Goldenburg declared that he would not give up the letters entirely. Grell was equally determined not to pay unless they were given to him.

'When I at length broke into the conversation I asked Grell for the letters I had written to him. I wanted to get him out of the room. He must have understood my look, for he at once said he had burnt them, but would make sure. He left the room. As soon as he was gone I played my final card with Goldenburg. I knew that the time had gone by for finesse; I told him that unless he gave up the letters I would suggest to Grell that he should declare them forgeries, and that I would bear him out.

'I think even Goldenburg was taken aback, for the revelation that I was playing double came as a shock to him. He laughed at me at first, but I could see that he had lost his temper. Then he swore at me for a Jezebel, and half rose as though he would strike me. But I was first. There was a dagger on the mantelpiece. For a moment I saw red. When I was again capable of thought I saw Goldenburg lying on the couch, motionless, and I knew what I had done.

'I struggled to get a grip on myself. At any moment Grell might return. I could not be sure of what he might do, and my whole idea was to save myself at any cost.

Goldenburg had fallen back on the couch. I had taken two steps to the door when there was a sound outside. I drew back behind a curtain, expecting Grell. Instead of that a woman came in. She was heavily veiled, and though I did not know her then I was positive it was Lady Eileen Meredith, for Goldenburg had hinted at some such dramatic surprise if Grell did not come to terms. I saw her stoop over the murdered man, and then Grell opened the door. He stared for a second, and then closed the door again just as Lady Eileen looked up.

'To him it must have appeared that she had killed the man. I expected her to scream, but she did nothing of the sort. She went out, closing the door softly. I followed her within a minute or so, for I began to have an idea how things might be turned to my advantage. I went straight back to my hotel, and made arrangements to secure a sort of alibi. But I wanted to know how things were going. I had told Grell that if it became necessary to write me under cover, he might do so at the *poste restante*, Folkestone. There it was I heard before I returned to London. He declared that he had killed Goldenburg, a statement I had the best of reasons for knowing was false. But it left me with an easier mind. I had no wish that he should be questioned by the police, for that might have given rise to questions as to why I was at the house, and how I left.

'That was why I helped him by every means in my power. I think now it would have been perfectly easy for me to have disappeared without raising more than a fleeting suspicion in anyone's mind. But we cannot foresee everything. And I believed that my safety lay in keeping Grell at liberty. What he thought of my motives for helping him, I do not know—he may have believed them to be gratitude, or something else. Anyway, he trusted me, and to make sure, I more than once hinted that I had an idea that Lady Eileen Meredith was the guilty person.

'It was I who supplied funds for the most part, and it was only when my resources threatened to give out, that we tried other methods. When I left for Liverpool, I was nearly at the bottom of my purse. The arrangement with Mr Grell was, that I should remain in hiding there until such time as he could obtain money to enable us to get out of the country. Then I was to join him. I got a wire from him at last fixing Dalehurst Grange, and knowing that the stations would be watched, I determined to motor down.

'This explanation should make the things clear you do not already know,—L.P.'

Heldon Foyle finished reading, and there was a moment's silence, broken at last by a gasp from Grell.

'It was she, then, not—not—'

'Not Lady Eileen Meredith,' interrupted Foyle. 'But do you confirm what she says there, Mr Grell?'

Grell reached out, and took the paper with a hand that shook. He scanned it quickly, and handed it back to the superintendent.

'She is right in everything she says about me,' he admitted. 'I did think—God forgive me!—that my own eyes were right. I believed that Eileen had killed that man. That it was influenced me in everything I did. Till this moment, I had no idea—' He wheeled almost angrily on Green. 'Why didn't you say why you brought me here?'

The chief inspector shrugged his shoulders. 'My instructions were to bring you here—not to give explanations.'

'I thought it best that you should learn all there was to know at your leisure,' interjected Foyle. 'Of course, we knew nothing of this'—he tapped the confession as he spoke— 'before you came in.'

Sir Hilary Thornton smoothed his moustache. 'It has been an unpleasant business for all of us,' he said urbanely, 'and particularly for you, Mr Grell. I can scarcely apologise for the trouble you have been caused, for, frankly, you have brought it all on yourself, though unofficially, I may say that I have never known a man behave with greater courage than you have in this matter. I am afraid that some of the things your fr—, your associates, have done, will have to be answered for, but anything consistent with our duty will be done for them. Perhaps Mr Foyle will tell us the story of the case now. You are at least entitled to that.'

CHAPTER LVI

A DEPRECATING smile came to the superintendent's lips. Robert Grell was studying him curiously. He recognised that he owed much to the blue-eyed, square-faced detective.

'Yes, I think I am at least entitled to that,' he echoed.

Foyle gave a shrug. 'As you like, gentlemen. You once complained, Sir Hilary, that I talked like a detective out of a book. This kind of thing makes me feel like one—except that, in this case, I cannot claim much credit. I only used common sense and perseverance.'

'Let us have it,' said Grell. He was beginning to be his own masterful self.

'Very well. It has all been a matter of organisation. You will remember, that in dealing with an intricate case no man is at his best working alone. However able or brilliant a detective is, he cannot systematically bring off successful coups single-handed—outside a novel. He is a wheel in a machine. Or perhaps, a better way to put it would be to say, he is a unit in an army. He is almost helpless alone.

'There are many people who believe that a detective's work is a kind of mental sleight of hand. By some means, he picks up a trivial clue which inevitably leads, by some magical process, to the solution of the mystery. I do not say that deductions are not helpful, but they are not all. A great writer once compared the science of detection to a game of cards, and the comparison is very accurate. A good player can judge, with reasonable certainty, the cards in the hands of each of his opponents. But he can never be absolutely certain—especially when he is unacquainted with his opponents' methods of play.

'Detection can never be reduced to a mathematical certainty until you level human nature, so that every person in the same set of circumstances will act in exactly the same way. Like doctors, we have to diagnose from circumstances—and even the greatest doctors are wrong at times. Specialist knowledge has often to be called in.

'When this case commenced, specialist knowledge had to be enlisted to fix our facts—and the one general difficulty which arose as always, was that we did not know which facts might prove important. As an instance, I may say that the finger-prints on the dagger were wholly misleading, and might have brought about a miscarriage of justice.

'It was necessary that we should collect every fact we could about the murder, whether great or small. That was one phase for the investigation where organisation was necessary. A man working alone would have taken months, perhaps years, in this preliminary work. Then luck favoured us. Our records—collected, of course, by organisation—contained a portrait of a man strikingly like you'—he nodded to Grell—'and a comparison of finger-prints told us that the dead man was not you, but Harry Goldenburg.

'Previously, the time of the murder had been fixed by Professor Harding as between ten and twelve. It was our business to find out who had been with Harry Goldenburg at that time. Among those persons was the guilty one.'

'I can't see how that helped you at all,' said Grell, his brows bent.

'In this way, and as a negative test. The alibi is a common-place of the criminal courts. Every person on whom clues might ultimately rest would be eliminated from the investigation if it could be proved beyond doubt that they were elsewhere at the time. You must remember, that we had not only to find the murderer, but to produce evidence that would satisfy a jury that we were right. But we worked, first of all, from such main facts as we had. You were missing. Ivan was missing. A mysterious veiled woman was missing. There was the pearl necklace that you had bought as a wedding present for Lady Eileen. There was the strange dagger used in the murder. There was the miniature of Lola on the dead man. These were the chief heads. There were scores of minor things to be dealt with.

'The matter was complicated, too, by the dead man's clothes. In the pockets, there were your personal belongings. A natural, but erroneous assumption was that they were your clothes. There is not much scope for individuality in evening dress. I confess I was misled and puzzled at first, but a little thought afforded the explanation, and, in fact, it would have been cleared up automatically in any event by the examination of the garments.

'Now, subtlety may be an admirable thing, but it can be overdone. I have never believed that, because a certain thing seems obvious, it is necessarily wrong. It was reasonably certain that one, or all of the missing persons, had knowledge of what had happened. It was extremely probable that one of them was guilty. Our starting-point was to find them. That was where organisation came in. The miniature helped me to bluff Sir Ralph Fairfield into an admission that it was the portrait of Lola of Vienna, and I purposely showed it to some newspaper men on a pretext. One of them commented on the likeness to the Princess Petrovska, who was staying at the Hotel Palatial, and I at once telephoned to the hotel, and discovered that she was supposed to have left at ten on the evening of the murder. A reference to the St Petersburg police gave us a few more facts about her. She became a possibility as the veiled visitor.

'The finger-prints on the dagger, although we should have adopted a different method had we known what we know now, helped us to narrow the investigation, for they apparently—and actually by luck—settled the innocence of several people who might have been suspected.

'Lady Eileen Meredith came to me with a story that seemed to implicate Sir Ralph Fairfield. There seemed just a possibility that she was right, for I could conceive jealousy might be a motive—though, of course, there was so far nothing to explain why the master of the house and his valet should take to flight. I took Sir Ralph's finger-prints by a ruse, and to me that seemed fairly satisfactory proof that he was not the man. Of course, I was then presuming that the finger-prints were those of the murderer.

'Then I received information that Ivan and a man my informant took for Goldenburg had been seen at Victoria Station on the night of the murder. I managed to find Ivan and, by a threat, got a partly formed opinion confirmed. He knew that the murdered man was not Mr Grell. I took from him the pearls that were to have formed a wedding present, and let him go after taking his finger-prints. My idea was to have him watched, for I felt confident that he was in touch with his master—whom I believed to be the murderer.

'But it was not enough to follow one line. We used the fact of the striking similarity of Grell and Goldenburg to advertise for the former under the name of the latter. The mere fact of throwing the description broadcast, was calculated to make any attempt to escape more difficult. Meanwhile, we were making inquiries about everyone concerned in the case by co-operation of foreign police forces, and particularly with the help of Pinkerton's agency in the United States. It was all organisation, you see—the individual counted for little.

'The first attempt to communicate with Fairfield failed, not through the working of any miracle on our part, but by patient watching. I stole a note from Fairfield, which gave us something to act upon, in the East End. Remember, the immediate object of our search was Robert Grell—not necessarily for the murderer. Do you follow?'

'I think I do,' answered Grell. 'You wanted, at least, an explanation from me.'

'Precisely. Well, on top of that, we got a typewritten letter, informing us of the kidnapping of Waverley. That letter was important, for its contents showed that we were up against people who were absolutely reckless. We were able to trace, too, a typewriting machine as having been sold recently to a man named Israel, in Grave Street, There were finger-prints on the letter, and they corresponded to those on the dagger. As a matter of fact, I recently found out that the letter had been written on paper given by you. You had torn a half-sheet from an old letter, and I can only presume it was one that had been written to you by Lady Eileen Meredith. For they were her finger-prints.

'We paid a surprise visit to Grave Street, and, although we were unable to lay our hands on anyone of much importance to the investigation, we hit on the cipher with which it was intended to communicate with your friends. Now, we had already, as you know, taken every precaution to stop supplies. It was obvious that, sooner or later, money would be wanted, and we rigorously watched the persons who were likely to be applied to. Up to this point, circumstantial evidence pointed clearly to you'—he nodded towards Grell—'as the murderer.

'Something of the sort happened, for Lola went to Lady Eileen, and we were able to lay hands on her. But we failed to get her identified as the veiled woman who had visited the house in Grosvenor Gardens. I will confess that, at that time, I never had any suspicion that she was the actual murderess. We had no adequate excuse for detaining her after she handed the jewels over, with an explanation endorsed by Lady Eileen Meredith. I had taken her finger-prints, and they did not agree.

'It was palpable that the attempt to baffle us was being shrewdly organised. I tried a different way of getting information—an attack, so to speak, by the back door. I enlisted the help of a criminal. He was acting more or less blindly, but by his help we stopped the burglary affair that was planned. In the pocket of one of the men we arrested, we discovered two advertisements, worded so as to convey a cipher key without exciting suspicion. We had them inserted, and naturally arranged to keep an eye on the office—for the word tomorrow suggested one to be inserted the following day.

'There is always wisdom in gaining the confidence of those concerned in a case if you can. I was trying hard to establish friendly relations with Lady Eileen and Sir Ralph Fairfield. Each was difficult to handle, but with Sir Ralph I succeeded to some extent. I used him to try and learn something from her. She realised that the cipher was known, and went to the newspaper office to try and stop the insertion of the advertisement that might enable us to find Grell. Of course she failed, and we got a message which had been handed in by Petrovska. One of our men followed her.

'We deciphered the message, and it enabled us to discover your hiding-place on the river. But the business was muddled, and you got away. We found the sheath of the knife used in the murder among other belongings you left behind. By the way, we understand that that dagger had belonged to Harry Goldenburg—how came it to be lying about your room?'

Grell shook his head. 'That is a mistake. The dagger was mine. It is possible that he had a similar one.'

'Yes, that is possible. But in the event, the point does not matter much. What was more important was, that we had driven you out of a secure hiding-place.

'Meanwhile, Pinkerton's had been hard at work on the other side of the Atlantic, and many episodes of your private life were minutely examined. Their detectives it was, too, who had discovered that Goldenburg and Petrovska had in some way been associated with you. What they found out pointed to blackmail. Here appeared an adequate motive for you to murder Goldenburg.'

Grell tapped impatiently on the table, but did not interrupt. Heldon Foyle went on.

'We could not blind ourselves to the fact that you were not the type of man who would commit an ordinary crime under stress of temptation. But homicide is in a class by itself. You might have committed murder. Indeed, there was the strongest possible assumption that you had done so.

'You will observe that there was nothing miraculous in what we did. One step led to another in natural sequence. On the barge, we got the letter that led to the tracing of Ivan at the gambling-house in Smike Street. We knew your finances were cramped. We were, as opportunity offered, limiting your helpers, so that we might force you to show yourself.

'That is what happened. You went to Sir Ralph Fairfield, and succeeded in dodging our men—so far. It was Fairfield's servant who gave you away. He came to Scotland Yard and, in my absence, was taken away by Sir Ralph. When I returned, I arranged to get Sir Ralph out of his chambers for a time, sufficient to allow me a talk with his servant. I then bluffed some idea of your mission out of Sir Ralph. I found you had been refused money.

'You had already applied once to Lady Eileen Meredith for money. There seemed a chance that, in your desperate state, you might do so again. I went to Berkeley Square. Lady Eileen had gone out. I got into her sitting-room on pretext of waiting for her. On the fire were fragments of a note from you, and I was able to make clear several words.

'That made me determined to examine her desk. I found a cheque-book, but the used counterfoils were not in her handwriting, nor did the amounts and the people to whom they were payable seem those that would be found in a personal cheque-book of hers. I searched the blotting-pad, and was able to make out the words Burghley and £200. The assumption I drew from that was startling enough, but it was still more startling to discover on the blotting-pad a finger-print which, as far as my recollection went, corresponded with those on the dagger.

'Up to that moment, the possibility that Lady Eileen might be the guilty person had not occurred to me. But now a rearrangement of the circumstances, apart from the finger-print, began to throw a new light on the matter. It would explain much if you, Mr Grell, were shielding Lady Eileen.

'I could think of no motive, however, and resolved to hold the matter over for the time being. Even if I had good cause for my suspicion, it was still essential to find you. You obviously held the key to the mystery.

'We found out that you had met Lady Eileen, and driven to Kingston—not by shadowing, for our man failed there—but by getting hold of the cabman who drove you. With the aid of the provincial police, we were able to trace you to Dalehurst Grange. I feared that you might be on the alert for any step taken by Mr Green, and so acted by myself in getting into the house.

'Your manner, when I confronted you, impressed me favourably. It was not that of a guilty man. But I could not let an opinion bias me, for, in spite of everything, you might still have been guilty. There was a great possibility that you were an accessory.

'One thing struck me. Your walk was uncommonly like that of Harry Goldenburg. Now, people may be uncommonly like each other in face and figure and be unrelated. But I have noticed often that little peculiarities of gait run through a family. I had thought you might be a relative of Goldenburg's, but not till that moment did I become certain of it. You will remember that I put some questions that might have seemed offensive. I wanted you to lose your temper—it was conceivable that you might blurt out something.

'I found it very difficult to place Petrovska. While you were asleep, I thought the matter over and formed an hypothesis. I put several questions to you later, and found that a woman had visited your house with Goldenburg. That was Lola Petrovska. Now, if she was not the veiled woman who came later, who was? For the sake of my theory, I put her as Lady Eileen.

'Very well. Lola and Goldenburg had visited you together. But she had assisted you since the murder, and she was hardly likely to do that if she was on friendly terms with the blackmailer and knew you had killed him. So it came to my mind that you might have used her in an attempt to get the compromising letters. And then it occurred as a remote possibility that she might, after all, be the guilty person, but, to assume that, it was necessary to explain away the finger-prints—for they were not hers.

'All this led to the supposition that the dagger had been handled by someone *after* the crime. That person must have been Lady Eileen—therefore she must have been the veiled woman—you see?

'But this was supposition, which a single fresh fact would destroy. I held on to you, and Lola walked into our trap. An interview with Ivan cleared up some of the vague points in the story, and confirmed my theory—you will understand that I was ready to drop it the moment it failed to fit the facts. Indeed, to make assurance more sure, I sent a story out to the papers, which I felt sure would convey to Lady Eileen Meredith that you were in great peril—and which, if she was guilty, might induce her to confess to save you. It had an effect rather different to that which I intended.

'Your clumsy attempts to take the guilt on yourself made me more sure than ever of your innocence. This morning we laid a trap for Lola. She was suddenly aroused out of her sleep, and I surprised her into what amounted to an admission of guilt.'

Grell rose from his chair with extended hand. 'I rather believe that I have made a fool of myself,' he said. 'You have done a great deal more than you adopt credit for. I cannot thank you now, but later—I suppose I am at liberty now. I must see Ei—Lady Eileen at once.'

'You will have to give evidence at the inquest,' said Thornton. 'That is all. The step this woman has taken will save us all a great deal of trouble. Of course, what Mr Foyle has told you is entirely confidential.'

'Of course.'

'Lady Eileen is here, if you would care to see her now,' said Foyle. 'Will you come with me?'

Grell followed the superintendent along the corridor. At the door of his own room, Heldon Foyle stopped and knocked.

'Here you are,' he said.

Robert Grell opened the door.

THE END

THE DETECTIVE STORY CLUB

"The Man with the Gun."

THE SELECTION COMMITTEE HAS PLEASURE IN RECOMMENDING THE FOLLOWING NOVELS OF OUTSTANDING MERIT

THE DETECTIVE STORY CLUB

FOR DETECTIVE CONNOISSEURS

recommends

"The Man with the Gun."

MR. BALDWIN'S FAVOURITE

THE LEAVENWORTH CASE

By ANNA K. GREEN

THIS exciting detective story, published towards the end of last century, enjoyed an enormous success both in England and America. It seems to have been forgotten for nearly fifty years until Mr. Baldwin, speaking at a dinner of the American Society in London, remarked: " An American woman, a successor of Poe, Anna K. Green, gave us *The Leavenworth Case*, which I still think one of the best detective stories ever written." It is a remarkably clever story, a masterpiece of its kind, and in addition to an exciting murder mystery and the subsequent tracking down of the criminal, the writing and characterisation are excellent. *The Leavenworth Case* will not only grip the attention of the reader from beginning to end but will also be read again and again with increasing pleasure.

CALLED BACK

By HUGH CONWAY

BY the purest of accidents a man who is blind accidentally comes on the scene of a murder. He cannot see what is happening, but he can hear. He is seen by the assassin who, on discovering him to be blind, allows him to go without harming him. Soon afterwards he recovers his sight and falls in love with a mysterious woman who is in some way involved in the crime. . . . The mystery deepens, and only after a series of memorable thrills is the tangled skein unravelled.

LOOK FOR THE MAN WITH THE GUN

THE DETECTIVE STORY CLUB

FOR DETECTIVE CONNOISSEURS

recommends

"The Man with the Gun."

THE BLACKMAILERS

By THE MASTER OF THE FRENCH CRIME STORY—EMILE GABORIAU

EMILE GABORIAU is France's greatest detective writer. *The Blackmailers* is one of his most thrilling novels, and is full of exciting surprises. The story opens with a sensational bank robbery in Paris, suspicion falling immediately upon Prosper Bertomy, the young cashier whose extravagant living has been the subject of talk among his friends. Further investigation, however, reveals a network of blackmail and villainy which seems as if it would inevitably close round Prosper and the beautiful Madeleine, who is deeply in love with him. Can he prove his innocence in the face of such damning evidence?

THE REAL THING *from* SCOTLAND YARD!

THE CRIME CLUB

By FRANK FRÖEST, Ex-Supt. C.I.D., Scotland Yard, and George Dilnot

YOU will seek in vain in any book of reference for the name of The Crime Club. Its watchword is secrecy. Its members wear the mask of mystery, but they form the most powerful organisation against master criminals ever known. The Crime Club is an international club composed of men who spend their lives studying crime and criminals. In its headquarters are to be found experts from Scotland Yard, many foreign detectives and secret service agents. This book tells of their greatest victories over crime, and is written in association with George Dilnot by a former member of the Criminal Investigation Department of Scotland Yard.

LOOK FOR THE MAN WITH THE GUN

THE DETECTIVE STORY CLUB

FOR DETECTIVE CONNOISSEURS

recommends

"The Man with the Gun."

THE PERFECT CRIME

THE FILM STORY OF

ISRAEL ZANGWILL'S famous detective thriller, THE BIG BOW MYSTERY

A MAN is murdered for no apparent reason. He has no enemies, and there seemed to be no motive for any one murdering him. No clues remained, and the instrument with which the murder was committed could not be traced. The door of the room in which the body was discovered was locked and bolted on the inside, both windows were latched, and there was no trace of any intruder. The greatest detectives in the land were puzzled. Here indeed was the perfect crime, the work of a master mind. Can you solve the problem which baffled Scotland Yard for so long, until at last the missing link in the chain of evidence was revealed?

LOOK OUT

FOR FURTHER SELECTIONS FROM THE DETECTIVE STORY CLUB—READY SHORTLY

LOOK FOR THE MAN WITH THE GUN